The Bogota Delusion

Adrien Trarieux

ISBN: 9798375652238

www.adrientrarieux.com

Falta mas de una persona para escribir un libro.
To all those that helped me along the journey.
From authentic detail, to proof reading, to writing advice,
to tech support.
Couldn't have made it to the end without you.
Los quiero mucho.

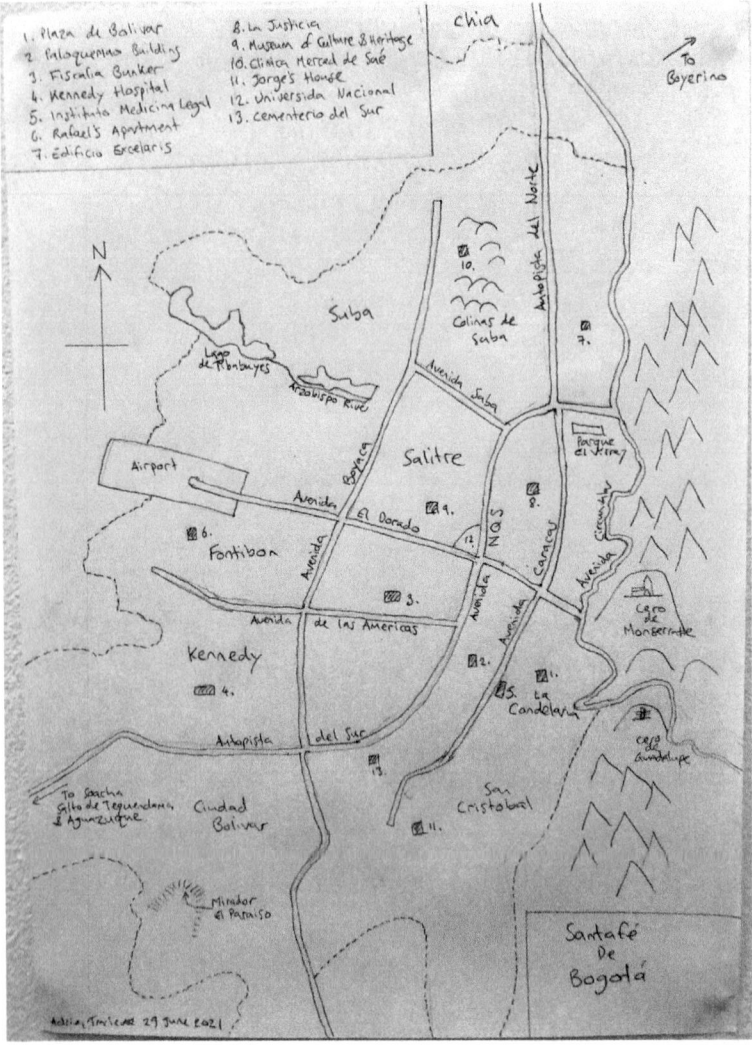

1. Uno

In the angry orange glare of the sodium lights the giant advertising panel blasted its slogan into the night in ugly red and yellow letters: *"Por una Bogota mejor."* There was a picture of a smiling politician next to the slogan. The smile looked artificial to Ernesto Obregon. It didn't match the look of cold detachment in the politician's eyes, almost as though someone else's smile had been pasted onto his face. The panel loomed crazily over the curve of the road ahead and its sinister glow seeped into the car as Ernesto drove past.

There wasn't much traffic on the Avenida Circumbalar. It was late December and, as usual, most people had left the city for the Christmas vacation. To his left Monserrate towered up to meet the black ceiling of clouds. The mountain dominated the city and the lights from the *Iglesia del Señor Caido* formed a golden halo at the summit. The rain on the windshield turned the lights of the other vehicles into coloured smears. Ernesto shifted in his seat and yawned, uncomfortable in the restricted driving space. The humidity in the car made the steering wheel sticky under his hands.

He shifted his focus momentarily to the reflection in the black window. A blocky lump of a face with sallow pockmarked skin stared back at him. Rugged eyebrows shaded a rough lump of a nose above the thick twisting serpents of his lips. He knew the effect that his intimidating appearance usually had on people and had often used it to his advantage.

In front of him an overloaded truck slowed without warning. He jerked the wheel to the left to avoid it, fighting the temptation to shout at the driver and sound the horn. He didn't want to draw attention to himself tonight. The junction he needed emerged from the haze of the highway. The rain was beginning to ease as the car penetrated the narrow streets of the colonial district at the centre of the city. Progress slowed to a crawl and pedestrians hurried past hunched under umbrellas.

1

The distorted voice from the call he had received earlier that evening, echoed through his mind again.

"Come to the asylum in one hour. Pick up the case. Take it to the address in the Candelaria." He had thought about questioning or protesting but the stakes were too high. If there were any doubts about his motivation or commitment the consequences would be very serious. Besides he would be paid for his efforts later on. Now, the suitcase was in the trunk of his battered green Chevrolet.

Ahead a traffic light turned red and a scrawny man in ragged shorts and t-shirt ran to the front of the queue of cars and started to juggle. The concentration showed on his face as he struggled to control the slippery wooden clubs in the drizzle. The juggler's friends passed along the cars tapping on the windows. When they reached him, Ernesto waved them away with a weary gesture. Then the light was green and the traffic rumbled into life again. At the corner of the next block Ernesto saw what he was looking for. On the sidewalk next to a narrow entrance was a yellow sign with the words "Parking Candelaria, *Hay Cupo*". He swung the steering wheel to the left and guided the Chevrolet through the entrance, down a ramp and into the underground car park.

In his office at the far end of the car park the security guard saw the Chevrolet ease into a vacant space next to a concrete pillar. He put down his newspaper and reached for the red cap that was part of his uniform. As he approached the car, the door swung open and the driver struggled out. The guard took an involuntary step backwards as the ugly giant of a man loomed over him. He was powerfully built with muscular arms and chest but his movements were precise and delicate. His eyes were a dull, indifferent black, almost lost to view in the blocky indistinct features. He was unshaven and his clothing was creased and stained. The glare of the florescent lights in the underground car park caused him to blink repeatedly which made him appear confused and almost uncertain of his reasons for being there.

"*Buenos noches Señor,*" the guard said loudly to break the awkward silence.

"I won't need long. How much is it to park for one hour?" The man's voice was weak and insubstantial as though it was an effort to form the words.

"It's two thousand pesos," replied the guard. "You can either give me the money now or take this ticket and pay when you're ready to leave." Ernesto grunted and fumbled in his pocket for some coins to make up the right amount. As he took the money the guard noticed the black markings of a tattoo on the back of Ernesto's right hand. The design was striking and consisted of a number of misshapen, concentric circles framed by eight triangular points. The guard stuffed the money into the leather pouch attached to his belt.

"*Muy amable Señor,*" he muttered as he stepped away, glad the transaction was concluded. Ernesto watched the guard closely until the man had returned to the office before turning his attention back to the car. He pushed the button to release the trunk and lifted the bulky top. Inside, the suitcase had shifted a little during the journey across town. His eyes scanned the hard plastic shell and he wondered what was inside. A robust looking combination lock prevented him firmly from indulging his curiosity. He gripped the handle and pulled the case towards him.

Outside Ernesto lit a cigarette, the harsh smoke filling his lungs and drowning out the unpleasant odours of the street. He peered at the building numbers. The delivery address was about three blocks away. He pulled up the collar of his jacket against the mountain chill and started walking, the case a dead weight at his side.

**

A siren cut through the Bogota night like the howl of a feral animal. Even though the source of the sound was not close, Angel shrunk back into the protective shadow of the alley. Behind him Ruben and his brother Paulito were bickering in hushed voices.

"*Ay hermano,* stop messing around with the *burundanga* powder. If you drop it on yourself now you'll be asleep before you close your eyes and I'm not going to carry you back to the tunnel." His voice was dry and raspy, the husky voice of a mature man rather than a fifteen year old youth. Years of smoking cigarettes and marijuana had leeched all the softness out of it.

"Back off Ruben. I know what I'm doing." Paulito was a

3

smaller version of his brother. He was lean and wiry with curly black hair and his thin face had a sharp, almost pinched look to it. A threadbare Colombian football shirt seemed to hang loosely from narrow, bony shoulders and he stared into the night with an expression that hovered between the guileless sincerity of youth and a dull, hungry scowl that made him look as old as time.

"Does that stuff really work?" Angel asked, smoothing some strands of his greasy neck length hair away from his eyes. Ruben scanned their surroundings, his eyes quick and sharp, tuned to the signals of the night.

"*Es un verraco.* I got it from El Chivo and you know he's reliable. Just a little bit is enough to put you out for a week."

"I'm taking this anyway," Angel replied reaching into his pocket and pulling out a dull looking blade. The cutting edge was chipped and rusty and the handle looked battered and worn.

"You won't need that. Trust me." A faintly contemptuous smile sketched across Ruben's face, twisting through the smear of dirt that stained his tanned cheek and delicate lips.

They had selected the site with care. The street was narrow here and the only source of light was a dim glow from a solitary street lamp at the corner of the next block. The entrance to the alley where they waited was partially concealed behind a large stack of crates and was almost invisible in the gloom. The rain had stopped now and a damp mist was beginning to rise off the streets. Metal shutters blocked off the windows and door of the only shop visible from their hiding place, a shabby looking jewellery store with a gaudy neon sign that read "*Palacio de Esmereldas*". The air was still and the smell of rotting refuse filled the alley.

A sudden scraping sound alerted them to the fact that they were no longer alone. Further down the alley a fire escape door creaked opened and a burly kitchen worker dressed in white appeared. He dragged a plastic sack filled with waste towards a skip at the other end of the alley. The three of them froze in the darkness, willing themselves invisible. If their presence was noticed now they would have to abandon the plan and return to their refuge empty handed. The kitchen worker progressed slowly along the alley trailing the shapeless mass of the bag behind him. He reached the skip and heaved the burden in before turning and striding back the way he had come. He was about to disappear into the doorway when something caught his attention and he stopped and stared intently into the shadows near where the three youths were concealed.

Time seemed to slow down for Ruben. He felt as though the man's eyes were fastened directly on him. How could the kitchen worker not have seen him? Any second now he was going to shout and raise the alarm. Ruben looked sideways at Angel and saw the blade was in his hand again. He started to reach for his own knife in case it proved necessary. Then a voice called from inside the building and the man in white turned away. The fire escape clanged shut and they were alone in the darkness once again.

For a few seconds none of them spoke, they just stared at each other in silence. Angel sighed and slumped back against the wall of the alley.

"Come on Ruben. We should get out of here. That *hijueputa* definitely clocked us. He'll be back in a minute with some of his friends and I could do without the hassle." He hawked and spat noisily on the ground.

"I don't want to stay here," Paulito blurted out, his voice panicky and insistent. "Let's go back to the tunnel," he pleaded, his thoughts fixed on the debris choked storm drain that they had claimed as their own. Hidden in among the rags and torn cardboard boxes Paulito had secreted a battered toy car, the last of the possessions he had taken from the orphanage when Ruben and himself had left for the final time. When the light was gone and the other two were asleep he would take it out and imagine himself playing in the bare concrete yard with the other children again. He wished himself there now, away from the stench of this foul and dangerous alley.

Ruben glared at the two of them, his dark eyes hardening.

"Are you hungry? Well I'm hungry. If we crawl back there now we're going to stay hungry." He wiped his mouth on the back of his hand. "If we don't get our hands on something worth selling, we don't get to eat. So stop whining and pull yourselves together. We're staying as long as we need to."

"Quiet!" Angel hissed at the two brothers, lifting up his hand. "I hear something."

A dark shadow moving slowly emerged from the mist like a wraith. The man was hunched over and dragged a case at his side. He stopped to look at the buildings around him and then strode forward with renewed purpose, heading towards the jewellery store. The three of them looked at each other in recognition. This was the opportunity they had been waiting for.

Paulito moved quickly into the dark chasm of the street. The man had nearly reached the entrance to the alley already. Clutching a square board to his chest with a fan of lottery tickets clipped to the front, Paulito shuffled forward with a furtive sideways movement, keeping his back to the wall.

"Please Señor, you must buy one of my tickets. I've got the lucky number for you right here. It's a sure thing for the *premio gordo de navidad.*"

The man stopped in his tracks, surprised by Paulito's sudden presence. He looked suspiciously at the boy in front of him in his dusty, ragged clothes.

"I've sold five winners already this week, Señor. It would be a shame to leave without buying one." The man was bigger than Paulito had first thought with powerful shoulders and a thick neck but the case he was carrying seemed to weigh him down. His face was hidden in shadows but Paulito could make out a strong, prominent jaw and the dark pools of his eyes. The man looked around cautiously and then grunted. He raised his free hand to wave the boy away, brushing past him to continue along the street.

The moment his attention shifted, Paulito shook the board with the tickets and a cloud of fine dust enveloped the man's head in a grey halo. He staggered back and dropped the case. Paulito jumped clear as the man lurched towards him coughing. The sound of running feet filled the street as the other two attackers arrived. Paulito grabbed the case while Angel and Ruben went for the man who was now on all fours. Angel aimed a vicious kick at his ribcage and the man collapsed in a heap. Ruben grabbed his arms but as Angel went to take the legs the man came back to life. He pulled his arm free and knocked Ruben away with an elbow to the face.

Angel registered a fleeting glimpse of the black smudge of a tattoo on the back of the man's thick hands before he felt their crushing force on his windpipe. The man's face was contorted into a snarling mask of rage and Angel felt a cold wave of terror flood his body. When would the *burundanga* take effect and put this guy to sleep? It wasn't working. He should have

6

known that Ruben and his crazy schemes would come to nothing. There was only one way out of this. He reached down and pulled out his knife. The man saw the danger in time and grabbed his wrist. Angel tried to force the knife home but the man's grip was vice-like below his hand. He felt his strength gradually fading and watched with mounting terror as the knife began to inch towards his own rib cage.

Then, as though a switch had been flicked, the man's sudden burst of energy seemed to be spent and the *burundanga* began to take effect. He seemed to have trouble focusing on Angel and the snarl of rage relaxed away from his face. Relief surged through Angel. Where was Ruben? They needed to hustle the guy quickly off the street so they could plunder what he carried.

As Angel turned to look over his shoulder, Ernesto was convulsed with a final spasm of strength and shoved Angel's wrist one last time. The youth shuddered as he felt the driving thrust of the rusty steel slip into his lower abdomen. He fell back and Ernesto dropped to his knees. But it was too late; the *burnudanga* had done its work and with a final sigh the big man collapsed on top of Angel.

Ruben staggered to his feet, blood streaming from a nose that was probably broken. He shook his head and ran back to where the man and the youth were lying motionless in the street. He rolled the unconscious Ernesto off his friend and looked round for Paulito who had managed to drag the heavy case half way back to the alley.

"Come back! Angel's in trouble. I need your help". Angel's breathing was distorted by a ragged wheezing and the handle of the knife stuck out at an odd angle from his body. "Get the guy's watch and wallet while I look after Angel," Ruben ordered as his younger brother skidded to a stop in front of him. Paulito rifled through the man's jacket while Ruben put his arm under Angel's shoulders and hauled him to his feet.

Light from the jewellery store leaked out onto the street and Ruben felt a sinking feeling in his stomach as he heard the scraping sound of the metal shutters being raised behind him. He looked at Paulito and saw panic in his eyes.

"Get the case quick," he hissed.

"What's going on? Is everything ok out there?" The voice and the footsteps were behind him now. Ruben did not turn and continued lurching down the street with Angel leaning heavily on his shoulder.

"Ernesto? Is that you?" Closer now. There was more than one of them. "Hey! What's going on? What are you doing? Come back."

Ruben knew he was out of time. Paulito struggled past him, both arms wrapped round the case as he grappled it towards the shadows of the alley

"It's too heavy. I need your help," his brother grunted, heaving the heavy burden with him. Ruben turned to look his friend in the face one last time.

"I'm sorry," he whispered. "I've got no choice." Angel's face contorted as he tried to protest, frozen into a rictus of pain. A final wheezing rattle came out and then he collapsed to the ground as Ruben released his grip. The pounding of running feet was close behind Ruben now. He ran off into the night without looking back.

**

2. Dos

The drumming of the rain on the roof of the parked car made the heavy air in the enclosed space seem to hiss with a static buzz. Rafael Alvarez felt his eyes begin to unfocus as he stared through the opaque windscreen at the wall of the empty, shuttered market hall on the Plaza Veinte de Julio.

The weather-beaten face of a leathery old *campesino* leered back at him from the mural on the wall opposite. Behind the *campesino*, a parade of impossibly oversized fruit and vegetables marched through an idyllic rural landscape of rolling hills and fields which was still just discernible through the drifting rain and night time shadows. The old man's inscrutable smile seemed to imply that he alone was the guardian of a promised land of satisfaction and plenty that was well beyond the reach of the vast majority of the people who trudged through the market on a daily basis.

The waiting was always the worst part, Rafael reflected bitterly. He had never got used to how it grated on his nerves. He supposed he resented the dead time, the imposed inactivity that lacked any restorative quality and left too much time for thought.

Rafael was intimately familiar with the area around the scruffy market hall that sat at the centre of the neighbourhood of San Cristobal, a few kilometres south of the centre of the city. From the car, he had a partial view of the bread shop at the corner of the street where his mother used to stop every day to buy *pan blandito*. The main entrance to the market, with its slanting, yellow sign that read *Bienvenidos,* was where Rafael and his best friend from school waited on Sundays to try and make a few extra pesos by offering to carry people's shopping to their cars. A simpler time that had disappeared forever into the past together with the grinding sense of hunger and tiredness that went with it.

The radio resting on the passenger seat next to him

9

squawked into life cutting into his thoughts and memories.

"You're on Alvarez. You know what to do." The clipped, distorted voice on the radio belonged to his colleague Miriam Hurtado. She was running the operation from an unmarked van on the other side of the plaza. Rafael clicked the button on the handset twice to acknowledge the message.

"Don't take any chances. You know how dangerous these guys are," came the tense reply. He glanced down, turning over his left forearm as he did so, to check the face of the watch strapped to the underside of his wrist. The gesture was more from habit than usefulness as the glass had cracked a long time ago and the hands no longer moved.

Rafael clambered from the car and jogged slowly through the gently drifting rain towards the dark bulk of the market hall. He barely noticed the dirty water from the scattered puddles that soaked into his trousers and shoes. The service door had been left open as arranged and Rafael passed quickly through into the cavernous gloom beyond.

He wiped the soft beading of moisture from the narrow oval of his face, drying his hand on the faded material of his dark raincoat. The cloying smell of over-ripe fruit and sawdust filled his nostrils. Yellow concrete pillars marched away into the gloom, supporting a framework of green steel beams that held up the transparent canopy of the roof.

Dripping a trail of water onto the broken, irregular tiles of the floor, Rafael hurried silently along the narrow alleys between the shuttered stalls, passing lowered metal grilles and empty refrigeration units that usually displayed meat and fish. At the corner of the hall, an archway gave access onto a concrete spiral stairway leading to the raised gallery on the upper level of the market.

Rafael emerged onto a narrow walkway with a metal railing running down one side. Beyond the railing, in the void under the canopy, he had a sweeping view of the corrugated roofs of the huddled stalls and shops below. Red plastic stars had been hung from the ceiling in an effort to make the market look festive and they spun slowly in the gentle breeze.

The walkway ended at a green metal door with ventilation slits let into its framework. A neon strip light had been left on above it as the agreed signal. He raised his fist and banged on the metal panel in the centre of the door. Footsteps shuffled in the gloom behind the entrance before the panel swung inwards a short way then stopped.

A cone of light spilled out onto the walkway and a rounded, sallow face peered out from the gap.

"I'm here to make a buy," Rafael announced. "Fidel sent me," he added after a pause, using the assumed name of the informant that had led them to this place. There was something vaguely ferret like about the head watching from the doorway. The man's eyes narrowed as he took the measure of the person standing on the walkway in front of him.

A thin, hard looking face, marked by a pair of striking pale brown eyes stared back. The features were suffused with an almost unnatural stillness, an absence of movement that was both compelling and slightly sinister. There were none of the usual ingratiating smiles or nervous gestures that marked most of the customers that came to do business at this door.

In the twilight gloom the man on the walkway stood immobile, waiting for a reaction, his face a collection of broken angles and planes that seemed to be carved from stone. The eyes appeared to simultaneously burn with a sharp, unsettling, intensity and yet also convey a sense of distance or absence, almost boredom. They seemed to glint a strange shade of yellow in the semi-darkness and the man at the door felt distinctly uneasy, as though he was being watched by a hawk ready to strike.

There was a short silence while they tracked each other nervously, then the sallow faced man seemed to make up his mind. He pulled his baseball cap down over his forehead and shrugged his shoulders.

"No man, you made a mistake. You're in the wrong place, *papi*. Nothing here to buy."

Rafael's face hardened as he realised that something was wrong.

The door started to swing shut and the man disappeared back into the shadows. At the last moment Rafael surged forward slamming into the panel with his shoulder. It snapped backwards, hammering into the man's face and knocking the baseball cap flying. He fell sideways clutching his nose and Rafael was through.

A narrow concrete passage led away in front of him, the walls stacked high with battered cardboard boxes. A musky odour filled the confined space as Rafael paced quickly forward. The man behind him remained sprawled on the floor near the door.

"*Cuidado! Es policía como el otro!*" he yelled from where he lay, his voice muffled behind the hand and thick with blood.

After a few steps, the passage opened up into the wider space of a dimly lit storage room. A pile of small cages had been stacked in one corner. All were empty except for one where a splash of brightly coloured feathers lay crumpled and unmoving at the bottom.

To his right, a battered table had been pushed against the wall. Spilling from an open cardboard box, a clutch of small figures, each about the size of his hand had been spread over the surface. He stepped closer, unsure of what they were. As his eyes adjusted to the gloom he realised that they were small crocodiles with their limbs and jaws tightly wrapped in sellotape. Most lay still with glassy eyes staring sightlessly up into the darkness but a few still twitched and struggled against the bonds that held them. Rafael picked one up, the skin cold and leathery against his palm.

A scraping noise came from behind a stack of crates further in the room. Rafael dropped the dead crocodile and turned to face it. From the shadows near the corner another man stepped into the light and moved towards Rafael. He was dressed in faded jeans and a white sweater and clasped a gun in his right hand which was levelled directly at Rafael.

"That's far enough," he growled, his lean, hatchet face furrowed into an aggressive snarl. Rafael raised his hands slightly. His own pistol remained where he had deliberately left it, in the glove box of his car.

"We know who you guys are," he said, keeping his tone neutral. "All this is finished." Rafael waved with his index finger loosely round the room as he spoke. "The animal smuggling, the protection money, all of it." He heard a shuffling as the other man rose from the floor and moved up behind him.

"There's nothing left. You're too late." The man glanced at his companion. "I say we waste this fool. No one's going to miss another shitty *tombo,* like that dirty snitch Fidel." He spat on the floor, a shiny gobbet of phlegm shot through with streaks of red.

Rafael tilted his head back, looking directly at the man holding the gun. His thin mouth was fixed in a firm line and a muscle pulsed at the corner of his jaw bone. He took a step forward.

"Come on then. Do it. What's the mater? What are you afraid of?" His voice was a grating hiss in the darkness of the cramped room.

The man's hand wavered for a moment then he raised the gun again so that the barrel was level with the point between Rafael's eyes. His knuckles showed white against the grip of the gun. He flashed a savage grin at the impassive investigator in front of him. Rafael closed his eyes, ready to welcome the moment of death, if that was to be.

The seconds passed and Rafael's eyes flicked open again. The hatchet faced man had still not fired. Rafael took another step towards him and he backed away. Then, as though something had been released inside him, the man swung from the waist and smashed Rafael across the forehead with the butt of the gun.

Rafael sank to his knees under the force of the blow. The room spun wildly around him. He put a shaky hand up to feel the curve of his forehead above the left eye. The tips of his fingers came away wet with a smear of sticky, red liquid.

The rapid slap of shoes on the concrete floor seemed to come from far away as the two men retreated towards the back of the room. There was a metallic scrape and Rafael had a blurry view of a fire escape door swinging outwards letting a wave of damp air into the enclosed space of the room. He watched from the floor as they shoved their way though and into the rainy darkness outside. Staggering to his feet, he weaved his way to the opening in time to see them clattering down the metal stairs and away into the night.

**

Rafael sat on the bumper between the open rear doors of the van holding a compress to the broken skin of his forehead. The area around the plaza was bathed in the flashing blue and red lights of a flock of parked squad cars. In the dancing, shimmering glow Rafael caught sight of Miriam Hurtado advancing towards him through the scattered groups of stony

13

faced officers. They quickly moved aside to let her past and Rafael could see that her sharp, angular features were twisted into an angry scowl.

She had a blue CTI cap jammed over her straight, brown hair, which was caught up at the back in a ponytail. Like Rafael, the acronym identified her as a member of the *Cuerpo Tecnico de Investigaciones*, the force of elite investigators that worked directly for Colombia's prosecutors in the *Fiscalia,* rather than the green uniformed *Polica Nacional.*

She stopped directly in front of him, glaring down in silence for a few seconds with her arms folded across her body.

"What the hell was that Rafael! You should have called for backup the moment you knew something was wrong." He flinched away from the sting in her voice.

"There was nothing I could do Miriam. They knew we were coming. Someone sold us out." His eyes flicked to the nearest group of officers, who stood conferring quietly a few meters away. Miriam seemed not to notice.

"Months of careful work and surveillance ruined," she fumed, pulling a piece of chewing gum from her pocket and shoving it into her mouth. "We've got nothing. No suspects, no merchandise, nothing!"

"It was probably Fidel and he's probably dead."

"It's a miracle they didn't kill you too. What were you thinking?" Rafael's thin, worn face tilted upwards, his pale eyes intense.

"I suppose I just don't care that much any more," he muttered before looking down again at the broken watch on his wrist.

"What is wrong with you? I know you used to be some kind of hotshot homicide detective but you've got to get your shit together." She chewed in silence for a few seconds, her lips pressed tightly shut. "Environmental Crimes might not be as glamorous as your old division, but what we do is important. The money these *cabrones* make from trafficking the animals goes into prostitution or drugs or whatever else they're into. No one cares because they think it's all about animals, but people get hurt as well." Rafael lifted the compress away from his forehead, revealing a wide patch of livid skin around the sharp line of the cut.

"I'm sorry Miriam. I made a poor decision, but I thought the

14

opportunity was going to slip away if I didn't do something."

"I still don't understand why you've been dumped in my department but I know what you can do. I know you can do better." She shook her head slightly, drawing in a deep breath as she looked down at him. "I want a full debrief ready for tomorrow morning. I want every lead, every theory, every idea you've got on where we can take the investigation from here. This isn't over."

She turned on her heel and stalked away across the plaza to talk to the captain of the unit of patrol men. Rafael watched her go then stood up from the van, planning to head back to his car. He'd taken a few steps when he became aware that an officer had detached himself from one of the groups and was following him across the plaza, no doubt another statement request or some more trivial admin to be addressed. He stopped walking to allow the man to catch up with him.

"So, it is you, " came a familiar voice from behind him. "I was wondering when I'd see you again Rafa." He turned to find himself looking at the calm and somewhat heavy features of Jorge Palacios. The smooth face with deeply scored lines on either side of the rounded nose were the same as he remembered. The air of self contained sincerity remained but his eyes looked sadder and there was a slightly pale tint to his normally ruddy brown complexion. Rafael could see that more grey hair was mixed in with the black at Jorge's temples under the green and yellow police cap he wore pulled down low on his forehead. A broad smile spread across Rafael's face as he recognised his old friend.

"You look like you need a drink, *mano*," Jorge declared. Rafael nodded vigorously and the two of them headed away from the plaza and into the damp streets of San Cristobal.

**

3. Tres

"So what happened to you in the market?" Jorge indicated with his beer glass towards Rafael's broken forehead before taking a large swig of the foamy, yellow liquid. Rafael shrugged.

"Could have been worse, a lot worse." The two of them leaned unsteadily against a makeshift serving counter set up on a row of barrels in the small, front room that was open onto the street. Despite the late hour, the space was packed with drinkers, probably because the owner had found a way to hook into the cable network signal and was showing a football match on a projector screen that he'd rigged up against one wall. A grainy close up of one of the players jerked onto the screen. His hands were raised in the air to protest the yellow card he'd just been shown.

"Two more here, *patron*," Jorge yelled at the barman above the noise of the booming commentary, raising his arm to draw the man's attention. "And bring us two *guaros* as well," he added, using the familiar term for aguardiente, the fiery, aniseed liqueur that was an unavoidable staple of any Colombian drinking session. "She was angry with you, the other *Fiscalia* agent." Jorge turned his face towards Rafael again as the drinks arrived.

"I needed to take some time away and it's been hard to find my way back in." Rafael's mouth set in a hard line. "I just can't seem to reconnect with how to do the job any more." Jorge placed his calloused hand on the younger man's shoulder.

"Well, it's good to see you again, my friend. *Salud!*" Mirroring Jorge, Rafael picked up the brimming glass of aguardiente and swallowed the clear liquid in a single mouthful. The bitter fluid seemed to coat the inside of his throat, warming his chest on the way down. He dropped the empty tumbler on the bar next to Jorge's.

"I remember when you qualified for CTI and left to join the *Fiscalia*," Jorge continued after wiping his mouth on the back of his sleeve. "I was pleased to see you moving up and doing something better but it was sad to see you go as well. The old Fifteenth Police Station in Restrepo is still the same as when you were there. *Comandante* Azuero still shouts at everyone and keeps threatening disciplinary processes if the arrest records don't go up." Rafael felt his head nod slightly as the alcohol and fatigue caught up with him. The corner of his mouth twisted into a half smile.

"When I look back on how naive I was when I came out of the officer training academy, it's a miracle I survived out there on the street. Do you remember those guys that attacked the bus over near Molinos. You and me were the first responders and they were still robbing the passengers when we arrived. They made a run for it and we chased them down to that drainage canal on Carrera Deiciséis." Rafael fiddled with a beermat as he talked. "Pablo Herrera was the backup and he wanted to go straight down there the moment he got off his motorbike. I was ready to go with him and you said we should wait for the rest of the squad as there was nowhere else they could go. Pablo wasn't having any of it. He stormed straight down into the ditch yelling "*Policia*" and they blew his face off with a shotgun. That was the first time I saw someone get shot."

"I remember Pablo Herrera. They tried to patch him up but he lost both his eyes. The last time I saw him he was selling *artesanias* on the Avenida Jimenez."

"It's different in the Fiscalia. I worked homicide before my…". Rafael hesitated as he struggled to find the right words. "Before my leave of absence." His pale eyes seemed clouded and distant as he finished the sentence. "Some of the things you see." He took another sip of the beer before continuing. "Worse than Pablo rolling about at the bottom of that ditch without his face. Sometimes it's hard to believe what one person can do to another. But I always found a way to keep it inside, to keep it separate. At least I did before." Rafael's voice trailed off and disappeared into the background buzz of conversation in the bar.

At that moment the blaring football commentary rose to another level as one of the teams scored. The long, drawn out middle syllable of the word 'goal' drowned out the other sounds in the bar and a small group of drinkers in one corner jumped to their feet cheering and clapping. Rafael din't recognise either of the teams. He guessed the match was from one of the many foreign leagues that were regularly streamed in Colombia. Probably Italian from the foppish, flamboyant look of the players embracing near the corner flag. When the noise died down Rafael turned back to Jorge.

"Enough about me. How are things with you?" A ready grin flashed over the older man's features.

"You know, same as always. Things don't really change for me. Claudia is still worried that I'm going to get myself shot. The boys are growing up fast. Julio is going to finish college next year. Mario is on the football team. He's getting pretty good and they made him captain for this season." Jorge's heavy brows knitted together as the grin passed away. "I drove past your old house the other day. The whole block has been boarded up. They're going to knock it down to build some new apartments or something."

"I didn't know that. It's been a while since I've been back in San Cristobal." A memory of the cramped, dimly lit bedroom he'd shared with his younger sister jumped unbidden into Rafael's memory. It wasn't possible to open the door fully before it jammed up against the frame of the bunk beds and you had to clamber over the storage box that was filled with a jumble of plastic robots, dolls, books and clothes to get out of the room. Jorge propped his chin on his hand, gazing past Rafael at the street outside.

"How's Gabriella?" he asked absently. Rafael opened his mouth to say something and then closed it again quickly. The skin on his fingers felt sticky from the spilled beer on the counter.

"I need to go to the bathroom," he said, stepping away from the bar before Jorge could reply. Pushing his way through the crowded throng to the back of the room and down some narrow stairs, the air became a thick blend of sewage reek cut through with cleaning chemicals. Rafael locked the door of the dingy cubicle behind him and slumped down onto the toilet with his head in his hands.

He was still for a moment before his right hand snaked out, groping for the pocket of his overcoat and the small bottle of pills that nestled at the bottom. Out of habit he gave the bottle a gentle shake, the dry rattle reassuring him that a good supply remained inside. He flipped the lid and tipped one of the chalky tablets onto his palm.

Telling himself that he didn't need the things, that he could stop taking them any time, just not yet, not today, he found that he'd already transferred the pill to his mouth. He gripped it between his front teeth for a heartbeat before tipping his head back and swallowing. A brief shudder trickled down his spine as the capsule slid past his Adam's apple.

The effects worked their way through his body like a slow wave. There was a gradual dimming of sound at the edge of his awareness. Then his eyes seemed sharper, bringing the details of the scummy toilet cubicle into stark relief. The faded scribble next to the empty toilet roll holder resolved itself into a name and phone number overwritten by the slur '*maricon*'. His limbs seemed lighter, stronger, more responsive to his directions. Most importantly, the pain and the panic seemed to drop away, leaving him cleansed and focussed.

He turned up the collar on his jacket and strode back towards the stairs, letting the door clack shut behind him. A man renewed, he was ready to talk about Gabriella now, to tell Jorge that she was fine, that she had a new job in a school or something, whatever lie he needed to hear. At the top of the stairs he picked out the heavy slab of his friend's back slouched at the bar and started to weave his way towards it.

He was stepping round a group of people gathered at a table when one of the drinkers staggered into Rafael slopping beer all over the front of his shirt. The man seemed to react in slow motion.

"I'm sorry," he mumbled, a vacant smile plastered onto his puffy face. Rage consumed Rafael like an irresistible sheet of fire, a sudden wave of white hot anger. He wanted to smash something, to hurt someone. His chest felt tight and his breath came in short bursts.

"What the fuck! Watch what you're doing, you fucking moron!" The man lurched backwards, his eyes wide with shock as he took in the furious snarl that flickered across Rafael's face below the ugly gash crossing his forehead.

"Look I'm really sorry, okay?" His hands came up, the palms facing towards Rafael. Before the man could say anything further, Rafael sprang forward, closing the distance between them in a single step. In the same smooth movement he grasped the front of the man's jacket and shoved him backwards onto the table behind. There was a rattling clatter as a series of glasses and bottles overturned and fell to the floor. A wave of spilled liquid washed across the surface and into the laps of the man's companions. They clambered to their feet muttering curses, not quite sure yet what had happened but angry enough to seek out the source of the disturbance, to demand recompense, to retaliate.

Rafael stood his ground, hands balled into fists, ready for the confrontation, welcoming it. His eyes flicked round the ring of livid faces, searching for which of them would make the first move. The stocky man with the wavy hair and the leather jacket. He was the one. His eyes were narrowed and his shoulders tense. He'd picked up one of the beer bottles and subtly manoeuvred himself past his companions to a position just to Rafael's left. Rafael turned his body slightly, anticipating the attack. He brought his left hand casually up to his face, as though he were about to scratch his nose. He felt the top of his bicep stiffen, now he was ready.

Then, just as he was set to strike, there was a sudden pressure on his shoulder from behind, a hand pulling him backwards. He flinched and spun to respond to the new threat. His shoulder slid down, his fist came up, his heart was beating wildly. At the last second he pulled him arm back as he registered that Jorge was the one pulling him away, his rounded face a tight mask of concern. Jorge shoved past Rafael and inserted himself between his friend and the group of men.

"There's no problem here, *caballeros*." He made it a flat statement leaving no room for response or argument. There was more muttering as they took in Jorge's police uniform. Most of them turned away shaking their head but the tension seemed to fade from the situation.

Jorge dragged Rafael back through the bar and out onto the street. The cool, damp air hit him like a wall of water and a a bubble of crazy laughter rose up through his chest and pushed past his lips.

"Wow, that was exciting." Jorge peered at him through the gloom, eyebrows drawn together in a puzzled frown.

"What was that all about? What were you trying to do in there?" The adrenalin draining from Rafael's body made him feel light and insubstantial. He fell back against the wall the moment Jorge relaxed his grip.

"She's dead Jorge. Gabriella's dead. She was supposed to go into hospital to give birth to my son and she fucking died, man." Another ripple of laughter started to press against his throat but was choked off in a wrenching sob. "My son died too."

Nausea flooded through him then and he fell forward onto his knees to retch into the gutter, while Jorge looked on, helpless.

**

4. Cuatro

High above the city a ragged group of *chulos* spiralled lazily in the powerful updraft from Monserrate. Milagros Santamaria watched the black and grey vultures dip and circle and thought to herself how amazing the grace and elegance of even the least of God's creatures was. She bowed her head and fell to her knees again reciting the Hail Mary under her breath. The steep gradient to the path at the top of the mountain was a formidable challenge. To her left a sheer wall stretched up out of sight while to her right the drop fell away to the gardens and the bottom of the mountain.

The pilgrimage had been Father Pivo's idea. After mass she had beseeched him for something she could do to show her devotion and to beg the Lord to intercede on behalf of her sick mother. The trek to the top of Monserrate on foot to pray at the *Iglesia del Señor Caido* was a time honoured tradition in Bogota and a powerful way to show her commitment. As well as a physically demanding climb, the path to the top could be dangerous due to the thieves that often waited to ambush travellers.

Milagros however was not concerned about thieves or attackers. She carried little of value on her trek and her faith in Jesus would protect her from harm. Condensation from the plastic water bottle she was carrying dripped onto the dusty ground as she unscrewed the top and swigged a mouthful of water. Less than halfway to the summit and the morning sun was already beginning to climb over the ragged line of the mountains to the east. The dusty heat of the day would soon build to an intense swelter and she had a long way to go. The prayer finished, she got to her feet again and continued the steady climb to her goal.

As she rounded the next switchback a curious sight awaited her. A plastic case lay abandoned in the middle of the path, its metal fixtures glinting in the sunlight. A large crack gaped across its hard surface and the lock had been broken off and thrown to one side, discarded. Milagros looked around but could see no sign of any apparent owner. The path was silent and empty apart from the buzzing of insects.

She approached cautiously half suspecting some kind of trap but reached the case without incident. Again she fell to her knees to better examine what was in front of her, reaching out carefully to lift the broken lid. It opened without resistance. At first she wasn't sure of what she was looking at, doubting the evidence of her own eyes. But, then with a deep intake of breath she realised the truth and felt a wave of panic surge through her.

The naked torso of a man had been packed carefully into the bottom of the shallow case. Red weals and marks criss-crossed his chalk white skin. Great, jagged gashes had been torn in the flesh where the head, arms and legs had been hacked off. A black tattoo adorned the torso's shoulder in a curious design of concentric circles framed by triangular points. Milagros crossed herself and her eyes filled with tears. The pain that poor soul suffered before his death must have been unbearable. What should she do next? The pilgrimage had been her commitment but the corpse in the suitcase changed everything. She tucked some loose strands of greying hair that had blown loose in the breeze behind her ear. Someone must be told about this terrible thing as soon as possible and the way back was easier than the way forward.

Her decision made, she gathered up her skirts and began to jog back down the path. The dusty city spread out before her in the hazy morning sunlight. A line of black clouds on the horizon signalled that rain was coming.

**

The restaurant was already full for lunch but Emilio Ortega had no trouble getting a table. The owner knew the prosecutor well enough and ushered him quickly through the busy dining area to an empty table near the window that he kept free in case one of his important regulars should put in an appearance. Ortega was, as always, dressed in an expensive, well tailored suit and his jet black hair was slicked back carefully against his skull. He ordered a mid-range bottle of wine and then waved the owner away dismissively while he settled back to wait for Calderon.

Ortega was an impatient man. He had fought his way into the inscrutable senior echelons of Colombia's powerful law enforcement agency, the *Fiscalia General de la Nacion*. He was now a Fiscal, a senior prosecutor with a large amount of autonomy to select his cases and direct and supervise the investigatorial efforts that went with them. Drumming his fingers on the table in frustration, he glanced at his watch before checking the entrance again. He was not accustomed to being kept waiting, especially by his subordinates.

Ortega had nearly finished his first glass of wine when he caught sight of his companion weaving his way through the clusters of white covered tables.

"I'm sorry to be late señor Fiscal. I was unavoidably detained at the divisional meeting." Guillermo Calderon was a portly man with a florid complexion and hid his rounded features behind a coarse, wiry moustache. He hovered at the edge of the table while Ortega continued to study the menu in frosty silence. Calderon was a sub-director attached to the Bogota section of the *Fiscalia* and commanded a unit of the investigators that worked directly for the country's prosecutors. "Gonzalez started off with one of his eccentric speeches and you know how he likes the sound of his own voice once he gets started." He gave a brief shrug by way of apology and handed his overcoat to the waiter. Ortega looked up slowly from the menu.

"Sit down Calderon. The *trucha al ajillo* is very good here." The sub-director was perspiring visibly despite the air conditioning. Next to the immaculately groomed prosecutor, the rumpled material of his brown suit and faded tie looked almost unkempt. The owner returned to the table, tried to push the unimpressive sounding daily special and then asked obsequiously if they were ready to order. "He'll have the special and I'll have the trout," commanded Ortega without looking at Calderon.

Calderon fiddled with his napkin. It was unusual for one of the Fiscals to summon him to lunch, particularly one of the more prominent prosecutors like Ortega. He had met Ortega before of course but their conversations had typically taken place in conference rooms or offices, never over a lunch table.

24

It seemed odd to Calderon that a Fiscal with the political skills of Ortega would have an interest in this case so quickly. From what he'd heard of the preliminary reports, the circumstances appeared highly unpromising. It was difficult to anticipate how the matter could progress from a dismembered torso on the mountainside into an accusation and a courtroom trial where the prosecutor could bring his skills to bear. Ortega's involvement in this matter made no sense to him and he wondered again what had attracted the man's attention. He supposed there were answers for these questions but none that he cared to explore further at this point.

The food arrived and they began to eat. The prosecutor cut his food into precise sections while Calderon attacked with his fork and shovelled large portions into his mouth. They ate in silence with the gentle tinkle of classical music playing in the background; the thin, precious sound of rich people's music, thought Calderon resentfully. As the plates were being cleared away Ortega turned towards him.

"I need to talk to you about my newest case, the body on the mountain. I want you to explain to me how you plan to run such a challenging investigation." Calderon felt the food sit heavy in his stomach. Ortega's directness had left him feeling outmanoeuvred and he scrambled to recover and deliver a credible response. With so many other urgent matters competing for his attention he had not given the question any real consideration. Being honest with himself he was probably not intending to do so.

"I'm not going to lie to you señor Fiscal; it's going to be tough to find the right investigator for this one, given the unusual circumstance. Suarez is on the rotation, but he's our lead investigator on street gang related crime and the Liberation Army are taking on the Black Eagles again for control of El Cartucho. We fished three of the Eagles out of a drainage canal in San Ines this morning so he's got his hands full dealing with that."

"And yet justice must be served and this case, like all others, must be properly investigated. Given its extreme nature I'm sure that, like me, you see the importance of closing this matter quickly. In fact, I would see a quick resolution as a personal favour to me. I'm sure I don't need to remind you of my status within this organisation for you to understand the value of doing me such a favour."

Calderon absently ran a finger over the wiry strands of his moustache as he considered the proposition. There was value here indeed, but also danger. Having the prosecutor as an ally could be an invaluable asset in the swift moving, often vicious, internal politics of the *Fiscalia*. At the same time, failure to give Ortega what he wanted ran the risk of creating an implacable enemy with the ability to harm Calderon and his unit in a hundred subtle ways. He moistened his dry lips with a slight flick of his tongue before speaking again.

"I do have one man who might be available. He was one of the best in my unit. An exceptional homicide investigator with experience of some of the most violent murders committed in the Bogota section. He has a rare talent of swiftly being able to grasp the essential details from any problem I've seen him encounter, as well as the vision and imagination to make connections where others see nothing." Calderon sighed and dropped his gaze to the table. "But he's a long way from his best at the moment. He's recovering from some personal issues that have taken a heavy toll. He's been deeply affected by…". Calderon's voice broke off as he struggled to select an appropriate euphemism. "Let's call it 'significant family bereavements' and leave it at that."

Calderon experienced a brief chill as he imagined momentarily being in the situation he was trying to avoid describing. "He's recently come back from an extended stretch on administrative leave and I've temporarily assigned him to support the Environmental Crimes Unit. He's investigating low-key animal cruelty cases and illegal pollution while he gets back on his feet. I'm honestly not sure he's ready to take on a case like this."

"Come on Calderon" exclaimed Ortega. "We both know that Environment Crimes was invented to improve the image of the *Fiscalia*. The conviction rates are non-existent and the work exists purely to generate favourable press releases." Ortega leaned forward over the table. "If there's no one else you don't really have much choice do you? Who is this damaged investigator anyway?" He made no effort to keep the sneer of sarcasm out of his voice.

"His name is Raphael Alvarez Carvalho. He was awarded a commendation after that nasty business with the police station attacks last year. He single handedly took down one of the terrorists before they could start shooting. It was in the newspapers. There was a ceremony with the Fiscal General."

"Yes, yes, I remember it. I'd like to meet him. Bring him to my office in an hour." The prosecutor dropped some money on the table and stalked out of the restaurant.

**

Investigator Rafael Alvarez of the *Cuerpo Tecnico de Investigacion,* raised his pale brown eyes from the monotonous report he was reading and looked out of the window. The sky was a delicate shade of purple grey and a light afternoon drizzle was just beginning to fall. He liked to watch the rain and gazed absently as the gauzy curtain of water began to soak slowly into the streets and buildings, gradually washing out the hazy yellows and greys and transforming them into darker shades of brown and black.

From the third floor of the concrete bulk of the *Fiscalia* building he had a view of Avenida La Esperanza and the ephemeral fast food chain outlets that had sprung up along the newly developed plots near the American embassy. At this time of day the traffic was beginning to build into a choked, snarling crescendo, crawling across the face of the city. A distant blare of car horns and the occasional strident yell could be heard faintly through the reinforced security glass of the windows, mixing into the muted background drone of the impersonal, open-plan office. Immediately below the window Raphael could see the high, metal railings festooned with razor-wire that formed a secure perimeter around the structure. It had been ten years since Pablo Escobar was gunned down on a Medellin rooftop but Colombia was still a dangerous place to be in the police. The *Fiscalia* building was known affectionately as 'the Bunker' by most of its cynical, jaded inhabitants.

Due to the dark lines scored faintly beneath Rafael's eyes, people frequently took them to be a deeper shade of brown than was in fact the case. In the direct focus of his gaze however, the striking, unusual pale colour became apparent; a delicate golden brown that was somewhere between amber and yellow. Rafael

27

seemed older than his twenty eight years. His pale eyes were set in a narrow, hard looking face and combined with the absent gaze to give him a detached, slightly cold expression. His skin was the rich brown mestizo typical of the Bogota altiplano. He had a strong, wiry build, close-cropped, deep brown hair and a curved, wedge-shaped nose. As he stood up from the desk, his straight, thin-lipped mouth was set in a resolute line that seemed to impart a sense of steely determination, a will of iron, almost uncomfortable on a face that was just beginning to pass the peak of youth.

Rafael had come to realise that life in the police was making him ill and earlier this morning he had reached a decision that one way or another it was time to leave. He raised his hand to touch the hard crust of dried blood on the uneven line running down his forehead. The incident in the bar last night felt like a new low point. Meeting up with Jorge and being back in San Cristobal had unleashed a flood of memories and he had lost his self control. Worst of all, he had ended up re-awakening the ghost of Gabriella.

It had been nearly a year now since she had died and in the early days it had been almost impossible to wake up and go about the basic functions of his life with the burden of that cruel day hanging over him. The endless, dismal corridors of the Kennedy hospital seemed to be forever burned into his memory. He had found himself sobbing uncontrollably in a stairwell, his unanswered prayers and futile tears etched into his soul. He would have have given anything, done anything in exchange for the lives of his wife and son.

But it was not to be. Fate, or God or whatever it was that determined the course of people's lives had decided against it and he was left bereaved; to make his way through life forever in the company of two insurmountable absences. Over time a kind of dull numbness had set in. But still, every once in a while he would suddenly feel what it had been like to hold his wife in his arms again. It wasn't exactly a memory; it was more like a physical sensation, an imprint the past had left on his body. These moments came less often now. He no longer wished to be dead but at the same time it cannot be said that he was glad to be alive. At least he did not resent it.

An insistent, reedy voice from behind cut through his thoughts and memories.

"Are you well señor? Can I offer you a *tintico*?" He turned to see one of the ladies who worked their way through the office supplying coffee to the investigators. Concern was etched onto her round, weathered face, framed with short silvery hair. She peered at him hesitantly, wiping a hand on her pink overalls while the other gripped the handle of the heavy metal urn of coffee. "You seemed very far away sir," she muttered apologetically.

"I'm sorry. Yes, a *tinto* would be good," he replied using the term for a mild, black coffee. He handed over a couple of small coins in exchange for a plastic goblet filled with the warm, dark liquid.

He took the coffee with him as he moved across the office, gathering up the necessary papers from his desk before stepping away. About half the operatives on the floor were in the blue uniform overalls of the CTI. The rest, like himself, wore casual plain clothes with some form of identification displayed clearly. He stopped at a set of metal storage shelves weighed down with cardboard folders and papers and glanced across the office to where Miriam Hurtado was sitting, typing rapidly into her computer.

Miriam was nearly the same age as Rafael. She was short with an angular face and features, which contrasted with a full generous mouth. She was focused intently on the screen as her fingers flashed over the keyboard and he could see the rhythmic movement of her jaw as she chewed a piece of gum. Unlike his own desk, which he kept resolutely bare, Miriam's was buried in a clutter of paper and personal objects, including a selection of family photos and a pot plant, which she called Suki.

He wondered how he appeared to Miriam standing forlornly near the storage shelves, a morose figure in a dark blue shirt and grey trousers who been forced to share the work she cared about because he was no longer able to do his own job. Miriam's hazel eyes shifted abruptly as she became aware that Raphael was looking at her. A faint look of exasperation moved over her face before she hid it quickly behind a tight smile and waved him over. He stepped towards her desk, footsteps muffled by the beige carpet tiles, still clutching the coffee and the papers.

"I've got the updated emissions reports for the agrochemical plant on the Avenida de las Americas. I've marked up the key sections on the carbon monoxide, lead and nitrogen oxide levels."

"Great, I'm just writing up the witness statement now. It's pretty clear they've made a deal with the local street gang to dump the chemicals in Lago de Amarillo next week." Miriam pulled the papers towards her, eyes darting as she scanned the top sheet. "Good work with the report on the raid at the market yesterday. I'm going to take the recommendations to Calderon this afternoon to authorise the surveillance."

"There's still no word from Fidel. My guess is we're not going to hear from him again. The guys from the warehouse have dropped him down a hole somewhere and he's never coming back." Miriam leaned back in her chair so she could look at him directly, a faint line appearing on her smooth forehead.

"Rafael, how are you doing? You've got that look where you just sort of go away sometimes. Are you still in there?"

"I'm good. I'm okay," he muttered. "I just feel really tired." He glanced down at his hands as the memory of his lapse with the pills in the bar flashed through his mind again.

"What are you doing later?" Miriam asked. "Me and a couple of guys from the technology department are going for a drink at Humberto's after work. Rosita is going to be there and you know she'd love to meet you. It's about time you came to celebrate a *Juernes* with us," she said using a term that combined the Spanish words for Thursday and Friday and was generally used for starting the weekend's festivities a day early.

It was the usual ritual where Miriam would invite him for drinks with the intention of introducing him to one of her female friends and he would invariably find a reason to decline. They had been working together for a couple of months now, since Raphael had been brought back from leave. His ability to make logical connections consistently astonished her, but he remained solitary and taciturn. Rafael smiled and was preparing a polite excuse for not joining them for the drinks, when Miriam turned away in her chair and looked across the office.

"Is that Calderon over there?" she uttered in a hushed whisper. Raphael turned his gaze to where Miriam was looking and saw the slightly overweight figure of the sub-director standing next to a glass interior wall deep in conversation with another man, whose back was turned. Calderon's presence in the open plan area was sufficiently rare as to be worthy of notice. It was more usual to be summoned to his dingy private office on the management floor.

"Do you know who he's talking to?" Raphael asked in the same tone.

"I haven't seen him before but someone I know over at Fiscal's offices told me that Ortega has a new assistant prosecutor. He doesn't look the type but I think that might be him." The man turned towards where they were sitting and Raphael saw immediately what she meant.

The other man had a stocky, muscular build, tough looking shifty eyes and a close-cropped black beard. His neck and arms were noticeably thick and he moved like a private security guard rather than a mid-level lawyer. His dark brown hair was combed forward and had a grey patch on the left hand side. While they watched he handed over a thin, manila folder to Calderon and then took his leave. His shrewd gaze seemed to linger on Rafael for a moment before he turned away. Calderon continued his progress across the office and they quickly noticed that he was heading straight towards them. Miriam stood up as Calderon approached and came to a stop at her desk glaring at both of them.

"Alvarez, Hurtado," he barked a cursive greeting. "What's the latest with the Biostar Chemical plant?" Miriam gave him a quick update on the progress and that they were ready to move things to the next stage. "Well it sounds like you've got things well in hand." Calderon paused for a moment, stroking his moustache as he took in and appraised the information. He turned to face Rafael, his eyes narrowing and his features going flat. "I just had lunch with Emilio Ortega." Miriam snorted with distaste.

"What does that hyena want today? There's always an ask when he's involved. " Rafael closed his eyes. He could feel what was coming.

"When does he want me to start?" he asked with a grave courtesy that seemed somehow mocking. Calderon was silent for a moment, a sour smirk twisting across his face under the moustache. Miriam looked at him sharply. "We saw you talking with Ortega's new deputy on the other side of the office," Rafael continued, "and now you're holding a folder with my name written on the front of it."

"You're right Alvarez. The funny thing is that Ortega actually wants to meet you." He dropped the manila file onto Miriam's desk with a slap. Raphael could see it had the golden puzzle piece logo of the *Fiscalia* above the oddly menacing motto of the organisation printed out in block capitals:

"En la calle y en los territorios - In the street and in the territories"

He had often wondered whether the purpose of the slogan was to threaten or to reassure. It seemed to achieve both objectives without much concern being given to who was on the receiving end. "You've been re-assigned. Read what's in here and meet me at the Paloquemao in half an hour." Without further discussion Calderon turned and strode away across the sterile landscape of the office.

**

The prosecutors had a floor to themselves in the Paloquemao Judicial Complex and Calderon was already waiting outside Ortega's office when Rafael arrived. The sub-director was fiddling absently with his tie and he glared at Raphael as the investigator sat down next to him.

"Now when we're in there I don't want you saying anything out of turn. I've had to assign this case to you as there's no one else. I don't want you getting any strange ideas just because the prosecutor has asked to speak with you directly. As far as I'm concerned it's entirely routine. We'll open the file, go through the usual process and then log it as unsolved. Is that clear?"

"I don't see how anything can be clear until I know more about what's involved."

"You see. That's what I'm talking about. You've been warned. Nothing out of turn."

Rafael was always struck by the unimaginative drabness of the Paloquemao building; a colossal, grey cuboid of concrete jutting up into the sky like a monumental grave stone that dominated the surrounding city blocks. The building itself and much of the surrounding area had been reduced to rubble by Escobar's monstrous bomb in December 1989. The drug lord's *sicarios* had packed five hundred kilograms of dynamite onto a bus and detonated it at the junction of Carrera 28 and Calle 18, one street away from the tower. The attack had been planned in an effort to take out the director of the State Intelligence Services, the DAS, who had been based in the building at the time. In the event, the director had escaped unhurt but the blast had killed at least fifty people and injured six hundred more.

Rafael had been fourteen when the bomb went off, finishing his ninth year at the *Colegio Antonio Nariño* in San Cristobal. His mother had moved the family to a small rented house in the modest south Bogota neighbourhood after the disappearance of his father the previous year. The faint roar of the explosion had been audible on the way to school in the morning, even from several kilometres away. Rafael distinctly remembered seeing the plume of smoke rising in the city to the north and the day being filled with the sound of sirens. In those days the feeling of fear was all pervasive. It felt like the balance of the country was tipping away from the old order and that a frightening chaos was taking over. Now the building had long since been reconstructed and the area served as one of the most important criminal courts of Bogota as well as the principle offices of the state prosecutors, the Fiscals.

The polished, mahogany door opened and the prosecutor's secretary ushered them onto a plush leather sofa before bustling off to get coffee. Calderon's portly frame sunk deep into the cushions. Rafael stared into space intrigued by the fact that even before he'd been told the details of the case, pressure was being put on him to deal with it quickly and not cause any waves. The secretary returned with the refreshments and then, in response to a buzzer on her desk, shepherded the two detectives into the prosecutor's inner sanctum.

"Gentlemen, I must thank you for taking the time to see me on this matter," Ortega announced, coming round his substantial desk to shake them by the hand. There was no irony in his voice despite the fact that they had been imperiously summoned at short notice rather than there being any voluntary element in their attendance. As Rafael shook the prosecutor's hand he noticed that the man wore a heavy gold ring with a green stone on the little finger of his right hand. "You may not have had a chance to familiarise yourselves with the full details of the file but I wanted to take the opportunity to personally meet the investigator who will be leading the case."

"Alvarez is the man I told you about earlier, sir. He is one of the best we have and shows an uncommon dedication to his work."

"Delighted to meet you investigator Alvarez. If you'll permit me to say, you seem very young to be a homicide investigator." The barbs in the opening exchanges had not been subtle, with minimal effort made to conceal the obvious disdain with which he was regarded. Rafael was tense and defiant, and avoided meeting the eyes fixed on him.

"Thank you sir. I have been privileged to serve our city in that capacity." He lowered his head in a gesture of acknowledgement, observing the political dance between the prosecutor and his boss.

"Yes, quite. Let's get to the details." The prosecutor settled into a high backed leather chair behind the polished expanse of his desk. A set of book shelves covered the wall to the right of the desk, filled with a comprehensive set of laws books. They seemed shiny, flawless, unused. An expensive view westwards towards the Candelaria and the gothic spires of the main cathedral could be seen from the window of Ortega's office.

"On the surface this appears a heinous and gruesome murder. In reality it is a homicide like any of the thousand or so others that tragically afflict our fellow citizens every year. It is almost certainly the result of *desplazados* from the country trying to bring their rural violence to the capital." Ortega leaned forward on the desk, making a steeple of his fingers. "Given its shock value I want you to be aware that this crime has the potential to generate political disturbance. The reason I've brought you both here today is to seek your assurances that you will not let that happen. I expect that you will deal with the crime in the normal way and not allow your investigation to be distracted by political agitations or attempts to sensationalise what is essentially another routine homicide."

"Don't worry sir. Alvarez knows what is required of him."

"Señor Fiscal, may I ask what it is about this case that particularly causes you concern." Calderon shot Rafael an evil glance.

"Certainly Investigator Alvarez. As you know this is a delicate time for Bogota. The government is keen to be seen to be doing something about the endemic street crime and the waves of refugees that sadly afflict our city. Our *'Bogota*

Mejor' campaign is finally beginning to bear fruit but certain elements in the media are dissatisfied with the way the campaign is being conducted. I fear that they would like to use this case as a talisman to derail our reforms. To prove that our measures are not working. Justice must take its course but we are very keen to see that justice is achieved quickly and without sensation. The way you conduct this case will be very important to a number of people and, as I said, I wanted to take the opportunity to meet the investigator personally and talk through my concerns."

"Very good sir. I shall try my best not to be a disappointment to you."

"I'm afraid I have another appointment. Gentlemen, I thank you again for your time and I look forward to a rapid and successful resolution of this case." Ortega stood as he spoke and it was clear they were being dismissed. Outside in the corridor Calderon grabbed Rafael's arm.

"You heard what the prosecutor said. Don't start that intricate brain of yours working on this one. Get an answer and get it quickly." Rafael shrugged him off and marched away, disgusted but intrigued.

**

5. Cinco

Rafael hailed a taxi on the street outside the Paloquemao building. A boxy, yellow Hyundai with number plate sticker decals on the side doors pulled up at the kerb almost immediately. As the taxi wove its way slowly eastwards through the afternoon traffic, Rafael's eyes were drawn to the plastic figure of the *Virgen del Carmen*, that hung from the rear view mirror, swaying with the movements of the car. The thin cord had looped itself round the neck of the miniature statue and the impassive face below its silver crown seemed to jerk and bounce from an executioners noose as the car lurched forward over the pitted surface of the road.

He sighed and pinched the skin at the bridge of his nose as he looked out of the window. The contradictions from his meeting with the prosecutor had left him perplexed and disorientated. Calderon had presented him as a highly-skilled investigator and the best man for the job, when they both knew that was a considerable way short of the truth. Ortega had seemed to be obtusely convinced by this version of his abilities. He had been simultaneously encouraged to investigate fully and then pressurised to close out the investigation in a short time frame. The whole situation felt decidedly dreamlike, as though reality had been suspended and some flight of fancy had plunged him back into the highly charged atmosphere of a murder investigation. And now here he was in the dented yellow taxi heading towards Monserrate and whatever was waiting for him on the mountain.

The memory of his last murder investigation floated back into his consciousness as he watched a scrawny looking youth on a motorbike with no crash helmet pick his way delicately between two enormous, rumbling buses. The woman's body had been found in the kitchen, a vivid spray of blood across the white tiles. It had been in one of the old houses in La Soledad, a few blocks from the *Parque Nacional*. He'd heard one of his colleagues describe the house as 'Victorian English style' without much of an idea of what that meant beyond what he had been able to see of the ornate, red-brick, two storey building in which the woman had been butchered. She had been stabbed so many times that her chest was little more than a bloody mush.

The husband, a wealthy stockbroker, had been missing so early efforts had focused on him as an immediate suspect. Rafael however, had been drawn towards the attitude of the woman who worked with him on the firm's trading desk. Something about her manner had not seemed right. Her expressions of grief struck him as inauthentic and her answers to his questions were too perfect, too assured.

Once she was in his focus it had not taken him long to unravel the sordid details. The intense love affair, the obsessive jealousy of the wife and the final humiliation when her lover refused to leave his family. His efforts to end the relationship had caused her to snap and take out her hatred on her despised rival in a frenzy of violence.

Rafael's hints that they were closing in on the husband led her to panic and she had been caught trying to flee the country. When she confessed to his murder as well, the forensics had been conclusive and she had been sentenced to a lengthy term in Colombia's extensive and punishing prison system.

Rafael walled himself away from the images of the dead woman. The reminder of what he himself had suddenly lost a few short weeks later was almost too sharp for him to bear. The taxi jerked as the driver braked suddenly to avoid being flattened by one of the buses which had changed lane without warning. The loud hiss of the bus's air brakes seemed to issue a sullen threat to keep away from its territory. In the back seat, a shiver of dread trickled down Rafael's spine. I'm not ready for this, a small, insistent voice echoed through his mind. I can't do it any more. I can't put the pieces together, I just don't care enough. What's the point of exposing myself to all the suffering and death? Surely there must be someone better than me to do this. Someone who isn't broken.

His hand was creeping towards the pocket of his trousers, where the pills waited for him. He watched its silent progress for a moment before snatching it back. No, not today. He wouldn't allow himself to indulge in their smothering comfort. It took an effort of will but he beat back the cloud of self-doubt that threatened to envelop him. The time for objections was past and it was too late to back out. One thing burned clear in his mind, now that he'd had a small amount of time to reflect. The implication that he was not capable of seeing the investigation through to a genuine resolution had irritated him. He felt the stubborn streak in him rise up and he silently vowed to himself that he would do everything within his power to find the truth of what had happened, to try and bring some small measure of justice to whoever it was that had been killed, even if the odds were stacked against him.

The grey clouds that covered the sky were beginning to darken by the time Rafael arrived at Monserrate. The car park at the base of the mountain was full and the taxi had been forced to leave him in the street. He counted out the bills to cover the fare and included a decent tip, pushing the money into the driver's outstretched hand before watching the taxi disappear into the evening rush hour traffic. The cable car and funicular railway that ferried tourists and visitors to the top had been closed off and the windows of the ticket office were dark and silent. A small group of green uniformed police waited outside to turn away any persistent sightseers. The air was beginning to turn cold with the coming night and the smell of damp earth carried on the breeze. Rafael pulled a blue jacket from the holdall he was carrying and slipped it over his shirt, the yellow CTI logo blazed prominently across the back.

He started alone up the steep path to the top of the mountain, the crunch of his shoes on the loose stones throwing up small clouds of dust as he ascended. Given the known dangers of the pilgrimage it was unusual to find anyone on the path. After dark it was almost always deserted apart from people who had a reason not to be found. In spite of that, he could see several small groups of people ahead of him and some passed him muttering on the way back down. Nothing like a death for brining out the crowds.

The mountains were a constant presence wherever you were in Bogota, a jagged wall running down the eastern side of the city. Rafael thought briefly of his childhood home in San Cristobal which had been right up against the foothills of the *Cerro Aguanoso* further to the south. He had a sudden vivid memory of chasing after a football with a group of the other scruffy children from the neighbourhood, careering past the

Asaderos, the make shift snack bars on the ground floor of someone's home, and the *Papelerias,* the newsagents and grocery stores, that lined the steeply sloping streets.   He wondered momentarily whatever had happened to the kids he used to know.   He didn't really have much reason to return to San Cristobal now that his mother had moved to Brazil to live with her cousins and since his sister had left for Miami to find work.   The last he heard was that she was working as a domestic helper for a fund manager who lived on Miami beach.

He remembered Monserrate as well, of course.   There had been any number of trips to the top of the mountain as a family, usually on a Sunday morning to pray for the soul of his missing father in the church at the top.   Another image floated up from his memory, of lighting a candle with his mother in one of the side chapels.   He recalled the intensity and emotion on her face as he knelt beside her, looking at the flame, and the strange guilt he experienced at not being able to feel anything himself when he thought of his father.   There had just been an empty void together with a simple acceptance that he was gone and that life would have to move on without him.

The air this high up was much clearer, with only a faint tang of the smog and car exhaust that clogged the atmosphere at street level.   Trees and bushes grew along the path on the downward side, clinging precariously to the sides of the mountain.   Rafael's eye was drawn to a metallic glint further ahead and as he got closer he saw that someone had pushed a crushed can of diet coke into a small gap between the bricks of the low wall that ran along next to the path.

The sun was setting through the brown haze that hung over the city below and the car headlamps were starting to come on, illuminating the streets with tightly-packed beads of moving light.   He could see the plan of the city spread out from where he stood with the main roads seeming to converge towards a point almost directly below him, like the uneven spokes of a bicycle wheel snapped in half.   His eyes followed the main north-south line of the *Avenida Caracas* through the buildings towards where it merged into the *Autopista del Norte* and left the city behind.   He could pick out the *Avenida Boyaca* heading towards the northwest, then moving counter clockwise around the wheel, the *Avenida El Dorado* and the *Avenida de las Americas* leading west towards the airport and his apartment in

39

Fontibon. The gleaming line of the *Avenida NQS*, the *Norte-Quito-Sur*, cut through the city to the southwest, passing through San Cristobal before heading down from the high Bogota plains towards the valley of the Magdalena river. Turning back to the trail he saw that the body of a dead rat lay sprawled out across the path ahead of him. He stepped over it carefully and continued his ascent.

Round the next switchback a small crowd of onlookers had gathered. A silent group of hollow-eyed people were being held back by a white line of tape across the path and a solitary patrol man in the green and white uniform of the Bogota police. Rafael blended seamlessly into the crowd and shuffled steadily to the front.

"It's terrible. The animals who did this cut off the guy's head." Someone in the crowd turned to whisper to their neighbour.

"Peoples' lives have no meaning any more. Isn't it your job to do something about it?"

Rafael had reached the front and the speaker, a shrunken middle aged man, was accusing the patrol man. He was almost shaking with anger and the patrol man looked scared and defensive. Rafael took the opportunity to duck under the tape and enter the crime scene.

"Hey, you can't go in there. No journalists allowed," the patrol man restraining the onlookers shouted at him. In his dark trousers, plain blue shirt and overcoat Rafael had to concede that he didn't look much like an investigator. Then the patrol man caught sight of the yellow CTI logo on the back of Rafael's jacket and realised his mistake. "Sorry sir. You're welcome to go ahead, if you can show me some identification."

"Give me a moment." Rafael turned slowly towards the man fishing his wallet out of his back pocket to show his *Fiscalia* card. As he handed it over he caught a glimpse of his photo behind the security laminate. The man staring back at him from the card seemed a stranger, a younger, happier version of himself who he barely recognised any more.

Beyond the tape Rafael stopped to survey the scene. Arc lights had been set up at intervals along the track, the glare of the harsh neon light throwing jagged shadows across the path and into the dense pine trees beyond. The suitcase stood apart in the middle of the trail, the broken lid yawning back like a dislocated jaw.   Men and women in white coveralls moved silently about, photographing, scraping and putting things into jars and bags, silent phantoms attending the dead.

"Excuse me. Is it ok to look at the case?" He stopped one of the ivory-clad crime scene specialists, a short woman with dark eyes and curly hair.

"You'll need to check with Lieutenant Ospina.   He's in charge until the *Fiscalia* arrive," she replied abruptly before striding off into the dazzling glow.   Rafael watched her go, wondering what to do next when an angry shout thundered from the barrier behind him, making him start.

"Don't ever tell me I'm wrong! Follow the goddam orders and move them back one hundred meters. I don't care if you need to use your gun to do it." Rafael turned his head to see a slender, young-looking officer leaning forward as he yelled at the patrol man who had asked him for identification. His arm was out and he was pointing past the tape line and back down the slope. A red flush played on the delicate cheekbones of his boyish face.   The man caught sight of where Rafael was standing and marched over to him.

"*Teniente* Mauro Ospina, Bogota Metropolitan Police, sir," he barked, raising his hand in a precise salute as he stopped. "I've been assigned as primary liaison officer for this incident." Rafael noticed the beginnings of a moustache shading his top lip. He glanced down at the cracked face of his watch as he introduced himself in turn, drawing a frown from the stiff shouldered young man in front of him.

So, things had moved faster than he'd expected and a watchdog had already been set on him. He wondered if Ortega was behind the move or if was simply down to the usual inter-agency rivalry between the *Policia Nacional* and the *Fiscalia*. There was no question that Rafael had jurisdiction and seniority but from now on his every move would be scrutinised.

"So, you're Alvarez," Ospina drawled, his hands held crisply behind his back. "Yes, they told me about you." His head tilted back and his sharp eyes seemed to glitter in the steely light. "Not to worry. I've been fully trained in crime scene protocol, so everything here is under my control."

"Have you managed to do much?" Rafael found it hard to keep the disdain out of his voice.

"Not yet sir. I've got the perimeter in place and set the

forensics team to work. Since then I've been waiting for the *Fiscalia* to arrive." The reflection from the yellow, hi-vis jacket that Ospina wore over his combat fatigues threw glints of brightness into the surrounding gloom.

"Well we're here now, at least I am. Are you ready to take a look?" Ospina gave a curt nod in reply and they turned towards the case. Darkness had fallen completely as the two of them approached the scene, stepping careful so as not to disturb any of the marks in the dust which were being carefully photographed and recorded by the phantoms. Rafael squeezed his hands into some plastic gloves and Ospina pulled out a flick knife from a pocket on his thigh which he snapped open with a sharp click. The unforgiving dazzle of the arc lights intensified the pale skin of the corpse so that it looked like an incongruous block of misshapen ice abandoned on the path in the cool night air.

"So, what do you see?" Ospina asked as they squatted next to the case. He held the knife steady in his right hand as he spoke.

"The torso is dry and the skin is waxy so probably not too long dead. I'd guess two or maybe three days. There's a puncture wound to the sternum which may have pierced the heart and led to death. The autopsy should give us more answers. The swelling and bloodstains around the groin suggest the injuries were inflicted while he was still alive."

"Jesus. What a way to go." Ospina blinked quickly and looked away. The faint red flush seemed to drain away from his face. Ospina watched Rafael through narrowed eyes as he worked. The investigator's thin face was an intense mask of concentration as he studied the remains. His pale, yellow eyes darted from one side to the other as he took in every detail.

"Were there any witnesses? Did anyone see anything?" Rafael continued to study the corpse as he spoke.

"Not really. Just the lady who found the case. She's waiting with some of my officers at the bottom of the path."

"This is interesting; what do you make of it?" Rafael asked, indicating a group of black marks standing out clearly on the corpse's pallid shoulder. "It looks like a tattoo of some kind," he added. "The circles and points almost look like a sun."

"I've seen these before. Not this design but you see it all the time with the *desplazado* kids in Ciudad Bolivar. It's a gang

42

symbol. As soon as they arrive in Bogota and realise there's nothing for them to do here the first thing they do is organise themselves into a gang, usually with a bunch of other kids from wherever it was they came from. The gangs all have a symbol and as soon as they're old enough they get it tattooed on themselves to prove they're committed to the gang."

To Rafael, Ospina sounded as though he was reciting from the academy manual. He doubted that the young man had spent much, if any time in Ciudad Bolivar. A thin frown appeared on Ospina's forehead and his eyebrows drew together.

"I've not heard of anything like this before though." Rafael nodded quickly as he felt the return of his old instincts in a rush. He was able to banish any thought of the torso as the remains of a human being and see it instead as a series of events leading up to this point, as a puzzle to be unlocked.

"Pass me your knife for a moment." Rafael took the knife before Ospina had a chance to respond. "Look here," he said using the knife to point at the beginning of a thin slit that ended close to the torso's armpit. "There's no blood or swelling so this was probably done after he died."

Rafael probed with the knife but the slit led down from the man's armpit and further progress was prevented by the body's position in the case. He pushed a gloved hand down the side to continue tracing the line.

"It stops just below the rim of the case and runs along the line of his rib cage."

"Hey, slow down a minute! I don't think any of this has been photographed yet." Ospina, interrupted, a slight note of alarm creeping into his voice.

"I'm sorry, you're right." Rafael withdrew his hand and wiped it unceremoniously on his grey trousers. "Excuse me, could you come and take the necessary pictures please," Rafael called to the short woman with the curly hair who he had spoken to on his arrival. She bustled over, holding a camera with some bulky flash equipment fixed to the top. The flash whirred and popped and the scene was caught in the hyper-real glare. When Rafael closed his eyes he could still see the suitcase with the yawning lid and the shrunken torso lying within. Rafael squatted once again next to the case.

"Let's see what this is all about," he said pushing his gloved hand back into the gap between the body and the case, following the line of the slit along the ribs.

"Go ahead. I'm not sure what you're expecting to find in there though," Ospina responded looking slightly queasy.

"The skin is loose here and the slit extends for the whole length of the torso." Rafael continued his commentary. "It's not fixed to the body at all. In fact if I lift here…" As he spoke he raised his hand from the corner of the case and the skin of the corpse peeled back from the corner like the page of an antique book.

Ospina turned away and vomited unceremoniously into the plants at the side of the path. Rafael's eyes were fixed on the corpse and what had been revealed under the peeled back skin. A gaping, empty cavity waited where the internal organs should have been. Heart, lungs, kidney and liver were all conspicuous by their absence. He took a sharp intake of breath and let the skin fall back with a dry sounding slap before turning to check on the incapacitated Ospina.

**

Milagros Santamaria was still waiting at the bottom of the mountain from where she had called for help. Her lined face was set with a brittle determination as she stood with a patrol man who was taking down her personal details to make sure she would be contactable later if needed.

"I've had enough for one day," Ospina declared as they reached the end of the path and the car park. "You can speak to the old woman if you want. I'll see you tomorrow morning at the Bunker." He turned and wobbled off into the night, still rattled from the encounter on the mountain.

Scattered raindrops fell from the overcast sky as Rafael approached Milagros. She turned away from the patrolman, a questioning look on her squarish, heavy face. She wore thick glasses with brown plastic frames and Rafael could see a few spots of rain glinting on the lenses. The brown of the glasses matched the colour of her shapeless dress and her greying hair was tied back in a severe bun. Rafael introduced himself, showing his *Fiscalia* card.

"Señora, I'm sorry you've had to see such a terrible thing. I understand that you'd probably like to get home but I'd be grateful if I could take a little more of your time."

"Whatever I can do to help, I will," she declared, looking him directly in the eye. To Rafael her voice sounded scratchy and fragile.

A shabby café was located at the end of the empty car park. A few plastic chairs spilled out onto the street but they headed inside to take a table out of the drizzle. They were the only two customers at this late hour and the owner looked distinctly unhappy to see them. A short balding man with deep set eyes and an unwelcoming scowl, he wiped his hands on his dirty apron as he took their order and then stomped away behind the counter. The legs of the chairs scraped across the tiled floor as they sat, a loud rasping that cut through the quiet atmosphere of the cafe. Moths circled the unshaded light bulbs and occasionally collided with them, making a soft pinging sound.

"So Señora, please tell me again how you found the body." Rafael asked once the owner had returned with the drinks, a black coffee for Rafael and an orange juice for Milagros.

"There's not much to tell. My mother is very sick, I don't think she is long for this world to be honest. I decided to make the pilgrimage up the mountain to the *Señor Caido* as a prayer to help relieve her suffering. I came round the corner and that suitcase was just lying there in the middle of the path, as though it was waiting for me to find it. I lifted the lid and the remains of that poor man were crammed inside." She raised a hand to her mouth as the reality of what she had seen weighed down on her again. "Who could do such a thing to another human being?" she asked, her voice shaking slightly.

Rafael shook his head, speechless. He didn't have any kind of answer for her and she looked away, taking a sip of the warm, acidy orange juice.

"Did you see anyone on the path, anything suspicious at all?" The question sounded hopeless even to him.

"No I'm sorry, when I realised what I was looking at I turned and ran. There might have been someone there but I'm afraid I didn't see anything. I wish I had something else to tell you."

There was a short pause as Rafael stirred his coffee, thinking. The whole thing seemed so hopeless. A body that no-one was missing with no way of knowing who it was and a witness who had seen nothing. Perhaps the prosecutor had been right to suggest that he finish the work quickly and get back to the mundane but less traumatic world of Environmental Crimes.

45

"You are a young man and yet you seem so sad." Milagros broke the silence looking at him carefully with concern showing in her eyes, behind the heavy lenses.

"I'm not expected to succeed," he muttered putting the spoon back on the table. "This is a murder I'm not expected to solve. I follow procedure, record the details and then it will be filed away as another unsolved Bogota homicide."

"I believe you will catch the evil men who did this terrible thing," she replied firmly. "I am sure of it. I can see it your face. The Lord wants justice and I will pray for you to prevail."

**

Rafael trudged wearily up the stairs to his second floor apartment. The hallway was dark and he had to fumble with his key to get it into the lock. The door creaked open to reveal the wreckage that was his personal life. The flat was small with wooden parquet floors and was located above a garage. Despite the late hour, the rumble of traffic outside was loud and unwashed dishes rattled in the sink. Dirty clothes were piled high on the sofa. He had stopped to pick up some empanadas from a street vendor on the way home and eaten them in his car. The dry pastry and greasy meat was not enough for a satisfying meal but enough to keep the hunger from his belly so he could sleep. As he entered the flat he let the wrapping fall to the floor. Since he'd lost Gabriella this was what his life had been reduced to. No longer able to look after himself; no longer caring that he was unable to do so.

He collapsed onto the sofa and pulled the bottle of pills from his pocket. Clasping it firmly between his index finger and thumb he held the small, plastic container up in front of his face. He stared at it for a long time in the semi-darkness until his eyes lost their focus and the dim cylinder seemed to blur into the beige wallpaper behind. Then he lowered his hand, allowing the pills to drop back onto the sofa next to him.

After a moment of stillness he reached towards his jacket again and removed his wallet from the breast pocket. Lying back he carefully took out a small passport photo of Gabriella that he kept concealed behind his driving licence. She looked out at him thoughtfully, her long, black hair swept back and her eyes dark and mysterious as she looked directly at the camera.

Her beautiful mouth was twisted into an expression half way between a smirk and a grimace as though she had thought to smile for the camera but then realised it was a passport photo and changed her expression at the last minute.

The months since she had been taken away from him had passed in a grey blur and the pain was still raw and burning. He put the photo carefully back into his wallet and fell asleep where he lay in his clothes.

**

6. Seis

Ciudad Bolivar spread away toward the horizon like a giant cancerous growth of ramshackle houses. So many wasted lives trapped in this decaying slum, Rafael reflected as they reached the top of the rise and the sombre panorama stretched out below them. Smog curled up in the hazy morning light, obscuring the mountains on the horizon. Jammed into the angle of Avenida Boyaca and the Autopista del Sur at the southern edge of the city, Ciudad Bolivar hadn't really existed until the 1980s. It grew up as the refugees from Colombia's brutal civil war, the *desplazados*, fled to the capital to escape the spiralling, arbitrary savageness of the perpetual internal conflict. Sadly, the more of them that arrived, the worse the conditions became and the area was a now byword for criminal gangs, drugs and violence. Nobody wanted to live in Ciudad Bolivar; those that did had little choice in the matter.

Rafael sat uncomfortably in the passenger seat of Jorge's ageing Ford hatchback. The adjusting control was broken and the back of the seat was jammed too far forward, forcing Rafael to lean over his knees. The seat belt on the passenger side was missing as well which meant that the drive through the chaos of the morning rush hour traffic had been even more intense than usual. Jorge was not a careful driver, darting into the lanes of moving traffic without warning and driving uncomfortably close to the slower and much larger buses and trucks as though trying to push them out of his way.

They had stopped outside the grey bulk of the Bunker and Mauro Ospina had clambered into the back seat. Ospina had grumbled about Jorge's presence for the expedition into Ciudad Bolivar but Rafael had insisted that the experienced police sergeant accompany them. Jorge was more familiar with the subtle dangers of the sprawling slum than anyone else Rafael knew. His friend had agreed reluctantly when Rafael explained what he wanted on the phone the night before. Now he stared impassively through the windshield, his grip tight on the steering wheel.

Ospina was wearing fashionable plastic sports sunglasses against the morning glare. The poor quality of the lenses and the spelling mistake on the brand name gave them away as obvious fakes. In the rearview mirror Rafael saw him turn his head to glance at the two men in front of him.

"You guys work together for a long time?" Jorge grunted in response his heavy features looking pale and indistinct in the bright morning sunlight.

"Yeah, we go way back. I knew Rafael before he joined the police. He was friends with my kid brother Nico. The two of them used to steal the fruit from outside *Viveres y Verduras* on the way home from school." Rafael grinned at the memory.

"Whatever happened to Nico? It's been years since I saw him."

"He works on a construction site these days. Last time I spoke with him he was pouring concrete for a new overpass on the Avenida Caracas." The three of them were dressed in plain, nondescript clothes. Ospina looked awkward and uncomfortable out of his combat fatigues but it would have been a dangerous provocation to walk around in a Bogota police uniform in this part of town.

"So what's your story, Alvarez?" Ospina leered, leaning forward through the middle of the car until his knife-like face was just behind Rafael's left shoulder. "I remember seeing you on the television when you got that medal from the Fiscal General. You looked like a chicken about to be eaten by a crocodile." He stifled a snort of laughter. "My friend who works in the Organised Crime department told me you were tipped for big things after that but then you sort of disappeared. How did you end up in charge of an investigation like this?"

"I've been trying to work that out for myself," Rafael muttered, resting his head against the cold pane of glass next to him. The memory of the surreal day that had been the reason for his award forced its way into Rafael's consciousness as he listened absently to Ospina's words. An appointment to consult with a ballistics expert had taken him to one of the less well protected *Fiscalia* branch offices in Chapinero, the city's financial district. He had been in the lobby, just through the angular frame of the metal detector when the shouting had started. The operator was frozen in the action of handing Rafael's gun back to him as three of the attackers burst through the glass front door. Time had seemed to slow down as he registered, the black masks covering their faces and the long, sleek shapes of the sub-machine guns they clutched to their chests.

Guttural shouts of '*Libertad*!' echoed through the lobby. There had been a series of dull pops and the head of a man in a suit standing close to him had disappeared in a cloud of blood. Rafael felt outside of himself as he watched his own hand jerk sharply upwards, clutching the gun he had just been passed. The muzzle lined up with one of the attackers and he squeezed the trigger. The man sprawled backwards onto the marble floor and Rafael dived behind the bulk of the security X-ray for protection. At that point the security guards had recovered from their surprise and shooting erupted from all directions. The other two attackers had fallen quickly after that, but not before a score of *Fiscalia* employees and civilians had been gunned down. It had all happened in less than a minute, but lying on his side behind the featureless plastic casing of the machine each second had seemed to stretch to an eternity as his heart hammered a crescendo in his ears. It had been the last time he had drawn or fired his gun.

As they descended into the warren of muddy paths and zinc roofed shacks, the bumpy broken tarmac gave way entirely to unpaved dirt road. There was less traffic here but Jorge was forced to pick his way around cracks and large potholes in order to make progress. Cars were gradually replaced by mule carts loaded high with ragged cargo that swayed dangerously.

"Turn left here," Rafael instructed.

"Can't we meet this contact of yours somewhere a little less hostile?" Ospina hissed from the back seat, his eyes darting about nervously.

"El Chivo never comes to see me. I always go to see him. That's how our arrangement works."

"I hope you know what you're doing. This is the kind of shithole where people disappear without a trace and no-one even notices or cares."

"Look, the chances are that if anyone in this part of town was involved with our man in the suitcase then El Chivo will know something about it. It's worth the risk."

El Chivo had been part of Escobar's crime organisation and had spent time working for one his top lieutenants, the notorious and oddly named Popeye. The Medellin cartel had relied on him to run a part of their operations in Ciudad Bolivar. After Escobar's death El Chivo had gone into business for himself and had considerable power and influence in this part of the slums. Rafael had been acquainted with him for more or less two years, after El Chivo provided vital information on one of Rafael's previous murder investigations in exchange for more lenient terms for one of his associates who had been detained by the *Fiscalia*. Since then Rafael had developed El Chivo into a valuable confidential informant who would provide information for money or favours in certain limited circumstances, usually where the wrong doings of his competitors were involved.

The street became narrower and Jorge was forced to slow the car as he followed the dusty path weaving through the flimsy wooden shacks. Ragged children ran to the side of the track to stare at the the car before turning and disappearing into the dark alleys between the houses. Groups of men lounged at street corners following the car with narrow, hostile eyes.

"Stop here" Rafael ordered as they reached a junction where several of the dirt roads joined to form a small open plaza. A makeshift cart with a tattered umbrella skewered through the middle stood abandoned in the middle of the space. No doubt the owner would return later in the day to try and sell some more of the sad detritus that was piled high on its flat wooden boards. The building in front of them was of more solid construction than the surrounding shacks with a concrete exterior and a tiled roof instead of the rusty, corrugated iron that served to cover the other shacks around them. A hand painted cloth banner held in place with frayed blue rope announced that they had arrived at Dona Julietta's bar.

A hard, wiry youth, not much younger than Ospina sauntered over to the car and tapped on the windscreen, lifting up his t-shirt to show the gun pushed into this belt. Rafael wound down the window.

"I'm here to see El Chivo." He looked the young man directly in the eyes as he spoke. "He knows I'm coming."

"We'll see," he sneered. "Wait here." Turning away from the car he headed for the bar and disappeared through the darkened doorway.

Ospina climbed out of the car and took several paces across the plaza, scuffing the dirt with his shoe as he stared around at the broken buildings. Jorge pulled out a flask of coffee from the glove box and offered Rafael a plastic cup. The piping hot liquid warmed his hands against the morning chill.

"If anything goes wrong in there, don't wait around for me. Just put your foot on the accelerator and drive." His nose wrinkled slightly and a tight smile played across his lips. "Make sure you get the lieutenant out of here. I'd hate to have to tell his mum if something happened to him." Jorge laughed and then shook his head gently.

"If it was the other way round would you leave me?" Rafael was silent in response. "Well then, I think you know the answer." Jorge took a sip of the scalding, bitter coffee, his eyes shifting to where Ospina stood a few metres from the car with his hand clasped behind his back awkwardly. "He looks a bit like you, did you realise that?"

Rafael turned to look at his friend, a sceptical frown playing over his forehead above his lopsided smile.

"Come on, I was never that much of a prick."

"That's not how I remember things." Jorge let out a low chuckle. Rafael's lips twitched into a faint smile and then his eyes grew distant.

"Look, I'm sorry about the other night. I didn't mean to unload my troubles onto you." His words were tinged with bitterness and his gaze dropped to the cracked screen of his watch.

"There's nothing to be sorry for. I can't believe you didn't tell me before." Rafael raised his left forearm, twisting back the wrist to show the watch to Jorge.

"She gave this to me you know, for my birthday last year. It was the first expensive watch I've ever owned." He sighed and let his arm fall back into his lap. "The day after she died I got so drunk I didn't even know my own name. I was so angry, so fucking sad that I needed to break something, to feel some pain. I was in one of those little bars in Fontibon and it was like a switch just flipped and I started smashing the place up. I threw a bottle of whisky through the window, smashed the TV with a chair, it was crazy. In the end they took me out the back and kicked the shit out of me. I got exactly what I wanted. When I woke up the next day, the watch was like this and now I can't bring myself to take it off. I know I need to let her go, but it's like I'm stuck. I can't go back but I don't want to move forward." Jorge placed his large, calloused hand on Rafael's shoulder and looked him directly in the eyes.

"Whatever you need. I'm here for you, *mano*, whenever you're ready." Across the plaza, the skinny figure of the youth emerged from the bar and made his way towards them with a deliberate, sullen slowness. He crossed the open space heading for the car without even a glance to where Ospina stood to one side.

"He's ready for you *jefe*," he said to Rafael, his voice flat as he leaned in towards the open window. Rafael pushed open the door and climbed out of the car, the morning air cold on his freshly shaved face. After a moment, Ospina moved to join them and the youth spun quickly to face him, his frame tensing and his hand moving towards his belt.

"Not you *parce*," he sneered glaring at the lieutenant with thinly veiled hostility. Rafael lifted his hands, showing the palms.

"It's okay Mauro. Wait in the car with Jorge and watch your back. I won't be long."

"Don't worry about me," said Ospina glancing about nervously. "I want to know everything you find out." He climbed into the back of the car, pushed his sunglasses up onto his nose and hunched down in the seat. Jorge leaned across to reach for the door. "Watch yourself in there. We'll be right here when you're done." Rafael pulled a brown leather jacket over the crumpled shirt he had fallen asleep in the night before. He took a moment to scan the deserted plaza and his eye was drawn to a twitch of movement in one of the broken-down shacks. For a moment he thought he caught a glimpse of a familiar flash of grey hair and a stocky silhouette through the darkened doorway, but when he looked again there was nothing. With a final wave to the car he turned to follow the youth across the dusty space and into the bar.

At this time of the morning the place was nearly empty. Two young men in football shirts were arguing over a game of billiards while an older man with a beard sat on a stool in a corner, reading a newspaper and nursing a glass of thin yellow beer. The tinny sound of Vallenato music came from a plastic cassette player perched at the end of the serving bar. The stale smell of spilled alcohol, sweat and tobacco smoke filled the room. Nobody looked at Rafael as he stepped up to the bar and ordered a drink.

"El Chivo is waiting for you in the back room," the bar tender announced as he twisted the lid from a bottle of beer and set it on the counter. Rafael picked up the bottle, dropped some coins into the man's hand and pushed through the beaded curtain that led to the toilets and the back room. He struggled down a narrow passage that was half filled with empty plastic crates and broken furniture.   The door at the end opened smoothly when he pushed it with his hand.

El Chivo was slouched in a rickety wooden chair and fiddled with a worn deck of playing cards. Although he wasn't a large man he seemed to fill the space in the small back room. Rafael felt like he was stepping into a cage with a wild animal.

"You look tired Rafael," El Chivo said without looking up.

"I don't sleep so well these days," he replied, settling into the chair opposite the informant. El Chivo's beady, close-set eyes glinted in the dull light from the single window high up in the wall.   He was somewhere in his mid thirties with sharp, angular features and a thin beard on his bony chin. A lifetime in the slums had left its inevitable mark on him in the form of deep scar that curled up from the corner of his mouth.

"So Rafael, how can I be of service this fine morning? The message I received yesterday said it was urgent." The sarcasm in his voice was ugly and obvious.

"Last night we found a corpse in a suitcase on the path to Monserrate.   It looks like he was tortured to death.   There wasn't much left of him.   Someone went to the trouble of removing his arms, legs and head, and also all the internal organs were missing."

"Are you sure you want to call in your favours for this guy? It's just another dead body.   It happens every day in our wonderful city."

"Look, I need something on this."   Rafael's pale eyes hardened. "Besides, I know about the guns you shipped in for the cartel last week and you know how this game works.   I know that you know something." El Chivo slapped the cards down on the table in front of him and let out a sharp braying laugh.

"Okay Rafael. I'll tell you what I know, but not because of the guns. It's because I like you, *papi*. You have an honest face. It's not much though so don't get excited." El Chivo moistened his thin lips with his tongue and took a swig of beer. "There's a man I know, just a kid really, goes by the name of Ruben Barraca. He's a *ratero*, likes to rob people on the street. Bags, watches, whatever. Sometimes he brings me what he steals, sometimes he takes it to the *casa de empeño* to sell. Most of the time it's quick and without violence but he's not afraid to get stuck in if that's necessary. A couple of days ago I sold him some *Burundanga* powder, you know, the stuff that sends you to sleep real quick. I heard from a friend of mine that he went to the Candelaria with his brother and his friend Angel. I heard that they went for some guy with a suitcase. I heard that they didn't find what they expected in that suitcase." El Chivo's eyes narrowed as he tried to gauge Rafael's reaction.

"How can I find Ruben? I need to speak with this kid."

"Well, that's the thing. No-one's seen him since yesterday. Something scared him real bad and he's disappeared down a hole somewhere. There's a lot of holes in Ciudad Bolivar and if he doesn't want to be found, he won't be." Rafael reached into his jacket and slapped a black and white photo face up on the battered table next to the cards. The torso in the case was frozen onto the grainy image, the detail standing out in the stark contrast, the tattoo a dark smudge on the shoulder.

"The guy who did this is completely deranged. I want you to do everything you can to find this kid and quickly. Without him I've got nothing." El Chivo was speechless for a couple of seconds. He picked up the photo and focused carefully on the detail. His eyes widened and he let the image fall from his hands.

"I can't help you Rafael. Get away from this business as quickly as you can." He stood up abruptly and left the room. The final slam of the back door closing announced his departure from the bar.

**

Back outside in the hazy morning sunlight someone had come to claim the ragged cart with the umbrella, which had disappeared from the plaza. A light breeze curled dust into the air and the smell of cooking meat drifted over from the huddled wooden shacks. Rafael was lost in thought as he trudged back to the waiting car. El Chivo was not a man to scare easily. He must have seen worse things in his time. What had caused him to react in such a way to the photo? It seemed like Ruben Barraca was the key. How would he find him without El Chivo? Still, there were other ways and means and at least now he had a name, which was more than he'd started with.

He stopped suddenly, staring at the grey car. Something wasn't right. The rear windscreen was a broken maze of jagged lines. Rafael broke into a jog, covering the open ground quickly. He reached the car and jerked the door open. Jorge was slumped forward against the steering wheel. Ospina lay prone and unmoving across the back seat, one arm trailing along the floor of the car. His sunglasses had ridden up onto his forehead and his eyes stared upwards, blank and unseeing.

Rafael reached out instinctively to touch Jorge's shoulder and the sergeant sagged off the steering wheel and to his side. Rafael caught him before he fell to the ground. A coin sized circle of blood darkened the front of Jorge's grey sweatshirt just below the left shoulder. Feeling the wetness, Rafael lifted his hand off Jorge's back, realising it was a soggy red mess. He looked again at Ospina seeing for the first time the ragged tear of the gunshot wound just below his left eye.

Rafael felt himself go cold. A choking panic took hold of him and his chest felt tight. The scene in front of him seemed unreal, like it was happening to someone else. He couldn't connect the deathly still casualties lying in the car with the two people he had left behind. How could this have happened? He had been in the bar for less than half an hour.

Pushing the fear to one side, he scanned the area around the plaza but there was no sign of an attacker. Rafael kicked the tyre of the car in frustration and slammed his hands onto the metal bodywork of the bonnet. It was then that he noticed the scratches in the paintwork. He lifted his hands and stepped back to get a better view. With a shock he realised that he recognised the design. Marked out in white gashes on the grey paintwork of the bonnet were the concentric circles and triangular points from the tattoo. He slumped down onto the ground, his thinking suspended, unable to process what he was seeing or understand how or why the symbol from the corpse had appeared on the car next to his stricken companions.

His attention returned to the car. It was his fault they had been shot. He had insisted on going to Ciudad Bolivar, despite the dangers. He had put them in harm's way. Ospina was clearly gone but automatically, almost without realising what he was doing, he reached out two fingers and placed them resignedly at Jorge's neck to feel for a pulse. Hope surged inside him as he felt a faint flutter and realised that Jorge was still alive. He bundled his friend back into the car and reached for the police radio attached to the dashboard. There was urgency in the response to his call for help but the nearest units were not close enough to make any difference.

He sat for a moment in silence, the panic rising again as he tried to work out what to do, various plans and scenarios cycling through his head. Then in a flash of clarity he realised the hospital in Kennedy was only a couple of kilometres away at most. With a struggle he shifted the big man over to the uncomfortable seat on passenger side where he himself had sat this morning on the way to the slum. It seemed like a lifetime ago. The car's sluggish, lethargic engine spluttered into life as he turned the key sharply. The wheels spun in the grit, throwing up a cloud of dust as Rafael pushed the hatchback down the slope at top speed in a desperate dash for the Autopista del Sur and on to the hospital, hoping that Jorge would be able to cling on long enough for him to get there.

**

7. Siete

Rafael perched uncomfortably on a sticky fabric sofa in a deserted corridor in the basement of the *Instituto Nacional de Medicina Legal*. The fluorescent strip lighting in the ceiling bathed the corridor in a wan, unnatural light. A wilted pot plant stood to the left of the sofa and a clock on the wall ticked loudly, slicing off the seconds in slow intervals. The autopsy for the suitcase body was due to happen soon and he was expected to be in attendance, waiting in this empty corridor in the basement for the pathologist to arrive.

Jorge's shooting dominated his thoughts. His friend's life was in the hands of the doctors now and hung in the balance. The pulse had been even fainter by the time Rafael had worked his way free of the tangle of traffic on the Autopista del Sur and raced up the Avenida Poporo Quimbaya to the Kennedy Hospital. The driver's seat behind him had been wet with Jorge's blood, a constant reminder of the need for haste as his friend lolled from side to side with the movements of the car. He had rammed the hatchback up onto the kerb outside the emergency department, almost hitting the blue and white sign and scattering a group of vendors selling coffee from carts under umbrellas. The doctors had come running as Rafael dragged the unconscious form of Jorge from the car, yelling that he was a police officer and that he had been shot.

Jorge had been surrounded by a flock of green-clad medical personnel, quickly hustled onto a gurney and borne away into the heart of the hospital. Even though nothing could be done for Ospina the doctors had taken him too. Rafael had had a fleeting view of the stark, white treatment bays with their dark blue dividing curtains and then the double doors had clacked shut, leaving him in the car park with a crowd of nonplussed ambulance drivers.

Someone had directed him to the waiting area and he had trudged reluctantly to the main entrance, navigating the gently curving corridors to the bleak, windowless room with its drab rows of threadbare, uncomfortable seats. At the reception desk a kind-faced nurse took his details and promised to give him any news on Jorge's condition. He had sat for a while with the hushed, anxious relatives staring into space and marking the time with cups of stale, tasteless coffee from the vending machine.

As the adrenalin began to fade Rafael realised that this was the same place in the hospital where he had sat waiting once the doctors realised there was a problem with Gabriella. He had been hustled from the birthing room, assured everything possible would be done for her and directed to this dismal area where he had been told to stay. He could see the same chair he had sat in while she had bled out in the operating theatre and died. A sense of deep gloom took hold of him then, his mood spiralling downwards as the images and memories from that awful day flitted through his mind again. Gabriella's pale, drawn face as she lay helpless on the bed, hair plastered to her head with sweat. The fear in her eyes as the doctors injected the anaesthetic. He was overwhelmed with an awful sense of history repeating itself as the doctors worked on Jorge while he was forced to kill time in this bland, sterile nowhere. It seemed anyone who spent an amount of time with him didn't have much of a future.

As the morning ground on there were scattered and infrequent updates on Jorge. He had been rushed into surgery. Everything was being done to save him and there was no alternative other than to wait patiently and see whether he would pull through. One of Ospina's colleagues in the *Policia Metropolitana de Bogota* had sought him out and he had given the man a statement, a succinct recounting of the events leading up to the shooting that contained all the facts but none of the answers. The man told him that a van with patrol officers had arrived quickly at the dirt plaza outside Dona Julieta's bar and rounded up some people at random from the nearby shacks for questioning. Rafael knew though that nothing would be found and no-one would know anything. This was the code of honour that kept these people alive in the barrio.

Shortly after that he had seen Claudia come barreling into the waiting area, her usually graceful, placid features twisted by grief and distress. She was accompanied by Julio, the older son who comforted his distraught mother with an arm round her shoulders. The resemblance to his father was striking, the same rounded nose and broad, solemn face. Rafael had lurked by the vending machine trying to stay out of sight. The thought of facing her accusing stare filled him with a heavy dread, so when an administrator from the *Fiscalia* called to remind him that the autopsy was due soon he was happy to use it as a chance to slip quietly away from the waiting room. He vowed to himself that he would call later to see what the news was.

The *Instituto Nacional de Medicina Legal* was a functional, six-storey red brick building on the edge of the Candelaria next to the Avenida Caracas. Its grounds blended into the *Parque Tercer Milenio* which had been laid out to replace a large zone of derelict land that had previously blighted the area near the historic centre of the city. Rafael hurried through the park, past the 'Monument to Disarmament' that had been erected near the entrance to the Institute. The three abstract figures that sat atop the plinth had been made from melted down firearms handed in by the inhabitants of Bogota. Their arms were spread wide as they were frozen forever in the act of releasing gunmetal black doves into the leaden sky. The base of the monument was obscured by a group of destitute, native *desplazados* who had chosen to make the site into a temporary camp, their ragged shelters and tents clustered around the statutes. The smell of cooking food and the screams of crying children drifted on the early afternoon air as he walked past, through the soulless glass doors and into the Institute.

Rafael felt a sense of palpable disorientation in the dim basement corridor. The lack of natural light and colour together with the monotonous beating of the clock made him lose all sense of place and time. The fatigue and tension from the last couple of days caught up with him then and his eyes blinked gently shut as he drifted into a fitful sleep. Thoughts and images flitted through his mind in rapid and baffling succession. The haughty face of the prosecutor assigning him to an unsolvable task; the narrow path twisting up the mountainside towards the suitcase and its gruesome contents waiting for him at the end; Jorge slumped against the steering wheel of the car, bleeding out onto the dashboard.

The squeak of the swing doors rubbing against the grey linoleum floor further up the corridor brought him awake quickly and announced the arrival of the pathologist. It seemed Rafael had only slept for a few moments and he rubbed his forehead to try and shake the sense of heaviness that remained. He watched the pathologist stride confidently down the corridor, dressed in surgical greens with an attendant following in his wake.

"Investigator…Alvarez." The man stopped abruptly at the sofa and consulted some notes on a clipboard. "You're here for what's left of the guy in the suitcase." It was a statement of fact not a question. "I'm Doctor Santiago," he announced crushing Rafael's hand in an iron handshake. "Let's get started. Follow me please."

The doctor was a robustly built man with broad, muscular shoulders. His hooked nose sat slightly off-centre between eyes that seemed to blink less than they should. The reflection of the lighting in the corridor was visible in the shiny bald crown of his head. He led the way through another set of swing doors with round portholes set at head height and into the black void of an unlit room. Rafael could hear the attendant fumbling for the switch, followed by an electronic buzz as more fluorescent strip lights fired up. The detail of a small sparsely-equipped mortuary jumped into life in the unforgiving glare. A bulky plastic bundle lay on a metal trolley with wheels in one corner. Santiago and his assistant manhandled it onto the dissection table.

Rafael leaned back against the wall as they began to unwrap the package. Autopsies had come to hold a secret fascination for him. He knew that for many, if not most of the investigators, they were an evil to be endured, but for Rafael the process of unveiling of the body's secrets had an all-absorbing quality. A person's final moments could be revealed in the measuring, weighing and dissecting of organs. The horrifying reality of pain, suffering and death were reduced to obscure medical technical terms. With the plastic covering pushed to one side, the sad, shrunken torso was revealed, still lying as it had been found, in the broken plastic case. Santiago fished out a cassette recorder from somewhere under his surgical robes and clicked the button to record.

"The torso of a white-skinned male lies in an unmarked broken plastic suitcase. The head, arms and legs have been detached. Initial impression is that this was done post mortem due to lack of obvious evidence of bleeding at the severed extremities. Genitals have also been removed. Swelling and bruising in the groin areas suggest this was done while subject was alive. Subject has a tattoo on the left shoulder. Concentric circles framed by triangular points."

Rafael thought again of the design carved into the bonnet of Jorge's car. There was no doubting the link and he silently promised that the people responsible would pay the price. The further he stepped into this case the more determined he became that this would not get buried as another unsolvable Bogota homicide.

"From the proportions of the torso I estimate the age at death to have been somewhere between twenty five and thirty five." Santiago clicked the recorder off and turned to fix Rafael with his unblinking stare. "There's not much I can really work with here." He snapped off his latex glove and drummed the top of his skull with his fingers, making a rhythmic tapping noise.

"Doctor, please do whatever you can. We have no idea who this man is or how he ended up in this terrible state. I'm really hoping there is something you can find here so I can start trying to find out who did this to him." Santiago stared at Rafael for a few more seconds before blinking and turning back to the corpse. The doctor and his assistant reached into the suitcase and carefully transferred the torso from the case directly onto the dissecting table. Santiago clicked the button on the recorder again.

"An obvious puncture wound in the centre of the chest is the probable cause of death. Bleeding and bruising around the wound indicate strongly that it was done while the subject was still alive." He pushed the little finger of his gloved hand into the slit. "Blade at least twenty centimetres in length and between four and five centimetres in width." His eyes widened in astonishment and he let the plastic cassette recorder clatter onto the linoleum floor. "Where is this man's heart?" he asked looking directly at Rafael.

Rafael pushed himself upright from where he had been slumped on the wall. He quickly pulled on some latex gloves and stepped over to where the doctor and his assistant waited for an explanation. His right hand reached for the incision near the arm pit, followed it down to the corner of torso and then he lifted the skin again.

"The heart isn't the only thing missing doctor," he said in an almost offhand manner as the empty cavity was exposed again.

"This body is little more than a shell," the doctor muttered, his eyes inscrutable above the surgical face mask. "Okay, out of the way Investigator. Let me see what I can tell you about this man."

The doctor and his assistant worked efficiently on the corpse. Details of the missing organs, the heart, lungs, liver and kidneys, were noted on Santiago's cassette recorder and scratched onto a body diagram by the assistant. They had all been removed with surgical precision after the man's violent death. The dry crunch of breaking bones filled the mortuary as the doctor opened the rib cage. Santiago's strong hands and muscular hairy arms moved quickly as the remaining organs were removed and a blood sample taken. The stomach was dumped unceremoniously into a plastic bucket and the assistant was despatched to get the contents analysed. Finally the doctor rolled the remnants of the torso onto its front.

"Ah now this is interesting," he exclaimed. "The subject has old scaring here at the top of the back and the bones of the shoulder look damaged." He took a shiny, steel scalpel and sliced through the layers of skin pulling them back and exposing the bones. "It's as I thought. Some time in the past this man's shoulder blade and collar bone were badly broken. They were never allowed to heal properly and would have been painful and lacked mobility." Santiago indicated with the scalpel, the light flashing momentarily across the blade. "He would have had a pronounced stoop and one of his shoulders would have been noticeably lower that the other. It's not much to go on but it might help you identify who this poor man was. I wish you luck Investigator Alvarez. You've got your work cut out for you with this one."

**

It was dusk by the time they emerged from the Institute and completed the short walk across the park to the Plaza Bolivar. The centre of the monumental square had been cordoned off around a giant plastic Christmas tree. Flashing lights had been strategically placed to draw attention to the advertising panels that ran around the enclosure attesting that the tree had been sponsored by the Mayor of the City with the kind support of the *Bogota Mejor* campaign.

Rafael had stayed in the mortuary to help Santiago clean up and wait for the results of the blood test and stomach contents. When the assistant had returned with the paper he had invited the pathologist for a drink. Now they sat in plastic chairs outside a bar overlooking the main square, staring silently at the people hurrying past in the amber glow. The rumble of cars and buses was a background roar occasionally punctuated by the blast of a horn and distant shouting. Santiago had changed out of his surgical gown and was wearing a light coloured jacket and an open collared shirt. He had lit a cigar as they took their seats and now the red point hovered in the gloom. A half empty bottle of aguardiente and two small glasses sat on the table in front of them next to a manila envelope with the various papers and results from the autopsy. Rafael still wore the same black shirt and tan trousers from the day before. He rubbed his face and felt the scratch of stubble on his cheek and jaw.

"I have seen many terrible things in my time in this city but I cannot remember a corpse in the same condition as this. You will, I think, find it very difficult to discover who this man was." Rafael stared silently at the body diagram that he had pulled from the envelope. The head, arms and legs had been scratched out in red.

"I think he needs a name doctor. It doesn't seem right to keep calling him 'the body in the suitcase' or 'the suitcase guy'. He was a person and someone did this to him. We shouldn't allow ourselves to lose sight of that." The doctor crossed his arms over his chest, looking at Rafael with his head tilted to one side.

"Very well, what do you suggest?" he asked evenly, a slight frown passing over his heavy features. Rafael paused. One name stood out clearly in his mind from the possible options. He twisted the wedding ring on his finger as he tried to think of an alternative. But it was no good, the name seemed to stick and he found himself speaking it aloud before he could stop himself.

"I think we should call him Adam," he said finally, using the name that Gabriella and he had been planning to give to their unborn son. "It's a strange thing," he said directing his gaze down at the table between them. "He was only found yesterday and it already feels like the investigation is engulfing me entirely. I've investigated murders before but I've never felt so completely that my future was somehow dependent on a single case, on finding out who did this to him and why." He ran a hand quickly over his wiry hair. "I was in Ciudad Bolivar earlier today. Someone shot my friend Jorge and then scratched the same design you saw on Adam's shoulder into the paint of the car." He quickly swallowed a glass of aguardiente, the spicy aniseed flavour warming his chest on its way to his stomach. The doctor's cigar glowed again as he took another drag. The bitter smell of the smoke drifted away into the dusk.

"There are only three things that I can tell you about Adam that may help mark him out as an individual. The tattoo on the shoulder you already know about. To me it looks like either a mechanical gear or maybe a star of some kind. Perhaps if you can figure out what it means it might lead you to who he was and how he died. Second, a long time before his death, he broke his shoulder and collar bone very badly. The break never healed properly and his right shoulder would have appeared twisted and hunched. Finally, the last thing he ate was a solution containing a massive amount of *yopa*."

"What is *yopa*?" Rafael interjected abruptly.

"It is a drug that was used by the indigenous peoples in their rituals. In small amounts it causes hallucinations and trances. In large amounts it causes the brain to cease working. The solution was in his stomach and large amounts of the drug were in his blood. In my professional opinion this man had very little idea of who he was and what was happening when he was tortured to death."

Rafael's mobile interrupted the doctor with an insistent beep. A message had arrived from an unknown number, the text solid black against the green back light: "Barraca brothers staying at uncle's house. Get there fast before they move again. Chivo." There was an address in Ciudad Bolivar at the end of the text. Rafael quickly made his apologies to the doctor and sprinted off to his car.

**

8. Ocho

At night Ciudad Bolivar oozed hostility. During the day the aggression and intimidation were potent but muted, bubbling below the surface in muttered words and glances but at night all the animals came out. Gangs of young men roamed the streets. Prostitutes at street corners whistled for business, their pimps ever present, just out of sight. Raucous laughter filled the air, cutting through the sound of latin hip-hop with its pounding, thumping beat.

As Rafael slipped through the shadows he felt like a refugee from another world. The weight of the gun under his jacket gave him some reassurance but not much. He had left his car in a well-lit public place near a row of ramshackle shops. As soon as he had stepped out he had been approached by a shabby man with missing teeth who had offered to 'protect' his car for a few pesos. The man's demeanour had made it clear that the offer wasn't optional.

A few blocks on foot felt like a thousand miles. He could feel unseen eyes on him as he moved through the darkness. This part of the city was someone's territory and he was an unwelcome intruder. Crossing one of the invisible borders that carved up the sprawling slum into parcels of property for the innumerable street gangs was a conspicuous risk.

An impromptu bar had been set up on the ground floor of the rickety building at the next corner. Flashing purple and green light spilled out onto the dirt of the sloping street, bathing the abstract graffiti faces that had been daubed onto the flaking plaster of the walls in a lurid glow. A bored prostitute lounged against the wall near the door playing with her mobile phone. She shifted uncomfortably in her short skirt and long black boots. Glancing up from the screen as he approached, she toyed with a strand of her hair. He walked past on the other side of the road without meeting her gaze.

A wall of sound surged into the night as the door creaked open behind him, this time he recognised the infectious, swirling rhythm of a well known salsa hit. Turning to look he found himself returning the stares of two young men who had stumbled out onto the street. One of them slapped the bottom of the prostitute in a familiar way, laughing at the string of curses she launched his way in reply.

They looked again towards where Rafael was standing a few meters away on the other side of the street. One of the youths put his arm around the shoulders of his companion pulling him in close. There was a whispered conversation followed by another burst of laughter. Rafael moved away quickly, anxious to put some distance between himself and the bar. He disappeared into the darkness, just another shadow in a city of shadows.

After a couple of hundred meters he arrived at an area where the houses had been abandoned. Broken concrete and brick shells lined the narrow dirt road with empty windows gaping black. He stopped to listen and heard the sound of trailing footsteps in the night. He picked up the pace but the pursuer seemed to stay with him. Ducking into an alley he reached for his gun and looked back down the street to see who was trying to follow him. The sloping dirt track spreading away below him was deserted and he turned away in confusion.

He felt rather than saw the swish of a metal bar aimed at his head and ducked away just in time. The bar slammed into the brick wall behind him with a shattering clang. Rafael recognised one of the men who had laughed at him earlier, his nostrils dilated in pain as he grunted from the shock. The man's companion stepped in and aimed a swinging punch at Rafael's head. Off balance from avoiding the bar he couldn't evade the flailing fist and it connected painfully with the top of his head. His vision lightened momentarily and the gun spun away from his hand.

The man with the bar leaned back to swing again but Rafael drove up from close to the ground and shoulder-charged him back into the chainlink fence that bordered the alley. The man dropped the metal bar and wrapped his arms around Rafael in an attempt to wrestle him to the ground. The basic close combat skills that Rafael had been taught in the army and then honed further in the police and the *Fiscalia* hovered at the back

67

of his mind like instinct. He knew that if his attacker succeeded in his efforts to throw Rafael to the ground he was as good as dead.

The second man came in from behind and landed a stinging blow to Rafael's kidneys. Rafael struck out with his right leg, connecting with the second man's midriff and he spun away doubling over. Rafael quickly reached down and pulled the legs away from the first, dumping him precipitously into the dirt. A sharp kick to the head put him out of action. He turned back to the second man who ran at him again. He blocked a punch with his forearm and then aimed a vicious kick to the side of the man's knee. Rafael had the satisfaction of hearing a crunching sound and the man was down, screaming in agony.

Rafael recovered his balance and wiped some blood from his nose. He paused to pick up his gun before continuing along the street. There was neither time nor purpose in trying to arrest his assailants so he left them where they lay.

The abandoned houses ended not far from where he left the two prone attackers behind and more low density, single-story shacks crowded in again on both sides of the street. Ahead in the darkness he could hear what sounded like the gurgle and murmur of running water.

Sure enough, a short distance further and the dirt track dipped where a dirty, swirling channel crossed the path, less a stream than an open sewage trough. Chunks of unidentifiable organic waste were washed past in the churning brown water and a sickly rotten smell filled the air. Rafael covered his nose and mouth with his hand and scrambled across the channel on several large stones that jutted out of the water.

On the other side, a few hundred meters further on, he could see the house he needed. The number was crudely painted onto a wooden post stuck into the ground at the front of the shack. Warped wooden walls and a corrugated iron roof provided scant protection against the chill of the mountain night. A light flickered in the window; someone was at home.

Rafael thought about the best way to approach the Barraca brothers. El Chivo had told him that they were connected in some way to the man in the suitcase and he had to find out what that connection was. He knew they had taken it from someone in the Candelaria and that they were now running scared. If he knocked on the front door they would probably be gone before he had a chance to even catch a glimpse of them. He decided that surprise and stealth were his best options here. He would stalk to the back of the shack, enter by force and keep them from running until they realised he was not a threat. Rafael thought again of Jorge slumped in the car earlier that morning and his own struggle with the two men from the bar. He was determined not to end up as another corpse in Ciudad Bolivar's foetid streets.

Before he reached the house, he ducked into an alley that opened up onto the main dirt track. The black walls of the shacks on either side loomed up in the darkness. A narrow strip of night sky stretched overhead. The bright pinpricks of stars shimmered in the thin air. The sound of a woman shouting and the starchy smell of boiling rice drifted through the thin walls on either side. A broader alley crossed the track between the two houses and ran parallel to the main dirt road. Rafael followed it along until he was behind the house where the Barraca brothers sheltered.

A dead animal, possibly a dog, lay in the space behind the house. In the darkness he could hear the buzz and skitter of insects. He was forced to step round it on the way to the back of the house, his feet crunching noisily on the loose dirt. The door was made of flimsy wooden boards with a piece of twisted wire serving as an improvised lock. Rafael pressed his ear to the rough planks and heard the low murmur of conversation. Someone was definitely in the house and it didn't appear they had been alerted by the sound of his approach. The musty stench of the dead animal hung in the confined space, filling Rafael's nostrils with its unpleasant odour. There didn't seem much point in hanging around. He took a deep breath and pulled the gun out from under his jacket. The heavy weight in his hand again gave him reassurance. Whatever was on the other side of the door, at least he was armed and ready to face it.

He steadied himself against the wall with his hand, lifted his right foot until it was level with the lock and brought it down with force next to where the wire was fastened. The fragile door splintered under the crushing force of the blow and flew inwards hitting the wall with a thump. Rafael was through the opening in a flash, the gun held steady in front of him.

A scrawny youth, little more than a boy really, was sitting cross legged on the floor, in front of a small television set.

Large hazel eyes, open wide with fear stared back at Rafael from a narrow pinched face. The moving colours and shapes from the cartoon on the screen played over his dark brown skin and tousled black hair. The boy had been shovelling rice and beans from a plastic plate into his mouth but Rafael's sudden entry caused him to drop his dinner to the floor with a clatter.

"Please don't kill me," he murmured in a thin, weak voice that was almost a whisper. The fork he had been using was clutched tightly in his right hand, frozen half way to his mouth.

"Don't move," barked Rafael at the frightened boy. "Where's your brother?" He hoped that surprise and shock would keep the boy where he was for long enough to answer his questions.

"He's not here. He went out to get food." The boy's eyes were fixed on the gun.

"Relax, I'm not going to hurt you. I just want to talk." With the lack of any obvious threat Rafael lowered the gun to point at the ground and looked round the shack.

The ground floor contained a single room. An uneven floor of wooden boards had been laid over the dirt. The corner near the door served as the kitchen. A pot with the remains of the rice rested on a small table next to an empty tin and a gas burner. Plastic buckets for washing took up another corner, some still filled with water, others empty and lying on their sides. The window at the front on the house had been covered with a frayed piece of tarpaulin held in place with a series of nails. A rickety wooden ladder led up to a second floor in the roof which presumably contained bedding and sleeping quarters. On the wall near the front door was a faded print of a famous painting of the last supper, mounted in an elaborate frame. They were available cheaply in religious merchandise shops throughout the city and were believed to ward off bad luck if placed near the front door.

"What's your name *muchacho*?"

"I'm Paulito. My brother is Ruben." The boy hunched his narrow shoulders and looked down at the ground.

"Listen to me Paulito. I can help you but I need you to trust me. I know about the man in the suitcase. I'm an investigator. I'm trying to find out who did this terrible thing and I need your help." Rafael squatted on his heels so that he was at the same level as the boy and put his hand on his shoulder.

"Paulito, why are you so scared? What is it you and your brother are running from?" Paulito fixed his hazel eyes on Rafael. He had the desperate, resigned look of a cornered animal.

"The man we stole the suitcase from, he killed my friend Angel. Stabbed him with a knife and we had to leave him there on the street. Now he wants to kill me and my brother too. He knows who we are and he knows where we live. Every place we go he seems to find us. We're not safe anywhere. When you came crashing through the door I thought it was him and that I was going to die." His voice wavered as he said the last words, the emotion of the memory overwhelming the boy.

"I need you to tell me everything you can remember, about the man, about the suitcase, everything. Help me catch him and this will all stop."

"You don't get it. It's not just him...". Paulito started to say more but then trailed off. His eyes focused over Rafael's shoulder. Rafael heard the creak of a floorboard behind him and quickly turned to identify the source of the sound.

He had a fleeting impression of something shiny, metallic and round before a crashing blow connected with the side of his face. Pain exploded through his head and he felt an overwhelming dizziness. Spun round by the force of the blow he lost his balance and collapsed to the ground. Momentarily stunned, his vision obscured by flashing lights in his head, he thought he could hear the sound of the running footsteps across the wooden floor.

"*Apurate hermano. Venga!*" The sound seemed to come from far away.

He shook his head groggily to clear his vision and just managed to catch a glimpse of Paulito disappearing out the back door. Another young man was just behind him and turned to look at Rafael before he too disappeared through the door. He shared the same curly black hair, lean build and narrow pinched features and Rafael guessed that he was the boy's brother, Ruben. He struggled to his feet, fighting dizziness and nausea and brushed the soggy remains of rice from his clothes and hair. The object that had been used to hit him was revealed to be the pan from the table which now rolled about on the floor as though mocking him. His nose had started to bleed again but he wiped off the blood with the back of his hand and staggered after the brothers.

Outside in the yard the night was like a black wall. After the relative warmth of the cabin the air felt cold on his skin. His eyes began to quickly adjust to the darkness of the night and vague shapes and shadows started to come into focus. The sound of pounding footsteps receded into the gloom somewhere to his left. He started quickly after them but was stopped by the revolting sensation of his foot sinking into something soft and clammy. He realised that, in his haste, he had stepped into the remains of the dead animal near the door and quickly pulled his foot free with a shudder.

Fighting the urge to swear loudly he stopped to listen again to be as sure as he could of the direction of the brothers' flight. Fainter than before but still audible, the sound of running echoed off the concrete walls and Rafael sprinted out of the yard in pursuit. The alley zigzagged along between the backs of the houses and quickly fractured into a multitude of smaller openings and other passageways. He caught the sound again coming from a narrow entrance on his right and dived after it, skidding on the loose ground as he changed direction. He was some way behind now and the brothers had the advantage of knowing the terrain, but he just about managed to maintain the pursuit. They changed direction often through the maze of alleyways and at one point the path between the buildings was so narrow that Rafael was forced to turn sideways to squeeze through. He had to stop and strain his hearing to catch their trail again over the sound of his own ragged breathing.

The pounding footsteps were louder now so he knew he was getting closer and he forced himself to ignore the burning fatigue in his legs and thighs. Finally, round the next bend, he saw the pale flash of Ruben's face in the shadowy gloom as the youth threw a desperate glance over his shoulder before disappearing into yet another dark opening. Rafael sprinted after him down some narrow steps with a drainage channel carved through the middle and was confronted by a dead end. The backs of houses rose up on either side and the alley was closed off by a brick wall that formed the back of a garage building. There was no sign of the Barraca brothers and no other doors or openings that they could have taken.

Rafael stopped in his tracks, his eyes scanning the rubbish-strewn alley for any obvious hiding places. He refused to believe that Ruben and Paulito had simply vanished into the night. In the sudden stillness a dog barked somewhere far away and then he heard a faint scrabbling sound coming from the darkness above him. They were on the roof of the garage! A stack of wooden boxes had been piled haphazardly against the wall and they swayed unsteadily as Rafael scrambled up them. From the top he managed to reach the edge of the roof and pull himself up, scraping his hands on the rough brick and concrete of the wall.

The thin, corrugated plastic roof creaked uncertainly, supporting his weight with difficulty. He lay prone for a moment, reluctant to get to his feet too quickly, half out of fear of falling through and half to take a moment to look for signs of the elusive Barraca brothers. A line of clothes stretched across the space, the tattered laundry swaying in the faint evening breeze and partially obscuring his view. He moved forward carefully, pushing aside a cluster of faded t-shirts, but it appeared the roof was deserted.

The stillness on the roof was shattered by the barking cough of an engine starting close by. Rafael sprang towards the sound but in his haste he pulled some of the damp garments with him, causing the entire line to detach itself from the wall. The spluttering engine rose to a whine as it ignited and then abruptly stopped as the motor cut out. Rafael extracted himself from the tangle of clothes and stumbled to the edge of the roof.

Below in the street he could see Ruben desperately trying to kick-start a battered motorbike. Paulito was perched behind him on the bike's mud guard clinging to his back. He looked over his shoulder, catching sight of Rafael as he jumped down from the roof. Paulito turned away again, urging his brother to get the bike started as quickly as possible.

With a final, frantic flail of the kickstand, Ruben coaxed the juddering engine into life again. The back wheel spun in the loose dirt as the machine wobbled away down the street. Rafael came to his feet quickly from where he had landed and began to sprint after the bike. As the distance increased and the bike accelerated away Rafael realised that he had lost the chase.

"You don't understand. I'm trying to help you." His final hopeless shout was drowned out by the buzz of the engine. He stopped running, gasping in great lungfuls of air with his hands on his knees. As he watched the red tail light recede into the night he wondered if he would see the Barraca brothers alive again.

**

9. Nueve

In his dream Rafael stood alone in an endless, grey corridor. The walls were narrow and featureless and a soft, hazy light suffused the space all around him. He started to walk, filled with a spontaneous sense of certainty that something important was waiting for him at the end of the hallway. If he could just reach it, some kind of crucial question would be answered, some essential truth would be revealed. The anticipation of discovery sent a thrill of impatience through him and he moved ahead with increased urgency.

As the walls shifted past he had a sudden feeling that something was different in the passage behind him. A terrible sense of dread stole over him and he turned to look.

The corridor was filled with a shapeless, black presence, blocking the way back. As he watched, the lights started to wink out in sequence, moving up the corridor towards him. He knew that if the darkness reached him something awful would happen.

He tried to run but his legs felt heavy and constricted. He had a sensation of wading through thick liquid and he seemed to inch down the corridor. Every time he looked over his shoulder the darkness was inevitably closer and he felt panic rising up inside. He made an effort to master his legs and put on a final burst of speed but they refused to respond.

Then, without quite knowing how, he found himself at the end of the corridor in a cavernous, white room. Heavy double doors flanked the entrance behind him and he managed to heave them shut with an effort before turning to look at his new surroundings. There were no other entrances or exits, no way forward. He knew instinctively that this was where he was meant to be, that this was where he'd find the answers.

A domed ceiling towered above his head and the walls seemed impossibly distant. The vast chamber was barren and stark, devoid of all adornment, an empty blank space. As he approached the centre of the room, he found he could suddenly discern a design marked out on the floor in what appeared to be black ink. It hadn't been there a moment ago. Rafael felt himself go cold with recognition. The concentric circles and triangular points. What was it doing here? What did it mean?

He watched as the middle of the design shimmered like water and turned midnight black. A shadowy figure appeared standing in the centre of the circle, its back to Rafael. Slowly it turned towards him and he found himself staring into the dead empty eyes of Mauro Ospina. The bullet wound was a puckered black circle marring his youthful face. The feelings he had experienced, finding Mauro dead so suddenly the day before flooded through him again. Horror, disbelief and guilt overcame him in a wave. He wanted to speak to Mauro, to ask him who had snuffed out his life so brutally. He needed to ask his forgiveness.

It was too late. The figure had dissolved and in its place Rafael found himself staring down at a headless torso without arms and legs. He felt himself sink to his knees and despair overwhelmed him again. He had failed Ospina. How could he expect to succeed for Adam? As in the autopsy, the front of Adam's torso yawned open again and he found himself confronted with the gaping body cavity. He felt his despair sink to a new depth. Adam was an empty shell. He had been stripped bare. There was little to suggest he had once been alive.

The centre of the design wavered again. The man without a head became a man without a face and suddenly Rafael knew he was looking at his father. Anger and sorrow rose within him. The jungles had claimed his father when Rafael had been little more than a boy, swallowing him as thoroughly as if he'd never been. Just another of the many Colombian soldiers who disappeared every year. In all probability Major Juan-Sebastian Alvarez lay in an unmarked grave somewhere in the endless ocean of trees. His fate was unknown and unknowable.

The images started to rush faster now, spiralling out of control, any consistency or structure disappearing. For a moment he was looking at Gabriella, sad and beautiful, like the last time he saw her. He felt the ache of her loss all over again. He called out to her but she didn't speak and seemed very far away. She was holding a baby in her arms, their baby.

Suddenly he couldn't see. All light was extinguished from the room. He knew instinctively that light itself had ceased to exist in the dream world in which he found himself. He stumbled around in the blackness, trying to find some way out. Then he was falling, rushing through space faster and faster. All sensation seemed to leave his body. His chest tightened in terror. Panic overwhelmed him and his mind rebelled at the situation jerking him awake.

A dusty brightness filtered into the bedroom from where he'd forgotten to close the curtains. Rafael stirred where he lay, on top of the covers of his empty bed. His mouth was dry and a dull ache spread through his face and jaw from the blows he had taken last night. He sat up, making a conscious effort to dispel the lingering sense of lightness in his limbs that made the room seem to move upwards around him.

He was back in his apartment and had managed to make it to his bed and remove most of his clothes this time before falling asleep. After losing the Barraca brothers in Ciudad Bolivar he had retraced his steps to the car without incident. He had been grateful to find it unharmed and when the man with missing teeth had pressed him for a few more pesos for 'excellent service' he hadn't protested.

Today was Saturday. Since Gabriella's death, Rafael never knew what to do with himself at weekends. He pulled on a t-shirt and stumbled into the kitchen to find some breakfast. The stack of dirty dishes was still waiting for him, piled high in the sink. He sighed and turned on the tap knowing he couldn't put off the washing up any longer. When he had cleaned enough things to make some breakfast he decided that the rest could wait until later and opened the fridge.

It had been a while since he had managed to buy any groceries and as a result the fridge was nearly empty. A carton of milk with a colourful cow on the packaging was just about usable. There were a couple of eggs in the door and a small knob of butter wrapped in too much foil packaging. He cleared everything out of the fridge and dropped all the ingredients into a plastic bowl that he'd just washed. He mixed in some flour from the back of the cupboard and a splash of water from the tap and then kneaded the mixture into thick dough.

He took chunks of the dough and squashed them into thick discs with his hands to make *arepas*. Heating what was left of the butter in a frying pan, he carefully placed the *arepas* into the melted oil. The smell of the dough cooking and crisping made him think of his mother. For a moment he was back in the kitchen of his childhood in San Cristobal watching her prepare the breakfast.

Often she would sing in her native Portuguese and he loved to listen to the sound of her lilting accent. The songs were about animals, dancing, superstitions and love. Brazil always seemed such a bright, colourful place. The language was so close to Spanish that he could understand most of the words and yet at the same time it was different and distorted, as though she was singing underwater. After his father disappeared she had sung less frequently and eventually decided on a return to Brazil, leaving Colombia when Rafael had been conscripted into the army.

Even Gabriella's death had not induced her to return. They had spoken briefly on the phone and she had been distant and cold. He suspected that his loss had resurrected the pain of her own. Memories of the bitterness he felt at the abandonment returned briefly before he pushed them aside. He wondered what she was doing now and if she was happy again.

The *arepas* were beginning to turn golden brown in the pan and he decided to make some coffee to go with them. He set a pan of water on the stove to boil and reached for the battered metal coffee jar at the back of the cupboard. There were a couple of spoonfuls of powder left and he scraped the bottom with a teaspoon to tip them out into the pan, vowing again that he would go shopping in the afternoon.

He took the *arepas* and coffee through to the lounge, the wooden floor cold on his bare feet. His gun lay on the coffee table where he had left it the night before. He moved it to one side and put down the cup of coffee and the plate. As he sipped the bitter black liquid memories of the dream floated back into his mind.

The most enduring image, the one that caused him most pain, was of Gabriella with the baby. Her death giving birth to their son had made the blow doubly grievous. It had left him numb, empty, detached. He felt like he was drifting between places, living one day at a time and clinging to what remained of life in case he drifted away. The sad truth was that all that was really left for him was his work, which is why Adam had become so important. He thought that if he could find Adam maybe he would find himself again.

Before the sadness could overwhelm him, he retrieved the bottle of pills from the crumpled pile of clothes in the bedroom. He swallowed one quickly, washing it down with a mouthful of coffee. In a few seconds his sense of calm returned. He was able to distance himself from his emotions and engage his ability to focus, even as he felt some vital part of himself falling away with the onset of the chemical stimulation.

His dark grey *Fiscalia* backpack rested to one side of the sofa, crammed with papers that he had brought home from the Bunker. He started to remove some of the documents and spread them out over the table, re-reading the details as he continued to drink his coffee. Soon the surface was buried under a jumbled layer of paper detritus. Photos from the path to Monserrate, showing the suitcase and the torso from different angles were mixed in among the various notes and reports that had been made at the crime scene. Rafael had managed to get hold of some of the preliminary details from the Bogota Police file on Jorge and Ospina's shooting. He held up the picture of the design that had been scratched into the car bonnet next to the photo of Adam's shoulder, wondering again at the similarity and what it might mean.

As he was rifling again through Doctor Santiago's disturbing autopsy report a small, white envelope slipped out and spilled onto the floor. The words '*Cuerpo de Monserrate*' had been scrawled across the front in spidery handwriting that he didn't recognise. He leaned down to pick it up, turning it over in his hands as he brought it towards him. He didn't recall putting it in with the papers as he'd cleared his desk. There were no stamps or postmarks so it must have reached him through the internal post. Someone who knew he was working the investigation must have left it for him to find while he was away.

He opened it carefully, lifting the sealed flap a small segment at a time. Inside was a single sheet of folded paper with a single sentence printed across the middle of the page. '*La Justicia, Annuncios de Desaparecedos,*' it read. He turned it over, but there was no more information. The rest of the paper was blank and there was nothing else in the envelope. He puzzled over it for a few minutes more before putting it down among the papers and turning back to the autopsy report, the coffee left to one side, cold and forgotten.

The morning passed away and his thoughts cycled back to Gabriella. She had died nearly a year ago now and he knew that soon he would have to decide what to do with his life. He had been determined to escape from Bogota, to go somewhere different and be someone different. But now he wasn't so sure. He sighed and looked round the apartment. A makeshift bookcase, constructed of wooden planks balanced on bricks, stood in the corner, next to a dead orchid in a plastic pot. Most of the books had belonged to Gabriella but a few had been his. A thin layer of dust covered them all.

Some friends had invited him to their house for dinner that evening. They were good people but they were really friends of Gabriella. He wasn't sure he wanted to go but had been unable to think of a good excuse. Anyway, he supposed it was all part of the process of coming to terms with his loss. He just needed to decide what to do with the rest of his day.

From the window he could see the road below was already filling up with traffic. The glass shivered in the pane and the occasional blast of car horns drifted up to the apartment. He tidied the clothes from the sofa and put them in a bag to take to the laundrette before heading to the bathroom for a shower. As usual, the water pressure was low and the pipes rattled and gurgled in protest but the hot water soothed away his aches and soon last night's exertions in Ciudad Bolivar were forgotten.

By the time he'd thrown on some jeans and a t-shirt he decided that he was going to go for a walk. As he was descending the stairs to the building entrance his neighbour on the ground floor came in clutching some oily tools from the garage. Rafael could never remember the man's name. They had introduced themselves when Rafael and Gabriella had first moved to the apartment but in the hurry the name had disappeared from his memory. Now, he suspected that they were both too embarrassed to say anything about the matter.

The man looked at Rafael with a guarded expression behind his thin beard. His blue overalls were stained from working in the garage.

"Morning neighbour." Rafael said quickly intending to pass the man and get out onto the street.

"Morning." The man returned his greeting and then seemed to hesitate. "Someone was here looking for you last night," he added after a short pause, almost apologetically.

"Really?" Rafael was a little surprised. It was unusual for him to have visitors he wasn't expecting, even more unusual for that to happen at night.

"It was a big guy with a patch of grey hair and bad skin. He said it was about your work and he needed to speak to you about your friends in the car." Rafael felt himself go cold as he recalled the silhouette he had seen before leaving Jorge and Ospina in the car to talk with with El Chivo. It looked like the shooter had tracked him down as well. He wondered how the man had managed to find him so quickly.

"Thanks. I'm sure I'll catch up with him later." He hoped he had managed to keep the nervousness from his voice as he stepped past his neighbour and out onto the street.

The sky had clouded over and the early sun had disappeared to be replaced by low, oppressive clouds. He wasn't sure where he wanted to go. He just wanted to walk, to have the sensation of travelling without knowing the destination. He felt the need to escape from the flat and his life, to leave his memories and the danger behind him. The impression of anonymity gave him a small measure of comfort. The distraction of the changing scenery helped to take his thoughts away from where he didn't want them to go. He found himself looking more closely at the faces flashing past, a hundred different people with a hundred different lives, all mashed together in the sprawling city.

The respite didn't last long and, almost against his will, Rafael's thoughts drifted back to the shooter. The man seemed to be able to glide through the city appearing when and where we wanted and then disappearing at will. He seemed to know exactly who his targets were and where they could be found. How did he get his information? He wondered if he was being watched now. The thought turned him cold and he stopped to look around.

A garbage truck had pulled over at the side of the road ahead and a man in red overalls was using a plastic broom to sweep the gutter with broad lethargic strokes. Dust and filth covered the truck but the words *"Ciudad Limpia"* were just visible through the grime. A man in faded jeans and a baseball cap hurried past carrying a guitar. His face was deeply lined and his eyes seemed hollow and empty. There were no immediate signs of danger so Rafael made a determined effort to put the notion out of his mind and carried on walking.

An empty growling in his stomach told him it was time to stop and get some lunch. On the other side of the road he could see a petrol station with a small grocery shop attached and he dodged through the traffic to reach it. A pot-bellied man with glasses was shaking the last drops of petrol from the pump into his car. He stopped what he was doing to watch Rafael cross the forecourt before turning back to the pump to check the price.

The door to the shop was rusty and Rafael had to shove it hard to get it to open. Inside, Christmas music played quietly in the background and faded decorations hung from the ceiling tiles. Hot dog sausages rotated slowly in a glass cabinet in the corner, the meat sweating steadily under the glare of the heat lamps. He pulled one out with the tongs provided and stuffed it into a stale bun before covering the whole thing with mustard. On the way to the till he picked up a bag of plantain chips and a can of beer from the chiller cabinet.

The man with the glasses was at the till in front of him arguing about the cost of the petrol with a bored teenager in a greasy polo shirt. The youth shrugged his shoulders and explained that he didn't have the authority to change the price on the pump. The last of the day's newspapers had been placed on a cardboard box next to the till. Rafael scanned the headlines while he was waiting for the argument to finish. He took in a sharp breath as his eyes were drawn towards the gothic lettering of a title near the bottom of the pile. The paper's name, blazed across the front was '*La Justicia*' and his thoughts whirled back to the mysterious envelope that had fallen out of his papers earlier this morning. The possibility seemed irresistible and he reached out a hand to pull the paper from the stack. Eventually, the man in the glasses left the shop with a final mutter of disgust. Rafael stepped forward and handed a couple of crumpled notes to the indifferent adolescent at the till without bothering to speak.

Outside, a plastic table and chairs had been positioned near the door. The sharp smell of petrol hung in the air and the roar of the passing traffic drowned out other sounds. Rafael spread the paper out on the table and started eating. The meat in the hotdog was soft and tasteless but the tang of the mustard disguised it well enough. The front page of the paper was almost entirely taken up with a photograph of a prominent politician giving a speech. He was wearing a red, blue and yellow sash over the right shoulder of his dark suit and one of his hands was squeezed tight into a fist raised up near his shoulder behind the microphone. The confident smile on his face contrasted sharply with the nervous frowns of the people in the audience. Rafael scanned the text at the bottom of the page. It contained the usual platitudes about how the answers to the many problems facing the country were simple and logical and if only people would vote for his party everything would be solved in short order. Versions of the same story appeared with such regularity that it was barely worth the effort to read them.

He put the hotdog down and opened the beer. Turning the paper over, he was confronted with more bad news on the sports pages. Millionarios de Bogota had been defeated by their arch-rivals America de Cali, a last-minute free kick deciding the game. The Millionarios supporters, unhappy with the referee's decision, had gone on the rampage, smashing up the football stadium and the surrounding district. He took a couple of mouthfuls of the beer to wash the taste of the hotdog out of his mouth and began flicking through the paper.

He skipped over the financial pages and the obituaries before he found what he was looking for. A gallery of misery and desperation stared up at him from the *'Annuncios de Desaparecedos'*, the missing person notices that formed a small but significant section in most of the newspapers in Colombia. Each advert was accompanied by a small black and white photo and a few words of description.

'Our son, Julio Ibanez, nineteen years old, went to visit a friend and never came back...'

'Francisco Ordoñez, husband and father of two, last seen going to work...'

The memory of his father stirred inside him for the second time that day and before he knew what he was doing he had read the details of half a dozen of the notices.

He continued scanning the page, not quite sure what he was looking for. Then he saw it. At the bottom of the second page, a photo of a young man smiled up out of the paper. His long, angular face seemed to mask an underlying tension. The twisted smile under his slightly hooded eyes seemed superficial and forced. His curly hair was brushed back from a square forehead and he wore thin, wire framed glasses. The caption read '*Un de Nuestros*' and confirmed that the man, Frederico Fernandez, had been a journalist working for the paper when he disappeared just over a month ago.

But it wasn't the writing that had attracted Rafael's attention. Even in the small, badly focused picture, he could see that Frederico Fernandez clearly had something wrong with his back. His right shoulder appeared to be twisted up and back. Rafael examined the picture intently. Was this what the message in the envelope had wanted him to see? Was it him? Had he found Adam? He had to know for certain. He paused for a few seconds, working out his options, then ripped the page out of the paper and ran off down the street, leaving the hot dog half eaten on the table.

**

10. Diez

The ponderous, grey exterior of the *Fiscalia* Bunker had been constructed without much thought for architectural quality. Blocky concrete pillars protruded from the main structure like the exposed ribs of some enormous carcass. The imposing façade was chipped and discoloured with bird droppings from the thousands of pigeons that inhabited the roofs. The monotony of the outer walls was broken only by the cold glint of a few widely spaced windows.

Rafael sprinted up the broad steps at the front of the building, his raincoat flapping behind him in the breeze. The uniformed security guard at the entrance peered at his identity card before reluctantly letting him through the revolving door and into the main lobby. Like most government buildings in Bogota, the Bunker was virtually deserted at the weekends. Most of the lights were off and the interior of the building was gloomy and dark.

Rafael's footsteps echoed through the labyrinthine corridors as he headed for the back stairs that led to the sub-basement. On either side of him, numerous locked doors shut out access to the rooms and offices beyond, adding to the sense of isolation. The sharp smell of disinfectant drifted through the half-light and further ahead Rafael caught sight of a janitor with a mop cleaning the seemingly endless shadowy passages. He wondered who else was in the building today.

A small window high up in the stairwell let in some much needed natural light as Rafael descended the two flights to the basement level. His route took him through the changing rooms which suited him well as he planned to pick up some equipment from his locker on the way. The odour of stale sweat and mould slid into his nostrils as he stepped through the entrance, taking in the rows of scuffed wooden benches and battered metal cabinets crammed into the space.

The door to his locker gave a rusty squeal as he pulled it open. Inside, his spare set of blue *Fiscalia* overalls and a heavy, black CTI tactical vest were suspended on a wire hanger taking up most of the room. Pushing past them, he rummaged through a battered cardboard box at the bottom of the locker. A flashlight and a small cloth bag with some picking tools were removed and secreted into the pockets of his overcoat before he closed the door softly behind him.

He reached his destination quickly, moving through the shadows like a wraith. The door to the archive room loomed out of the darkness ahead, a solid metal barrier at the end of the corridor. He tried the handle and, as expected, it was firmly locked.

He wasn't normally allowed into this part of the building but today he was determined to make his own access. With a final check of the corridor to make sure he was indeed alone he selected a tension wrench and a cylinder pick from the bag. This was certainly not the most difficult lock that Rafael had ever broken into but it was the first time he'd tried something like this inside the *Fiscalia*.

The consequences of discovery would be severe but he felt the risk was justified. He knew from past experience, that any requests made to examine the files would likely take weeks to grind their way through the agency's ponderous bureaucracy. There was also a good chance that Ortega would act to block his application, given the prosecutor's mysterious fixation on closing out the investigation with a minimum of disruption.

Rafael's hands moved with purpose and determination, using the pick to check the number of pins, inserting the tension wrench to exert force on the cylinder then moving back in with the pick to slowly push the pins up. He grimaced at the scraping and clicking sounds as he worked, fearing they could attract the attention of a patrolling security guard. One by one the pins snapped into place, the tension placed on the cylinder stopping them from falling back. With a final clunk the door opened and Rafael was through in an instant, closing it silently behind him.

The darkness in the archive room was nearly total and the musty smell of paper files filled the thick, muggy air. Rafael switched on his flashlight sending crazy shadows spiralling onto the walls. The ceiling was lower here and in places the tiles had

86

been removed completely, exposing the air conditioning ducts. Rows of metal shelving, piled high with archive boxes, surrounded him and stretched away as far as he could see. In the dancing beam of the flashlight the back wall of the room was not visible.

The labels at the end of each row were faded and peeling and it took him some time to locate what he was looking for. The section where the missing person records had been dumped was a sprawling mess. There seemed to be no order or reason to the placement of the boxes and many of the files were covered with a silvery layer of dust. Rafael wondered briefly if any information about his own father's disappearance had been collected and entombed here among these endless, silent racks.

He was forced to turn sideways to squeeze into the narrow space between the shelves. Searching along the row he was relieved to find that the newer files were organised according to month reported missing and then alphabetically by family name. The boxes covering the period of the journalist's disappearance took up a whole stack of shelves. It seemed incredible that such a large number of people could have gone missing in such a short period of time.

As he got closer to the right section Rafael could see that the reference system had been disarranged and he was forced to rummage through a number of boxes before he found the right one. The plain cardboard folder with the details on Frederico Fernandez seemed to have been deliberately concealed and was crammed within the covers of another file. Several scraps of torn paper slipped to the ground as he pulled it from the box. Frederico's full name and a date of birth had been printed onto the front in thick black pen.

Leafing through the muddled contents Rafael quickly located another photograph. A young man in jeans and a red sweatshirt stood self consciously in front of a stone wall. His hands were pushed deep into his pockets and his right shoulder appeared twisted out of place. He pulled the folded newspaper page out of his pocket and looked again at the blurry black and white photo of the missing journalist. They were definitely the same person. Now to find out if Frederico Fernandez was really the man he was looking for.

The sound of voices from outside the door interrupted Rafael's thoughts and he quickly extinguished the flashlight. In the silence of his head the thumping of his heart was thunderous. For seconds that seemed like hours he stood motionless in the darkness but, to his relief, the voices passed on down the corridor without stopping. The warning served as a timely reminder that Rafael wasn't supposed to be in the archive room and he decided it would be more prudent to examine the folder back at his desk on the third floor.

The lights had been switched off in the open plan office and the jumbled maze of screens and cubicles seemed a uniform shade of grey in the dim light from the scattering of dusty windows that opened on to the outside. Rafael could hear the low drone of a cleaner hoovering the beige carpet tiles somewhere on the floor. He slipped past the rows of empty desks and chairs, making his way silently to the corner near the window where his own desk had been set up. The cleaner had tidied the papers he'd left scattered about into a neat pile and moved his chair away so that the floor could be cleaned. Everything else appeared as he had left it the day before.

He emptied the contents of the file, spreading the papers out over the laminate working surface. Frederico Fernandez had been twenty four years old when he disappeared. He was the youngest child of a large, relatively well-off family. His father had worked briefly in the previous government. After spending a couple of years at college he dropped out and started working for 'La Justicia', a left leaning newspaper that focused on the many social inequalities in Bogota and elsewhere across the country.

His bank statements showed that his wages from the paper were modest but a monthly allowance paid by his father meant that he had been able to rent a smart apartment in north Bogota. There were more photos: Frederico on the beach wearing shorts and sunglasses, Frederico with a group of friends at a bar, Frederico standing in a park with his mother and father. His smooth, youthful features smiled up out of each of the pictures and there was no mistaking the irregular posture of his back.

Sifting through the papers, Rafael felt a thrill of excitement when he came across a sheet of medical records on a curling, yellow carbon copy. A note in the spidery hand of some unknown doctor explained that Frederico took painkillers regularly to ease the chronic pain in his back and shoulders. Further down the page the cause was confirmed as a broken shoulder and collar bone that Frederico had suffered as a teenager in a riding accident at his parents' ranch. The fall had been severe and had left a permanent mark on him in the form of his twisted shoulder.

It was enough for Rafael. Of course, he would take the file to Dr Santiago on Monday to get a more definitive confirmation but he felt certain he now knew the identity of Adam. He leaned back in the chair and closed his eyes, letting the new information settle and thinking about what he would do next. His satisfaction was interrupted by the realisation that finding Frederico against all the odds was only one piece in a larger jigsaw puzzle. Rafael still needed to figure out who had killed him and why.

His thoughts turned to the strange tattoo that he had seen on Frederico's other shoulder, the interlocking circles and triangular points. Rafael searched through the stack of papers again but couldn't find a single mention of it. In fact, looking again at the photo of Frederico on the beach he could clearly see that on the part of his back where the tattoo should have been there was nothing but unmarked skin. It must have been done in the two months since he disappeared and was clearly the strongest link yet to the murderer.

Something else was puzzling him and he frowned slightly as he tried to identify what it was. Frederico had been missing for quite some time now but there was nothing in the file detailing any progress in the investigation or identifying the officer who had been assigned to the case. Even in the most hopeless situation, the investigator would have carried out some basic enquiries, to cover his back if nothing else. Leafing through the file again confirmed his suspicions. Anything that could have provided a link to the investigator had been removed. Someone had got to the file before he had.

He wondered if this could be the work of the same man who had shot Jorge and Ospina in Ciudad Bolivar, his opponent with the patch of grey hair and the thin beard who always seemed to be one step ahead of him. The Barraca brothers had indicated that more than one pursuer was hunting them down. If the man had been able to obtain Rafael's address as well as remove papers from a missing person file in the *Fiscalia* Bunker, then his adversary must have some powerful connections.

Sitting there in his office, the realisation hit him that someone from inside the organisation could be working against him. He would have to move quickly and watch his back every step of the way. The only thing he could do was follow the thread through to the end and hope that he got there before he was stopped.

He felt a strong sense of urgency rise inside him. Given the situation it would be foolish and maybe even dangerous to pause now. The address and phone number for Frederico's apartment were written on the inside cover of the folder. The file also contained a white envelope with a key inside. Rafael scribbled the details onto the envelope, stuffed it into his pocket and quickly left the building.

**

11. Once

The Saturday afternoon traffic in Bogota was horrendous as usual so Rafael pushed his way on to the packed *Transmilenio* bus system. The articulated, double length buses had their own exclusive lanes which made progress through the city fairly rapid. He wedged himself between a fat man trying to read a newspaper and a woman gossiping loudly into her mobile phone. They both muttered in irritation but Rafael didn't take any notice and eventually they shifted aside to make room for him. He spent the journey trying to ignore his discomfort and nervously scanning the other passengers for anyone that resembled the vague mental profile he'd built of Jorge's would be killer. There was no sign of the assassin however, and the bus reached its destination without incident.

The light was beginning to fade when Rafael arrived on foot outside the journalist's apartment building. It was a boxy, ten-floor tower with a sign at the front that revealed its name to be *"Edificio Excelaris"*. Red bricks glowed in the setting sun, mingling with yellow from the windows as the residents began to switch on their lights. A metal railing surrounded the property and from where he was standing Rafael could make out a path that led through a well-tended garden to the main entrance. The smell of recently cut grass drifted on the evening breeze. Security guards in dark blue uniforms sat behind a polished wooden desk in the lobby. To the side of the building a sloping concrete ramp led down towards an underground parking garage. A wooden barrier attended by another guard blocked the way onto the ramp.

Rafael considered his approach. Given the uncertainties of the situation it would be preferable if he could get into the building without alerting the guards to his presence. The lobby didn't look promising and scaling the fence while remaining unnoticed was unlikely. It looked like the only viable option was the parking garage with its single guard and more accessible entrance. He moved closer to get a better look and then quickly ducked behind a low wall at the sound of a car approaching in the quiet residential street. In his dark overcoat the gathering dusk rendered him practically invisible where he crouched, concealed about ten meters from the guard and the entrance. A well-polished SUV turned into the short driveway leading to the car park. It stopped at the barrier and the silver-haired driver wound down his window and beckoned the guard over.

"Buenas noches Señor Martín," the watchman began with a deferential greeting.

"Thank you young man. Remind me of your name?"

"Miguel Torres, Señor."

"Listen Miguel. I need you to do a favour for me. My son is coming to visit me from Medellin tomorrow and I need another parking space."

"Of course, Señor. I'll make the necessary arrangements for you."

"I appreciate that Miguel." The driver dismissed the guard with another wave of his hand. He stepped away to raise the barrier and the SUV passed smoothly down the ramp, disappearing into the darkness of the underground car park.

Rafael retreated to the other side of the street. The beginning of a plan was forming in his mind and he quickly thought through the options and pitfalls before deciding it could work. Keeping the lobby in sight, he made sure he also had a view of the guard and the entrance to the parking garage. The night had taken hold by now and the evening air was distinctly chilly as he pulled out his cell phone and the white envelope on which he'd scribbled Frederico's details back at the Bunker. He quickly keyed the number into the phone and listened to the faint static as it searched for a connection. With mounting excitement, Rafael turned to watch as the call went through and he heard the electronic buzz of the ring tones. Outlined in the soft lights of the lobby he could clearly see one of the guards reaching out to pick up the receiver.

"Edificio Excelaris, can I help you?" The man's voice sounded tired and bored.

"Can I talk with Miguel Torres please? I need to speak to him urgently on a personal matter."

"One moment." The guard put down the receiver on the wooden desk and started walking towards the lobby entrance and the short path that led to the parking garage. Simultaneously Rafael crept back to his previous vantage point behind the low wall, taking care to remain out of sight. The voices of the guards carried clearly in the still night air.

"Hey Miguel. Someone needs to speak to you urgently on phone."

"Who is it? Did they say what it was about?"

"No, I didn't ask but it sounded important. Come on. They're on the line now, back at the lobby." The guards moved away together and Rafael waited a couple of seconds before vaulting over the wall onto the driveway. He swiftly ducked under the barrier, entered the parking garage and stopped on the downward sloping access ramp before he went too far underground. He'd kept the cell phone connected and now he pressed it to his ear, waiting for the guard to reach the phone.

"Hello, is that Miguel Torres of 257 Avenida de la Libertad?" Rafael said quickly as he heard the receiver being picked up.

"No, that's not right I live in Soacha, near the Autopista del Sur."

"Excuse me sir. I must have the wrong number. Sorry to have troubled you." He hung up quickly and jogged down the ramp before Miguel Torres could return to his station.

The sleek shapes of expensive, well-maintained cars filled the basement. The odour of petrol and exhaust fumes hung faintly in the air. On the far side of the garage Rafael could see an elevator and he strode through the silent, gleaming ranks of upmarket vehicles without looking to the side. The elevator doors opened with a metallic whisper when he pressed the call button. The interior was larger than he had expected and was adorned with marble and glass. A full-length mirror had been fixed opposite the doors. He stepped inside and pressed the button for the ninth floor.

The gleam of the overhead lights was dazzling and and he felt strangely out of place in the crisp, clean world of the elevator. He found himself examining his crumpled reflection in the mirror. The lines at the corners of his eyes appeared more deeply carved in the intense light and shadows gathered at the edges of his face and under his cheekbones. A smudge of dirt showed up on the shoulder of his overcoat where he had thrown himself to the ground behind the wall outside and his faded jeans and creased grey t-shirt seemed to hang loosely on his thin frame. He ran his hand over his short-cropped black hair and wondered idly what Gabriella would think if she could see him now.

Rafael barely noticed the smooth deceleration as the elevator glided to a stop and was slightly surprised when the doors swished open again. He stepped through cautiously and found himself on a well-appointed landing. The marble floor had a strip of carpet running down the centre which muffled the sound of his footsteps. A stairwell with a polished wooden handrail stretched away towards the roof. He could hear the faint conversation of the security guards echoing up from the lobby. Abstract modern paintings were fixed to the walls and a number of sturdy doors were spaced at intervals around the landing.

Conscious of how conspicuous he would appear if one of the doors opened and the residents emerged, he moved swiftly away from the elevator. The entrance to Frederico's apartment was indicated by solid bronze numbers screwed into the frame. A spy hole had been bored through the wood at eye level and Rafael checked it quickly to make sure the other side was dark. He fished the key out of the envelope and, with a final glance along the landing, inserted it into the lock and opened the door.

The first thing he noticed as he stepped into the apartment was the stuffy smell of stale air. Shutting the door softly behind him he groped along the wall until he found a light switch. Subdued spot lights illuminated a short hallway leading to a living area. Open doors led off to either side. He caught a glimpse of a small bathroom to his left and a compact kitchen to his right. The floor was covered in a plush green carpet blazoned with a garish, swirling pattern and Rafael's feet sunk into it slightly as he stepped along the hallway. A large television and a comfortable looking sofa took up most of the space in the living room. Floor to ceiling windows opened out of one of the walls and Rafael could see the city's lights spread out below him. An expensive view, a view to savour.

A breakfast bar joined the lounge to the kitchen he had seen through the door earlier. He stepped around it to find himself in a well-designed and tidy room. A dishwasher and washing machine testified to the fact that Frederico certainly wasn't short of money. Crockery and cutlery was neatly ordered and tidied away and other expensive gadgets were dotted about; a microwave near the fridge, a blender in the corner. Rafael thought of his own basic, untidy kitchen and wondered what his life would have been like if he'd been rich.

Looking somewhat at odds with the otherwise orderly surroundings, a curling newspaper lay folded on the kitchen table. Rafael picked it up and began leafing through. It was a copy of *La Justicia* from just before Frederico was reported missing. Perhaps it was one of the final things he read before leaving his home for the last time, thought Rafael grimly. Most of the articles were about poverty in the slums with some criticism of American foreign policy thrown in for good measure. He stopped abruptly when he came to a prominent, full page story about a cultural institution in Salitre, near the city centre.

Under the headline, "Disappearing History", the article alleged that a number of sacred indigenous artefacts had disappeared gradually from the Museum of Culture and Heritage, as the place was known, over the course of the year and called for a thorough investigation by the authorities. The missing objects had all come from the museum's extensive collection on the Muisca, the Indian tribe that had been the original inhabitants of Bogota, and the article included some limited details on their history and background. After some fierce early resistance, it seemed they had been largely wiped out when the Spanish Conquistadors arrived en masse in the sixteenth century and their existence survived solely in some of the more unusual place names dotted around the capital.

What had caught Rafael's attention was that the article had been written by Frederico and his profile photo was printed at the top of the page next to the headline, the same photo from the missing person notices that Rafael had taken from the petrol station earlier that morning. He was unable to suppress a broad smile. The fact that the file in the archive room had been cleaned out made finding something meaningful about Frederico's work and recent activities all the sweeter. He wondered whether there was any kind of link between Frederico's death and the museum. Somehow a group of antiquarians and archaeologists didn't seem like the kind of people who would torture a man to death and then remove his internal organs but even that thought couldn't dampen his satisfaction. He removed the page with the story, folded it carefully and put it into his pocket.

Back in the lounge he found another door that led into the bedroom. This room was dominated by a neatly-made double bed with dark green covers that clashed slightly with the carpet. A large painting of horses on a green canvas was fixed to the wall above the bed creating a gloomy, slightly sinister atmosphere in the room. There was a glass desk at the foot of the bed under a window. A flat panel computer screen and a keyboard were the only objects on the desk, while underneath it the blocky shape of the accompanying computer processing unit was planted into the carpet like a tombstone.

As he sat down he could see that the window opened onto an internal ventilation shaft. He imagined Frederico sitting in the same space staring at the blank wall opposite and shivered involuntarily. Rafael reached down to push the on button and the computer emitted a violent buzzing noise which sounded unnaturally loud in the ghostly silence of the apartment. The monitor blinked into life and its soft glow lit his face. A little grey box appeared in the centre of the screen asking for the password. Rafael took a couple of moments to consider before pressing 'enter' to see whether Frederico had actually set a password. A red circle with a white cross in the middle popped up. 'Password Incorrect' said the writing on the screen.

He tried some obvious passwords then, Frederico's name, family members, dates and places of birth, various combinations, forwards, backwards and with the letters mixed up. Each time the 'Password Incorrect' box was his only reward. He pinched the bridge of his nose and closed his eyes. He was certain Frederico had stored valuable information on his computer; if not why protect it with a password, and it was frustrating to be so close but not be able to access what he needed. He was confident he could crack the password eventually, with more thought and time, but he was getting nowhere fast at the moment so he decided to check the rest of the apartment more thoroughly.

Back in the kitchen, Rafael went through all the drawers and cupboards. The most interesting thing he found was a small quantity of mouldy food in the fridge. Similarly, a search of the bathroom turned up nothing beyond a stack of pain killers in the medicine cabinet, which made him think of the stockpile of pills in his own bathroom. He'd just about given up hope of discovering anything further of value when he decided to look round the bedroom one more time.

He was checking through the drawers again when he found that one of them didn't open properly. There seemed to be something obstructing it. He pulled it out of the housing and emptied the contents onto the bed. As he turned it over he could see that a plain, manila envelope had been carefully taped to the bottom. His excitement mounted as he tore open the envelope and pulled out the contents. Rafael couldn't prevent a sharp intake of breath as he looked at what he held in his hand. It was a small dog-eared business card with the words *Nuevo Templo del Sol,* the New Temple of the Sun, printed across the middle in bold typeface. He had no idea what it meant but what had really taken his breath away was the design in the top right-hand corner of the card. Concentric circles surrounded by triangular points, identical to the tattoo on Frederico's shoulder and the symbol scratched into the car when Jorge and Ospina had been shot.

The electronic beeping of his cell phone made him jump and he dropped the business card in surprise. He searched in his pocket to retrieve the device and his heart sank when he saw the number on the display. It was the friends who had invited him round for dinner. In his excitement at discovering Frederico's identity and then getting into the apartment he had totally forgotten his dinner appointment. Looking at his watch now he knew there was no way he could get to their apartment in time. In fact, they were probably calling to ask if he was nearly there or if he could pick something up on the way. The thought of making excuses filled him with despair so he put the phone down on the desk and waited until the beeping and vibrating had stopped. It seemed to take an eternity in the hollow silence of the empty apartment.

**

12. Doce

The photocopier rattled and clicked as another sheet of paper was sucked into its mechanical interior. Nathalie Rodriguez pushed some loose strands of hair away from her eyes and looked up from the pile of admin forms that were collecting on the photocopier's out-tray. The bulky machine gave off an unpleasant, chemical odour of hot toner and Nathalie wished that she was at home with her son. Victor was eighteen months old and Nathalie had been forced to leave him with her mother while she was at work. It would be time to feed him again now. An image of his little face formed in her mind, his mouth working over the carefully chopped food, his eyes filled with the curiosity of new sensations.

The whirring of the copier stopped abruptly, interrupting Nathalie's thoughts. She picked up the pile of still-warm papers and looked out of the window for a moment. It was a typically overcast day in Bogota with a layer of grey cloud lying like a dirty blanket over the city. Three floors below cars and buses jostled for position in the street. The growling of engines formed a background rumble that was clearly audible over the click of people typing.

Nathalie's desk was near the filing cabinets and it was necessary to pass through the rest of the office to get there. Twenty more desks were squashed into the narrow space, pushed together like crates in storage. The widely-spaced skylights hadn't been cleaned properly for some time and the light they let in was cloudy and opaque. The low heels of her office shoes made a dull thump on the grey carpet tiles as she passed. Her sallow faced colleagues were slumped in their seats, staring blankly at their computers and muttering clipped sentences at each other.

She dumped the pile of forms onto the last clear corner of her desk. The rest of the surface was lost under an assortment of paper, computer equipment and stationery, in sharp contrast to the empty desk facing it where a faint layer of dust clung to the monitor screen.

The desk had belonged to Nathalie's colleague Frederico Fernandez. Nathalie had liked Freddy. He had been lively, kind and curious, joking with everyone in the office and always asking questions. She had worked as his assistant and then he had disappeared, just not turned up in the office one day about two months ago. Of course the police and the family had been involved but that had all been dealt with by the paper's management. Now all that was left of his time at *La Justicia* was the bare desk.

Nathalie sighed and took a small mirror from her handbag to check her hair. The face that looked back at her from the small circle of glass was pale and smooth with delicate, almost vulnerable, features. She had always considered her lips to be a little too thin and she frowned at the slight shadows that marked the areas beneath her chocolate-coloured eyes. Victor's crying had woken her several times during the night. Her slightly-wavy, shoulder length black hair was untied and she pushed it back in to place behind her ears again.

The sharp clack of a door being closed firmly caused her to glance up from the mirror. A small office had been marked off at the end of the floor behind greasy-looking glass partitions that didn't quite reach the uneven ceiling tiles. Someone had attempted to fix a blind made of beige cloth strips across a section of the glass wall but a number of the strips had fallen over time, allowing a partial view into the office.

Nathalie could see the paper's editor, Gustavo, talking with a slim man dressed in tan trousers, a black shirt and grey tie. Gustavo reclined in the padded chair behind his desk while the man seemed slightly uncertain, standing uncomfortably near the glass door. The overhead lights in the office and the smudged glass of the partition made Gustavo's bulky face seem further away and it was difficult to see the wispy hair receding back from his forehead and his close-set eyes. Gustavo seemed to be nervous and was moving his arms about rapidly behind the desk. With a vague gesture of his arm he pointed down the office towards where Nathalie was sitting.

The man turned to follow the gesture and seemed to catch her gaze. She had a glimpse of a lean face with a high forehead. The eyes and eyebrows seemed very dark and she noticed the dark shadows underneath the eyes. His mouth was a firm line with lips pressed together and she had an impression of impatience or disappointment. The man nodded and Gustavo pushed out from his desk and opened the door.

"Nathalie could you come in here for a minute please." Not quite sure what to expect, she paced over to the office and joined them in the murky space enclosed by the glass walls.

"This is Investigator Raphael Alvarez of the *Fiscalia,* " rasped Gustavo, indicating the man with the thin face. Closer up Nathalie could see that his clothes were creased and the tie knot had started to work itself loose. The office smelled of stale coffee and the door closed shut behind her with a dry click. "*Agente* Alvarez has some questions about our missing colleague Frederico. I've already told him we co-operated fully with the officers back when Freddy first disappeared but it seems he wants to review all the details."

"Sometimes it can help to discuss things again. Information that was forgotten can come back." The man's voice was soft, almost apologetic in contrast to the stern looking features and Nathalie noticed that his eyes were actually an unusually light shade of brown, almost yellow.

"I don't know what else I can tell you," she replied. "We spent a long time talking to the other investigator. He took all of Freddy's papers and files." Raphael looked up sharply.

"Can you tell me about him, the other investigator I mean? What can you remember about him?" She looked puzzled by his question.

"Well, it all seems like a long time ago now," she said. "But I'll tell you what I can. He was tall, taller than you. Older as well, with a patch of grey in his hair, at the front, here." She put her hand on her forehead at the left side. "He had a moustache and a beard but they were very thin and you could see his face through them. Is there any news about Freddy? Does anyone know what happened to him?" Raphael opened his mouth to reply but was interrupted by the shrill ringing of the telephone on Gustavo's desk. The editor picked up the receiver and pressed it to his ear.

"I have to take this," he grumbled after a few seconds of listening. "Why don't the two of you step out for a while. And Nathalie," he added as they moved towards the office door.

"Remember you don't need to answer any questions if you don't want to."

**

The noise from the street hit them like a wall as they pushed out through the glass doors of the lobby into the dry, dusty heat of the Bogota afternoon. A jumble of cars, motorbikes and overloaded trucks filled the eight lane *autopista*, weaving in and out of each other like a shoal of dirty, roaring fish creeping slowly in the direction of the airport. Nathalie led Raphael to a precarious-looking footbridge over the sprawling river of vehicles.

They navigated through the street vendors that had colonised the bridge and waved away the various attempts to sell fruit and lottery tickets. On the other side of the bridge, at the corner of a side street was a badly finished two-storey building that seemed to lean against the more sturdy apartment block next to it. The ground floor was open to the street and in the gloomy light of the interior Raphael could make out packets and bottles stacked to the ceiling on fragile shelves. A faded red panel hanging above the entrance read: *Cigarreria Buen Punto* in bold yellow italics. The O was formed from the thumb and index finger of a stylised hand. Nathalie turned to look at Raphael, a spark of challenge in her eyes.

"We go here after work sometimes. It's not much to look at but the *empanadas* are pretty good." Without waiting for a reply she plunged inside. Raphael paused for a heartbeat then followed her in. Past the entrance he could see that the shop was narrow and went back for the length of most of the building. About half way along, a set of glass fronted cabinets had been set against one wall filled with the more expensive bottles of alcohol.

A small area of the floorspace had been cleared next to the cabinets and half a dozen plastic tables and chairs had been set up. Nathalie was sitting at one of the chairs watching as Raphael stepped past a stack of tins to approach. He was struck by the elegant, almost fragile beauty of her features offset by the determined mouth and the challenging eyes that radiated a certain strength and courage. She certainly didn't seem scared

101

or intimidated by talking to the police. There were no other customers and they had the tables to themselves.

"So what do you want to know?" began Nathalie after the shop attendant had prised herself away from her telenovela and slouched over to their table with two beers in plastic cups.

"Well, let's start with you. How did you know Frederico Fernandez and why has your boss sent me out here with you to talk about him?" He smiled to show the last part of his question was not meant as a serious accusation.

"I was friendly with Freddy but we weren't really friends. I worked with him on his last investigation. My desk was next to his and I talked to him everyday."

"What were you working on?"

"Freddy had this thing about the Muisca Indians. They were here before the Spanish arrived apparently. Did you know that Bogota is named from a Muisca word? That was one of the things he used to tell me every couple of days." She paused to take a sip of the beer, her eyes fixed on a point above Raphael's left shoulder. "The biggest collection of Muisca objects is held by a museum near the university in Salitre. It's called the Museum of Culture and Heritage. Freddy spent a lot of time there. I went with him a couple of times to help him interview the head of the anthropology department. His name was Ignacio Perez I think, *Professor* Ignacio Perez - he reminded us of that every time I met him. They were great friends to start with. I think the professor was pleased to get all the attention. Then Freddy started to push him about things going missing from the collection."

"What kind of things?"

"Well that's the strange part. He started out planning to write a story about how the museum was building links with the remaining Muisca Indians. Then one day he came back to office and started talking about things going missing. He had me go through all the photos and records from the Muisca section with him to see if we could prove that some of the items had gone. The pieces that caught Freddy's attention all came from one group, called 'Offerings to the Sun'. Golden knives and arrows and strange shaped pots with human figures on them." Nathalie paused and put her half-empty cup back down on the table. A small pool of moisture was spreading from the condensation running down the side.

"But what about you detective? What are you doing looking at all this again? And you still haven't told me if there's any news about Freddy. Where did he go? What happened to him?" Raphael was silent for a couple of seconds. She saw the corners of his mouth tighten and the yellowish eyes seemed to look through her as if he was gauging whether to trust her.

"Look I can't tell you anything yet. We've still got to do more tests and depending on the results we'd need to talk with the family first." He paused for another second. "But you should prepare for the worst."

"Oh! That's terrible." Nathalie's pale hand moved to her mouth. She blinked quickly and Raphael could see the glimmer of moisture in the corner of her eyes. "I was really hoping he would be ok - that he just needed to go into hiding for a while." Raphael waited while Nathalie wiped her eyes with a tissue from her handbag. "I think I need something stronger to drink." She raised her arm and turned to the shop assistant. "Two aguardientes here please." Nathalie drained the spicy, aniseed liquid in one go after the shop assistant had deposited the two tumblers on the table. Raphael left his untouched for a moment then did the same.

"The phrase we're trained to use is: 'sorry for your loss', but I know how inadequate that sounds." His mouth softened and the yellowish eyes seemed to take on a milder tone. He leaned forward and for a moment Nathalie thought he was going to take her hand.

"No I'm fine. I'll be fine. What else do you want to know?" Nathalie sat back in the chair and brushed a strand of her brown hair out of her eyes. He saw her lips pressed together into a tight line and took another sip of beer as he considered how to continue.

"Did you and Freddy work together for a long time?" He asked with a cautious glance.

"I've been at the paper, at '*La Justicia*', for coming up to two years now." A grimace of sarcasm twisted her mouth when she used the paper's name. "My cousin helped me get the job after my partner left. She's into all that left-wing, trade union stuff, a 'true believer' as we call them in the office. She knew there was a job at the paper and she put me in touch with Gustavo. I started out doing assistant work around the office and then about six months ago he asked me to work for

Frederico as well. I was so excited at first to do some real journalism work, to try and make a difference, but I suppose I should have known better. Freddy was easy to work with but he was under so much pressure to come up with stories. He worked all the time and often at late hours. It's really hard to keep up with that when you've got a child at home."

Her voice got fainter and she looked down sadly at the tabletop. "He started to change in the couple of weeks before he went missing. He hardly smiled any more. He didn't come in to the office much and when he did he looked like he hadn't slept. He got a tattoo. He didn't want to show me but I could see the tape they put over those things through his shirt. Freddy was the last guy you'd ever expect to get a tattoo."

"Do you remember the last time you spoke with him?"

"Yes, it was about two months ago. He called me at home in the middle of the night to talk about work. I don't think he even realised what the time was. He sounded drunk or something. His words were slurring and he was talking really quickly. The phone woke up my son Victor, so we couldn't talk for very long. He kept saying he needed to go to hospital, but that he was fine, there was nothing wrong with him. He said something about a *Clinica Santa Carmen*. My mother is called Carmen so the name stayed in my memory.

I mentioned that to the other investigator, the man with the grey hair and the thin beard but he didn't seem interested. We looked it up after Freddy didn't come back to work. There isn't a *Clinica Santa Carmen* anywhere near Bogota. The nearest one is in Cartagena, on the Caribbean coast where they do plastic surgery for rich people. I have no idea what Freddy would be doing in Cartagena or why he'd go to a cosmetic clinic. It doesn't make any sense." She drained the last mouthful of beer. "I'm not sure I've got much more to tell you. I hope some of this was useful. If you'll excuse me I really need to get back to work."

"Yes, thanks. You've been really helpful. I'm going to follow up with the Museum of Culture and Heritage and I'll see if I can find anything about a *Clinica Santa Carmen*." They stood together, the plastic chairs scraping against the bare concrete of the floor. Nathalie could see that the hard, closed look had returned to Raphael's face. He seemed to turn in on himself as the conversation ended.

"Please don't say anything about Freddy being dead yet. It really is too early to be sure. I'll confirm officially as soon as I can and I promise I will get in touch with you personally to let you know." Raphael reached into his wallet to pull out a contact card. "If you think of anything else you can reach me on that number." He paused for a moment and reached back into the wallet. "One last thing. Do you know anything about this." He handed over the business card he had found at Frederico's apartment with the circles and triangles. As she studied the card her eyes widened slightly and Raphael was struck by their rich brown colour which seemed to shine with the remains of her tears.

"Yes, I recognise this. Come with me." She turned suddenly and started heading for the exit. Rafael left some money on the table and followed her out. She was silent as they crossed back over the footbridge and into the lobby of the office building. "Wait here please. I'll be back in couple of minutes."

Raphael sat down heavily on the single threadbare sofa and contemplated the yellowing front pages of *La Justicia* that had been put into frames and hung on the walls. He hadn't realised how tired he was and the fatigue and the alcohol suddenly caught up with him as he sat in the airless lobby with the dull moan of the traffic from the *autopista* outside.

He had appreciated the conversation with Nathalie more than he had realised. It had been some time since he had sat with an attractive woman and drunk a beer. He felt the sadness rise up unbidden as his memories of Gabriella returned and he wondered again what his life would have been like if she had not been taken away from him. He pulled away from the loop he had been down so many times before. There was no moving forward that way and he pushed his thoughts back to the work, back to the case.

The discussion with Nathalie had opened a lot of doors and he felt a surge of excitement as he reflected on the new information. He'd started out with a mangled torso which he'd named Adam without any real hope of finding out more. Now he knew that Adam was Frederico and that Freddy had been involved in some curious things. He wondered how Calderon would react when he learnt Raphael was making progress with a case he wasn't meant to solve.

105

The ding of the elevator bell made him look up again and he saw Nathalie striding towards him.

"Here, take this. It's the only thing left from Freddy's papers." She passed him a small, black, leather-bound book with the familiar symbol of circles and triangles inlaid in silver on the front cover. "I found it in the corner under his desk. It's almost as though they didn't want to take it with them."

Raphael pulled back the front cover and read: *Testamento del Nuevo Templo del Sol* printed in blocky letters on the first page. He quickly flicked through the rest of the book, which seemed to be filled with densely printed, almost illegible text. A faint handwritten message had been scribbled near the back cover. He smiled and the placed the book carefully into the pocket of his jacket, to study later. With a final goodbye to Nathalie and a promise to get in contact with any news, he shoved through the glass doors and back out onto the street, hoping to see her again soon.

**

13. Trece

As Raphael climbed out of his car his eye was caught by a Che Guevara mural picked out in black outline against the white end-wall of a row of houses on the other side of the street. It was clearly a smaller copy of the more well-known mural that decorated one of the faculty buildings at the nearby *Universidad Nacional*, itself based on the famous photo of the Cuban *"Guerillero Heroico"* by Alberto Korda. There was a faint odour of tear gas in the air and Raphael guessed that another of the frequent student protests at the university had spiralled out of control.

The approach to the Museum of Culture and Heritage was through a small open area which had been planted with wiry grass. Stunted trees lined a short gravel path which took an oblique route over the patchy lawn to the entrance. The palm fronds waved about madly in the strong wind that had blown up overnight from the east and Raphael's gaze was drawn to the shredded remains of a plastic bag caught in one of the branches. The building itself stood alone and a set of shallow, white steps led up to a single metal-framed revolving door. The squat, linear architecture was devoid of any external decoration as though it didn't want to distract from the value of the exhibits contained within.

Raphael had stayed up late into the night, searching through the strange book that Nathalie had given him yesterday. It was cheaply printed with the cramped typeface crowded onto thin pages through which you could see the outline of your finger as you held the corner. There was no structure or order to the text but Raphael had surmised from what he had read that it set out some kind of obscure religious revelation. Some of the passages returned to his mind now as his feet crunched along the gravel path. "The current order is not what was intended"… "The time of the false religion of the Spanish is coming to an end"…"The people of this land will rise from their knees"…

107

"The blessed Sun will shine His light upon us all. He will bathe in the blood of his enemies."

On the blank page on the inside of the back cover, someone had left what looked like an address, in scratchy, black handwriting. The details were hard to make out but it seemed to be in a small village called Boyerino just north of the city and Raphael planned to make the drive out there later that day. Now the book was nestled carefully in the pocket of his overcoat again. He could feel the weight of it against his thigh as he strode up the short flight of steps.

The revolving door pushed Raphael into a high-ceilinged entrance hall where, in contrast to the outside, some effort had been made to embellish the space. Ornately carved pillars with abstract geometric shapes marched away into the dim light provided by the skylights far above. Garish posters advertising the current exhibitions were pasted up along the walls. A security guard was hunkered down behind a desk in one corner. Part of the space had originally been given over to a drab gift shop that had since closed down and the stacks of empty shelves lingered in the shadows behind the metal grilles that covered the windows. Small groups of people moved across the hall and the hushed echo of quiet conversations formed a persistent background hiss in the dry, stale air.

Raphael stopped next to the gift shop as his eyes adjusted to the gloom. There had not been many opportunities to visit a museum growing up in San Cristobal. He remembered the one time his class from the *Colegio* had been loaded up onto a bus and then marched forcibly round the *Museo Nacional* with its endless galleries of portraits and dusty Simón Bolívar memorabilia. One of his classmates had tried to steal a camera from a foreign tourist and they'd all been escorted out and put quickly back onto the bus before anything worse could happen. With a sigh he stepped up to the reception desk and reached for his identification badge.

**

Professor Ignacio Perez drummed his fingers against the frame of the wooden lectern and then rubbed the stubble of his white beard thoughtfully. He gazed out over the empty wood-frame chairs spread out in ranks across the parquet floor of the hall. From where he stood on the low stage at the front of the room, the final rows of seats and the entrance were lost in the shadows under a raised viewing gallery. He needed to change the end of the speech. Something better would be needed to secure the future of his research, and the museum's fundraising reception was coming up fast. There would be a group from the university funding council and that awful man Yoposa was likely be there as well. He shuddered thinking of the last time he had been in a room with Yoposa. The man's strange accent and mannerisms had a way of making a person feel uneasy, as though he was trying to constantly emphasise all the differences between you rather than find the things you had in common. And all the problems that had been caused by their last agreement had still not quite gone away.

Ignacio cleared his throat and began again, the rich timbre of his voice echoing through the empty space.

"We will shed new light on Colombia's archaeological treasures and make the heritage of the original inhabitants relevant to all the people of this country. Your generous donations will allow this crucial work to continue." A faint rustling sound caused him to stop and peer into the gloom at the back of the hall. His heart jumped in his chest as he saw a figure detach itself from the shadows and step towards him. A young looking man with a narrow, hard face emerged into the dim light of the hall.

His dark brown hair was cut short and the thin mouth and straight eyebrows gave him an almost fierce expression, as though he were secretly angry at some unseen offence. The man was carrying a raincoat slung over one arm and his shoes clicked on the parquet floor as he stepped towards the stage.

"I'm sorry. I didn't mean to surprise you. One of your staff told me where to find you." The voice was soft, almost hard to hear in the expansive space of the hall. Closer up Ignacio could see that the man's eyes were an unusual shade of pale brown, almost yellow and that dark lines marked the face under the eyes. "I am Investigator Raphael Alvarez of the *Fiscalia* and you, I think, are Professor Ignacio Perez." Ignacio adjusted his tie and shifted uncomfortably in his dark brown suit jacket.

"Yes I suppose you are right. What can I do to help you, Señor Investigator?"

"I want to talk with you about Frederico Fernandez". Ignacio swallowed in a throat suddenly dry.

"Yes I remember him. A most persistent young man. Let's go to my office where we can talk more freely. Please walk with me." Raphael watched in silence as the stout professor stepped down from the stage, his white hair and beard framing a well-lined, nut-brown face. The mahogany double doors of the hall clacked shut behind them and Ignacio led the way into a complex network of corridors and rooms.

"My offices are in the Londoño wing of the museum, which is where the indigenous history galleries are located, with our extensive Muisca exhibits. It was the Muisca that brought me into contact with Mr Fernandez - with Frederico. How is he by the way?" Raphael walked on for a few paces without replying.

"That is a good question Professor. I was hoping you might be able to tell me. No-one has seen Frederico Fernandez alive for over two months." Ignacio blinked quickly and looked at the floor.

"Well, I'm sorry to hear that. I didn't see him again after he wrote those lies about me in his newspaper." They descended a wide marble staircase and passed into a softly-lit exhibition hall. Glass fronted display cases filled the room and Raphael could see files of bulbous, brown pottery locked away behind the dusty screens. A middle-aged man in glasses strolled among the exhibits peering at the stylised images of fish and animals picked out on the beakers and jugs in vivid white paint. In another large case in one corner a skeleton with leathery patches of brown skin crouched next to more broken pots, the arms, thighs and ankles bound tightly with wire cords. An elaborate head dress fashioned from ceramic beads and copper circles decorated the skull and the jaw bone was pulled back in a silent scream. Raphael stopped next to the skeleton.

"So what happened to him?"

"I told you I don't know. I liked Freddy, I really did. He had a quick mind and a real interest in the past. But when he accused me of stealing things from my own museum that was a step too far. He didn't have a shred of proof and I hope you haven't come here to repeat those baseless accusations." Ignacio felt the colour rising in his cheeks. His voice had become louder and the man in glasses had ceased his inspection of the pottery and was glancing at them furtively from the other

110

side of the room. Ignacio saw that the detective was looking at him with a twisted smile.

"No, I mean our friend in the case here." The professor took a breath and calmed himself. His hand was trembling slightly.

"Oh him. They found him when a group of children went missing in some caves near Sogamoso. The searchers broke through a wall and there he was waiting for them, pretty much like you see here. The story goes that one of the children was never found again and that is the price that was paid for having him back in the world." Rafael cocked his head to one side sceptically.

"He has been mummified," the professor continued. "It was a common practice among the Muisca. His skin was dried out with resin to preserve the likeness. His internal organs were removed and originally emeralds were placed on his eyes and navel. The emeralds sadly did not make it out of the cave." The professor gave a half shrug. "The Muisca revered the bodies of their chiefs and fiercest warriors. They were displayed on important feast days and were used to intimidate enemies on the field of battle. This mummy was donated to the museum in the 1960s and has spent most of his time since in this case. So as you can see, there's no crime for you to investigate here." Ignacio allowed himself to return the investigator's sardonic smile. Raphael stepped away from the case and nodded, a faint look of amusement still playing over his features.

"Tell me more about your work Professor Perez. What is your field exactly?"

"I am one of this country's pre-eminent professors of ethnography, paleo-anthropology and archaeology," he stated without any hint of false modesty.

"So what does that involve? What do you do?"

"Let me show you some of the things I'm working on here." He led the way out of the gallery, along a corridor and through a reinforced metal door into another darkened exhibition room. In contrast to the previous gallery this room was virtually empty with a single, large, circular tank of thick perspex forming an area of focus at the centre of the room. Raphael could make out some small, gold figures clustered around a flat rectangular object.

"This is our version of the famous *Barco Muisca*. It is not as embellished as the more well-known example in the *Museo de Oro*, but it is still an exceptional piece of pre-Hispanic art and gold working." Ignacio's voice seemed to float out of the semi-darkness and took on a hushed, ethereal quality as he continued to describe the precious objects in front of them.

"It is a representation of El Dorado, the golden man, the legend that brought the Spanish conquistadores from their coastal bases on the Caribbean into the interior of the continent. When it was time for a new chief of the Muisca, a new *Zipá*, to take on his responsibilities, he was first required to make the appropriate offerings to the gods. He was taken out on a raft into the middle of the Muisca's sacred lake, which most people think was located at Lake Guatavita up in the mountains about fifty kilometres north of here. The lake is almost perfectly circular, surrounded by pine forest. Some theories argue it was formed by a meteorite impact. For the Muisca it was a perfect representation of the sun on Earth, a great shining, circular mirror, and it was a fitting place for their chief to be offered to the sun.

The *Zipá's* body was covered in golden dust so that he became a great, shimmering, golden man and then at the height of the ceremony he was immersed in the waters of the lake. The Muisca legends say that at that moment the man's soul was taken by the great sun god, *Sué,* and that what came back from the waters was not a man but a living representation of the sun to guide and lead the people. There was a throng of priests and other important people of the tribe to witness the miraculous transformation and when the new chief emerged from the waters they threw a great horde of golden objects into the lake in celebration and thanks." Ignacio stepped back from the glow of the spotlights in the display case. A firmer note of pride had returned to his voice.

"It was me that discovered this precious collection of objects for the museum just under five years ago. We were working on the original manuscript of the the chronicles of Juan de Castellanos, who was with the conquistadores in 1537. In one section he describes the temple that the Muiscas built at Lake Guatavita, a beautifully carved platform out in lake which they used for astronomical calculations and worship. No one had been able to find it before and it was thought to be a myth. We

112

were able to use a new X-ray technique developed here in the museum to reveal that in the original version of the manuscript Castellanos included detailed notes on where to find the temple, which were then erased and lost as the text was copied and distributed.

I took my team to the area he described. The water is much lower today and it is right on the shore of the lake. I knew we were in the right place straight away and when we started digging I was proved right. We found the foundations of the temple platform and a whole array of objects and finds, a lot of which are on display in the other galleries. Finally after months of careful digging down into the lake shore we saw a glimmer of gold. Another day of work and we were able to pull this spectacular gold boat and its attendants from the heavy, black mud and back into the light of day for the rest of the world to enjoy here in this museum. So this is what I do, Señor Investigator. A bit like you, I try to bring the past back to life to see what it can tell us about the present."

After the gold room they walked on in silence for a spell before passing through a set of glass-panelled double doors and into a cloister round an open court. A fountain with an abstract modern sculpture decorated the court and the tinkle of the falling water sounded loud after the hushed atmosphere of the galleries. On the far side of the cloister Ignacio entered a code into a keypad. A click sounded and Raphael followed him through a heavy door marked 'Private'.

Away from the public areas the ceilings were lower, with sharp strip lights throwing a bright glare onto bare whitewashed walls that had been overpainted with a distasteful shade of light green up to shoulder height. An odd chemical smell pervaded the air and Raphael could feel an acrid tang at the back of his throat. They came through an archway and into a cavernous storage room filled with wire cages and shelving. A bric-a-brac of archive boxes, stuffed animals wrapped in thick plastic sheets and disused furniture stretched away into the gloom.

"This way please." Ignacio's voice seemed unexpectedly loud in the broad space and Raphael saw the flash of the professor's white hair as he started to ascend a tightly-coiled spiral staircase towards a decking level near the high ceiling. They seemed to float upwards through the abandoned layers of neglected objects, as their feet clattered on the cast iron steps and the cage supporting the stairway rattled and shook.

"What is all this stuff?"

"Storage area for the collection. Only a small percentage is on display at any one time. The rest waits here in the dark, until it is needed again"

On the upper level, they paused briefly in the Restoration department so Ignacio could confer with an assistant who was meticulously scraping particles of dirt from what looked like a small golden bird figure. Further along they passed a lab area, walled off behind a glass screen. Technicians in white jackets hurried about with glass tubes and trays while computers whirred and machines hummed and bleeped. After the lab, at the end of a long, narrow corridor, they arrived at a door with "Ignacio Perez - Anthropology" stencilled onto the frosted glass. Ignacio fiddled with the key and they entered the office.

The room was cramped and the air smelled stale and dusty. One wall had been given over to storage units with stacks of wide, shallow drawers that stretched to the ceiling. Some of the drawers had been left partially open and Raphael could see fragments of bone and a row of colourful preserved beetles resting on a delicate white fabric lining. A sturdy bookcase covered the opposite wall. The books were stacked and piled in a haphazard manner with some resting horizontally across the top of others. Notebooks and loose-leaf sheets of paper were pushed in among them. A roughly carved wooden sculpture of a man stood in the corner near the small window. The flat stylised features and rigid ceremonial pose with arms straight at the sides suggested something tribal about it.

"I see we have company." Raphael said with a grin. "Is this another Muisca piece?"

"A memento of my youth, Investigator. When I was a young man I studied with the famous anthropologist, Gonzalo Urrego. I spent months at a time living with the Miraña Indians in the *Amazonas,*" replied Ignacio settling himself into the spartan chair behind his desk and moving a stack of papers.

"The Miraña are animists. They make no distinction between the spirit world and the real world. For example they would say that this carving has a spirit which is as real as the spirit that you or I would have, or even the spirit of Frederico

Fernandez." He sighed. "So how is it you think I can help you?"

"Let me explain the situation for you. About two months ago, Frederico published a damaging article about you in *La Justicia* and then disappeared without a trace. What do you think happened to him?"

"I didn't know he was missing. No-one contacted me before. And I made a point of not reading what he wrote about me."

The surprise sounded genuine. Raphael took a moment before replying, thinking carefully how to proceed. Clearly the other investigator, his rival, had shut down the search before reaching the professor. Whether that was to protect Frederio's killers by limiting the inquiries or whether it was to protect the professor himself remained unclear.

"I have been asked to review the case again and follow up on all possible leads. Even though you didn't read the article, you knew what it was about. How did that make you feel?"

"Freddy was like one of my best students. He seemed to have a genuine interest in who the Muisca were and how they had lived. When he turned on me it felt like a betrayal." The volume of Ignacio's voice climbed higher as his anger returned. "He came to my office one evening. There was an attractive young lady with him, his colleague I think. I'd met her a few times previously. I knew something was different from the moment he sat down, right in that same chair where you are now. He looked terrible, like he hadn't slept properly in a long while and he seemed to be in some kind of pain. She kept looking at him as though she expected him to fall apart at any moment." The professor scratched his beard absently.

"Then he started talking about some elaborate theory of how things were going missing from the museum and how I was personally responsible. Well, I'm assuming you've read his article. Obviously I told him it didn't make sense and that it was all rubbish. Why would I steal things from my own museum? He kept insisting he had evidence but he wouldn't tell me what it was. I think we shouted at each other for a while and then they both left. I never saw him again after that. Now you tell me he is missing. What happened to him? Is there any news?"

"There's nothing I can tell you at the moment. As I said, I've been asked to review the circumstances for the *Fiscal*. So

115

let's talk more specifically about some of the items in this museum." Raphael made a show of reading from a small piece of paper he took from his pocket. "Let's talk about something called 'Offerings to the Sun', is that the right name for it?"

Beads of perspiration stood out on Ignacio's forehead. This investigator knew more than he had realised. He sat in silence while Raphael's questions continued.

"We seem to be talking about a special group of knives, arrows and pots all made of gold. What can you tell me about them? If we go through all the boxes in that storage area are we going to find those things?"

"There are over twenty thousand individual Muisca items in the collection of this museum. You'll forgive me if I'm not intimately acquainted with the whereabouts of every one of them. I'll have someone look into it and we'll get back to you. Now, if there's nothing else I'm due to present my next lecture over at the university."

Ignacio pushed back his chair and started to stand.

"One more question Professor Perez; what do you know about this?" Raphael asked, carefully taking the small black *Testamento* from his raincoat. Ignacio's face seemed to empty of expression when he saw the inlaid symbol on the cover. His grasp was unsteady as he reached for the book. So it did all lead back to Yoposa after all. Ignacio suddenly felt very old as he sadly noticed the spots on his hand that came with age.

"Where did you get that?" The professor's voice was a barely audible whisper now.

"Freddy had it. It was left with his things at the newspaper. I can see you recognise it. Why don't you tell me what you know?"

"Look, I really can't talk to you about this now. I must get to my lecture."

"Please professor. This is important. It might help us understand what happened to Freddy. I know you had your differences with him, but don't you want to help?" Ignacio seemed to struggle to respond.

"I will say that even a member of the *Fiscalia* should tread very carefully if you have any dealings with the *Nuevo Templo del Sol*," he said finally. "But please, I really do have to go." Ignacio waited to one side of the door, indicating that the conversation was over. Raphael stood in turn and picked up his raincoat.

"Can we talk again Professor Perez? Where are you going to be if I need to find you?"

"That's going to be more difficult I'm afraid. I'm leaving Bogota tomorrow. I'm expected to supervise the work and review the latest finds at one of our archaeological digs. It's in a place called Aguazuque, west of here, on the way to Tolima. It's not far though and you can find me there if you need to." With that Ignacio scribbled directions on a scrap of paper and ushered Raphael from his office.

**

Back outside white clouds scudded across the sky and Raphael's raincoat flapped in the wind as he descended the steps at the museum's entrance. A street seller with a cart loaded with avocados shuffled towards him hopefully. Raphael felt like he was breaking the surface back into the real world after a surreal journey through an exotic land of mummies, gold and spirits. Ignacio clearly had more information than he was ready to share at this point but he didn't seem like the kind of person with the will or the resources to torture a man to death and leave his body in a suitcase.

The grudging warning about the enigmatic *Nuevo Templo del Sol* had left him feeling uneasy, but he was not to be intimidated. The *Templo*, whatever it was, and its mysterious emblem that seemed to have been his constant sinister companion for the last week, had obviously had some involvement in Freddy's horrific death. Raphael was more determined than ever to discover what that role had been and how an obscure quasi-religious organisation was capable of inspiring such fear. It was time to drive to Boyerino and uncover whatever clandestine enterprise it was that this Temple was engaged in at the isolated village location.

Raphael's thoughts were interrupted by the buzz of the cell phone in his pocket. He pushed the button to connect the call and heard the thin, metallic sound of Miriam's voice over the faint, background distortion.

"Where have you been? Calderon is looking for you. He keeps asking me where you are. I can't cover for you much longer."

"I'll be back later this afternoon. I'm having trouble with the car again. I'm on the way to the garage now to get it fixed." He wasn't sure why the lie had come so easily; perhaps an instinct that it would be better to avoid giving an account of himself to Calderon for a while longer, until he had a clearer idea of what was involved. There was a pause on the other end of the line and Raphael could hear the muffled hiss of electronic static as he waited for Miriam to reply.

"Raphael, what are you doing? Are you alright?"

"I'm fine Miriam. Don't worry about me. There's something important I need to follow up on. Did you manage to find anything about a *Clinica de Santa Carmen?*" There was another brief pause and Raphael could imagine Miriam pulling papers towards her as she prepared to share the results of her research.

"I got in touch with my contact in the licensing department over at the Ministry of Health. There used to be a 'Clinica Virgin del Carmen' in the *Colinas de Suba*, near Avenida Boyaca. It was a small public mental health facility integrated into the wider medical services for the north of the city. About two years ago there was some kind of scandal. Nothing was proved but public money was disappearing and the Medical Oversight Board of Cundinamarca determined to remove the funding and close the hospital."

Miriam was talking more quickly now, the satisfaction from being able to share the information apparent in her voice.

"Then something unusual happened. Some kind of confidential agreement was made and all the clinic's assets were transferred to a private trust company. The problems with the money disappeared and the trust company agreed to keep the facility open and run it as a private psychiatric rehabilitation centre; they even agreed to keep on treating the same patients. My friend sent me the licensing approval papers and it's all here. The only thing they did change was the name. It's in exactly the same place but now it's called *Clinica Merced de Sué.* What an odd name. What do you think it means?"

"Thanks Miriam, you're the best. Let's talk later."

"Ok Raphael, I don't know what you're up to, but stay safe."
There was a dry click as the call disconnected and Raphael
trudged back towards his parked car.

**

14. Catorce

Raphael crunched the gears as he shifted down to take another bend in the steeply ascending track. The midnight blue Toyota Landcruiser pitched to the left, the noise of the engine loud as it climbed into the curve. This far away from the main roads the track was virtually empty and he had an uninterrupted view of spindly pine trees and the slope leading down to the green, open fields at the bottom of the valley. The wind had blown away the cloud cover and a hazy afternoon sunshine was just starting to break through. Raphael pulled his sunglasses from their case and set them carefully on his nose.

The Toyota had been with him for three years now. He still remembered the thrill of getting his first unmarked departmental car shortly after joining the CTI. It had already been several years old with a couple of discernible dents in the bodywork when the keys were handed over to him in the basement garage of the Bunker. The Landcruiser was a pretty generic car in Colombia and it was not unusual to see at least one or two of them if you drove around the streets for more than ten minutes. But Raphael hadn't given any attention to the car's defects that day. It belonged to him and he had indulged in the noise and energy as he revved it up the ramp, out of the garage and straight home. He had washed down the outside and carefully cleaned out the interior before loading a selection of gear into the back, including a simple fingerprint kit, a roll of yellow and black police tape and several boxes of ammunition.

The radio was tuned to a local rock station and the unmistakable opening chords of Hotel California rolled out of the speakers. As the song flowed on he was struck by a sudden memory of Gabriella sitting in the passenger seat, her brown skin glowing in the sunshine and her honey-coloured hair blowing about in the draft from the open window. It had been one of their first holidays together, just after they got married and they had driven down the mountains to Melgar to enjoy some time in the balmy, tropical weather at the resort there. Her English had been much better than his and she had sung along with snatches of the lyrics. He could almost hear her voice now as the Eagles reached their soulful crescendo "...we're all just prisoners here, of our own device." Then the voice of the commentator cut through the music with the mundane details of a traffic bulletin and the memory was gone as abruptly as it had come.

After a quick lunch of *tamal* purchased from a street stall near the museum, he had taken the *Autopista del Norte* out of the city. The stewed mix of chicken, pork and vegetables had taken the edge off his hunger and he threw the banana leaf wrapping out of the window as he drove. The three lanes of afternoon traffic had limped sluggishly past the sprawling shopping centres, car dealerships and fast food restaurants that dominated the scrubby land at the margins of Bogota. Through the screen of stunted thorny trees that had been planted down the middle of the road he had seen that the traffic was even worse going the other way. Just past Chia he had taken a nondescript turning to the right and then driven up into the hills and mountains to the east.

Now he was approaching the village of Boyerino and he slowed the car to a crawl. The road ahead curved and Raphael passed a succession of low, modest houses with whitewashed walls and uneven, tiled roofs. An improvised cafe was positioned at the edge of the street ahead, little more than a group of flimsy tables arranged under an awning outside of one of the buildings. Even at this late afternoon hour there were no customers and the place seemed to be closed.

As he passed the cafe he noticed that some kind of monument had been set up on the other side of the road. A tall, rectangular obelisk rose up from the centre of a small open area, where a number of tracks from elsewhere in the village met. An unusual bronze sphere had been fixed to the top and it seemed to glow a dull red in the reflected rays of the afternoon sun.

The Landcruiser's tyres shuddered on the dried, rutted ground as Raphael pulled up onto the verge at the side of the road further ahead and cut the engine. He felt the slap of the wind on his face as he climbed from the car and the pungent smell of animals was in the air around him. The place seemed deserted apart from some scrawny cows standing in a field next to a handwritten sign that read '*Se Vende Este Lote*'.

There didn't seem to be any immediate cause for concern, but given the uncertainty of what waited here a level of caution seemed in order. Raphael returned to the Landcruiser and removed his service weapon from the glove box. Like most CTI investigators he had been issued with a standard Colombian-made Indumil Cordova 9mm pistol. He checked the ammunition clip carefully before slotting the weapon into the shoulder holster under his left arm. For good measure he also pulled out his metal CTI identification shield and slipped the chain round his neck. The solid weight of the pistol was a reassuring presence as he strode down the track further into the village, tucking the shield away under his shirt as he walked.

Round the next bend was the first sign of inconsistency, something that suggested this place was different from any other small village in Cundinamarca. Half way along the lane was a modern concrete building that stood out in stark contrast to the small traditional houses that made up the rest of the village. The building was fashioned from angular white blocks and rose above the surrounding dwellings like a monumental sarcophagus, its grim outline dark against the cloudy sky. Arched full-length windows had been let into the structure at regular intervals, the openings covered with opaque blue-tinted glass to prevent any view into the interior. At the rear a small tower had been erected, surmounted with what looked like an uneven bronze sphere, similar to the orb on the monument in the small plaza he had passed on the way. The entrance was guarded by an impressive gateway that was very much closed and locked tight.

Raphael studied the structure in silence for a few moments. The place resembled an industrial, fortress-like church which, he reflected wryly, should probably not have been a total surprise. While driving to the village he had half imagined a more involved search to find what he was looking for, or that Boyerino would contain nothing unusual, just another dead end. As it was he had little doubt that what he was looking at was the *Nuevo Templo del Sol* itself, or at the very least some kind of major centre for the enigmatic organisation. A lot of paths seemed to lead here. He assumed this was where the small book had originated, with its incoherent messages of rage and hatred. He wondered if this was where Frederico had met his gruesome end. The journalist seemed to have some links to the Temple, not least the strange tattoo on his shoulder, but quite what his involvement was remained to be seen. The place certainly had a formidable reputation and Rafael felt his pulse quicken as he stepped up to the gateway.

There was certain to be some kind of security or surveillance system but Rafael could see no sign of it from where he stood. Rather than attempt a direct approach straight away, he decided to circle around and get a better sense of the layout. He followed the perimeter fence away from the gateway along the road. After about fifty meters the grounds ended and he found a narrow track leading away between the boundary of the Temple and the next property. The metal railing was replaced with a solid brick wall on the right hand side, the other consisted of the uneven stones of the village houses. The high walls blocked out most of the light and a smell of damp earth emanated from the alley. Further in, Raphael could just make out a heap of rusted farm tools piled up to one side.

He took a final look around before plunging into the gloomy opening, walking briskly now on the springy ground. The alley twisted gently and the village house on his left fell away quickly, opening out onto a patch of clear ground. The perimeter wall to his right continued for some distance past the back of the houses and Raphael could see that the temple compound was far larger than it had seemed from the relatively narrow profile that faced the street in the village. Stepping back, he caught a glimpse of the top of the strange, squat tower with its ugly metal globe like a giant rotting fruit.

Up ahead, a dense stand of tangled trees and bushes grew right up against the bricks. On an impulse he pushed through the heavy brambles and leaves into the thicket. The shadows here were deep and it took him a few moments to register a particularly gnarled eucalyptus tree rising up into the darkness almost flush with the wall. Still not entirely sure what he was doing, he grabbed the lowest branch and pulled himself up off the ground. The tree's limbs were spaced evenly and he climbed quickly, the bark rough against the skin of his hands. He reached a comfortable fork and stopped for a moment, the aromatic, minty smell of the leaves filling his nostrils. From his vantage point he now had a clear view down into the compound.

From this angle he could see the rear of the main temple building. It was a symmetrical copy of the front facade, including a monumental doorway that led out into the enclosure. A ceremonial pathway led in an arrow-straight line from the rear doorway to a curious round wooden structure with a conical roof made of reeds. The walls seemed to be coated with brightly-coloured clay and it was surrounded by a colonnade of wooden pillars rising up into the reed roof. The crudely made structure formed a strange contrast with the precise lines and angles of the larger building. Half way between the two, at the mid-point of the path, a paved area had been constructed around two roughly-hewn circular stone slabs. The blocks had been laid side by side, almost touching and the honey-coloured surfaces were pitted and weathered. A number of plain outbuildings were scattered around the rest of the yard, mostly set up against the walls and away from the central area.

Raphael felt his curiosity surpass his caution, as he wondered at the purpose of the circular structure. It looked to a certain extent like a large village hut but clearly had some kind of special relationship with the main building given its central position. He could tell, even from this distance that significant care had gone into its construction and that while it was made from basic materials it looked well-kept and maintained rather than shabby or run-down. The round stones were also intriguing. He could think of no obvious reason for their presence in the compound. They looked somehow incomplete as though waiting for something to be set atop them, like plinths for missing statues.

He waited a few minutes more as the red afternoon sun drifted towards the horizon but there was no sign of any movement. The yard and the structures remained deserted. Even from this side of the building there was still no sign of any security and Rafael decided he would take his chances. It was time for a closer look. A thick branch ahead of him grew out over the top of the wall and he moved along it now, crawling hand over hand. On the other side, he swung down and released his grip, hitting the ground with a soft thump. His heart was beating fast as he looked around. He was inside and all remained still and silent. No shouts of alarm rang through the air and no-one challenged his presence.

Raphael rose slowly from his crouched landing position and started to make his way across the space, trying to stay in the growing shadows as much as possible. The hut structure loomed larger as he approached, stepping softly on the balls of his feet. He ducked into the gloom beneath the colonnade, feeling the rough texture of the clay walls abrasive against his back as he followed the curve round towards the entrance. Ahead, the black square of the doorway was oriented to receive the last of the light from the crimson sunset. The wind rustled gently against the reed roof as he reached the edge of the opening and peered cautiously round.

It took several moments for his eyes to adjust to the darkness inside the building. At first he could make out little beyond the plain timber planks on the floor and a row of wooden pillars following the inside curve of the wall. A few heartbeats later and an intricately carved inner wall emerged from the gloom. It appeared to be blocking off a circular central room right at the heart of the structure. Another dark opening directly opposite him showed the entrance.

Suddenly he froze in place as he realised he could distinguish what appeared to be the silhouette of a man standing between two of the pillars. He looked closer, hardly daring to breathe. Further details resolved themselves and Raphael could see that the man's stillness was too absolute, the pose too rigid. He appeared to be wearing some kind of ceremonial outfit, with a white linen robe, an elaborate circlet on his head and curiously, an ornate golden panel that covered the lower half of his face, like a mask. A few more seconds passed and he understood that he was looking at some kind of statue or display figure.

A sense of relief washed through him and he stepped through the shadowy entranceway towards the figure. Closer up he could see that the linen robe was delicately embroidered with gold thread. The man's face remained enigmatic behind its golden face plate but the eyes seemed to have been carved with an expression of burning anger, beneath scowling brows. The statue stood on a raised platform with a short inscription engraved on it. He read the legend '*Tisquesusa*' marked out in curling italic script and wondered what it might mean. The style of the clothing and jewellery made him think of the Muisca objects he had seen earlier that morning in the museum.

Turning away from the figure he focused his attention on the inner room. Hazy red fingers of light from the sunset reached across the floor towards its entrance. He had a partial view through the doorway and could see that something large occupied the gloomy space beyond. From this angle he could make out a segment of what seemed to be an enormous disc hanging down from the ceiling. Further details and patterning had been carved onto the disc but he was unable to see clearly what it was intended to represent. The wooden planks of the floor creaked softly as he stepped across them.

Raphael felt a gust of wind blow in through the opening behind him. He could see the dust stir in the ethereal air and then his eyes were drawn towards the disc. It had also been caught by the draught and the flat face spun gently towards him. Suddenly it was aligned with the open doorway and the surface flashed a blinding red, reflecting the dying light of the sun. Raphael had a microsecond to register that the carvings showed a monumental stylised image of the sun before he was forced to look away.

At that moment he heard a mechanical click and the crunch of a footstep behind him on the dry ground of the yard outside. The entranceway went dark as a figure blocked out the last of the sunlight and a gravely voice barked out, "*No te muevas.*"

His eyes flicked towards the snub outline of a pistol pointing at the centre of his chest. The man holding it was powerfully built and a good head taller than Raphael. His face was broad and blocky and the expression was impassive and unreadable. Raphael could see the black markings of a tattoo on the hand holding the gun, the circle and triangular points that had become such a familiar emblem. He could tell from the steady grip that the giant of a man knew how to use this weapon.

Raphael raised his hands slowly as he cursed inwardly. In his keenness to explore the hut structure he had left himself totally exposed. For such a big individual the gunman had moved as silently as a cat and now he had Raphael completely at his mercy.

"Ok, take it easy. Look, I'm a state agent," said Raphael gently. "I'm going to reach for my ID now." His fingers felt for the chain around his neck. He yanked the cord and the CTI shield came loose from his shirt. The giant blinked in surprise and studied the badge in silence for a few seconds.

"Come," he grunted eventually, waving the gun to indicate that Raphael was to exit the building. They walked in silence across the yard towards the doors of the main temple, Raphael in front with his hands slightly raised and the big man behind with the gun levelled at his back. He directed Raphael to open a small door to the left of the monumental entranceway and they passed over the threshold and into the larger building. The air inside was cool and dry and Raphael caught the sharp tang of some kind of resin or incense. The last of the sunlight was fading away now and the cavernous interior was largely obscured in darkness. Several lamps hung down on chains from the vaulted ceiling far above leaving widely spaced points of light in the echoing gloom. Rows of wooden benches covered the marble floor, arranged around a raised platform in the centre of the room, directly under where the tower disappeared into the shadows above. A metal tripod stood on the dais with a tendril of grey smoke rising into the still air, the source, no doubt of the resin smell that Raphael had noticed on entering.

Their footsteps echoed on the marble tiles as they walked forward. He was directed to a narrow staircase rising away from the ground level and up to a raised gallery that followed the wall round. Raphael considered his options as he climbed the stairs with his hands still raised. The man had not taken his gun and he could feel its weight under his left arm, the raised bump of the hammer rubbing gently against the lining of his jacket. At the same time, there appeared to be no immediate threat so he decided to wait a little longer before making any moves to defend himself.

They arrived at a plain wooden door and the giant with the gun issued another gruff command that he should enter. He grabbed the handle, pushed the door and stepped through into a brightly lit room. Floor to ceiling windows give a panoramic view over the dusky hills and down towards Bogota. Far away, the lights in the towers of the financial centre were just starting to tun on. Airy, golden drapes framed the windows, with the stylised sun pattern marked out on them in black, matching the design of the tattoo on the back of the big man's hand. The rest of the room was nearly empty, apart from a large, ornately carved desk in the centre. Standing behind the desk, a strangely dressed man was talking on the phone as they entered.

"Yes it is urgent. Please have him call me back on this number immediately. Be sure to tell him who I am." The man had an expressive, mobile face and shoulder-length black hair. He was wearing a white tunic made of thick linen with geometric designs worked into the cloth at the neck and shoulders.

As he put the phone down, Raphael could see that on the little finger of his right hand he wore a heavy gold ring with a large green stone. Rafael had a fleeting impression that he had seen a similar ring somewhere else, but before he could focus on the recollection the moment was gone. The man turned his gaze onto the giant with the gun and spoke to him in a lilting, sing-song voice.

"Thank you Ernesto. Please leave us now." The big man turned without another word and stalked from the room. Raphael found himself alone with the long-haired man. The shifting, liquid gaze refocused onto him and he felt a mix of scorn and scrutiny from the figure in front of him.

"Please take a seat, Señor Investigator. We watched you through the cameras as you wandered about. Would you care to tell me what it is that you are doing in our temple?"

"Yes, this in an interesting place, your temple as you called it. What is it that you do here?" Raphael kept his tone mild as he sat in the offered chair in front of the desk.

"Our temple, the New Temple of the Sun, exists to guide people back to the true religion of this land. I am Gael Yoposa and I am the high priest, I suppose you would say, of this institution. To many of our deepest devotees like Ernesto we are the supreme source of hope and guidance in a confused and troubled world."

"Tell me about Tisquesusa," Raphael asked quietly.

"So, you have dared to walk in our innermost sanctuary and have looked on the face of the great Muisca chief, the last *Zipá* of Bogota." Yoposa's face was taut as the level of anger in his voice rose.

"When the Spanish arrived, over three million of my ancestors lived in peace and prosperity in a nation stretching from Boyaca in the north to the *Paramo* of Sumapaz in the South. Tisquesusa ruled over all. He had brought the Muisca clans together and been anointed at the ceremony of El Dorado at Guatavita. When the Spanish invaded his territory Tisquesusa sent his armies against them, his best *Guecha* warriors, but they didn't stand a chance with arrows and slings against armoured men with guns and they were wiped out." The man's eyes were bright and hard with something Raphael couldn't read.

"After he realised the situation was hopeless, he tried to save the people and evacuated all the towns but it was no use. He was eventually cornered at his last stronghold in Facatativa. He made a glorious final counterattack against the invaders but it was no use and he was cut down brutally in the dark. Our people were ground to dust and even the use of Chibcha, the native language was prohibited by the Spanish king. Today I think you would call it 'genocide'." Yoposa's emotion had worn itself out telling the story and his voice was soft, almost a whisper as he finished.

"We will soon be recognised as the descendants of the Muisca and given the same rights and privileges of other indigenous peoples in Colombia." His eyes snapped back to Raphael as he finished this last sentence. "Now, I have answered your questions, but you haven't answered mine. Why is it that you are here?" Raphael took a moment to collect his thoughts. He kept his tone neutral and his gaze level as he responded.

"I am investigating the murder of a journalist called Frederico Fernandez. He was tortured and dismembered and part of his body was left on Montserrate. What do you know of him?" Yoposa's dark eyes were hard as he levelled a flat, blank stare at Raphael.

"I have never heard of this man. So, what is it that you think gives you the right to jump over the wall of our private property and start interfering in our most sacred spaces?" Raphael opened his mouth to answer. He was ready to refer to Frederico's tattoo and the vituperative *Testamento* book that was still resting in the pocket of his rain coat.

Just then, the crashing ring of the telephone on the desk cut through the room. Yoposa snatched up the receiver quickly and listened in silence for a few moments. He looked up at Raphael with an odd smirk.

"It's for you," he grinned holding out the handset. Raphael frowned in confusion and placed it rather uncertainly against his ear.

"Do you know who this is? Tell me who I'm talking to," an angry bark demanded immediately and Raphael closed his eyes in resignation as he recognised the nasal and slightly oily voice of *Fiscal* Ortega.

"This is Raphael Alvarez," he replied quietly.

"Of course it is." Ortega's voice had taken on the dangerous aspect of honeyed venom. "May I call you Raphael? You can call me 'Sir'. I bet you don't know what to say right now, Raphael".

"That's right sir, I don't."

"Do you remember when we met in my office at the start of this business? I warned you then that it was imperative that this murder was solved quickly and without sensation. I believe those were the exact words I used." Rafael let the silence hang for a few more seconds before responding.

"I remember you saying that sir."

"Okay Raphael, I'm going to make this very easy for you. I'm going to tell you exactly what's going to happen now. I don't know what wild notion made you enter the private premises of my close personal friend and respected community leader Gael Yoposa. You can have no conceivable professional reason for being there. Your investigation, and the brief I gave you, has no jurisdiction and no involvement with him and his organisation. You're going to apologise to him and then leave. Is that clear?"

"Yes sir, it is." There was a click as the line disconnected. Raphael found himself looking up into the liquid gaze of Yoposa who was still smirking in amusement.

"Goodbye Investigator Raphael Alvarez of the *Fiscalia*," he intoned and raised his hand in an ironic salutation. In silence Raphael pushed back the chair and strode from the room.

**

15. Quince

Raphael's eyes were drawn irresistibly to a fly darting about near the discoloured ceiling tiles. The fly's movement seemed designed to both attract attention and to elude capture, as it sketched lazy triangles in the air with rapid, baffling changes of direction. Despite the cool weather a fan stirred the air gently and its rotations caused a nearby blue sign, suspended on its wire cords, to sway to the same sluggish rhythm. The solid white letters on the sign read '*Sala de Espera*' and Raphael was slumped into a moulded plastic seat almost directly underneath. The waiting room was located just next to the main entrance of the *Clinica Merced de Sué*, a sprawling, run down complex of buildings that covered the best part of a city block in the northern suburb of Suba. The stillness was punctuated by a regular thump as a bored-looking nurse stapled different parts of a form together from behind a glass counter. A dying pot plant occupied a corner of the room and a television set had been fixed to the wall above it. The sound had been turned off but silent images from a news update flickered across the screen.

In an immaculate white suit and a broad brimmed hat the figure of the President of the Republic appeared. He was pictured striding through a jungle setting before coming to a stop in front of a row of blank-faced men in combat fatigues to address the camera directly.

"He's turning Colombia back into a real country," muttered a well-dressed young man with the distinctive accent of a '*Paisa*' from Medellin. "He's going to destroy those parasite guerrillas and push them back under whatever rocks they crawled out from." An older man with rounded features a few seats away, snorted loudly in contempt.

"Yes, yes, I'm sure victory is just around the corner, like always. More money and sacrifice and the war will soon be won."

131

"What do you mean by that? This country has been on its knees for too long. You can't believe the communists are the best for the future? Cuba and the Soviets are done. It's time for those fools to realise when they're beaten and put down their guns."

"Well, maybe. Look, at my age I've seen it all before. The president may tell us he's going to save the world but to me he looks like just another paramilitary. Mark my words, sooner or later we'll find out that he's no different from the rest of them. It wouldn't surprise me if him and his friends have got their hands in the drug trade somewhere along the line." The young Paisa bristled with outrage and turned to face Rafael.

"What about you *señor*? Surely you agree that Colombia can change for the better. It's the old cynics like him that leave us stuck in the past repeating endless cycles of fighting with each other."

Rafael sighed inwardly. He was sick of the fighting and death which had been such a prominent feature of life in Colombia for as long as he could remember. The general inclination of most of his countrymen tended towards exaggeration and extremes which flowed through into their preference for entrenched political absolutes. The president was either the saviour of the country or he was a drug-dealing criminal. He preferred to avoid being pinned down and forced to pick a side when both options were bad. The superficial attraction of simple solutions was usually a mirage. Situations were usually more complicated in real life but in his experience trying to find a reasonable middle ground usually left both sides unhappy. He tried anyway.

"I think some things seem better but it's too early to be sure that the president is going to win the war in any meaningful sense of the word. I just don't think he's in a position to understand the injustices that drive some of these people to fight." Sure enough both the Paisa and the older man seemed dissatisfied with his reply and they turned back to stare at the screen in silence.

After the bruising encounter with Ortega and Yoposa at the Temple Rafael had been summoned to Calderon's dingy office the next morning to give an account of himself.

"I've let you run with this for longer than I should have Alvarez. I got the call from Ortega last night. He was as angry as a demonic viper," the sub-director had growled from the depths of his padded chair and let the silence hang for a few seconds.

"Tell me where you are with the case."

Rafael studied Calderon from the other side of the sub-director's impossibly disorganised desk. His ruddy face was set hard and despite the early hour his functional brown suit already looked crumpled. Rafael decided to adopt the manner he had developed from his days of military service for talking to the senior officers. He straightened his shoulders and fixed his eyes on the wall behind Calderon where a large calendar covered in scribbled notes hung next to a small crucifix.

"I've established that the body on the mountain is one Frederico Fernandez, a journalist for the *La Justicia* newspaper. Fernandez disappeared just over two months ago and there is an open file on him in the missing person archive in the basement. I went to talk to his colleagues. He was investigating items going missing from the Museum of Culture and Heritage in Salitre just before his disappearance. I had some preliminary discussions with an anthropology professor at the museum but they were inconclusive. His colleagues indicated that he may have been attending a psychiatric clinic in Suba." Calderon's heavy eyebrows drew together into a hostile scowl.

"The torso had a distinctive tattoo on its left shoulder," Rafael continued. "Both Fernandez's colleagues and the anthropology professor suggested a link to the *Nuevo Templo del Sol*. I was also passed a small book of scriptures from the Temple which was in Fernandez's possession. This led me to conclude that a visit to the premises of the Temple would be an appropriate next step in the investigation. I believed the property to be empty so I effected an entry. It became apparent that was not the case and I was taken for a brief interview with the high priest before Fiscal Ortega's call."

He had recited this clipped summary in an emotionless monotone then waited stony faced and still for whatever the judgement was to be. Calderon shook his head slowly and seemed to deflate a little as some of the anger left him.

"You continue to surprise me Alvarez. It was made abundantly clear that you were expected to conclude the investigations on this case and close it as unsolvable without undue delay. Instead you seem to have made a considerable

133

amount of progress." Calderon absently moved some of the papers on his desk as he continued to reflect. He sighed and looked up again at the impassive figure of Rafael.

"Ok Alvarez, keep following the trail. But I warn you, this is the final chance. Visit the clinic and then follow up with the anthropologist, but keep it subtle. Ortega has stipulated that you're to stay away from the Temple at all costs. Is that clear?"

Rafael considered protesting for a moment. So much about the Temple remained unknown and the links to Frederic Fernandez's murder were almost tangible. Instead, because of Ortega's connections with the high priest, it was deemed to be off limits. The futility of the situation filled him with fatigue and disgust. He looked down at Calderon and nodded almost imperceptibly.

"I want regular updates from you Alvarez," Calderon had grumbled. "Don't drop off the grid again or I'll send the Special Operations commandos after you." He turned back to the papers on his desk. "I will arrange for a formal notification to be made to Fernandez's family. You can get back to work."

After his debrief with Calderon, Rafael had been to see Miriam. He had invited her for breakfast in the basement canteen of the *Fiscalia* Bunker. They had found a vacant spot at one of the long tables and got stuck into the decent-sized portion of *Calentado*, a mix of rice, beans and minced beef topped off with a fried egg, that was the breakfast menu for the day. Breakfast was always popular and there was a noisy crowd of CTI operatives packed in around them. Miriam raised her voice as she shared the latest news from home.

"Well, Diego's going to be off work for a week. The silly berk fell off a ladder trying to fix the cable on the roof for the television. He wouldn't wait for the technician because he was determined not to miss the match against Peru. Now he's hobbling around with a bandage on his leg telling everyone he got a sporting injury." She snorted in disgust and rolled her eyes. Rafael smiled at the thought of the long-suffering Diego.

"I heard it was an exciting match. Juan Pablo Angel got a *golazo* and we're looking good for World Cup qualification." She mumbled an indifferent response around another mouthful of the *Calentado*. "How's it going with Biostar Chemicals?"

"Yeah, I'm not sure we're getting anywhere. It would have been good to have you back on the work again. The surveillance has been inconclusive and there haven't been any more developments. I'm staying with it though. I think we need to work up another informant. How's your case? Did you manage to follow up on the clinic I found for you?" There was a note of concern in her tone, lurking behind the apparently casual nature of the question. Rafael smiled again in an effort to dispel her anxiety.

"Well, I've been on something of a cultural adventure. I went to a museum and met an anthropology professor and then took a trip out of the city to visit an indigenous religious organisation. I got a warning from Ortega and Calderon though. Apparently the priest is a friend of Ortega's, so I'm not allowed any further contact. Instead I'm planning to head over to the clinic later this morning to have a look round, ask some questions and see what surfaces." Miriam finished the last of her coffee and slipped a piece of gum into her mouth, pushing away the empty plate at the same time. "Seriously Miriam. Thanks for your help with the research. This is the strangest, most convoluted investigation I've been involved in for a long time and I feel like I'm out there on my own." Miriam leaned forward, a serious look in her eyes.

"Be careful Rafael. I heard from my contact in Internal Affairs that they're preparing a misconduct charge against you. Don't take any more risks with this one or they'll leave you to hang."

He had left Miriam in the canteen and driven north towards the low ridge of hills that thrust up through the north western zone of the city, like a whale breaching through the surface of the ocean. The uppermost parts of the ridge that were too rugged for buildings had been abandoned to the bracken and pine trees and at the highest point the spindly barb of a television mast soared above the rumbling bulk of the city. A blanket of grey clouds had come down again overnight from the mountains to the east and Rafael was wearing a dark brown leather jacket over a threadbare yellow sweater against the cool morning air.

The original town of Suba with its elegant plaza and church had been just on the far side of the hills. The streets and houses had long since been absorbed into the urban sprawl of Bogota and in the 1950s Suba had been officially declared as another district of the capital. The city's implacable grid system broke down into winding lanes and open vistas as Rafael climbed into the *Colinas de Suba*, as the hills were known. Ramshackle low-rise houses and stunted trees lined the roads and it had taken Rafael some time to locate the *Clinica Merced de Sué* in the impenetrable tangle of streets. Eventually he found the place, surrounded by a high, white perimeter wall that had long since been given over to the livid, abstract graffiti of the local gangs. The heavy-set, uniformed security guard at the main gate had directed Rafael to the adjacent waiting room and now he found himself tracking the movements of the evasive fly near the ceiling again.

He had made an appointment under the pretext of searching for a care facility for a putative father suffering from progressive dementia. Rafael tried to remember his own father but his image was as thin and indefinite, as wavering as that of a ghost. He was long since gone, vanished into the lush jungles of Cauca province as surely as if he'd been swallowed by the sea. Rafael supposed it had been an occupational hazard of life in the Colombian army. Juan-Sebastian Alvarez had risen to the rank of major and was in charge of a small fighting unit. One day he had climbed into a helicopter with his squad to follow up on reports of a force of guerrilla fighters moving into the area and had simply never come back. No body had ever been found despite numerous search parties. The Major had been marked down as presumed killed in action and, barring a short, military memorial service, that had been the end of the matter as far as the army was concerned. Rafael had been six at the time and all that were left to him were fragments and impressions. A tall, craggy man with a hard, brash confidence, precise gestures and a tone that demanded obedience. Of course, in this case the vagueness of his memories provided him with a perfect blank canvas on which to project an imaginary father who could help him gain access to the clinic and perhaps establish if Frederico Fernandez had any connection to this place.

The crackle of his name being read out over a loud speaker snapped Rafael back to the present. He stepped up to the glass counter and the nurse pushed the release button for the security door.

"Follow the main path to the administrative building. Take the stairs to the first floor and *Directora* Florez will meet you in her office there," she intoned in a nasal drone. "Please minimise your contact with the patients and don't do anything to disturb them during your visit." Rafael had been able to make out very little of the clinic from outside or while sat in the waiting room. Before entering he had circled the structure slowly in the Landcruiser and seen that the graffitied perimeter wall enclosed the entire complex, rising to a considerable height all the way around, more like a prison than a medical facility. The waiting room was part of the gatehouse structure and the one narrow window was high up on the wall and faced the outside.

It was with some surprise then that Rafael found himself looking out at an overgrown, almost tropical garden, as the green metal door swung slowly outwards. Palm trees and hibiscus bushes with bright red and yellow flowers were spread out across much of the open space. A wide packed-earth driveway cut through the garden, leading from the imposing gateway on his immediate left to a sprawling group of whitewashed two-storey buildings that Rafael supposed was the main wing of the asylum. The area was filled with movement and sound and Rafael could make out groups of eccentrically dressed people strolling along the numerous, narrow paths and trails that wove through the garden. A tall, statuesque lady in a light blue robe was talking loudly into a clearly broken mobile phone. A portly man with wild curly hair and a blue peaked cap on his head scampered across the driveway on all fours, barking like a dog. As Rafael advanced he noticed another group assembled in the yard in front of the buildings, gesturing in the air and making rhythmic chanting noises. They were led in their movements by a placid orderly in a white jacket buttoned up one side to the neck.

The central building was surmounted by a wooden clock tower and a faded sign next to a clump of garish yellow sunflowers proclaimed it to be the administrative block to which he had been directed. It was fronted by a broad, open colonnade that ran the length of the structure and was slightly raised up from the garden level. A pattern of faded brown and white checkered tiles covered the floor and blue painted doors and windows gave access into a cool shady interior.

Rafael stepped onto the colonnade, looking for an indication of how to reach the first floor and the *Directora's* office. A loud scraping sound cut through the general hubbub and Rafael saw a short wiry man in a thick poncho bent almost double over a plastic chair which he was pushing forcefully across the tiles as an improvised walking frame. A janitor in paint spattered overalls with a brown baseball cap pulled low over his eyes was mopping the floor in slow, lazy circles and looked on in indifference. Rounding the corner of the building, and moving at a steady pace, a stern dark-haired nurse came into view pushing a battered wheelchair along in front of her. Hunched down in the chair with a red plastic safety helmet strapped low over his head was a chubby, round-faced man with vacant eyes. He was bundled up in a padded overcoat with a wooly scarf knotted tightly at his neck and was smiling serenely at the world in general.

As Rafael watched, another man emerged from the shadows of one of the doorways into the gloomy, grey light outside on the colonnade. He was tall and thin with a pale complexion and surveyed the scene in the garden with quick, darting movements of his prominent, slightly protruding eyes. The man was wearing a white doctor's jacket over a light blue shirt and he carried a clipboard in his right hand. The nurse came to a stop in front of him and the doctor crouched down so that his face was level with the man in the wheelchair. He talked with the patient quietly for a few moments and Rafael couldn't make out what was said but then he straightened abruptly and said in a louder voice "Well, you look much better than yesterday Edgar."

As he turned away, the doctor caught sight of Rafael loitering near the corner of the colonnade.

"Can I help you *Señor*? You don't look like one of my patients." The man's voice was dry and a cynical twist curved across his mouth when he spoke.

"Yes, yes please," stumbled Rafael. "I'm trying to find *Directora* Florez's office. My name is Rafael Alvarez. I have an appointment with her to discuss my father."

"I'm guessing you've never been in an asylum before. You've got that slightly startled look of someone who's not been in close contact with psychiatric patients and the alternative realities in which they live."

"Yes, I have to confess this is not what I expected. To be honest, I'm not sure what I did expect but still, I find myself surprised by…" Rafael paused to select the right word, "…by the level of freedom that you allow here."

"Come with me. Edgar and I will show you the way and you'll be able to see something of our modest facility as we go." Rafael didn't seem to have much choice so he fell into step beside the doctor who began pushing the wheelchair back along the tiled floor of the colonnade.

"I am Doctor Juan Oliviera, the chief psychiatrist of this clinic. So what is it you'd like to know?"

"How are the patients treated here? Why are they left free to roam about?"

"We find that wherever possible it is best to leave our patients to express themselves in the manner they like best, as long as it's not harmful to themselves or others." The doctor smiled indulgently and led the way through one of the open doorways into a spacious studio area. The room was filled with rickety wooden tables on which paints and crafting materials had been spread about in all directions. "We call it 'creative therapy' and as you can see we have the resources here to allow our patients to develop their artistic instincts further, if they are so inclined." The man in the wheelchair, Edgar, began to move his arms about to get the doctor's attention.

'Show, show, show mine doctor!"

"Ok Edgar, that's what we'll do." Oliviera's voice was clear and precise, the note of sarcasm gone as he spoke to his patient. The doctor moved over to a wooden easel near the corner and came back with a large canvas. He made a point of showing the painting carefully to Rafael in front of Edgar.

A crude representation of a man had been painted onto the white background in bright colours and thick lines, like a picture a child might make. Where the figure's head should have been were two circles cutting over each other, one red and one black. The circles had been painted over so many times that they had almost gone through the material. Rafael looked at Oliviera, unsure what he should say. The doctor nodded slightly, to let him know it was alright. Rafael spoke directly to Edgar, adopting the same manner the doctor had used.

"That's very good. Is it a picture of you?".

"Yes, yes that's right. Me and my, my, my demon." The man grinned at him, his head moving slightly from side to side.

"Edgar is a paranoid schizophrenic," Doctor Oliviera explained. "He sees and hears things that are not real. In Edgar's case, the delusions take the form of a red demon who tells him what to do. We're using a course of medication to help control the condition, which is starting to have some promising results. We don't hear so much from Viruñas any more, do we Edgar?"

"He, he mostly leaves me in peace now," the stocky man nodded in agreement. Rafael looked back to the doctor.

"What about the wheelchair? How did that happen?" Oliviera sighed and ran his hand over his slightly receding hairline.

"Edgar's is a typical Colombian story. His parents died when he was very young and he was sent to live with his grandparents in the country near Villavicencio. They owned a smallholding in the *Cordillera Oriental* growing a moderate amount of coffee and sugarcane. One day a group of paramilitaries arrived and levied a fine on Edgar's grandfather to support their efforts at 'protecting' him from the communist guerrillas. Edgar's grandfather couldn't or wouldn't pay and the paramilitaries began beating him with wooden poles. Edgar tried to stop them and ended up taking the best part of the beatings." The doctor paused, a hard look darkening his face.

"He was beaten so savagely that he ended up with the injuries that put him in the chair, including a badly fractured skull and a broken pelvis that never healed properly. We think that the blows to the the head and post traumatic stress may have been a trigger for the schizophrenia. He is still able to walk but we find that the medication together with his injuries makes him clumsy and uncoordinated so we allow him to use the chair for his own comfort and safety.

The family fled to Bogota and tried to cope but not long after they moved to the city they asked if we could help look after Edgar. That was quite some time ago now and he's been with us ever since."

"That's a sad story Edgar. One day I hope that things like that won't happen any more in this country." The Doctor moved his slightly unsettling gaze back to Rafael.

"So Mr Alvarez, tell me more about your father. How do you think we can help him here?" Rafael quickly brought to mind the account of his father's condition that he had devised for the purpose.

"My father was an army man. He served in the sixteenth infantry battalion in Tolima until he retired three years ago. He was injured in combat and has never been the same since. He often finds it difficult to remember things that are happening around him, like turning off the stove, but he can remember things from when he was a small boy, a long time ago now. He gets confused very easily and sometimes doesn't recognise members of his own family. Sometimes he's violent and he lashes out and breaks the things around him. He's been to psychiatric institutions before but the results have always been inconclusive. My sister and I are all he has left and we've come to the point where we don't believe we can properly care for him anymore. This place was recommended to me by a friend of mine, Frederico Fernandez, do you remember him?"

Doctor Oliviera had been inspecting the paintings again but he looked up sharply at the mention of the journalist's name. He frowned deeply and seemed momentarily at a loss for what to say. Edgar stirred in his wheelchair.

"Yes, yes, yes, I remember him. He was always very kind with me," he blurted out with enthusiasm.

"That sounds like Frederico. Do you know why he decided to attend the clinic?"

The doctor seemed to recover his composure and cut in abruptly before the conversation could continue.

"Well, I think it's time we finished up with the tour. I'm afraid we don't allow discussion of the confidential details of our other patients. Edgar, please head back to the treatment room, I'll see you there later. Mr Alvarez, please come with me. I'll take you to the *Directora's* office now, so you can discuss your father's care needs with her."

Oliviera led the way back to a hallway in the centre of the building and up a flight of creaking wooden stairs. Rafael was left to hurry along in his wake. The doctor moved so quickly that further conversation was precluded. On the landing, a reception desk had been planted across the passage in front of a closed white doorway. Oliviera addressed the large, middle-aged, blonde assistant behind the desk.

"Good morning Dafne. Mr Alvarez is here to see Carolina. He has an appointment to discuss his father with her." Dafne blinked in surprise, her heavy frame shifting behind the desk

"I'm sorry. *Directora* Florez has been called away for an urgent meeting. She will not be able to see you today."

"That's a shame. Very well Dafne, please take Mr Alvarez directly back to the main entrance." The doctor turned quickly to Rafael and shook his hand in a blur.

"You'll have to make another appointment to meet with her I'm afraid. Perhaps we'll see you again some other time." And with that he spun on his heel and strode off down the corridor. Rafael was again left wondering at the sudden change of atmosphere at the mention of Frederico Fernandez. Oliviera had seemed friendly and open at first but had closed down almost instantly as soon as the discussion had turned to the journalist. His instincts told him that Oliviera wanted to say more and he promised himself that he would follow up on the doctor's vague parting words and find a way to talk to him again. He sighed and turned to follow the hefty receptionist back through the garden to the entrance of the clinic.

**

16. Dieciséis

The lid of the saucepan rattled gently as a puff of steam escaped from the cooking rice. Nathalie Rodriguez stirred the chicken legs that were poaching slowly in another pot and quickly turned the plantains over as they started to caramelise.

"Mama, don't let Victor play near the television," she shouted through to the other room of the apartment to make herself heard over the background noise. "Give him one of the toys from the cupboard instead."

"Don't worry yourself *hija mia*," her mother's voice came back. Concentrate on the plantains instead. I think you're burning them." Nathalie sighed and in spite of herself glanced down at the plantains again. To her annoyance, it looked like her mother was right, so she turned down the heat.

Her wavy black hair was tied into a compact bun at the back of her head while she worked at the stove. Through the small kitchen window of the second-storey apartment Nathalie could see that the sun had set and the street lights were starting to come on outside. Her apartment was in a modest neighbourhood called Modelia, which was part of the wider Fontibon district near the airport.

"Dinner will be ready in about ten minutes", she shouted again and picked up the knife to start chopping coriander. The chime of the doorbell sounded loudly through the apartment. She put down the knife, wiping her hands on a towel and strode into the hallway. "I'll get it Mama," she announced over her shoulder as she unbolted the door and turned the latch.

Standing uncertainly on the stairwell landing was the figure of Rafael Alvarez, looking forlorn and closed in on himself. She was struck again by the strange yellow eyes with their faraway gaze, almost like a cat lost in the gloom, and the tight line of his mouth fixed in some indeterminate middle distance between resolution and sadness.

"Investigator Alvarez, thank you again for agreeing to visit me. Please come in." He stepped over the threshold and followed her into the golden, glowing light of the kitchen.

"That smells good," he remarked stopping by the small square table where two places were set either side of the baby's high chair.

"Well, thank you. It's just a simple recipe my mother taught me to make, although I'm sure she'll say I haven't cooked it properly." She smiled fondly to show the complaint wasn't meant seriously.

"I heard that *nena.*" Rafael turned to see a slender woman of about fifty with a strong, slightly weathered face and fine hair dyed a deep shade of auburn watching them from the doorway. The corners of her full lips were turned up slightly in an amused smirk as she held the baby in her elegant hands. The sight of so many people in the kitchen seemed to have energised him and he kicked his short legs in excitement.

"Mama, this is Investigator Alvarez of the *Fiscalia.* He's the one I told you about, who came to visit us at work."

"Nice to meet you, Señor Alvarez. I am Raquel, I see you already know my daughter." The similarities to her daughter were striking and Rafael had the disorienting impression of looking into the future at the same person.

"Please, call me Rafael," he said modestly, feeling that the formality was starting to get in the way.

"And this little *guapo* is my son Victor," Nathalie added, taking Victor from her mother.

"Well hello little man. Pleased to meet you too" said Rafael leaning forward to address the baby. Nathalie saw a momentary flash of sadness pass over his face after he had spoken to the baby, but it was gone before she could say anything.

"We'll leave you two to talk about work for a minute," said Raquel taking Victor back again as she left the room. "Don't forget to check the plantains Nathalie." Rafael waited for a moment until they had left the room and then looked back at Nathalie. She could see that his face was serious again now.

"Can we sit down for a moment?" he asked softly.

"Yes, of course. Please take a seat." She indicated one of the places round the battered kitchen table.

"You asked me to come and talk to you about about Frederico Fernandez." She nodded lightly.

"I'm sad to say that I can now confirm that he is dead. The family was notified earlier today. I have been asked to lead the investigation into his murder, which is why I came to talk with you earlier this week." She looked down at her hands and felt a wave of sadness wash over her. The news was not unexpected given her previous discussion with Rafael, but to have confirmation that Frederico was not just dead but had been murdered was still something of a shock.

"Thank you. Thank you for letting me know." She laid a hand on his for a second, then lifted it, although he had the odd sensation that it was still there. "Would you like to stay for dinner with us, I mean if you don't have other plans?"

"Well, yes thank you. That would be very kind, if it's not too much trouble." It was Rafael's turn to be surprised. He hadn't been sure what to expect after Nathalie had called him earlier that afternoon. He had imagined himself leaving shortly after confirming Frederico's death with a vague promise of contact if more information became available. The idea of staying in the pleasantly warm kitchen for longer and eating a decently cooked meal for a change was hard to resist.

"I'm about to serve, so please stay where you are." He watched Nathalie in silence as she transferred the food from pots and saucepans onto three mismatched plates with quick delicate movements. Raquel and Victor were summoned again from the lounge and the plates were placed carefully on the table. Nathalie had cooked an *arroz mixto* with shredded chicken stirred through rice and mixed in with olives and chopped green vegetables. A slice of avocado and the fried plantains completed the dish.

For a short while the clatter of knives and forks filled the kitchen, mingling with the background noise of the television drifting through from the other room. A small plastic bowl of food had been prepared for Victor and he busied himself bashing his spoon against the tray of the high chair. The simple blend of flavours tasted superb to Rafael. The texture of the rice was light and fluffy and the chicken had been cooked perfectly. For a moment he was lost again in memories of happier times as he thought of the evening meals he had enjoyed with Gabriella, before she had been taken away from him. As if reading his mind, Raquel looked up from her plate and fixed him with an inquiring look.

"So, Rafael, tell us about yourself. Are you married?" she asked abruptly. His heart sank. The inevitable questions about his background had emerged early this time. He supposed that it was far enough in the past that he should no longer care how people reacted, but he still felt the familiar trepidation rise within him. His face hardened as he responded.

"I was for a time. I'm afraid my wife passed away giving birth to our child." There was a shocked silence and then Nathalie exclaimed, "That's terrible. I'm so sorry to hear that. Mother, your directness is too much sometimes." Rafael seemed to close in on himself. He fixed his eyes on the plate and wouldn't meet their gaze. He looked so lost sitting there in his threadbare yellow jumper and for a moment Nathalie thought he was going to stand up and leave.

Raquel seemed to sense she had stepped over a line and with an embarrassed cough she said, "Yes, I'm sorry to hear that too and I'm sorry for my intrusiveness. I suppose though that you and my daughter have something in common in being alone."

Rafael looked up from the plate and saw that Nathalie's face was now a mask of sadness as Raquel continued speaking.

"Victor's father may not be dead, but he might as well be for all we know of him. Luis was from Baranquilla originally and he disappeared back there shortly after he learned that Nathalie was pregnant. He said he was going to look for work and that he'd get in touch with us when he had a job, but that never happened and we never heard from him again. It's been over two years now and my guess is we're not going to hear from him again. I always told you *hija*, not to trust that *costeño*."

"I'm sorry to hear of your troubles too," said Rafael gently. Nathalie composed herself and smiled softly.

"Well I think we're doing just fine without him and I have other things to focus on now, looking after Victor." Nathalie was pretty to begin with but when she smiled now he found himself suddenly struck by her beauty.

"Rafael, there is something else I wanted to talk to you about this evening." Her sad smile had faded and been replaced with a slight frown of nervous concentration. "I think your visit earlier in the week prompted something with our editor Gustavo. He's suddenly taken a much more active interest in Frederico and he wants *La Justicia* to look more closely into the disappearance and death of one of its own journalists.

146

"He's asked me to follow your investigation and cover the story for the paper. We know each other already and I worked most closely with Frederico so maybe I can be of use to you and help you find out what happened to him and how he was killed. So, what do you think? Is there some way I can be part of your investigation?" Rafael's instincts told him he had found an ally to help oppose the hostile forces lined up against him. He put down his knife and fork to reflect for a moment before coming to a decision.

"I'm still at the early stages of trying to piece together who Frederico was involved with and what he was doing before he was killed. I spoke with the man you told me about, Ignacio Perez, the anthropology professor at the museum. I don't think he murdered Frederico but I'm certain he knows more than he was ready to tell me when I went to visit him yesterday morning. My next step is to go and see him again to try and convince him to tell me more of what he knows. But to do that, I'll need to leave Bogota for at least a day. Perez will be on an archaeology dig to the west in Cundinamarca at a place called Aguazuque. I'd be very happy if you were able to come with me, but it's quite a drive so I completely understand if that's not possible at short notice."

Nathalie glanced uncertainly at Victor, who seemed oblivious that he had become the centre of attention. He scooped another spoonful of rice into his mouth and cooed happily. Raquel looked up from her plate and spoke quietly.

"You should go Nathalie. This sounds like an important piece of work. A chance to do something more useful than being someone's assistant. I'll happily look after Victor while you are away."

"Oh thank you Mama! Are you sure that's ok?"

"Of course *hija mia*. I'll take any chance I can to spend more time with my little grandson." A broad smile spread over Raquel's faintly-lined face as she looked happily at the plump little boy in the high chair.

"Then it's settled," said Nathalie brightly, meeting Rafael's gaze again. "I'll call Gustavo tomorrow morning before we leave."

"One thing I'd request," Rafael cut in softly. "There are a lot of people who want me to fail at this investigation so that Freddy's death is filed as another unsolved homicide. I don't

147

want to interfere with whatever it is you decide to write but if there's any way you can help keep the investigation alive for as long as possible, we'll have more of a chance of finding Freddy's killer."

"Of course. I'll do whatever I can to help catch the person who did those terrible things to Freddy."

"This calls for a toast," Raquel declared abruptly, rising and moving towards the battered cabinet that stood at the side of the room. She took out a dusty, half-full bottle of whisky and three small glasses, pouring the brown liquid when she came back to the table. Nathalie raised her glass and looked Rafael directly in the eye.

"To success and justice for Freddy. *Salud*!" They drained the liquid down in one mouthful, the fiery burn of the whisky making Rafael's eyes water for a moment. The meal came to an end shortly after that. Victor was getting tired and fussy and it was time for his bath. Rafael took his leave after agreeing the arrangements for the trip with Nathalie.

Back outside on the street, under the orange glare of the lamps with the cold night air on his face, Rafael felt an unfamiliar energy flow through him. It was different from the chemically induced vigour provided by his pills, which remained unopened and unused in his pocket. His arms and shoulders felt light and strong, as though he could lift up the cars around him or punch through walls, and the ache in his forehead that was his constant companion seemed to have lessened and almost gone away. At first he thought it was just the after-effects of the whisky. It took him several more steps to work out that it was happiness and contentment.

**

17. Diecisiete

History had always been something of an enigma to Rafael. The past was a complicated concept in Colombia, more of a political consensus than a definitive set of facts and events. It was the engine that drove the violent and bloodthirsty arguments that were still being played out today with the guerrillas and the paramilitaries continuing to kill each other and those around them indiscriminately. Rafael had always felt a nebulous detachment from those extreme passions. To become so involved in abstract notions and ideas to the point that you could be driven to maim and murder strangers in their service seemed an alien concept to him. Of course, as the son of an army officer and a member of the police force, certain judgements and assumptions would always be made about his viewpoints. But given the facts of his background, with his father having vanished from his life at such a young age and his mother a foreigner returned now to her own country, he felt that history had somehow passed him by, that he had nothing to do with it and it had nothing to do with him. It was then with a sense of fascinated curiosity that he watched as the past was quite literally brought into the pale light of day all around him.

Rafael and Nathalie stood side by side in the mid-morning haze looking down into a shallow trench that zigzagged across the low hillside. Spread out unevenly across the bottom, the archaeological labourers worked alone or in small groups, hunched over the ground, picking at the soil with slender trowels and delicate brushes. Rafael watched as a bucket of earth was carried over to a nearby sieve in a large wooden frame where it was the job of another worker to rub the clods over the fine grille, reducing the spoil to powder and verifying that nothing had been missed. His eyes were drawn to the movement of the man's gloved hands as he pulled something from the dirt, brushed off the dust and grit and held it up for examination. From the vantage point at the edge of the trench

Rafael could see what seemed to be a broken piece of ceramic head clasped firmly in the man's grip. The stylised, flat eye slits and sharp nose of the face were clearly visible and seemed to impart an expression of stern irritation and astonishment, as though it thoroughly disapproved of its abrupt disturbance from the earthy ground in which it had lain for so long. As he continued to watch, the head was nonchalantly stuffed into a clear plastic bag, a location code was scribbled on the label and the package placed carefully into a large plastic storage crate.

"This place reminds me of what was left of Armenia after the earthquake," Nathalie remarked softly, sweeping her gaze over the barren, broken ground that stretched away for several hundred meters to the chain link fence that surrounded the site. A few wispy strands of her dark hair had worked their way loose from her ponytail and seemed to float about her face in the faint breeze that was blowing up from the valley below them. She wore graceful, metal-framed sunglasses against the glare and was dressed in faded dark grey jeans and a red and black checked shirt.

"I was away from the city when it happened," she continued, tucking a lock of the stray hair behind her ear. "My cousins were working on a coffee farm in Salento, up in the hills and I had been sent to visit them. The quake was pretty bad up there too, but we were spared the worst. We had just finished lunch outside in the field when the shaking began. It only lasted about ten seconds but I remember feeling paralysed with fear and then the complete silence afterwards for about a minute before the screaming started."

"I remember that day too," Rafael replied quietly. "We felt the quake in Bogota. I was driving on the *Avenida Primero de Mayo* at the time and everyone just stopped and got out of their cars. It's one of the strangest things I've seen. We all thought the overpass would collapse or something. That was the year I got married." Nathalie met his gaze and the corners of her mouth turned up slightly in a sad smile.

"It was nearly a month before they would let me return to Armenia," she continued. "By the time I was allowed back a lot of the rubble had been cleared and the city was full of empty spaces. My house was gone, the whole neighbourhood had gone. Mother was all I had left and we moved to Bogota shortly after that to start a new life. There didn't seem to be anything left for us back there." She lowered her face and pressed her lips together. "One memory that has always stuck with me from that time was the teams of workers picking carefully through what was left to make sure that no human remains were missed. That's what I was thinking of just now while we were looking at those men working at the bottom of the trench. It's funny how, even though it was over six years ago I suddenly felt like I was just there."

"I know what you mean. I feel that all the time. I think some memories are just so powerful that they take you away before you even realise it's happened." The skin around Rafael's jaw tightened. "But then you realise that you can't change the past and the only way through life is forward and so you keep moving to see what happens next."

He turned towards the rising sun and advanced along the rim of the trench towards where a group of the workers were gathered below. Nathalie followed, the loose earth crunching and shifting under her feet. One of the men straightened up at the sound of their approach. Rafael could see the film of fine grey powder coating his creased skin and the faint, acrid odour of sweat hung on the morning air.

"Could you tell us where to find Professor Perez?" he shouted down into the trench to make himself heard over the tapping and scraping sounds of the excavation.

"*Sí señor*. The *Patrón* is working on the other side of the site, near the ruins of the gatehouse." Rafael waved a thanks and turned to follow the direction the man had indicated. They walked in silence for a while, climbing towards the crest of the small hill over which the archaeological dig was spread. Rafael could feel the heat of the day beginning to build on the skin of his face and hands. He doubted that the long-sleeved grey t-shirt he had chosen to wear that morning in the darkness of Bogota would prove to be a wise decision.

Below them, away from the summit of the hill, trees and scrub stretched off into the distance all around. The sunlight glimmered on the waters of the Bogota river at the bottom of the valley, far beneath. The low buildings of the small, shabby town of San Antonio could just be seen through the haze, a few kilometres distant, on the next ridge. Further west, dark clouds were gathering on the horizon from the direction of the Magdalena, building to a roiling, black wall that threatened storms later in the day.

Over the crest of the hill, the character of the site seemed to change completely. The side they had climbed was largely barren and featureless apart from the deep trenches that snaked across the ground like dark gouges. On the other side the ruins were exposed to the surface and a network of low walls and building remains spread out around them. A darkened tarpaulin had been rigged up to provide some shelter to the workers and marked clearly where the digging continued. Nathalie and Rafael headed steadily down towards it, forced to occasionally deviate and weave around the various barriers and obstacles presented by the ruins.

"When I saw the professor at the museum in Bogota, I knew he was holding things back," said Rafael as they paused for a moment next to a broken heap of bricks and rubble. "He told me about meeting Freddy and you when you went to interview him about the missing Muisca pieces. He said that Freddy's article was all lies and that there was an argument."

"That's right. I remember he practically threw us out of his office and threatened all sorts of terrible things if we published the article. At that point Freddy was barely functioning any more. I was amazed that he could pull himself together enough to stand up to Perez's intimidation."

"When I told him about Freddy's disappearance he seemed to be genuinely surprised and claimed to be completely unaware that anything had happened to him after the article was published. Last time I saw him I wasn't in a position to confirm that Freddy was dead. This time I'm going to push him a lot harder. I'm going to need to say some things about Frederico and how he died. You should be ready for that."

"Do whatever you need to do. I'll be fine." Nathalie adjusted her sunglasses on the bridge of her nose. "What can I do to help?" she asked resolutely.

"At some point I'm going to ask him about the missing items. Last time he was evasive on that point too. I want you to challenge him with the research that you and Frederico did to see if we can get him to say more."

"I'll never forget all that time I spent working through the catalogues and the cross-checking with the museum records. I know what to do."

The approach to the black tarpaulin led through a narrow

gulley where the ruined walls closed in about them and Rafael and Nathalie were forced to walk in single file. Rafael was picking his way over some broken slabs when a voice rang out from above and to his left.

"Investigator, up here. Good to see you again. I trust you made it here okay?" In the glare of the sun above him, Rafael could make out a silhouette at the top of the wall looking down at them. He shaded his eyes with his hand and the blurry shadow resolved itself into the portly figure of Ignacio Perez standing with his hands on his hips. The enthusiasm of his greeting had sounded genuine. "Please, come and join me. There's a gap in the wall just ahead of you and a way up the slope."

Rafael and Nathalie followed his directions and quickly scrambled up the narrow track to where he was waiting. Closer up Rafael could see that Ignacio was totally transformed from the dusty, defensive professor he had met in Bogota. His broad face seemed filled with energy and enthusiasm and his eyes sparkled as he watched them approach.

"Well this is a surprise," he exclaimed as they reached him, shaking Rafael's hand warmly. "I didn't expect to see you so soon, and you've brought the young lady from the newspaper. Remind me of your name again *señorita*."

"I'm Nathalie Rodriguez. I used to work with Frederico Fernandez. We came to see you about the items going missing from the museum." Her eyes flashed in challenge.

"Yes, I heard about Frederico. The investigator was telling me last time that he seems to have disappeared. I was sorry to hear that." Ignacio was wearing a loose green linen shirt, khaki shorts and a broad-brimmed hat made of woven cane strips that he pushed back from his forehead now as he turned to stare at the valley spread out below.

"Professor, we need to talk with you again," Rafael began firmly, focusing his gaze directly on Ignacio. "I've driven all the way from Bogota this morning. Frederico Fernandez is dead and I think those missing objects have something to do with it. I need you to tell me what you know." Ignacio sighed and turned to face them both again.

"Do you know how long people have lived in this place? The first hunter gatherers moved onto this site over twelve thousand years ago. Think of that investigator. Colombia has existed as a country only for about two hundred years. The Spanish were here for about three hundred years before that. Jesus Christ himself walked the Holy Land about two thousand years ago and ten thousand years before that you have people living on this hill using stone tools, hunting animals and cooking them on fires. I've always felt a powerful need to know who these people were, to know how they lived, to know what happened before my time on the earth." He paused for a moment, as if searching for something in the air around.

"I find it much more difficult to make a connection with the everyday things of our own time. I'm sad to hear that Frederico is dead. I did wonder if that was how the story was going to end when you came to see me last time. Sadly, a lot of people disappear in Colombia and they don't usually turn up alive and well. I can only repeat to you what I said then. I didn't have anything to do with whatever happened to him and I don't think I can help you."

"Do you know how Frederico was killed?" Rafael threw back angrily. "First, he was tortured and mutilated horrifically, then he was stabbed through the heart. After he was dead, his body was chopped up into pieces, his organs were removed and part of him was left in a suitcase on the path to Monserrate." Nathalie's hand went to her mouth and she looked away. Ignacio on the other hand seemed unmoved but his face had become slightly paler and more drawn.

"Whoever did that to him is still out there," Rafael continued. "It could happen again. Can you live with yourself knowing that you didn't help us when you had the opportunity? Are you going to be able to look at yourself in the mirror and say I knew what happened but I did nothing?" Ignacio took a step backwards. His shoulders seemed to slump.

"Walk with me a moment," he said softly. He led them in silence across the rocky landscape. All around them the remnants of mud brick walls pushed up through the earth, like broken teeth through gums.

"This is an impressive place, don't you think?" Ignacio began again after a while. "It was one of the last Muisca towns to hold out against the conquistadores. Where we were standing was part of the walls near the ancient gateway. After Tisquesusa was killed in Facatativa, the surviving warriors came here, determined to fight a final battle and exact a heavy price for their lives.   The conquistadores felt that they had already won and were in no mood for negotiations.   The last of the Muiscas were quite literally blasted into history here and their remains are scattered all over this part of the site together with the musket balls and cannon shots that slaughtered them." Ignacio took a sip from a metal water bottle that he carried on his belt, as the sun climbed towards its zenith in the sky above.

"I'm sorry Rafael, I really am.   You know Freddy and I had our differences but I was not responsible for his death.   You will need to look elsewhere for the answers to your questions.   I think you're intelligent enough to know what I mean."   Rafael's head inclined slightly and his gaze became opaque.   It was several moments before he spoke again, the buzzing of insects loud in the air around the three of them, over the crunching of their footsteps on the loose ground.

"Yes," he replied eventually.   "I went to the *Nuevo Templo del Sol* in Boyerino.   I was able to talk briefly with Yoposa, before I was told in no uncertain terms to stay away.   He strikes me as an intriguing and difficult man.   What do you know about him?"

"I suppose it's true that Yoposa and I have something of a history," Ignacio continued warily.   "I gather you have heard about the goals of his organisation, to resurrect and reestablish the religion of the Muiscas in Colombia.   Given our shared interest in the past, he has been a regular donor to the museum.   However an interest in the past is really all we share.   My objective is scientific.   I study history to know what happened, in the hope that it can help us understand better what happens in the present.   Yoposa and his associates are trying to twist the past, to take it as a literal and spiritual template for how to live in the present.   Part of it is political as well, of course.   He's aiming to establish himself as the legitimate descendant of the Muisca's legacy in order to take advantage of the indigenous recognition laws.   He's certainly wealthy and well-connected and the Temple's activities may go well beyond the religious and community aspects that they present to the public, but I wouldn't know anything about that."

"I'm more interested in what you do know, rather than what you don't." Rafael interrupted drily.   "Let's get back to the missing objects, to this 'Offerings to the Sun' collection. Nathalie, will you explain to the professor what it was that

155

made Freddy so sure they had disappeared from the museum?"

"I don't know what it was that gave him the idea that something was missing," Nathalie looked directly at the professor as she spoke. "But I remember in the last few weeks before he disappeared it became something of an obsession for him. He managed to get hold of a copy of the catalogue of all the Muisca objects in your museum. I went through all of them with him and we cross-referenced everything with the exhibition records to verify the last time each one had been seen in public. We came across the 'Offerings to the Sun' fairly early on. It stood out as one of the more impressive collections that we couldn't trace." She narrowed her eyes and seemed to recite from memory.

"The group consists of two highly stylised ceremonial knives made almost entirely of gold. The larger knife has a heavy semi-circular blade and a handle shaped in the form of a crowned, abstract face. The notes describe it as an unknown Muisca god or king. The second knife is slim and long with a serrated edge and the figure of a man is represented on the handle. Both the knives are heavily inlaid with turquoise and emeralds. Fifteen matching gold spear heads are included with the group, each decorated with the emblem of the sun. A large vessel shaped like a reclining man is also part of the collection. There is an opening in the man's chest presumably for pouring or collecting liquid and the handles are again stamped with the same sun emblem."

"Thank you Miss Rodriguez," Ignacio replied quietly. "I'm impressed. That is an excellent description of the collection. I am familiar with the pieces and have had the opportunity to study them intimately. You probably also know that they were discovered in the Temple of Chiguasuqué in Tunja in the 1930s and purchased by the museum from a private collector ten years ago." Nathalie nodded quickly before continuing.

"The 'Offerings to the Sun' objects were last on display in the museum just over six months ago. According to the catalogue records they were then removed for scheduled restoration work. While in storage they were supposedly transferred on loan to the Ethnographic Museum of Cali. When we contacted them, there was no record of the collection ever having arrived there. The funny thing was that the authorising signature on all the release forms was your own. That was the evidence Freddy was talking about when the two of you fought and you wouldn't hear him out. But I think you already knew that."

The midday sun was glaring down fiercely from the sky as Nathalie stopped talking, turning the barren ground into a furnace. The faint ringing of bells could be heard in the distance through the heavy air, from the direction of the church tower in San Antonio. Ignacio lifted a hand in acceptance.

"Very well, I'll tell you what I know about the objects. But please, let's get out of this heat first." Rafael turned to see that the workers were beginning to depart the site in small groups or alone, drifting towards a large canvas shelter that had been set up near the fence. "Stay for some lunch with us," offered Ignacio. "We'll talk again afterwards. I promise that once we've eaten I'll tell you as much as I can."

Nathalie turned a questioning look to Rafael who shrugged in agreement and they followed the professor over the dusty ground to join the workers at the shelter. Inside two large trestle tables had been set up, one for the food and another with benches alongside for the workers to sit down and eat. A plump woman in a brightly-coloured headscarf was unloading food from two large plastic crates and placing it carefully onto the surface of the table. There was cold rice, salad, bread, empanadas with cheese and a large plate of cold and cured meat. The workers had formed a line and shuffled slowly forward to help themselves using paper plates and disposable cutlery.

It was a relief to step out of the intense sunlight into the cool of the shade offered by the shelter and Rafael felt the beads of sweat that had collected on his forehead as the three of them joined the line. The insects had sensed it was lunch time too and were drawn inexorably to the food, buzzing about the line of dusty men and the trestle table in a constantly shifting cloud. The cold meat seemed to be the main attraction and Rafael could see several hornets and wasps crawling on the slices, their tiny jaws moving in a frenzy as they chewed the salty protein.

A small group of collapsible chairs had been set up in the shelter, to one side of the tables. Ignacio, Rafael and Nathalie took their food and sat down, balancing the plates on their knees. The muted conversation of the workers buzzed around them and after a few minutes Ignacio looked up from a mouthful of rice.

"How was your journey out here?" he asked. "Did you pass the *Salto de Tequendama*?" Rafael nodded, recalling the overpowering smell and the gauzy mist as they came down the stretch of road from Bogota that ran past the roaring cascade of water and the slowly decomposing remains of the abandoned hotel, in the steely early morning light. "They say the waterfall was created by Bochica," continued Ignacio "one of the Muisca's legendary heroes, who used his staff to break the rocks and release the water that covered the Bogota Savannah."

"The view is spectacular," Nathalie replied politely. "I've lived in Bogota for five years now and never had the opportunity to visit before." Ignacio smiled broadly, placing his plastic knife and fork on his empty plate. "Another story I've heard is that groups of defeated Muisca warriors leapt to their deaths from the falls to escape the Spanish conquistadores. They were turned into eagles half way down and flew to their freedom in the blue sky." Rafael snorted skeptically.

"These days, with all the sewage and pollution in the river Bogota the stench is so bad that even the suicidal would do well to stay away."

The black clouds had drifted closer and the occasional rumble of distant thunder could be heard from the west as the last of the workers finished eating and headed back towards the site. The three of them were left alone in the shelter with the stout woman with the headscarf as she busied herself clearing away the remains of the food. The wind had picked up and the light had started to grow dim. Rafael put his plate and glass on the ground and looked pointedly at Ignacio.

"So Professor, you promised us an explanation. Where do you want to begin?" Ignacio stood up from the chair and took several paces towards the edge of the shelter. His gaze seemed to drift off into the middle distance as he surveyed the broken landscape all around them and the approaching clouds.

"Very well investigator, let me start with a question. What do you think is the purpose of the 'Offerings to the Sun'? To what use did the Muisca put these highly prized objects?"

"Well, from what I've told you about how Freddy died it won't surprise you to learn that I think they might have somehow been involved in what was done to him. As for the Muisca, I really have no idea. That's your area of expertise after all." Ignacio turned back to face where Rafael and Nathalie were still sitting in the plastic chairs.

"One of the cornerstones of Muisca religion was human sacrifice," he began sombrely, raising his voice to be heard over the increasing noise of the rising wind. "It was considered to be one of the greatest honours to be selected for the ritual, to become one of the people's appointed messengers to the gods. Those chosen were provided with every comfort and luxury until the final day came." A strong gust blew in from the west, directly behind where Ignacio was standing, whipping his thin white hair up about his head.

"The victim was tied securely to a pole and spears were pushed into their arms and legs. Human blood was considered sacred and as it dripped down it was collected into the vessel, which was placed underneath the pole for that purpose. Once the victim was weak from loss of blood, the small serrated knife was used to remove parts of the body that were offered separately to the gods. First the nose, ears and tongue were removed, followed by the sexual organs. Finally, when the point of death was close the victim was taken down and placed on the altar. The high priest would use the heavy semi-circular blade, the *Tumí*, to punch through the sternum and pierce the heart, ending the victim's agony."

Rafael and Nathalie were stunned into silence as Ignacio finished his explanation. His green shirt seemed black against the gloom outside the shelter. To Rafael, he looked like an ancient magician who had conjured up the storm from beyond the edge of the world. Another crack of thunder echoed though the air, closer now.

"What about the internal organs?" asked Rafael quietly after a few moments had passed. "Were they part of the ceremony as well?"

"Well, the heart was considered sacred. It was removed from the body after death and used for other ritual purposes. The Muisca believed that if you possessed the heart of someone you possessed their deepest essence and you could direct their spirit to perform your will."

"What about the other organs?" Rafael insisted. "Was there a use for the lungs, kidneys or liver?" Ignacio bowed his head, thinking.

"I can't recall any references to those parts of the body in any of the sources I've read, so I couldn't really say. The Muisca had a fairly rudimentary knowledge of human anatomy. They understood about the heart and blood as I said. They had a vague notion that the lungs were connected to air and breathing but I think the liver and the kidneys would have been a mystery to them."

The first fat drops of rain began to fall from the black sky, leaving coin-sized craters where they landed on the dusty ground. Quickly a hissing downpour sprang up all around them and the world outside the shelter was reduced to a shimmering torrent of water and noise. Rafael tilted his head back to look Ignacio directly in the eye again.

"So where are the knives and the rest of the pieces now Ignacio? How do you explain your signature on those transfer forms?" Ignacio blinked quickly and returned Rafael's gaze.

"Well, do you have possession of these forms? Can you prove I moved the missing objects under my own authority?" Rafael turned to look at Nathalie who stared vacantly at the ground, crestfallen. Her reply was almost lost in the seething rumble of the rain.

"They were with Freddy's papers," she replied softly. "Everything was taken after Freddy disappeared."

"I thought that might be the case." A slight smile floated over Ignacio's fleshy lips. "Otherwise I suspect our friend from the *Fiscalia* here would have turned up with an arrest warrant rather than some general questions about Freddy and the Muisca. I hope that if things get to that stage you will take into account that I've willingly co-operated with every area of your questioning." Rafael felt his frustration rise. Ignacio had realised the weakness of his position and he was blocked again.

"Look, don't misunderstand me," Ignacio continued in a conciliatory tone. "I want to help you find out what happened to Freddy, I really do, but please let me check a few things of my own before we talk further. I am due to return to Bogota at the start of next week. Let me contact you after I'm back and I will tell you what you want to know."

The rain had settled down into an even rhythmic pattering now and streams of water ran steadily over the archaeological site, turning the dusty ground to mud. Rafael looked grimly out at the falling water, wondering what to do next.

"Don't drive back to the city in this awful weather," Ignacio urged. "The roads will be dangerous by now. You should both stay in San Antonio for the evening. I know a place and I can drop you there. I will call you again in Bogota as soon as I'm ready to talk." In the absence of any better options Rafael reluctantly agreed.

**

18. Dieciocho

Ignacio gave them a lift into town and left them in the main plaza as the daylight was turning a deeper shade of grey with the approach of evening. He told Rafael that one of the workers from the site would come to the hotel he had recommended the next morning and give them a ride back to where Rafael had parked his car. Some kind of renovation works were underway and the centre of the plaza was closed off behind a flimsy green plastic barrier. A rusty yellow excavator stood silent and unmoving next to mounds of sodden gravel. Water dripped down from the leaves of the two large cedar trees that grew in the middle and presumably provided a pleasant shade when the weather was better. A squat stone-built church took up most of one side of the plaza, its plain facade topped by a housing for the bells they had heard at the site. They were still now but clanked softly in the wind blowing up from the valley. Opposite the church was a small branch of a supermarket chain and a cafe with its metal shutters pulled down. The rain seemed to have cleared everyone off the streets and the plaza was deserted.

Rafael took all this in quickly as Nathalie and he jogged through the falling rain towards the garish sign of the hotel, picked out in dim neon strip lighting. It was a run-down, two-storey building on the corner where the main road entered the square, a few meters from where Ignacio had dropped them. An unusual pattern of pale green diamonds had been painted onto the whitewashed walls, which were marked by brown water stains and showed patches of the underlying brickwork where the coating had peeled. A mangy-looking stray dog, soaked from the rain, watched as they splashed through the puddles towards the entrance.

Rafael and Nathalie stood dripping water onto the worn tiled floor of a cramped reception hall where a makeshift counter in the form of a low wall had been built to one side of the door. The place smelled strongly of damp and stale cigarette smoke.

162

The counter was empty so Rafael rang a small bell and after a few moments a baffled middle-aged woman with a smooth face and glasses on a chain round her neck came bustling out from behind a string curtain to see what they wanted. Rafael explained they had been visiting the archaeological site and had decided not to risk the drive back to Bogota that evening. His request for two rooms for one evening only drew a knowing look from the woman but she handed over the keys and after being told they had no baggage she suggested they buy dry clothes and any overnight essentials from the supermarket on the plaza. A set of narrow stairs led to the upper level and further down the passage Rafael could see through a wedged-open fire door to where an empty pool was filling up gradually with murky rainwater.

Nathalie's phone didn't work. It seemed there was no network coverage this far out from the city, so she negotiated with the lady to use the landline phone in the reception area. She needed to call her mother to check that Victor was alright and let her know that she wouldn't be back until tomorrow. Rafael felt a fleeting moment of envy at having people who wondered where you might be and what you might be doing. It passed as quickly as it had come and he resolved that he would not allow the unfortunate fact of his solitude to bring on resentment of others. Rafael headed back out in the rain to the supermarket while Nathalie used the phone and they agreed to meet up later back in the hotel lobby where a threadbare sofa had been pushed into a corner next to an unplugged primitive television set. He spent a tedious half-hour browsing round under glaring lights with insistent tinny music in the background but after a thorough search of the half-empty shelves he managed to find more or less what he needed.

When the time came he headed over to the waiting area feeling somewhat self-conscious. Nathalie let out a snort of laughter when she caught sight of him.

"You look like you're ready for the pool," she smirked.

"I suppose you're right," he conceded, laughing as well at the ridiculous figure he made in the oversized pair of shorts and cheap red football shirt that were all he had been able to find in the supermarket's limited clothing section.

"Mind you, I don't look much better," commented Nathalie with a faint look of disgust, indicating the tightly-fitting sleeveless t-shirt and blue leggings that she had purchased herself.

163

The lady from the reception bustled over again when she saw them both and suggested pointedly that they have dinner in the hotel as the cafe on the plaza had closed down permanently earlier in the year. The hotel restaurant turned out to consist of three small tables in a cramped room at the back of the hotel. A vase of dusty artificial flowers stood on one of the tables and a faded picture of the *Salto de Tequendama* waterfall decorated the wall nearest the door. The only thing she could offer them to eat was some *corrientazo* that had been left over from lunch. Rafael found that he was was suddenly very hungry and agreed readily. She brought them each a bottle of beer and left to attend to the food. Rafael realised abruptly that it was Thursday again and his thoughts flitted involuntarily to Miriam in the *Fiscalia* Bunker. He wondered how her *Juernes* plans were going this afternoon and he thought she would be pleased that he was sat in the hotel drinking with Nathalie.

The *corrientazo*, when it arrived, turned out to be a piece of chewy beef, some cold potatoes, and chopped vegetables mixed through with rice and beans. They ate in silence for a while.

"This is as bad as the food from the *Fiscalia* canteen," said Rafael with a smile.

"Yeah, it's pretty hard work isn't it," agreed Nathalie with a grimace. "Still I suppose it's better than a bag of crisps from the supermarket." Outside, the storm was picking up and the rattle of rain sounded loud against the window. Nathalie looked up, her face serious again.

"Rafael, I wanted to ask you, do you think what the professor told us about human sacrifice is what happened to Freddy?"

"I don't know, I sincerely hope not. From what I saw of the body though I'm sorry to say that some of the injuries are consistent with what he described."

"That's awful, I can't imagine what he must have gone through. What kind of psychopath could do that to another person? The Muisca don't exist any more, Ignacio said so himself. Sacrificing someone to their gods doesn't make any sense." Nathalie shook her head faintly in disbelief. In the soft yellow light of the restaurant Rafael was struck again by how attractive she was.

"What are you going to do next?" she asked him quietly. Rafael sighed. He felt like he was pacing round in circles, always sideways and never forwards. The answer to what had really happened to Frederico Fernandez always seemed tantalising close but remained out of reach.

"I don't really know, I'm starting to run out of options. My superiors at the *Fiscalia* have absolutely forbidden me to contact Yoposa or to investigate the Temple further, which seems crazy. I'm hoping that I can discover something conclusive enough to force them to stop ignoring the obvious. Maybe Ignacio will give us something concrete when he finally makes up his mind on what to tell us." Rafael looked directly into Nathalie's pensive, deep brown eyes.

"What about you? Where do you think this leaves you with the paper?" Nathalie frowned and looked away.

"For me the hardest thing is Victor. Everything I do is for him. He's not old enough to understand yet, but I keep thinking what life will be like for him growing up without ever knowing his father. I was never really in love with Luis and I don't think he was ready, so when I turned out to be pregnant I wasn't really surprised that he never came back. For a while I kept asking myself if I could have done anything different to give Victor a better life. Now I think we're better off without Luis after all and what a *cabron* he was to walk out on me and his own child. Sometimes it makes me want to cry but then I think life isn't so bad and you just have to keep on going."

She smiled fiercely at him and blinked away the hint of a tear from her eye. His heart beating fast, Rafael placed his hand on top of hers on the table top. Nathalie stared down at his hand where the flesh touched, feeling an electric pressure that both lured and frightened her.

"Tell me about your wife," she asked impulsively.

"Are you sure you want to hear about that? It's just more sad memories."

"Yes. I want to know what she meant to you." Rafael sighed again and his eyes seemed to look inward.

"She was beautiful, to me she was perfect. I find it's the little details that stand out strongest in my mind. The bits and pieces you never bothered to put into words. How she used to drink her coffee in the morning, the way she looked reading a book, her eyes when she thought something was funny. I remember how we used to plan for our future, how we mapped out our life together. Then I remember the end, when they told me she wasn't coming back and I knew I was going to be on my own. You put all that together and you get the feel of a person, enough to know how much you miss them." He paused and lifted his hand to his temple, rubbing the taut skin softly as his eyes narrowed.

"When I wake up it's like she's not there because she's just stepped out of bed or something. But then I remember and I know she's never coming back. I'm tired of waking up in the morning thinking she's still there."

They had finished eating by that point and the intensity of the conversation seemed to have left them both drained. So, as the woman cleared away the plates, they headed for the stairs and agreed a time to meet in the morning for the drive back to Bogota. Later, back in his room Rafael found himself sitting the dark thinking about Nathalie. He seemed to see her smooth, delicate face floating next to Gabriella's and he wondered what they would have made of each other had they been able to meet in real life. He had loved Gabriella intensely and he imagined that after everything that had happened she would want more than anything for him to be happy.

Rafael held up the bottle of pills in front of his face, the glossy cylinder barely visible in the shadows. It had been a couple of days now since he'd last taken one and the numbing, dislocating effect was beginning to fade leaving him feeling raw-edged and more connected to his immediate emotional responses. He put his hands on his knees and rose heavily from the thin, uncomfortable mattress aiming for the paler rectangle of gloom that indicated the door to the narrow, cell-like bathroom.

A gentle knocking on the door stopped him in his tracks. The sound of his heart was loud in his ears as he stepped back to the door and pulled it open. There, in the dim light of the silent hallway stood Nathalie, her head tilted slightly to one side. One of her arms was crossed over her body holding the other at the elbow. They studied each other wordlessly for a moment, then she came to him quickly and he held her in his embrace, revelling in the feel of her, the warmth and the smell of her hair, rich to his senses. The door closed softly behind them, cutting out the light and leaving them in soft, welcoming darkness.

**

19. Diecinueve

Rafael watched as the heavy, metal disc tumbled through the air, spinning end over end before it hit the soft clay with a resounding thump. The thrower groaned; his disc was further from the centre than a number of the others which meant he had not scored any points. Rafael took a sip of beer from the bottle in front of him on the bar and looked around. He was in the right place. Dr Oliviera's message had specified to meet him here, at this *Campo de Tejo*, in Suba close to the *Clinica Merced de Sué*. The building looked like it had previously served as a warehouse of some kind. The interior space was open with a high ceiling and a concrete floor. A row of *tejo* boards were set along one wall in their wire protective cages, with the throwing alleys marked out on the floor in yellow paint. Gaps between the corrugated metal roofing panels let in the occasional drips of the rain and puddles collected in the corners.

Rafael scanned the area again quickly but the doctor didn't appear to be here so he returned his attention to the players. It was still early on a wet and gloomy Friday evening so only two of the boards were currently in use. One group seemed to be a local team having a practice session while they waited for their opponents to arrive. Their matching green and yellow shirts were bright and gaudy in the harsh glare of the fluorescent strip lights that illuminated the playing space. They swigged briskly from the beer bottles lined up on the table to one side and took turns to throw the hand-sized metal discs, the *tejos* from which the game took its name, along the alley towards where their board had been set up.

Tejo was a relatively simple game to play and was second only to football in its popularity across Colombia. Indeed it was often described as 'Colombia's unique national sport' by the organising federation as well as the numerous beer adverts and commercials that featured *tejo* as part of their sales pitch. This *campo* was no exception and was prominently sponsored by one of the major Colombian beer brands which had covered almost every available space with its red and gold advertising.

At one end of the alley a flat wooden board was set at a forty five degree angle. The board was filled and covered with soft clay which at the start of the game was levelled to a smooth flat surface. In the centre of the frame, flush with the clay, a metal pipe was fixed so that a ring of metal formed a central target to aim at. Players took turns to throw their *tejos* underarm along the twenty metre alley from the throwing area at one end. Around the edge of the pipe were placed the *mechas*, small paper triangles filled with gunpowder. Hitting a *mecha* square-on with a *tejo* usually caused an explosive bang and signalled the end of the round. Rafael had always been a fair player of *tejo*, a legacy of many boozy evenings spent at the local bar with his comrades from the Fifteenth Station in San Cristobal. The memories made him think of Jorge, still in the hospital after the shooting in Ciudad Bolivar last week, and he resolved to visit his friend again as soon as the opportunity presented itself.

The metal grille covering the doorway was pulled open and Rafael saw the slender, agile figure of Doctor Oliviera slip through the entrance and into the club. Dark patches showed on his brown raincoat where it had been soaked through by the insistent drizzle. He carried a furled umbrella and water ran down onto the floor to mingle with the puddles in the corners. A flat cap was pulled down low over his hair, leaving his eyes and forehead in shadow. Oliviera deftly removed his hat, shaking more stray water droplets onto the floor. He blinked at the brightness of the bar and catching sight of Rafael advanced towards him with quick deliberate steps. As Oliviera ordered a beer Rafael found himself wondering what the doctor's purpose was in asking to meet him here.

Rafael had not realised that a message was waiting for him until he arrived back at his flat in the early afternoon and plugged his phone onto the charger. The device had beeped insistently and the familiar voicemail cassette icon had flashed onto the screen. The message itself had been ambiguous with Oliviera's voice sounding hesitant and uncertain. He had made a vague reference to Rafael's friend, presumably referring to Frederico Fernandez. He had then gone on to express a desire to talk with Rafael about his visit to the clinic and finished with a request to meet at the *Campo de Tejo las Colinas* at around six this evening. Rafael had been unsure what to make of it and had felt reluctant to make the trip up to Suba. He was tired after the long drive back from San Antonio and didn't relish the prospect of another late night.

His parting from Nathalie had been neither awkward nor problematic. They had developed a comfortable equilibrium with each other almost immediately the next morning, neither wishing to push the other too hard to explore how they viewed the events of the previous night. It seemed to be too early to ascertain where either of them wanted to take the relationship and the drive back to Bogota had been punctuated by discussions of other topics. Nathalie had seemed slightly withdrawn as they agreed to meet up again in a couple of days time and had given him a distracted wave when he had left her in Modelia near her apartment.

Now the doctor was raising his beer bottle in a salute and regarding Rafael cryptically with his expressive brownish-grey eyes.

"Thank you for coming," Oliviera began hesitantly. "I wasn't sure I was going to find you here."

"I got your message late," replied Rafael tersely. "I was away from the city yesterday and almost didn't make it." He paused and turned to face the doctor. "But I'm glad I could come," he continued, making a conscious effort to inject a friendlier tone into his voice. "You mentioned my friend Frederico Fernandez. What is it you wanted to tell me about him?"

The doctor hesitated again. His long fingers picked distractedly at the label on the beer bottle as he decided how best to begin.

"When was the last time you saw him?" he asked at last. The image of the mutilated torso and the face from the photographs of Frederico that he'd managed to retrieve from the missing person file tumbled quickly through Rafael's mind. He restrained his urge to strike the doctor and decided to play along a bit further to see where the conversation went.

"I think it was about two months ago, back in October," said Rafael inventing something quickly, based on his memory of the timelines. "I went with him to the Museum of Culture and Heritage in Salitre. Do you know it? I was helping him with some work he was doing on the Muisca Indians." Rafael

169

paused to see if his fabrication had had any impact but the doctor's stony face left him uncertain if there was any connection between the two parts of this intractable puzzle. "He seemed absolutely fine at the time and I was surprised to hear he needed help," Rafael continued picking up his beer again. "Can you tell me what he was doing in your clinic doctor. Why were you treating him?"

Oliviera seemed to react to the insistence in Rafael's voice. He stood up smoothly, an effortless motion that caught Rafael by surprise.

"This was a mistake," he muttered quietly. "I'm sorry to have asked you here, but I must go now." Rafael's arm shot out and he grabbed the doctor at the elbow as he made to turn away.

"Sit down *malparido*," he growled. "You're not going anywhere." With his free hand he reached into his jacket and pulled out his wallet. He flashed his *Fiscalia* identification with contemptuous brevity and then allowed a little time for Oliviera's fear to take effect. Everyone has some reason to be afraid of the police and fear can be spent on something quite unrelated to what has created it. "Now we're going to talk about Frederico Fernandez and you're going to tell me what's really going on here." Oliviera slumped onto his stool, his face becoming pinched and pale.

"I thought something like this would happen," he muttered to himself. "I suppose part of me wanted it to happen." He breathed deeply and put his head in his hands. "It's true, we treated a young man called Frederico Fernandez at the clinic. He was brought in by the Directora, raving and delusional. We were told he needed some time to recover himself and to keep him in isolation for a while."

They both turned sharply to the entrance as the door grille banged open again and a group of burly men trooped into the club. One of them caught sight of the doctor and raised his arm in greeting.

"Some of the orderlies from the clinic," he explained. "Look, there's danger in this," he whispered urgently. "Not just for me but for you as well. Let's go somewhere more quiet so we can talk in peace. Please come with me back to the clinic. We can talk privately there." Rafael agreed warily and they stood up together and headed for the door. The sharp bang of a *mecha* detonating followed by the ragged cheer of the players sounded behind them as they stepped out into the chill dampness of the night.

**

Drops of rain hung in the air outside the *Clinica Merced de Sué*, drifting through the orange glow of the street lights as they approached. Rafael's face was cold and his wet hair was plastered against his forehead. He could taste the acrid tang of the rain on his lips and he licked it away. Next to him Oliviera was a dark shadow hunched down in his raincoat. The umbrella was useless against the sideways floating drizzle so he had left it rolled up at his side. Oliviera led them away from the main entrance which was now dark and closed, following the line of the perimeter wall along the street. The indecipherable scrawl of the red and black graffiti stood out starkly against the background of the wall, a jumble of nonsense words and convoluted images.

At the next corner the wall curved outwards and a small, concrete security post had been built into the brickwork next to a wider arched doorway, closed off by a metal shutter. It appeared to be disused, with the single window boarded up and given over to the graffiti. Behind it, in the angle where it met the wall, a cramped metal turnstile had been installed and it was toward this that Oliviera directed his steps. Rafael watched surreptitiously as Oliviera clicked the code into the adjacent keypad, his eyes locked onto the doctor's fingers as he committed the numbers to memory. The turnstile pushed them out in a part of the hospital that Rafael didn't recognise from his previous visit. It seemed to be separate from the garden and the main buildings he had seen last time, although it was hard to make out anything for certain in the deep gloom behind the perimeter wall.

The area seemed to be used as some kind of storage yard as well as serving as a small car park. Stacks of crates and barrels loomed up in the darkness of the enclosed space and two empty cars were stationed in among them; a polished, black Mercedes saloon and a boxy Nissan hatchback.

"This way please." The doctor's voice was a hushed whisper and his face was pinched with anxiety. He led the way out of the yard and through a set of double doors into a long, poorly-lit corridor. The worn grey linoleum under their feet squeaked faintly at their steps and Rafael's nose twitched at the sharp smell of antibacterial cleaner. A long window covered by a mesh grille ran along one side of the corridor and Rafael could see a row of white iron bedsteads inside, stretching away into the gloom of a dormitory.

The bulky shapes of the sleepers twitched and turned restlessly, drawing the eye with their sudden movements. A number of the occupants were tied down with cloth restraints and a dull groaning could be heard over the sound of their footsteps. An orderly in a white jacket paced slowly between the beds, his flashlight bobbing and jerking in the darkness as he checked the patients. Further along, on the right hand side, a lattice of heavy iron bars blocked a passageway leading deeper into the hospital. On the far side, a hulking security guard sat at a wooden table, flicking through the crumpled pages of a newspaper.

"What's down there?" Rafael asked quietly.

"That's the secure section where we detain any of our patients who become dangerous or violent for any reason." The doctor spoke in a nervous mutter, his eyes darting to the entrance. "Access is limited and I'm not usually allowed to visit that part of the hospital myself."

A fire escape door blocked the way ahead and the doctor pushed the horizontal metal bar to unfasten it with a heavy clunk. Rafael followed him into a damp concrete stairwell that disappeared both upwards and downwards. The doctor didn't hesitate and stepped quickly onto the upward flight with Rafael close behind him. The loosely-fitted handrail shook and rattled under his grip. Another door at the next level led out into a more opulently decorated part of the hospital. In the dim glow of the widely-spaced lamps Rafael saw a polished wooden floor running alongside a railing that overlooked a flight of stairs. He realised suddenly that they had come out onto the landing where he had taken his leave of the doctor the previous time.

The empty desk of Dafne, the secretary who had guarded the *Directora's* office, sat squarely across the end of the hallway. Behind it a faint line of light showed underneath the white panelled door and a muted buzz of conversation could be heard from where they stood. Oliviera moved quickly in the other direction, back along the darkened landing and stopped in front of a narrow door about halfway along. He fiddled in his pocket before removing a cumbersome bunch of keys, unlocking the door and apprehensively motioning the way through.

A cramped, cluttered office was revealed when the doctor pushed a light switch and the room was illuminated in the dusky glow of a single dim lamp on the desk. Patient files were spread across the surface in an untidy heap. An overloaded filing cabinet took up one corner, the drawers yawning open and spilling yet more papers onto the floor. Oliviera cleared a pile of books and documents from a collapsible chair in front of his desk and indicated for Rafael to sit.

"I suppose that story about your father was a lie," began Oliviera leaning back in his chair and tilting his head. Rafael nodded faintly, his face impassive as he fixed the doctor with his pale yellow eyes.

"Frederico Fernandez is dead," he snapped in a quiet, cold tone. "He was horribly tortured and then murdered. But I think you knew that already." Rafael let the silence hang for a moment. "Now, you need to tell me what is going on in this place."

The doctor leaned forward, reached into the drawer of his desk and pulled out a clear bottle of cheap whisky. His hand shook slightly as he sloshed the brown liquid into two scratched glasses.

"I was here before, you know, when this place was still part of the public healthcare system." Oliviera's wistful voice seemed to float out of the darkness.

"That was a simpler time. I lived to help the patients, to bring some order and balance into their lives. To bring them back to themselves. But even then I never quite escaped the fear of being discovered."

The doctor took the whisky with him as he moved to the single narrow window and pulled up the bottom panel. A flame flared in the gloom as he lit a cigarette, blowing smoke out towards the darkened garden.

"Of course everything is different now. It's hard to properly understand what this place has become. For the new owners the patients are assets to be cultivated and then harvested when the time is right. They own me as well, in a way so comprehensive I can't see how I could ever break free." He flicked ash through the opening, gazing out over over the sweep of gently rustling trees. "If I were to tell you, if I even could tell you, I'd need some kind of guarantee. How do I know you can protect me?"

"You don't, but I can. Anyway, you don't really have much choice. If I arrest you for obstructing my investigation, I'm sure someone will find out pretty quickly, assume you're co-operating and take measures against you. They shot my friend the day after we found the body, because they were worried about who we were talking to." The doctor drank down his measure of whisky in one gulp, shuddering at the taste.

"What exactly is the hold they have on you?"

"It's a sad and fairly sordid story of youthful mistakes with enduring consequences." The cynical twist had returned to the doctor's mouth. "Are you sure you want to hear it?"

"I insist."

"Very well." The doctor's voice hardened as he struggled to subdue his self-pity. "After my student years, despite the fact that I had become secretly addicted to morphine, I was considered to be most promising. A man with a future. During my first residency I did a thirty six hour stretch in the Emergency Room, so I went out and got more than a little drunk." Oliviera stubbed his cigarette out on the ledge and tossed the butt out of the window. He moved back to the desk and poured himself another draught of the whisky with a wry smile on his face.

"Then I got called back. There had been an explosion at one of the fuel refineries near the airport and they brought in thirty casualties. Eight people died that night, not because of the accident but because I prescribed the wrong dose of painkiller. I got five years in prison for medical negligence and involuntary manslaughter. At least I got off the morphine. All things considered, I think I was treated pretty leniently."

In the silence that followed the doctor's confession Rafael thought he could hear the faint clicking of footsteps moving along the wooden floor of the landing outside the office.

"I had to pay a hefty bribe to get through the reference checking and obtain a job here. But the owners found out my secret when they took over this place and are using it to control me. If it were to come out there would be another disciplinary hearing and I'd most likely be looking at a medical malpractice charge. That would be the end for me. I told myself a long time ago that I would not go back to prison, no matter what."

Rafael leaned forward in the chair, his steady gaze on the doctor.

"Tell me about these new owners and what it is that happens here and I'll see if I can find a way to make all that go away." The doctor took a deep shuddering breath.

"I don't know Rafael, I don't know." The doctor's voice wavered with uncertainty and a gleam of hope.

Suddenly there was a rapid, cursory tapping on the door before it swung swiftly inward, causing them both to jump. Framed in the light from the hallway was a tall, fierce-looking woman wearing an expensive, well-tailored black trouser suit. High heels added to her imposing figure and her black hair was cut short, framing the elegant but stern features of her face.

A well applied layer of makeup made it difficult to discern her age and the effect, in the dim light, was to give the impression that she was made of ceramic or porcelain.

"Oh it's you Oliviera. I thought I could hear people talking, and I was right." The doctor looked at her speechless, the glass in his hand hovering over the desk. The woman's voice was husky and authoritative and she glared at them both. "Who are you skulking with in here?"

"*Directora* Florez, this is Rafael Alvarez," he stammered. "We were reviewing some files together. He is planning to send his father into our care and he wanted to work through a few questions."

"Well it's late and I'm leaving shortly," she snapped. "I need to talk with you before I go." She turned her steely gaze on Rafael.

"Mr Alvarez, I'm afraid you will need to leave now. You really shouldn't be in here at this hour. The hospital is closed to visitors." Oliviera looked down glumly at the table. The woman stepped quickly over to the railing on the landing, her heels clicking on the wooden floor.

"Ramirez!" She raised her voice to carry to the bottom of the stairway. "I need you to come up here and escort someone to the front gate." She turned back to Rafael. "I hope you'll forgive my intrusion and Oliviera's poor judgement in bringing you here so late. You'll have to find some other time to go through your questions."

The bulky, athletic figure of Ramirez, another of the clinic's security guards, loomed outside the doorway and Rafael stood abruptly to go with him. The man's angular, impassive features and deep-brown skin made him seem carved from wood as he waited in silence on the landing. At the threshold Rafael paused and turned back to where the doctor was slumped sullenly in his chair.

"Thank you for your help with my questions doctor. I'll remember what we talked about tonight and I'll think carefully about how things can go away if you really need them to. I hope we can talk about that again soon." With that he stepped out of the room to where Ramirez was waiting to conduct him back through the darkened hospital and out into the night.

**

Rafael rested his hands on the soft plastic grip of the steering wheel and peered absently through the rain-spotted windscreen at the untidy tangle of overhead cables that crisscrossed the dark canyon of the empty street. Further along from where he was parked a broken sofa had been left on the pavement next to a shapeless pile of black plastic bags that were gradually disgorging their foetid contents onto the tarmac through a series of rips and tears. The twin beams of a car's headlights sparkled in his rear view mirror, pinpricks of brightness in the murk. The glare got steadily stronger as they approached, illuminating the untidy interior of the Landcruiser and then faded into the distance as the shadows danced inside the car. From where he was hunched down in the well-worn driver's seat he had a clear view of the shuttered archway and the boarded-up security post where he had entered the clinic earlier that evening.

The drizzle had stopped but the moisture hung heavy in the air which remained sharp and cold. The inside of the car smelled stale and damp and Rafael's forehead felt heavy from fatigue as well as the beer and whisky he had drunk with the doctor. He felt his eyes drift out of focus and he found his thoughts turning inevitably towards the events of the last few days. The key to who had murdered Frederico and why he had been killed was wrapped up in what had happened at this clinic and how it was linked to the *Nuevo Templo del Sol*. He was certain of it but the details eluded him as he tried to make the pieces fit together in the silence of his thoughts.

As he shifted in the chair Rafael became aware of the slim shape of the *testamento* book pressing against his thigh from where it rested in the pocket of his coat. He pulled it out and flicked through the pages idly, skimming over the invective verses while keeping one eye on the closed metal shutters. It was hard to make out the words and sentences in the faint glow of the street lights and he stopped reading, just taking in the general impression of the book as he flicked back and forth. That was how he came to notice the odd circle about half way down one of the pages. It was faintly drawn, more a scoring on the paper than a definite mark but as he held the sheet up in front of his face he could see there was definitely something there; a ring clearly surrounded a letter 'y' at the end of a line.

He looked at it puzzled for a few moments and then clicked on the car's interior light next to the rearview mirror. Holding the book up to the dim glow, he began to work his way through it, turning the pages slowly and examining each one carefully. A few pages further forward he found another faint circle around another letter, just as lightly drawn as the first but equally tangible. He rummaged in the pocket of the car door and quickly fished out a cracked biro and a scrap of paper. Starting at the beginning, he continued his examination of the book, noting down each of the marked letters while outside the car on the street the silence settled in more thickly as the night wore on.

When he had finished he found himself looking at a fifteen-character nonsense word formed of a jumbled mix of letters, numbers and symbols. It took him several moments to work out what it was but then he realised that he was almost certainly looking at Frederico's password. His thoughts quickly returned to the journalist's apartment and the computer which had blocked his progress on the previous visit. He wondered again what files might be locked away inside the squat plastic box. What was it that Freddy had discovered that had led to him being tortured and murdered in such a brutal manner? What connections had he made that had caused them to act against him in such a definitive way? He grinned in the darkness as he held on to the slip of paper realising that he finally held the key to answering some of the elusive questions and puzzles that had confronted him at every step of this investigation.

A sharp grating noise cut into his thoughts, shattering the silence on the empty street. Rafael's eyes flicked up from the paper to where the metal shutter closing off the entrance to the clinic was rising slowly into the housing of the archway. After a few moments of motion and noise, the mechanism fell silent again and he watched with mounting excitement as the sleek shape of the Mercedes saloon nosed its way into the night. The headlights turned towards him and approached slowly. He hunched down further into his seat, his eyes just level with the dashboard. As the car cruised steadily past where he was parked he had a clear view of the white oval of the driver's face. As he had hoped, it had been the steely features of the *Directora* behind the steering wheel of the Mercedes, focused intently on the road ahead of her. Rafael waited a few more seconds as the car drove past him, tracking the red points of the tail lights in his rearview mirror. Then, as the Mercedes reached the corner of the block, he started the engine and turned quickly and quietly across the street, hurrying in the same direction.

Traffic was light and Rafael was able to keep a steady distance between himself and the *Directora's* car as they passed through the narrow curving streets of Suba. The cracked, uneven roads sloped gradually downwards as they moved out of the hills, past neglected shops and houses and onto the Transversal 76. A carpet of glittering orange and white lights stretched away southwards as they rounded a curve, the panorama of the city spread out below them. He kept the Mercedes in view as they reached a gloomy area of red brick apartment buildings laid out carefully over a well-manicured open space dotted with trees and bushes. She picked up speed as they crossed the overpass above Avenida Boyaca and onto the Troncal Suba and Rafael was forced to weave past a series of slower moving vehicles to keep up. The concrete blocks lining the segregated lane for the Transmilenio buses ran along the left side of the road, reducing the room for manoeuvre and he was close to losing sight of the red pinpricks of the Mercedes' tail lights. Then the traffic bunched up again and Rafael was almost directly behind her as they forced their way into the twin lanes of slow moving cars cutting across at Avenida Calle Cien.

It was easy now to stay with the Mercedes as they passed down a short stretch of the Autopista del Norte and threaded

178

their way into the spider's web of link roads and on-ramps before coming out in the quiet streets of the exclusive neighbourhood near the Parque El Virrey. Most of the space under the overpasses had been fenced off behind a multitude of canvas screens to make temporary shelters for the homeless of this part of the city. The dizzying contrast of life in Bogota still left Rafael with a sense of breathlessness sometimes. The rich lived like twenty first century gods with every modern convenience that money could buy while the poor were left to pick over the detritus that was left behind.

The *Directora's* driving was slow and cautious now and Rafael sensed they were nearing her destination. The car swept calmly down a nearly empty tree-lined avenue and Rafael dropped back so as not to make his surveillance obvious. Suddenly, as it passed a buseta minibus, Rafael completely lost sight of the car. It seemed to have just disappeared into the night. He cursed and moved forward quickly, the Landcruiser's engine growling in response to the pressure of his foot on the accelerator. His eyes darting all around, he scanned the darkened streets urgently looking for a sign of the Mercedes but it was nowhere to be seen so he pulled up to the kerb.

He thumped the steering wheel in frustration. It had to be around here somewhere, he was sure of it. Well-dressed pedestrians strolled about in the hazy gloom, wrapped up in raincoats. The green expanse of the park lay along one side of the street. Moisture hung thickly in the leaves of the trees. On the other side a parade of upmarket shops was situated on the ground floor of the buildings. The darkened displays contained a mixture of watches and stylish designer clothing entwined with gaudy Christmas lights and gift boxes decorated with ribbons and bright paper. The corner of the street was occupied by an expensive-looking Italian restaurant with prominent, full-length windows and an outside dining terrace screened off behind potted plants.

Rafael realised what had happened when he saw the entrance to a discrete underground parking garage leading down from the pavement under the structure of the restaurant. Then, with a surge of excitement, he saw a figure he recognised leaning against the wall next to the darkened opening, a few metres from where he was parked. It was the big man from the Temple; the giant with the tattoo on his hand who had

179

ambushed him in Boyerino three days ago. The man's face was impassive and his bulky silhouette loomed above the passersby in the street around him. He remembered Yoposa referring to the giant as Ernesto. The disappointment at losing the *Directora's* car evaporated instantly. What was he doing here lurking outside a classy restaurant in the Zona Rosa? His mind raced to put the connections together and he turned his attention quickly to the window of the restaurant.

From his vantage point he had a clear view through the broad pane of transparent glass and there, sure enough, as he had hoped, was the imposing form of Carolina Florez in her black trouser suit picking her way carefully though the busy dining space. He watched closely as she made her way to a corner table close to the window. Waiting for her there, his sharp features standing out even in the soft lighting of the restaurant was the unmistakable figure of Gael Yoposa. He had put away the eccentric tribal garb that he had sported when Rafael had seen him at the temple and was wearing a more conventional western-style business suit. His long hair was tied back in a neat pony tail. Yoposa stood as Florez approached the table and they embraced warmly. The waiter hurried over with the menus and Rafael observed silently as they leaned over the table talking earnestly and clinking glasses. They were clearly not meeting each other for the first time.

In the dark of his car Rafael grinned happily to himself for the second time that evening. He was sure of it now, his ideas moving beyond conjecture to certainty. There was a definite link between whatever it was that happened at the clinic and the wider activities of the Temple. He felt he had put together the two largest pieces of this mystery and had made another significant step towards understanding what had happened to Frederico. His hand twisted the key in the ignition and the engine of the Landcruiser revved loudly as he accelerated away into the Bogota night.

**

180

20. Veinte

Carlos Morales was a tattered wreck of a human being. He thought he was probably forty five years old but he was no longer certain on that point, or on much of anything these days. In any case, his straggly grey beard and thin, deeply creased face made him look much, much older. His posture was bent and broken as he shuffled aimlessly along the dirt tracks and rutted streets of El Mirador del Paraíso in Ciudad Bolivar.

Carlos had enjoyed his time in the 'viewpoint of paradise'. It was certainly preferable to most of the other areas of Bogota in which he had spent a large part of his adult life. For one thing, the '*ollas*', the 'waves' hadn't reached this far up and away from the centre. *Olla* was the name that the homeless of Bogota used for the group they were usually forced to be a part of. An *olla* provided you with a patch of territory; it gave you food to eat and work to do. Most importantly it gave you access to whatever substance you were using to escape the mundane horrors of your daily existence.

But the *olla* was not a charity; you were expected to contribute in return. You were required to hand over most of any money you made from either begging or scavenging or stealing. Someone was always watching you and if you didn't pay or you couldn't pay you were out of the *olla*, which usually meant a savage beating and expulsion from the area it controlled.

Carlos was done with the *ollas* and his dirt-encrusted lips twisted into a feral grin as he thought of his newfound freedom. He had picked the perfect place to eke out the last of his days. This was as close to paradise as he was ever going to get. Through eyes almost sealed shut with grime he squinted into the hazy morning sunlight.

He was certain of one thing at this moment; he needed his next fix of alcohol and drugs and he needed it fast. His hands had started to shake uncontrollably and he hugged himself in an effort to try and still the tremors. The pain in his forehead was like a blaze of lightning and worse, the memories had started returning. He could feel them hovering just behind his eyes, demanding his attention and focus. His bare feet were stained a deep, grainy black, all sensation long since gone as he kicked through a pile of refuse and trod unfeeling on jagged metal and broken glass.

At the next corner a jumbled confusion of merchandise had been spread out over a wooden plank on the street outside one of the shacks. The owner of the makeshift shop surveyed his eclectic mix of goods from a flimsy chair, his eyes sharp as he scanned the street for potential customers or threats. A small pile of ragged clothing lay next to a stack of tins and a collection of coloured wires and cables were tied in ordered bunches to one side. Carlos trudged closer under the man's watchful gaze. His filthy, hollow face was a familiar sight to the owner since Carlos stumbled past every couple of days to buy the few pathetic things he needed to stay alive.

The man's nostrils twitched involuntarily as the overpowering stench of Carlos's unwashed body reached him. A few mumbled words and some dirty coins dropped into the man's outstretched hand and Carlos had what he needed; a large plastic bottle of homemade *chicha* was handed over. The dirty brown liquid sloshed noisily as Carlos quickly stashed it away inside the ragged folds of his tattered overcoat. The sour-tasting fermented maize drink would not be strong enough to get him to where he needed to be but it would get things started.

Almost as an afterthought Carlos bought a tube of glue to keep his high going when the alcohol had worked its way through his system. It would have to do until he could get hold of some heavily adulterated cocaine from one of El Chivo's dealers later. Carlos took his purchases and shuffled back through the dusty streets towards where the city ended; the shacks and roughly-built houses simply petered out on the faded dirty brown grass of the Bogota Altiplano. As he walked he drank the *chicha*, swigging great mouthfuls and gulping them down hungrily.

Outside a miserable broken-down hut a little girl stood, watching him pass with wide, curious eyes. Before he could stop himself his thoughts had jumped to his own little girl, to his Isabella. One day, a lifetime ago, when he had still been a young man, he had come home from his work of loading cargo onto the Magdalena river boats so drunk that he could barely speak. His daughter's crying had started almost the moment he walked through the door, a piercing, wailing noise that had filled the one room they all shared.

The blind rage had taken him then and he had hit her without any thought of his own strength. The wailing had not stopped and he had hit her again and again. It was not until his wife had grabbed his arm desperately that he realised that Isabella had stopped moving. It was only later, when his wife had started screaming in her turn that he understood what he had done. He had beaten his own daughter to death.

He had gone to prison then, a blur of violence and wasted time in which to endure the horror and self-loathing from his unspeakable crime. When he had eventually been released there had been nothing and no-one waiting for him so he had drifted inevitably onto the streets. That had been at least ten years ago by his reckoning but time had become meaningless to him and any accurate measure of the passing days had been lost in the fog of his uncertainty.

He was halfway through the bottle now, the dirty liquid soaking into his beard where it had dribbled from his mouth. The alcohol was starting to do its job and the memories began to fade. His hands shook less and the pain in his face had started to subside. He took a deep, long sniff from the glue for good measure, his eyes blurring as the pungent solvent worked its way into his sinuses.

At the edge of the city a small patch of dirt had been levelled and the space had been given over to the rusting carcasses of abandoned buses and trucks. Carlos weaved his way through the dusty shells towards where he had set up his shelter. He didn't have the wherewithal to build himself a shack but he had rigged up a blue tarpaulin that he had found on a refuse heap. He had chosen a stunted tree near the edge of the canyon that divided El Mirador from the rest of Ciudad Bolivar and hung the ragged sheeting up with scraps of rope and wire. From his perch he had a vantage over the jumbled heaps of buildings that disappeared into the hazy smog hanging over the city. One of his motives for selecting this spot was the solitude. No one came out here. There was no reason to; nothing was here.

That expectation of seclusion, together with the dulling effect of the alcohol and solvents, was why Carlos didn't see the man until he was almost in front of him. It took him several moments to realise what he was looking at, his eyes struggling to focus on the amorphous shape facing him. The figure was slumped against a decaying bus tyre right next to Carlos' shelter, his head sagging languidly forward into shadow, the arms lying motionless at his side. Carlos took a cautious pace towards him and then stopped.

"Clear off!" His rasping yell sounded shrill and fearful in the clear morning air, the gusting wind taking most of the force from the sound. He brandished the bottle menacingly.

"Go on, *largate*! Get lost, this is my patch." Nothing, no reaction. The man didn't move as the wind blew scattered scraps of plastic across the brown grass like confetti. After glaring at the intruder for a few more moments, Carlos settled down against his tree to see what the man would do next. He felt his mood changing as he took another large swig of the *chicha*. The man was clearly wasted, he decided after a while. He had probably stumbled out here to sleep off the effects of his own drinking binge. Ciudad Bolivar was abundant with drugs and alcohol; everyone here was trying to get away from something. Well, Carlos knew exactly how that went. He smiled broadly, showing the blackened stumps of his teeth.

"Alright then, you can stay awhile brother," he grated eventually. "But no touching my stuff." As the sun climbed higher into the sky Carlos felt himself loosening up further. He started to talk about whatever flitted into his mind, rambling incoherently about random incidents from his past and speculating wildly about what his future might hold. At one point he found himself singing ragged snatches of some half-remembered tune and then laughing wildly at the ridiculousness of it all. His companion was a good listener. He endured Carlos' ranting in stony silence, his head resting gently on his chest.

"One time, I was in Manizales and they had the best powder I've ever sampled." Carlos' tone was reflective as he started reminiscing again. "There was almost no flour in it. It was incredible, one sniff and I was so high I felt like my ears were going to explode. Then I had a massive panic attack and spent the rest of the afternoon curled up on the floor." He cackled loudly to himself again, head tilted back and *chicha* spraying from his mouth. "You know you're alright *jefe*," he announced to the stranger when he had recovered. "You can stay for a bit longer if you've a mind to. I'm in the mood for company."

Carlos staggered to his feet, holding out the near-empty bottle and shaking it gently.

"I know what you need *amigo*. A swig of this stuff and you'll start to feel alright again." He approached over the broken ground, stepping closer to where the stranger remained slumped a few paces from the shelter.

"Time to wake up," he declared reaching out his left hand and giving the man's shoulder a vigorous shake. Rather than opening his eyes though and enjoying the *chicha* with Carlos, the man toppled sideways away from the bus tyre to lie prone and still on the dry brown grass. The head seemed to flop away at an unnatural angle and now that he was out of the shadows Carlos could see that the man's red t-shirt was stained wet with a deeper crimson from the sheet of blood that ran down from the gaping slash at his neck. Something was very wrong with the wound and Carlos couldn't bring himself to look at it too closely. Instead, he fixed his eyes on the man's white face. He looked almost peaceful in death, at rest with his eyes closed. A mop of curly black hair spread out above his youthful features which had a thin, pinched look in the crisp, clear daylight.

Carlos sat back on his heels, a wave of sadness running through him. He watched the corpse for a short while trying to figure out what to do next. A fly buzzed about his head and then settled on the sheen of blood soaking the man's chest. His companion was dead, there was no doubt of that and he had been so for some time by the look of him. There was nothing that could be done to help him. But Carlos was a survivor and through the alcoholic fug in his brain he thought he saw an opportunity to help himself. He crawled over to the corpse and ran his hands over the man's clothes, rifling through his pockets and checking his shoes. At the man's waist he uncovered a slim pouch-like bag closed with a zip which he tore open, tipping the contents out onto the grass. The pickings were slim; a handful of coins and notes, a chipped, rusty flick knife and a set of keys for a Honda motorbike. He pocketed the cash and dropped the other items back down next to the corpse. The money was enough to buy himself a bottle of something stronger than the *chicha* he had already consumed this morning.

Carlos heaved himself to his feet again and looked around. The patch of scrubby ground next to the canyon remained silent and deserted. It was time to go and find Pepe, El Chivo's main dealer in this part of Mirador. El Chivo made most of his money selling dope to the slack-faced addicts of Ciudad Bolivar. But it was also well known that he would occasionally pay for information if it was fresh and valuable enough. Carlos was gambling that news of a dead body in one of his territories would certainly be enough to secure him a few more pesos from Pepe. Perhaps the dealer might even hand over a small bag of white powder to reward him for the message. Carlos trembled with anticipation as he imagined how good the cheap cocaine would make him feel. He would be able to spend the rest of the afternoon cocooned away from his misery in a numb, hazy blur. Quickly now, chuckling to himself again and rubbing his filthy hands together, he picked his way through the desolate buses and back into the tangled streets of Ciudad Bolivar.

**

"Well, Azuero's got it in for you, my friend. He keeps saying he's going to knock the crap out of you and then try to knock some sense back in, if you ever show your face at the Fifteenth Station again. He's still furious that we went to Ciudad Bolivar without any backup. I'd stay well away from him for a while if I were you."

Jorge's mouth curved upwards into a sheepish grin and he shifted awkwardly on the cushions that propped him up on the sun lounger. Then a serious look returned to his broad, solemn face.

"For my part, I'm just glad you managed to get me to the hospital in time. The doctors told me it was a pretty close thing. The bullet went through my lung and they had to break my ribs to get to the injury." Jorge shuddered and raked a hand through his hair. "Apparently my heart stopped twice and they had to bring me back with the defibrillator."

Rafael put down his bottle of beer carefully on the edge of the wall that ran round the terrace. He glanced up at the wispy white clouds that scudded across the sky and then fixed Jorge with an intense look, his eyes shining slightly in the muted, delicate light.

"I'm so relieved it didn't go the other way. I thought you were dead for sure when I found you in the car with Ospina. I feel truly fortunate to be able to sit here with you, my friend." Rafael placed his hand gently on Jorge's shoulder. "*Se vio como un roble*," he declared with a grin, using an expression that suggested his friend's resemblance to an oak tree. "How do you feel?"

"Like I've been run over by a truck!" Jorge let out a snort of laughter and shifted again. "Claudia! Bring me a beer!" he yelled. "It's a beautiful day, the barbecue is lit and I haven't got anything to drink woman." Rafael laughed in turn and swept his eyes around the narrow patio where they both sat in the weak December sunshine.

The flat roof of Jorge's modest house in San Cristobal had been adapted, like most of the houses in the street, to provide a small amount of outside space at the top of the building. Discoloured plastic sheeting had been rigged up to provide some shelter at one end, near the door where the stairway led back into the house.

Along one wall some loose wooden shelves had been set up and given over to a variety of brightly-coloured plants and flowers. Rafael recognised some delicate orchids in pots, a coffee plant with its distinctive red berries and an orange bush in a larger container on the floor. The heavy black barbecue occupied one corner and the rich smell of the burning charcoal was all around them. The smoke curled gently upwards from the flames before it was snatched away by the stiff breeze.

Jorge leaned forward on the sun lounger and rested his forearms on his thighs.

"So what happened?" he asked quietly. "With the guy in the suitcase I mean. I know a few things but they haven't told me very much." Rafael retrieved his beer from the wall and took a long swig.

"There's a lot to tell," he began briskly. "It turns out our man was a journalist called Frederico Fernandez, who worked for *La Justicia*. Trying to put the pieces of his life together has been an intriguing puzzle. Over the last few days I've found myself talking with an archaeologist from Salitre, a psychiatrist from a clinic in Suba and the leader of some kind of Indian revival religion from a temple out near Chia. I think I'm getting closer to figuring out who killed him and why and I'm sure all three of them had a part to play. I'm betting one of them was also responsible for shooting Ospina and you." Rafael sat back in the collapsible chair that had been set up for him next to Jorge's sun lounger, his face an inscrutable mask.

"It's funny, the events of that morning keep running over in my mind." Jorge's voice was a hesitant murmur. "I watched you walk into the bar. I drank the coffee, I fiddled with the radio, then I looked in the side mirror. I could see the guy striding towards the car and I knew something was wrong. He had his hood up and I couldn't make out his face. I watched the gun come up and I tried to move but he was too quick. I remember the pop and it felt like I'd been skewered by a spear. I couldn't breathe and I couldn't move. He must have thought I was dead. I heard him scratching something on the car then someone shouted and he ran off."

Jorge's hand moved involuntarily to his shoulder and he gently massaged the spot where the bullet had entered.

"Each time I remember, I keep telling myself that it's going to be different and I'll see who it was holding the gun. But no, it's the same every time. There's just a blur where his face should be."

"I know this is difficult, but did you see if he had a tattoo on his hand?" asked Rafael, thinking of his encounter with Ernesto in the Temple.

"It's hard to remember, but I'm certain I saw his hand clearly as he raised the gun. I'm sure there wasn't a tattoo Rafael. I hope that's useful."

The door onto the roof terrace swung open and Claudia emerged into the sunshine carrying a tray of marinated meat for the barbecue. Her glossy shoulder-length hair seemed to glow a faint shade of red where the gauzy light from the sun shone through it, framing her graceful rounded face with its full lips and bright, sparkling eyes.

"I hope you two aren't talking shop," she remarked tartly, setting the tray down on a small table next to the grill.

"Yeah, maybe we were a little," grunted Jorge, a lopsided grin flashing over his face.

"Jorge, you've only been out of hospital for two days. You've been signed off for a month. No more working for you." Claudia's scolding was gentle, her hands on her hips as she looked down at her husband. "And I expected more of you, Rafael Alvarez."

She smiled softly to show that the rebuke was not meant seriously.

"It's good to see you Claudia." He grinned at her as she perched anxiously next to Jorge.

"It's good to see you too Rafael," she replied, reaching over to embrace him in a warm hug. "I can't thank you enough for getting him to that hospital. The thought of what might have happened otherwise is almost too much to bear."

She released him and turned to the barbecue, setting the slices of meat onto the smoking grill. The hiss and sizzle of the burning fat was loud and Rafael felt his mouth watering with anticipation at the succulent food to come.

"How long are you going to stay out there in Fontibon, all on your own?" Claudia asked abruptly, moving a piece of chicken away from the flames. "You should think about moving back here to San Cristobal. At least there are people here who know who you are." Rafael glanced down at his hands.

"It's an interesting idea Claudia. I'll give it some thought, I swear."

"Stop hassling the man, Claudia," Jorge cut in. "What happened with my beer?"

"No beer for you Jorge," she replied bluntly, handing him a large glass of blended juice that had sat unnoticed on the tray alongside the meat. Rafael smiled broadly again and looked out across the jumbled rooftops that bristled with television aerials and satellite dishes.

The distant, angry buzz of a motorcycle engine flickered faintly at the edge of Rafael's hearing, jarring against the calm of the quiet residential street. While Jorge and Claudia continued bickering gently in the background, the droning rose to a crescendo and the bike got closer.

Rafael watched idly from the vantage point of the terrace as the bike sped over the crest of the ridge and down into the shallow dip in which the street was situated. To his surprise the rider lurched to a stop on the corner outside Jorge's house and pulled off his helmet. He recognised the same arrogant scrawny youth who had escorted him into Dona Julietta's bar just over a week ago. The young man directed his gaze straight up to the

189

roof terrace where he could see the smoke from the grill and the people moving about.

"I'm looking for Rafael Alvarez," he called out in a clear, loud voice. "If you're there I need to speak with you urgently. I have a message from El Chivo." Rafael lifted his shoulders in a half shrug and stood up from the chair.

"Look, I'm not sure what this guy is doing here but I think I need to see what this is about." After a moment Jorge stood stiffly as well and glanced meaningfully at Claudia.

"It's okay Jorge," she sighed. "I understand. Go if you need to. Just promise me you'll be careful this time." The two of them descended quickly through the house to stand outside on the pavement facing the rider.

"El Chivo has something important he wants you to see," the youth announced in is his familiar sardonic drawl. "He told me to take you straight there. You should follow me now and drive fast so you can keep up."

"What's going on? What does El Chivo want?" Rafael demanded, crossing his arms. For an answer the youth flailed his leg to activate the kick starter and revved the engine of the bike.

Jorge and Rafael were left with no choice but to climb quickly into the midnight-blue Landcruiser and pull out after him onto the street. He took them on a twisting, circuitous route across San Cristobal, deliberately staying off the main roads and thoroughfares. The direction was inexorably westwards and a tense frown crossed Jorge's face as they started to climb up into the hills of Ciudad Bolivar. The figure of the youth on the bike continued to swerve and jink in front of them as they plunged into the twisting dusty lanes at the edge of the city. The trail led them further uphill and into the lofty neighbourhood of El Mirador.

Eventually, at the end of a narrow dirt track lined with wooden shacks, the rider swerved his bike to the side and stopped.

"This is as far as you can drive," he explained, pulling off his helmet once again as Rafael and Jorge jumped down from the Landcruiser. He put two fingers in his mouth and gave a shrill whistle. In response two more youths emerged from the shadows between the shacks.

"No one touches the car or the bike," he ordered and the other two nodded curtly, settling in to watch the vehicles. Their guide turned away and led them further into the maze of ramshackle huts. Jorge looked increasingly pale and nervous as they moved away from the relative safety of the street. Eyes followed their progress and stray dogs and chickens scattered out of their way. They passed quickly through a dirt yard crowded with rusted buses and out onto an open space near the edge of the ravine. Further ahead Rafael could see a group of men waiting for them, silhouettes dark against the afternoon sun.

El Chivo stepped forward from the group, a taut smile sketched over his narrow face. He was wearing a thin yellow sports coat and had both hands shoved in the pockets to keep it from being blown about in the breeze.

"Well here you are," he announced fixing them both with his steely glare. Rafael and Jorge returned the gaze in silence, waiting for him to explain. Rafael could see that the other men were in the same mould as the young motorcyclist. Some carried sticks and bars, most had guns at their waists, the handles deliberately left visible in the waistbands of their trousers and shorts. El Chivo shifted to face Jorge, sizing him up before speaking.

"First of all, I want you to know that we had nothing to do with what happened to you last time you were up here in Ciudad Bolivar. It wasn't me or anyone connected with my organisation that was responsible for you being shot." He grinned again and the twisted scar down the left side of his face gleamed pinkly in the sun against the darker brown of his skin. "Besides, I don't like having cops gunned down in the middle of my territory. It's very bad for business."

A blue sheet of canvas attached loosely to a stunted tree nearby flapped noisily in the wind.

"What do you want El Chivo?" Rafael demanded his eyes on the wiry gang leader. "Why drag both of us all the way across town on a Saturday afternoon?"

El Chivo took a pace backwards and motioned with his arm to a wretched shape lying bundled on the dry brown grass.

"I wanted you to be one of the first to see this." Rafael felt a wave of sadness pass through him. He slowly approached the broken figure of Ruben Barraca's corpse, his feet crunching on the loose ground. The body was lying on its side, slumped next to a discarded bus tyre. The face seemed almost calm in death, his youthful features composed and peaceful. Rafael closed his eyes for a moment recalling the last time he had seen the young man disappearing into the night in a different part of Ciudad Bolivar as he desperately tried to catch up with him.

This was exactly the moment he had feared then and to see it come to pass left him filled with a sense of futility and helplessness. The cause of death was evident; a deep gash ran across his neck just below the jawline. Looking closer Rafael could see that in addition, where the wound sagged open, the killer had gone to the effort of yanking his tongue through the gaping slash. The ritual post-death mutilation was known as the 'Corte de Corbata', the 'Colombian Necktie', and was a deliberate message that the victim would have nothing further to say; his tongue had been repurposed as decoration for his lifeless corpse. The sound of the wind echoed mournfully through the canyon.

"Look, this guy can't be here," El Chivo interrupted Rafael's silent observation, his voice hard again. "I have interests and activities in this area that I can't afford to be disturbed. It was inconvenient enough having my bar shut down." He shrugged apologetically again at Jorge before continuing. "When the police find him, in a couple of days time, he's going to look a lot tidier and he's going to be in a different part of town. But before that happens I wanted you to know. I wanted you to see what they had done to him."

Rafael inclined his head. Another lead in the investigation had been snuffed out. Someone who could help him understand what had happened to Frederico Fernandez had been silenced. At the same time it seemed there was only one body up here at the edge of the city and Rafael's thoughts turned to the younger brother, to Paulito. He wondered whether the boy was still out there running and hiding or whether he had already been found and had suffered the same fate as his brother. The sun was a hazy white ball behind the low hanging clouds. A plastic bag floated by on the breeze.

"One more thing Rafael." El Chivo had to raise his voice to be heard over the rushing dancing air. "We're finished with this business. I've done what you wanted and more. I consider I've paid what I owe you for this one. From now on you're on your own." The youth who had guided them here indicated it was time for them to go as El Chivo turned and walked away along the cliff, leaving his men to attend to the corpse of Ruben Barraca.

**

21. Veintiuno

The time for careful surveillance and stealth had passed. The sight of Ruben Barraca's mutilated corpse left Rafael feeling that his chances of resolving or even surviving this investigation were slipping away fast. Jorge looked pale and exhausted by the time Rafael drove back to San Cristobal. Claudia ran out onto the street to hug her husband as they climbed out of the Landcruiser. They invited him in for dinner, to share in what remained from the barbecue but Rafael had lost his appetite for both food and company so he declined. A sense of urgency filled him as he left San Cristobal behind, a need to advance the investigation before someone moved against him.

Ever since he'd found the stripped-out file on Frederico in the basement of the Bunker, he'd suspected that someone from within the *Fiscalia* was working to block him. It was most probably the same man who had shot Jorge and Ospina a week ago in Ciudad Bolivar and had been remorselessly tracking down the Barraca brothers ever since. It appeared he had caught up with Ruben and was likely closing in on Ruben's brother Paulito, who seemed to be the last person alive who could tell Rafael what had really happened with the suitcase and how it had ended up on the path to Monserrate. But Rafael had something his rival didn't know about. He reached into his pocket and felt for the piece of paper on which he had scribbled what he was certain was Frederico's password. The page crumpled at his touch; it was time to find out what secrets it unlocked.

Night had fallen while he was driving across the city to the rich neighbourhoods and upmarket apartment buildings north of the Zona Rosa. He parked the Landcruiser several hundred meters away from Frederico's block, on the opposite side of the street. Rafael was determined to take no chances this time and he carefully removed his black CTI tactical vest from the boot of the car before pulling it on over his grey long-sleeved sweater. He checked the ammunition in the Cordova pistol at his waist and for good measure donned a dark blue baseball cap emblazoned with the gold puzzle-piece logo of the *Fiscalia*.

The neat, well-maintained gardens surrounding *Edificio Excelaris* were mostly lost in shadow as Rafael strode along the short path leading up to the glass door of the building lobby. In the sallow light of the marble-lined entrance hall he could see a single guard stationed behind the deep brown slab of the polished wooden reception desk. The man's gaze was fixed on the glowing screen of his mobile phone and his fingers darted over the minute buttons as he tapped out a message. He looked up in surprised as Rafael pushed through the door, quickly putting down the phone as he took in the details of the other man's uniformed combat gear. Rafael held his identification up clearly in the guard's line of sight.

"I'm a State Agent," he announced flatly. "I need access to one of the apartments in this block with immediate effect." The guard scrambled with the papers behind the desk and seemed unsure how to respond. He looked to be about the same age as Rafael who suddenly recognised the short-cropped hair and serious, clean-shaven face of Miguel Torres, the man he had phoned to divert away from the parking garage on his previous visit to the building.

"It's okay *Vigilante*." Rafael smiled faintly, softening the hardness of his expression. "You can call your superior for authorisation. This is a solicitation for entry made under the powers of the Criminal Justice Law which allows an investigating officer to access a property believed to be connected with a homicide investigation."

Rafael glanced round at the lobby while Torres spoke into his radio. There were some cut flowers on a low glass table next to an opulent sofa. The musky, sweet smell of the pollen made Rafael's nose tingle and he felt a faint irritation at the corners of his eyes.

"What is this about *Agente* Alvarez?" Torres asked nervously as he clicked the button on his radio to end the conversation. "We haven't been told anything about a homicide investigation in the building." Rafael made a show of reading the name tag sewn onto the front of the man's uniform so that Torres would not be surprised at the use of his name.

"Miguel, I need you to use the master security key to open apartment 905 for me. I need access to the residence of Frederico Fernandez." The guard disappeared into a small room behind the desk for a few moments before returning with a heavy bunch of keys on a chain.

"Follow me please," he said leading the way to the stairwell. Rafael quickly found himself in the familiar marble and glass interior of the elevator and he idly watched the floor marker changing as they swished silently up to the ninth floor.

"So, are you usually stationed at this building?" Rafael asked to break the silence.

"Yes, I'm here pretty much every day," Torres replied quietly. Rafael could see the man's face in the reflection of the polished doors and noticed a slight frown pass over his brow. "Now that you mention it," he continued after a short pause, "there was a day last week when I was told not to come in. I remember I was ready to leave for my shift and then I got a call from the watch supervisor. He told me that something had come up and that I wasn't needed. It was strange because they even agreed to pay me for the lost day, which has never happened before. Anyway, I'm sure it's nothing." A half grin sketched across Torres face and he shook his head slightly. "It's probably the idea of a murder investigation that's making me over-suspicious."

"It's hard to say," answered Rafael with a slight shrug of his shoulders. "Let's go take a look at that apartment." A chime sounded, the doors hissed open and they stepped out onto the ninth floor landing. They approached the door, their steps muted by the strip of plush carpet. Torres knocked loudly, the deep thumping echoed around the hallway but was greeted by complete silence from within the apartment.

"What are we going to find in there?" he asked, fumbling with the keys. "I've never seen a dead body before."

"I don't think you need to be alarmed," Rafael replied softly. "This is entirely routine." Nevertheless, outside of Torres' line of sight, he rested his hand on the grip of his pistol. The door swung open onto blackness. Torres reached for the switch in the hallway. There was a dry click but nothing happened; the apartment remained in darkness.

"Well that's odd," Torres muttered to himself, trying the switch a few more times. Rafael pulled a flashlight from one of the pockets on his tactical vest.

"Let me take a look please," he commanded, moving past Torres and into the doorway.

The beam played over the green swirl of the carpet as Rafael stepped cautiously along the corridor. After a few paces the whisper of his feet on the soft floor changed to an audible squelch and he realised that the carpet was sodden with water. At first glance, under the dancing beam of the torch, the bathroom on the left seemed undisturbed. Then Rafael saw that the ceramic lid on the toilet cistern had been removed. The mechanism had been damaged and the water had leaked in a steady stream out of the bathroom and across the hallway.

Rafael swung the circle of light towards his right and took in the shattered remains of the kitchen. Smashed plates and kitchen implements sparkled in the glow. The door to the fridge yawned open and the remains of food and shredded packaging spilled onto the floor. The microwave had been partly disassembled, the casing removed and shoved into a corner. The damage was worse as Rafael advanced further into the apartment, Torres a few steps behind him. The sofa in the living room had been slashed open and the stuffing from the cushions had been ripped out. Books had been torn apart and loose papers flapped lethargically in the breeze from the open window. The television had been overturned, the screen cracked and broken.

Rafael felt the last of his earlier optimism evaporate as he surveyed the wreckage. Someone had beaten him to the apartment and the trail was being removed as quickly as he could follow it.

"How could this happen?" asked Torres, his voice a shocked whisper in the gloom. Rafael could see the whites of his eyes in the faint grey light seeping in from the full-length windows. "How could someone get in here, destroy the place and leave without anyone noticing? We keep records of anyone who's not registered as a resident." The guard's surprise and outrage seemed a little overdone to Rafael as he recalled that the security hadn't been particularly difficult to evade on his previous clandestine visit to the building. "I don't understand how it's possible. I need to alert the watch supervisor straight away. Excuse me *Señor Agente.*" Rafael nodded silently and Torres bustled away shutting the door to the apartment behind him with a dull thud.

Alone in the dark, Rafael slipped his hand back into the pocket of his trousers and took out the slip of paper with the password. He turned disconsolately towards the black oblong of the bedroom door, stepping over the amorphous mounds of foam from the sofa.

As he had feared, a similar state of disrepair awaited him in this room as well. The glass desk had been shattered leaving a glittering carpet of broken shards that crunched under his feet. Great jagged slits criss-crossed the mattress which had been thoroughly searched through, the metal springs visible through the gaping rents. The computer and its accessories were nowhere to be seen. All that remained was a single power cable snaking across the carpet to show where the main unit had stood previously. Rafael sat down heavily on what was left of the bed, staring at the empty space.

He wondered again what Frederico had uncovered and how it had led to his death. The tattoo on his shoulder confirmed that the journalist had been involved with the Temple, but how and to what extent remained a mystery. He had been investigating Ignacio Perez and had accused the archaeologist of misappropriating the Muisca sacrificial knives from his own museum. From Ignacio's description of the ritual it seemed likely that Frederico had then been killed himself using the same set of implements. He had also been a patient at the *Clinica Merced de Sué.* Oliviera had asserted that he had been raving and delusional when he was brought there and Edgar recalled spending time with him.

Rafael's witnessing of the meeting between Yoposa and Florez at the restaurant last night had confirmed that there was some kind of connection between the Clinic and the Temple. Various people had been keen to warn him off the Temple. El Chivo had recognised the tattoo symbol, before Rafael had known about Frederico. Ignacio had also seemed intimidated by the design when they met at the museum. Ortega had forbidden him from investigating further. He considered the possibility that Yoposa might have stepped in to take ownership of the Clinic at the time of the scandal. It was a compelling idea but like all his thoughts it remained speculation in the dark.

Without proof and evidence he couldn't advance further. And with the removal of the computer, the apartment seemed to be a dead end.

Rafael crumpled the password note and shoved it back into his pocket as he stood up to leave. He was turning to go when he passed the torch idly over a pile of papers that had spilled out of a filing box at the bottom of the open wardrobe. The beam of light stopped moving as he froze where he was. His instincts were telling him that he'd just seen something important but he couldn't quite place what it was.

Slowly he moved the light back across the room and over the papers. Stepping closer to the wardrobe, he leaned down towards the sheet that had caught his eye. Under the concentrated light of the torch he found himself looking at a grainy black and white photo of some kind of indigenous idol. Its heavy, animal-like features were frozen into an eternal snarl and an impressive studded circlet adorned its head. Reaching his hand out, he pulled the print clear and saw that the head was in fact the handle of a large ceremonial knife with a semi-circular blade. Another *Tumi*! His excitement mounted as he knelt down and began to rifle through the documents. Perhaps something of use remained here after all.

Most of the papers were indecipherable nonsense; disjointed fragments of notes and pictures that looked like they came from Frederico's early research into the Muisca and the collection at the Museum of Culture and Heritage. Near the bottom of the pile he was rewarded by the discovery of a letter from the Ethnographic Museum of Cali. It was a response to an enquiry from Frederico and confirmed that they were not the recipients of the Offerings to the Sun collection. Inside the same envelope was a poor-quality photocopy of the original transfer form for the items, together with the signature of Professor Ignacio Perez scrawled in black at the bottom. Enthralled, Rafael continued to search through the stack, hopeful of finding something further that might help him.

He barely noticed the soft click of the apartment door opening again but heard clearly the squelching tread on the wet carpet in the corridor.

"I'm in the bedroom Miguel," he announced. "There's some useful papers here that I need for the investigation. Can you help me carry them to my car please." There was a slight darkening of the gloom as the faint glow of the city lights from the lounge was blocked out. Rafael raised his eyes quickly expecting to see Miguel Torres. Instead a stocky figure in dark clothes stood at the doorway. A hood had been pulled up over his head and the bottom of his face was obscured by a black cloth mask. The eyes glittered in the darkness and in the man's right hand Rafael could see the cold gleam of a long, serrated knife.

He froze for a moment, his heart hammering in his ears. Then from his crouched position next to the papers he reached sharply with his right hand towards the gun at his waist. The attacker surged from the doorway as he pulled the pistol free, smashing at Rafael's hand with a powerful blow from his left forearm. Rafael's fingers were stunned from the impact. The gun was knocked from his grasp and went skittering across the floor into the dark. The follow-up blow from the hand with the knife was almost the end for Rafael. A deep, rapid lunge was directed straight at his chest. He managed to twist away at the last moment and was saved by his tactical vest. The point of the knife sliced into the reinforced fibres and slid down the side, tearing a deep groove in the material.

Rafael swung a heavy two-handed blow that connected with the top of the man's head as he swept past. He grunted and shrugged off the effects before advancing again. The torch had rolled away from the fighting and projected a disorienting cone of light onto the wall near the bed. They circled each other warily, both watchful for any sign of an opening. Rafael adopted the combat stance he had first learned in the army, knees bent and shifting his weight forward onto the balls of his feet. His left hand was raised for protection near his eye while the right was held in reserve, ready to smash forward if an opportunity presented itself.

Rafael's eyes were fixed on the knife as it swept from side to side in the man's grip. There was no suggestion of the tattoo which might have indicated that he was up against Ernesto, although he seemed to be about the same size as the big man from the Temple. The attacker used his build and longer reach to gradually force Rafael back towards the corner of the room. He feinted left and then quickly dived in with another powerful lunge but this time Rafael was ready.

He leaned sideways to avoid the swinging blade and then stepped in close towards the man's body while he was fully extended from the strike. Rafael jammed his left arm up against the inside of the man's bicep, gripping him fiercely at the shoulder joint while his right hand closed about the wrist holding the knife. Rafael put his whole body weight against the knife hand, pushing from his shoulder. The attacker, off-balance and clearly surprised by Rafael's desperate gambit, couldn't stop the slow steady advance of the knife back towards his face. He twisted and tried to pull backwards but with a final jerk the tip of blade pushed into the skin just below the right eye. Rafael felt it scrap along the bone of the cheek. The man let out a fearful, agonised shriek. The slice across his face seemed to spur him to a final desperate act. He hooked his right leg around Rafael's planted foot and swept it backwards causing Rafael to loosen his grip and topple sideways towards the wall. The face-mask was ripped away as the knife fell to the floor.

Rafael had a momentary glimpse of a broad face with a closely-cropped dark beard, a furious snarl frozen across the taut lips. The man looked familiar from somewhere but he couldn't place him in the split second before the attacker turned and ran precipitously for the door.

Rafael pushed himself quickly back on to his feet. He darted to the corner of the room and grabbed his gun before sprinting through the darkened apartment in pursuit.

Out on the landing there were spots of blood on the white marble of the floor and a clattering echoed up the stairwell as the man descended at pace. Rafael glanced at the lift, quickly ruling it out as a viable option and then plunged down the stairs after the attacker. He raced out into the lobby and stopped short. Sprawled on the floor next to the sofa was the prone form of Miguel Torres. A pool of crimson blood was seeping slowly outwards from where he lay. Rafael crouched beside him and quickly reached out a hand to touch his neck. The skin was clammy and there was no sign of a pulse.

He pressed his forehead into the palm of his hand, fighting back his anger and frustration. Miguel Torres had no involvement in Rafael's investigation of Frederico Fernandez. He knew nothing about the Muisca or the Nuevo Templo de Sol. He had just been in the way, collateral damage to a ruthless enemy. Rafael wondered sadly about the man's family as he rolled the corpse over. Torres had been slashed deeply across the throat, a dark red gash from which there was no recovery. His blood had sprayed out across the white marble as his life faded away. Rafael reached for his phone to call for more police to secure the scene and an ambulance for the body. He looked up to where the glass door was slowly drifting shut on its self-closing hinge. The path and building entrance were empty and dark. The attacker had disappeared into the night.

**

22. Veintidós

This far away from the front of the room, the sound of the words was reduced to a muted droning that hummed and murmured sluggishly in the air. The units of meaning were rendered incoherent and obsolete by distance and poor acoustic design. From where he sat, squeezed uncomfortably onto a folding chair in the last row of the lecture theatre, Rafael had a dizzying view over the top of a sea of heads falling away and narrowing as they got closer to the stage that dominated the lower part of the wedge-shaped room. The portly figure of Ignacio Perez paced about on the platform below, diminished by the distance between them.

The air was warm and stuffy. Rafael watched through half-closed eyes as the professor waved his hands about to emphasise a point and then scribbled a fragmented note onto the oversize blackboard behind him. The young woman in the seat next to him turned her head slightly and glanced at Raphael from the corner of her eye. She was not much younger than him but came from a very different world. Like almost all the students in the room her skin was a smooth, lightly tanned white. Her delicate features were regular and pleasing but seemed infused with a cold indifference. In his plain brown trousers, faded black shirt and bland tie he certainly looked out of place among the gilded youthful students packed onto the benches with their discrete designer labels.

He made a conscious effort to extinguish the resentment that he felt start to rise up in him. The rundown classroom of *Colegio Antonio Nariño* slid unbidden into his mind and the discussion with *Professora* Delgado about progressing further with his education. She had been vocal in her encouragement but when the matter of fees had been raised with his mother she had been equally unequivocal in her refusal. It was just not conceivable within their very limited budget and Rafael had felt the possibilities of his future reduce to match his social station.

203

Instead he had been compelled to carry out his military service and from there progressed into a career with the police. He wondered again what path his life might have taken if he had been a scion of a wealthy family like those surrounding him; or if his father had never disappeared and a different set of possibilities had presented themselves.

On the stage below Rafael could see that Ignacio was now reading from a stack of notes balanced on the corner of the lectern. He strode to the table in the middle of the stage and took a sip from a glass of water, gesturing and pointing like a miniature automaton. Occasional snatches of meaning drifted up to the back of the room.

"So we can see Durkheim's theories on the division of labour are borne out in the ancient Muisca iconography..."

"A clear and unambiguous progression is presented in the pre-contact artefacts and architecture in the archaeological record..."

"It is an inherent misnomer to assert that a structural hierarchy is inconsistent with social egalitarianism...".

It seemed the professor was drawing to the end of his lecture. Rafael's neighbour snapped her expensive-looking laptop closed. A ripple swept backwards in the sea of brown, black and blonde hair as Rafael could see the audience starting to rise to their feet. Students headed for the exits on the top row, alone or in groups while Rafael remained seated, hunched down in his dark raincoat. The hall was filled with the hubbub of conversation as the young men and women discussed the crucial points of the lecture, their next class or some salacious university gossip.

Ignacio waited at the front of the room, standing to one side of the table. A pair of students had approached the stage to seek the professor's opinion on a particular point. A young man in a baggy turtle-neck sweater was caught up in an animated discussion with his tall, pale friend. Ignacio smiled at them paternally as he continued to gather up his papers while they talked. When the hall had nearly cleared Rafael began to descend the widely-spaced stairs towards the front of the room where he caught the end of the conversation.

"I disagree that it is valid to equate ethnicity in any way with the remains of material culture."

"Whereas I believe it can be a useful shortcut to assign a presumptive identity to a group of people based on the character of their day-to-day possessions. What's your view Professor?" Turtle-neck was asking as Rafael arrived.

He stood to one side with his arms folded as the conversation continued for a few moments longer. The Professor weighed in with a balanced response that suggested there was value in both perspectives but also pointed out the limitations of each. He suggested further reading for both of the students and then turned towards Rafael.

"Please excuse me gentlemen," he apologised. "This has been a fascinating debate but I need to speak urgently with the *Fiscalia* agent you can see waiting there." The two young men glared angrily at Rafael. He could sense the instinctive disdain and hostility to the powers of the state that was part of the basic constitution of the aspiring left-leaning intellectual.

"Is there anything we can help you with Professor?" asked Turtle-neck, the bolder of the two.

"There's no need to worry, Nelson. I'm assisting the investigator with one of his cases. I'm sure he just has a few more questions for me." He turned his slightly patronising smile on Rafael and nodded. Nelson and his friend pushed past Rafael and with final backward glances proceeded towards the exit at the back of the hall.

"*Agente* Alvarez, I didn't think I'd see you again so soon," began Ignacio. "I was planning to contact you but it seems you have found me first." Rafael shrugged then stepped up onto the stage to stand with the professor. It felt slightly intimidating to be exposed at the front of the room facing the rows of seats soaring upwards, even though they were almost empty.

"I'm going to get straight to the point here Professor. I've got something that I want you to take a look at." Rafael reached into the inside pocket of his raincoat and pulled out a white envelope. He carefully removed the copy of the transfer form and spread it out on the table in front of Ignacio.

"What is this?" the professor asked in a clipped tone. "What do you want from me?"

"I believe that's your signature at the bottom of the paper." Ignacio maintained a stony silence. "It's what we talked about when I saw you at the archaeological site last week," continued Rafael. "This is the form you signed to authorise the transfer of the Offerings to the Sun collection to the museum in Cali. Just before the objects disappeared."

The professor stared grimly at the paper, his lips pressed firmly together. After a few moments he seemed to come to a decision and raised his head to look Rafael directly in the eye.

"Very good investigator, I concur. That is exactly what you have here." Ignacio picked up the brown leather satchel containing his papers and swung it over his shoulder. "Please walk with me," he said heading towards one of the exits at the side of the stage. He pushed the metal bar to release the door and it swung outwards into a high-ceilinged whitewashed corridor. Rafael followed close behind the Professor as he paced quickly along the short featureless passage, their footsteps loud on the woodblock floor.

"You know I have enough here for an arrest warrant," Rafael announced calmly to Ignacio's retreating back. "We've talked a few times now and you've told me that you weren't responsible for Frederico's death. I believe you, but I also know you're holding something back. Something important. It's time to tell me what you know Professor. I won't ask kindly again."

The passage ended, joining another broader corridor. Tall, metal-framed windows ran down one side letting in the bright, pale daylight and providing a pleasing view over the open green spaces of the university campus. The sky was a constantly changing blend of clear, crisp blue and dirty white clouds. Ignacio stopped walking at the junction and turned back to face Rafael.

"I told you I was planning to contact you and it's true. I've been to see my lawyers to discuss some matters connected with but tangental to Frederico's death. On their advice I am proposing to make a deal with you. I will make a full statement and confession of my involvement in certain irregularities connected with the transfer of registered antiquities in return for immunity from prosecution." Rafael blinked quickly and narrowed his eyes, looking down at the floor as he considered.

"I agree that is an acceptable proposal," he replied evenly. "We can have the lawyers draw up the terms and the *Fiscalia* legal department can review and sign off. My over-riding concern in all of this has always been to find who was responsible for Frederico's torture and murder." Rafael ran his hand through his hair and fixed the professor with his pale yellow eyes.

"The only condition I have is that you need to tell me what's going on now," he continued, emphasising the last word. "Matters have become overwhelmingly urgent. One of the only witnesses was found dead at the weekend and last night, someone tried to kill me with this." He reached into his coat again and took out a plastic evidence bag, holding it up in front of Ignacio. The serrated knife used by the anonymous attacker in Frederico's apartment swung from his grip at the bottom of the bag. Ignacio took a step backwards, his mouth open in astonishment.

"*Madre mia*! I can't believe it," he gasped. "That is the second sacrificial blade from the collection, for extracting the sacred body parts. How did you get it?" He stretched out a hand to touch the knife and Rafael quickly wrapped it back up in the bag and returned it to his pocket.

"I was at Frederico's apartment last night," Rafael explained. "I needed to check some details but the place had been broken into and ransacked. I was searching through some papers when I heard someone enter the apartment behind me. It was a man in a mask holding that knife. He was strong and quick and he tried to stab me. Luckily I was able to fight him off and he made a run for it but the building security guard was not so fortunate. He's dead as well." Ignacio seemed to recover his composure, his round face was slightly paler than usual as he spoke again.

"Have you tested it for poison?" he asked urgently. "It was common Muisca practice to coat their ceremonial blades with a contact neurotoxin. Their traditional preference was the Batrachotoxin of the Golden Poison Frog. It was regularly traded up the Magdalena River from the coastal forests of the Caribbean and it's extremely lethal. The muscles are quickly paralysed and the victim usually dies from cardiac failure shortly after."

"*Carajo!*" Rafael hissed, the exclamation almost involuntarily as he recalled how close he had come to being cut by the knife. Only his tactical vest had saved him, turning the blade away at the last second. He wondered what had happened to the attacker, remembering the man's desperate run to get away after a relatively minor wound to his face. There had not been any reports of a dead body that matched the sketchy physical characteristics he had observed from the attacker. But then he hadn't thought to check. "Thanks Professor. I'll see if the *Fiscalia* laboratory can find anything, after we're done here."

The two of them turned into the wider passage and began to pace along its length. Doors were spaced regularly along the side facing the windows and opened onto a range of laboratories, classrooms and smaller lecture halls. The corridors hummed with voices as groups of noisy young adults moved between the rooms and to other parts of the building.

"So let's hear it Professor," Rafael began after they had walked a short distance. "It's time to tell me what happened to the knives." Ignacio sighed and his face twisted into a bitter smile.

"Very well Rafael, I'll confess my sins. Then you can grant me absolution with the stroke of a pen." He took a few more paces in silence, looking towards the ground. His heavy brow creased into a frown.

"I suppose it all begins and ends with the museum to which I've dedicated such a significant portion of my life. Budgets for cultural institutions aren't what they were and it probably won't surprise you to learn that the government is cutting our funding again. I sometimes feel like I have ceased to be an anthropology professor and that the most important part of my job now is trying to constantly raise money for the museum." Rafael was surprised at the harshness and anger in the other man's tone.

"I first came across Gael Yoposa at one of the charity dinners organised by the Archaeological Association of Colombia. I suppose he thought I would be naturally sympathetic to his organisation and its obsessive, revivalist goals. He was exceedingly generous to start with, which I realise now was an effort to establish his credibility and more importantly to build up our reliance on his donations. Then he started to reduce the money." Walking beside the professor, Rafael could see that the stout man's hands had clenched into fists.

"I suspect that he made efforts to contact our other donors to get them to similarly cut back on their funding. I can't prove anything but I believe threats and intimidation were involved.

It wasn't long before the museum was back in financial difficulties. We were looking at reducing the staff and even considered selling some items from the collection to cover the costs. It was at that point when Yoposa came to me with his proposal." Rafael could see the end of the corridor up ahead. Another crowd of students was coming towards them and he followed as Ignacio stepped to one side to wait near one of the windows while they passed.

"Yoposa had a fascination for the Muisca relics, as you'd expect," Ignacio continued as the last of the students disappeared into a classroom behind them. "He seemed genuinely aggrieved that the artefacts were kept on display in a state-owned institution rather than in the custody of what he considered to be the rightful heirs to the Muisca culture. He confronted me regularly on that point and implied that he was doing his best to hold back some of his more hotheaded acolytes from taking action to 'liberate their history', as he put it."

"Wait, are you saying he threatened you?" interrupted Rafael. Ignacio returned his gaze and a wry smile played across his lips.

"In the end, I have to admit, it was the incentive that moved me rather than the menace. Yoposa came to me with an offer that was beyond extravagant. It worked out as about the equivalent of half the annual budget for the entire museum. What he wanted in return was for us to 'share ownership' as he called it, of some of the more evocative ritual items in the collection. He proposed to hold them in trust for the museum and would return them after a specified period.

The Offerings to the Sun collection was our test case. I created a false paper trail to cover its temporary removal from the museum. Yoposa paid the money and I gave the knives over to him. To be more accurate they were left in a carefully concealed parcel for one of his associates to pick up at an agreed location. As well as paying for the museum's ongoing operating costs the money funded some incredibly valuable research into early Muisca society."

As Ignacio was speaking the two of them stepped out of the corridor and into the building's expansive entrance hall. A polished concrete stairway curved gracefully upwards to the higher floors. People milled about talking quietly or waiting for someone and the buzz of conversation echoed through the open space. The imposing wooden doors to the Social Sciences Faculty Building were wedged open and a uniformed guard sat at a discretely placed desk just to one side.

"So why couldn't you tell me this before?" Rafael asked as they passed through the crowded space. Ignacio let out a derisive snort of laughter.

"Look, the *Fiscalia* is not exactly renowned for its integrity! Honestly, I was worried that if I gave myself over to the custody of your organisation, word of it would have quickly got back to Yoposa. Also the impact on my position at the museum would have been significant." Rafael gazed quizzically at the professor as they approached the doors.

"Let me get this straight. You're now ready to formally testify that you loaned the objects, including the knife I was attacked with, to Yoposa and his organisation in return for a cash payment."

"That's right Rafael. I am ready to do the right thing now. And, as part of my deal I want zero custody time. I don't want the risk of Yoposa finding a way to get to me."

"So how does this all link back to Freddy? How does it help me catch his killers?"

"You already know my history with Freddy. Clever lad that he was, he worked out what was going on and published it in his newspaper article. I think we both believe that Yoposa and the Temple were directly responsible for what happened to him. My testimony gives you solid evidence of their possession of the artefacts and cause to formally investigate further."

Outside the main entrance the dirty clouds had prevailed and the sky was blanketed with a familiar grey overcast. The air smelled damp and Rafael assumed there would be rain before the afternoon was finished. The two of them stood side by side at the top of the steep flight of stone stairs that led from the redbrick exterior of the Institute building to join the campus roadway that ran through the university grounds. Opposite, across a paved open plaza, the ultra-modern facade of the university admin building loomed up into the gloomy afternoon. The roadway was moderately busy with a mix of pedestrians and cyclists that formed the bulk of the traffic inside the university campus. A few cars circulated slowly and Rafael could hear the high-pitched whine of a motorbike engine in the distance. He raised his arm and the professor shook the offered hand.

"Let me know when you're on your way to the *Fiscalia* building with your lawyer tomorrow morning. I'll find a discrete way to get you inside and we can sign the papers."

Ignacio nodded, turning away towards the steps. He paused half way down, looking back to where Rafael stood above him.

"Isn't that funny, I haven't even done the hardest part but I feel as though my whole body is lighter already. See you tomorrow *Agente* Alvarez." He flashed a cynical grin and with a final wave of his hand quickly jogged down the remaining steps to merge into the gangs of walkers moving slowly between the buildings.

Rafael swept his gaze along the line of the busy road as he considered what to do next. He fiddled with the plastic bag in his coat pocket, conscious of the possibility that the knife inside was in fact poisoned. His instincts told him something was wrong though it took a few moments for him to realise what had attracted his attention. The whine of the motorbike was noticeably louder, like a stubborn mosquito at the edge of his consciousness. His eyes were drawn to the sleek, powerful machine as it got closer. It seemed to be travelling faster than the surrounding traffic, weaving around the pedestrians and slow-moving cars. Rafael could see the rider crouched low over the handlebars, a passenger clinging on tightly with his arms wrapped around the driver's body. Both their faces were concealed by dark crash helmets, the visors snapped down tightly. The passenger was weighed down with a bulky backpack, which stuck out behind him like a hump.

Rafael searched for Ignacio in the crowd. He could see the professor's tell-tale wispy hair about half way across the plaza, on the way to the admin building. The motorbike was closing fast. The passenger had unslung the backpack and was rummaging about inside. Rafael took a step towards the professor, then another and started to run down the stairs. He was near the bottom and was about to shout out a warning when the bike drew level with Ignacio. The passenger's hand flicked out of the bag and Rafael could see the stubby barrel of a sub-machine gun. There was a sudden, violent spray of automatic gunfire. The professor jerked about frantically and then collapsed in a heap.

For a fraction of a second there was absolute silence. Then the hysterical screaming started and seemed to come from everywhere at the same time. People scrambled madly in all directions to get away from the bike. Rafael heard the fierce pitch of the bike's engine revved to maximum as it skidded away along the road. He was sprinting desperately across the plaza. Ignacio was a ragged heap on the paving slabs in front of him. Rivulets of blood were streaming away from where he lay motionless on his back, arms spread wide. He knew straightaway that nothing could be done and that the professor was gone and with him, probably his best chance of taking the investigation directly to the Temple.

It was the second time in less than twenty four hours that Rafael found himself confronted with the corpse of someone who had been alive moments before. A young woman standing next to the professor had been hit in the leg by a stray bullet. Her screams cut into his thoughts and jerked him back to the present. He pulled the tie from around his neck and wrapped it tightly around her leg as an improvised tourniquet. In the distance he could hear the shrill wail of sirens getting closer.

**

23. Veintitrés

A dull, percussive drumbeat rattled through the damp air as Rafael stepped over the glossy puddles towards the front entrance of the Bunker. To his left the gold, blue and red horizontal bands of a voluminous Colombian tricolour were pulling wildly against the chill breeze, each snap of the giant flag pounding out another beat. The grey concrete of the building was the same colour as the overcast sky, almost as though the building was seeking to merge itself into the background, to make itself invisible. The corners of Rafael's mouth twitched at the irony of the thought; an organisation with an ambiguous mandate hiding in plain sight.

He merged into the morning crowd funnelling over the plaza towards the steps that led up to the entrance. All around him people shuffled forward with dull eyes and pinched looks as another working day began. A team of blue-uniformed guards was working the crowds at the entrance. Rafael's ID card was thoroughly inspected by an unsmiling young man in a peaked cap when his turn came. The guard held the card up between finger and thumb at face level and made an exaggerated show of checking that the picture was a match for the owner.

"*Siga Senor,*" he barked after an uncomfortably long pause, handing the card back to Rafael and stepping out of the way.

There was a long line in front of the newly installed Juan Valdez coffee franchise in the lobby. A fleshy man in a loose-fitting white shirt had placed a complicated order involving flavoured syrups and the server was bustling about trying to figure out what to do.

"Just give the man a *tinto* and let's get moving, *coño,*" someone shouted from further down the line, triggering a chorus of grunts and complaints along the queue. The man at the front flushed crimson and clenched his fists. He insisted in a loud voice obviously meant to be heard by the grumblers that he ordered the same thing all the time and didn't understand why it was a problem today.

Rafael pushed aside his craving for caffeine, deciding that the coffee stand was more trouble than it was worth this morning. He jostled his way towards the bank of elevators on the far side of the reception area. The cobalt-tinted skylights coloured everything with a sharp blue tinge giving a harsh, almost electric effect to the faces of the people striding about. Their eyes were vacant and downcast as they focused on getting quickly through the transitional space of the lobby. Rafael was reminded of the quiet, purposeful activity of robots as they stepped carefully round each other, heads down looking at mobile phones, muttering softly.

The sound of his name being called cut through the quiet murmur, snapping him out of his reverie. He turned to see Miriam standing a few paces behind him. She had managed to secure a coffee from the server before the system had broken down and clutched a dark red paper cup adorned with the abstract white logo of a moustachioed man and his mule. A tired smile played across her lips as she lifted a hand in greeting, her angular features looking pale in the sharp light. The two of them were swept into the same lift when the doors swished open with a ding. Rafael found himself pressed up against the back wall close enough to Miriam that he could smell her subtle, slightly flowery perfume.

"You look exhausted," he began, instinctively adopting the hushed pitch used by people in crowded lifts everywhere.

"It's crazy at the moment," she replied in the same tone, a frown creasing over her gently curving forehead. "I've got more cases than I know what to do with and the work keeps piling up. Calderon assigned Lopez to the unit but the guy is worse than useless. He's so old-school I think he'd be happier shooting jaguars than protecting them from trafficking." Miriam snorted dismissively and took a sip of her coffee. "I know Environment Crimes is seen as a bit of a joke but I swear, with the way the work is going, I think it's going to be one of the biggest departments in the *Fiscalia* in five years time." Rafael nodded his head vaguely and gave a noncommittal grunt.

The lift jerked to a stop and Rafael and Miriam threaded their way through the other passengers and out into the crowded warren of desks on the third floor.

"You look pretty tired yourself Rafael," she remarked as they walked side by side past a glum-faced woman using the photocopier. He gave a vague shrug and took a few more paces in silence.

"It's been a tough couple of days," he responded evenly. "I thought I was making some progress with my investigation, the murdered journalist in the suitcase. I had someone ready to testify. He was going to provide some concrete evidence against one of the main suspects. But then he was gunned down yesterday, outside the university, right in front of me, just after I'd finished speaking with him." Miriam raised her hand to her mouth in astonishment, her eyebrows curving upwards above her chestnut brown eyes.

"You were there?" she asked incredulously. "I mean, someone told me about the shooting but I didn't realise it was part of your work. I'm sorry Rafael, that must have been awful." He moved to look at her in turn, sadness etched onto his narrow face.

"It's a mess. I'm not sure what to do next or where to go from here." Miriam reached out a hand and placed it reassuringly on Rafael's upper arm.

"Well, I hope you figure it out. If anyone can, I'm sure it's you."

She stepped away ready to head towards her desk on the other side of the office then suddenly turned back. Moving in close to him she spoke in a rapid whisper so that her voice didn't carry to any of the other operatives sitting close to where they were talking.

"Did you hear about Ortega's deputy, Antonio Saloman? He was in the department talking to Calderon when you were re-assigned away from Environment Crime?" she muttered urgently. Rafael shook his head slightly. "They found him in the evidence room, dead on the floor. Apparently he had a cut on his face and his body was full of some kind of deadly poison. Someone told me he drowned in his own saliva. The whole section is closed off now. I don't know if it was anything to do with you or your case but watch your back Rafael."

Then she was gone leaving him to puzzle out the implications of what she had just revealed to him. He stumbled to his desk in a kind of daze, not really seeing the people or things around him. So it had been Ortega's man Saloman who

215

had attacked him in Frederico's apartment. It matched with what he remembered of the man's looks from the brief glances he had snatched from across the office and the half-seen face in the gloom as the mask had been ripped away.

He considered quickly where else Saloman might have been working against him as he remembered the emptied file on Frederico in the archive room. Perhaps it had even been Saloman who shot Jorge and Ospina in Ciudad Bolivar the day after the discovery of the body. Rafael collapsed into the chair at his desk, still barely conscious of what was going on around him. It seemed to make little sense that Ortega would select him to work on the case and then deliberately have one of his associates undermine everything he was doing.

Then he remembered the pressure to close down the investigation quickly and the reluctance to allow him to go anywhere near Yoposa and the Temple. He wondered for a moment whether there was more to the relationship than the typical desire of Colombia's rich and powerful to protect and do favours for their friends. Perhaps Ortega was a fully committed member of Yoposa's organisation and its revivalist hatred. If so, Rafael's position was even more precarious than he had feared.

It took a monumental effort to drag his mind back to the present and focus on the task in front of him, rather than continue to lose himself in endless speculation. He unlocked the drawer to his desk and took out a large folder, spreading the contents over the working surface. Among the jumble of papers was the autopsy report with its scribbled red lines and the clinical details of the horrific injuries suffered by Frederico. A scattering of crime scene photos from the path to Monserrate rested next to his left hand showing the battered suitcase and its miserable contents. He leafed through the sparse remains of the missing person file on Frederico, taking a moment to scrutinise the faded picture of the journalist that was included with the file.

The knife in its plastic bag was still nestled in the pocket of his coat. He extracted it carefully and deposited it onto the surface of the desk, on top of the photocopied transfer form and his notes from his discussions with Doctor Oliviera. If it had indeed been responsible for the death of Ortega's deputy he was going to need to think carefully about how to explain his possession of it.

He stared intently at the items, trying to feel a connection and willing them to reveal how they fitted into the story of Frederico's murder and more importantly what was missing. What was the final detail that joined them all together and unlocked the puzzle of who had been responsible and why? He let all the pieces sift through his mind for a few minutes, waiting to see if he would discover something he had missed, hoping that something would speak to him and suggest a coherent course of action.

A shadow fell across his desk and Rafael looked up to see a uniformed agent looming over him.

"Come with me please, Investigator Alvarez," the man demanded flatly. The laminated ID badge hanging from a cord around his neck showed him to be a member of the building's internal security team. Something in the man's blank hostile gaze filled Rafael with apprehension. The air conditioning was turned up but his involuntary shiver was due to something more than the cold. He stood up stiffly from the desk, leaving the documents and photos where they lay.

"What's this about?" he asked quietly. The people around his desk were turning to look at him.

"I have orders to escort you to the basement conference room. Please leave everything where it is and come with me immediately." Rafael cast a last glance at the knife in its bag and stepped away. He trudged across the open plan following the broad back of his escort. Miriam caught his eye as he passed through her area of the office. Her arms were crossed over her chest and a look of shock and sadness flashed across her slender features as he walked past.

The agent stopped at a secure doorway and took out a red keycard. Access was not usually permitted to this area for the majority of the operatives on the floor. Rafael took a final look at the office, momentarily considering some kind of wild flight and knowing instantly it would be both futile and damaging. Instead he sighed in resignation and stepped though the door with his escort. The man maintained a stony silence as they entered a lift, staring impassively at the ceiling as the numbers clicked inevitably downwards.

217

The sinking feeling as the elevator descended into the bowels of the building matched the lightness in Rafael's stomach. He was certain that some kind of reckoning was coming. They emerged, when the lift ended its journey, into an empty, narrow basement corridor. A strip of bright neon lights ran down the centre of the low ceiling, bathing the area in a harsh, pale light that reflected off the whitewashed breeze blocks that lined the walls. The rush of the air conditioning was noticeably louder at this level and Rafael knew they were not far from the holding cells in the most secure part of the building.

Round a precisely right-angled turn, a solid-looking door was set into the left hand wall. The agent checked a small viewing window at head height and then swiped his red access card again. There was a metallic beep and a click before the door swung outwards into the corridor. Rafael stepped cautiously over the threshold into a spacious and glaringly bright meeting room dominated by a polished wooden table that took up most of the floor. Spindly metal-framed chairs on wheels were spread around it at wide intervals. The people that made use this room were clearly accustomed to plenty of space. A black speaker phone lurking at one end of the table put Rafael in mind of a squat, ugly spider. A red light gleamed on its surface like a single malevolent eye.

Guillermo Calderon had seated himself at the end of the table furthest from the door, a small pile of papers spread out in front of him. His slightly unkempt appearance looked almost out of place in the immaculately arranged room. The lean, predatory figure of Emilio Ortega leaned stiffly against the wall behind Calderon's right shoulder. His arms were crossed over his chest and he watched Rafael through narrowed eyes as the investigator stood near the entrance, his chin raised in defiance. Calderon glanced at Ortega and broke the silence with a dry cough.

"Sit down Alvarez," he rasped. "You have been summoned here to give an account of your investigation." Rafael pulled out one of the metal-framed seats and flopped down, leaning back in the chair with his legs pushed out in front of him. His thin lips twisted into an angry sneer. After Miriam's warning he knew he was due for some kind of reprimand and was determined to go down fighting. He was tired of tip-toeing around the politics of the *Fiscalia* while he tried to uncover the truth. Calderon fixed him with an unfriendly glare.

"Yesterday afternoon, prominent anthropology professor Ignacio Perez was gunned down in your presence outside the Social Sciences Faculty building in the university in Salitre," he began brusquely. An image of the professor's broken body flashed back into Rafael's mind as he glanced down at the dark wood of the table. "How did that come to happen? What's your explanation?" barked Calderon, his moustache bristling. Rafael looked from Calderon to Ortega and back again, his yellow eyes hard.

"He was ready to testify that he had been pressured into selling Muisca sacrificial artefacts to Gael Yoposa and the Nuevo Templo del Sol." Ortega snorted, a sharp dismissive sound in the quiet of the room. "I had just made an agreement with him. He was supposed to visit the Bunker today with his lawyer and make his statement."

He shook his head slightly at the senselessness of it all. "I can only conclude that someone learned of the professor's intention and wished to silence him before he could provide his testimony." Calderon grunted and picked up one of the pieces of paper in front of him.

"Let's talk about what happened at the victim's apartment the day before. I have here your report of the incident. According to this you were attacked by an unknown assailant while searching for evidence at the address." He held up a black and white photo of the face down corpse of Miguel Torres, arms spread wide on the lobby floor of *Edificio Excelaris*. The blood spreading out from his neck showed as a dark stain of midnight black on the glossy surface of the picture. "I can see the results, but I'm unclear how this episode helped move you forward in the investigation." An ugly sarcastic grimace flashed across the sub-director's fleshy face. Rafael inclined his head, his gaze dropping to the table again.

"The man surprised me in the apartment. He attacked me with a knife. I was lucky to survive. I'm certain the security guard had nothing to do with the case. He must have got in the attacker's way and paid the price." He flicked his eyes to where Ortega leaned against the wall. "I managed to wound the man with his own knife causing him to flee. I wonder how he's coping with the effects of that wound."

Ortega seemed to stiffen, his lean face pale and angry. Rafael kept his voice calm and even.

"It turns out that the knife he used to attack me, and let's not forget, to kill Miguel Torres as well, was one of the blades that Professor Perez sold to the Temple. It seems a strange coincidence that it came to be in the hands of my attacker. Unless of course he was connected to the Temple and was working under their direction."

"Preposterous!" barked Ortega. "How much longer are we going to listen to this nonsense Calderon?" Rafael continued as though the prosecutor hadn't spoken.

"Incidentally, it seems most likely that the same Muisca knives were used to inflict the horrific injuries that ultimately killed Frederico Fernandez. Before he was killed, Professor Perez explained to me their ritual use in Muisca sacrifice. The wounds and injuries suffered by the victim are surprisingly consistent with the methods he described." Ortega was struggling to contain himself. His hands tightened into fists. Calderon turned to him, raising a hand in placation.

"One more thing I want to clarify with Alvarez, señor *Fiscal*," he declared, smoothing his moustache with thumb and forefinger. "In one of your preliminary investigation summaries you stated that it was of the utmost importance to locate and secure two known youth criminals, Ruben and Paulo Barraca. Is that still the case?" Rafael nodded silently, guessing what was coming next. "The body of Ruben Barraca was found dumped by the side of Calle 80 in Engativa earlier this morning. His throat had been hacked out a few days previously. The pathologist is still working on an exact time of death."

Rafael sighed and raised a hand to his forehead. He was surprised that El Chivo had managed to hold on to Ruben for so long. From Calderon's description it sounded like he had cleaned up the worst excesses of what had been done to the young man. He felt certain that Calderon would have mentioned something if the *corbata* mutilation had remained a feature of the corpse. It would have served as another weapon to attack Rafael's handling of the case. El Chivo had made a shrewd choice in Engativa. The scruffy suburb in the north-west of the city was far enough away from Ciudad Bolivar to deflect any suspicion that might land on the informant and his operations.

Calderon adjusted his tie.

"Another murder connected with your investigation. It seems your leads are disappearing faster than you can follow them up, Alvarez. So, after all this, after three more bodies in as many days, do you have a plan? Do you have any feasible ideas on how to take this investigation forward?"

"Well, I confess sir, I find myself in something of a dilemma. By my reckoning, any reasonable reading of the evidence justifies immediate further investigation into the *Nuevo Templo del Sol* and Gael Yoposa." The prosecutor stepped forward and banged both his palms down on the meeting table.

"Enough!" he roared into the stunned silence of the room. "I won't stand for any more of this fantastical nonsense theory of sacrificial knives and long-dead Indians." Rafael and Ortega glared at each other wordlessly, hard looks filled with dark thoughts and hostility.

"Well I don't know where this is going," Rafael spat back at the prosecutor, "but this investigation has been a farce from the very start. You've been more interested in setting up barriers for me than showing any interest in the truth of what happened to Frederico Fernandez. Now you know where the evidence points and you want to shut everything down because you don't like the answers. It's pathetic."

The prosecutor's hooded brown eyes were locked on his. Rafael felt a calm settle through him dissipating the anger, as he waited for the prosecutor's response.

"You have used this investigation as a pretext to repeatedly make unfounded, unjustified threats against a man who has done nothing but good in this city. His organisation has helped more people and changed more lives for the better than the three of us in this room will ever be able to appreciate." Ortega lifted his hands from the table and settled himself in the chair next to Calderon. He leaned into the backrest and surveyed Rafael along the length of his smooth, aquiline nose. Rafael was put in mind of a hungry lizard watching its next meal.

"You have comprehensively failed at the task I set you to do Investigator. Instead of closing things down, this case is spiralling out of control. The media are starting to take an interest. People are starting to ask questions."

"I know that your friend Yoposa was involved in this murder. You can try to twist things any way you want but it's only a matter of time before the truth comes out." A frosty silence settled over the room. "Very well sir. If you're unconvinced by what I am saying, what do you suggest?" Rafael made no effort to keep the sarcasm out of his voice. "What are your directions for taking the investigation forward?"

"This investigation is over," barked Ortega in response. "I'm using my executive powers to close the file. Reasonable enquiries have been exhausted." He stressed the first word of the sentence. "There is a lack of any feasible lead that merits further investigation or follow up."

Calderon opened his mouth to protest but it was Ortega's turn to hold up one of his slim, well-manicured hands. "As of now you are back on Administrative Leave *Agente* Alvarez. I want him escorted out of the building immediately," he added, turning to Calderon who looked uncomfortable with what had happened in the last twenty seconds.

Rafael shook his head in disgust, the bitter smile fixed in place on his narrow lips. He tossed his gun and ID card onto the table with a dull thump and turned to leave before the internal security agent could step back into the room.

**

24. Veinticuatro

Rafael stood in the quiet shade of the yew tree, watching as the old man in the black suit took another shuffling step along the row of tombs. The man clutched a walking stick in one gnarled hand and a shapeless bunch of flowers in the other. The flimsy plastic wrapper reflected the weak sunlight in scattered flashes among the shadowed grey pathways. He seemed to be bent against some invisible burden, his thin, lined face inclined towards the ground, sparse grey hair lifted in the gentle breeze, shoulders stooped and fragile. Rafael felt for a moment that he was looking at an image from the desolate future that was most likely waiting for him at the end of his days, where he was left isolated and alone with a grief and loneliness that were to be his only companions.

Then, as quickly as it had come, the feeling passed. A small group of the old man's family and relatives came round the corner of the high concrete wall in which the tombs rested. A plain-faced woman in her thirties, who Rafael supposed was the man's daughter, took his arm at the elbow, supporting his weight as he struggled along. A few paces behind, a morose man in sunglasses scuffed along with two more women dressed in sober shades of brown. The man wore a black leather jacket over a black t-shirt with a heavy-metal band logo. He jerked his head silently in time with a rhythm that only he could hear. Rafael watched them pass, struck again by the thought that unlike most Colombians, his own future would probably not involve crowds of friends and relatives. His life had been a path towards solitude and yesterday's events at the Bunker were another step along that road.

His own destination was ahead and he felt foreign and alone as he slipped along the path under the yew trees like a shadow. He passed the whitewashed remembrance chapel open to the air behind its barred grille, an indecipherable Latin inscription chiselled out along the lintel beneath the feet of the white stone angels who guarded the roof. The high rise concrete canyons of the newer part of the cemetery rose all around him. About half the spaces in the wall were open and unoccupied, lending the area a provisional unfinished quality as though some kind of badly planned construction project had been abandoned half way through. Although it was quiet and peaceful, the buzz and roar of the city was never far away, a low constant growling in the background even here.

Gabriella's tomb was slightly below head height mid-way along the row. A small vase had been fixed to the front of the slab next to a faded photo behind a grimy glass screen. Her name was picked out in embellished, gothic script on a black metal name plate. Rafael took out the small spray of red flowers he had purchased from a stand at the entrance to the cemetery and pushed them carefully into the top of the vase. An empty feeling of sadness took hold of him again as he reflected he had only ever made a handful of visits to the grave in the months since Gabriella had died. The tomb in the honeycomb slabs had been mainly paid for by her family. He had been too overwhelmed to have much involvement in the decisions or how they had been carried out.

Memories of his wife tumbled through his consciousness. He spoke to her in his mind again telling her all that had happened to him in the last couple of weeks. The body in the suitcase and his mix of excitement and uncertainty at being put in charge of the case. His meeting with El Chivo and the shock of Jorge's shooting in Ciudad Bolivar. The discovery of Frederico Fernandez as the victim and the progression of discussions with the archaeologist, the asylum doctor and the high priest as he circled closer and closer to the truth. He hesitated for a moment but overcame the barrier of his own reticence and recounted his meeting with Nathalie and their night together, certain in the end that Gabriella would be happy that he had met someone who could help him heal. Finally he reached the end of his description with the acrimonious confrontation in the conference room yesterday, culminating with him being cut loose again, to drift through the city with neither reason or purpose.

He felt his thoughts shift to what the future might hold for him. It was time to think about what life outside of the police might mean. His ideas of where to go and what to do were jumbled and roughly formed as they tumbled through his head. A nebulous image of leaving Bogota to spend time with some distant cousins in Tolima. A vague notion of taking work in a security company out there. Whispers of uncertainty rose to haunt him, repeatedly questioning his decisions and actions. He stepped again through every aspect of the case, every choice he had made. Where had it all gone wrong?

He was unaware of the passing of time as he crouched motionless in front of the grave until the crunching of footsteps on the gravel path behind him brought him back to himself. Raising his eyes from the tomb he suddenly realised that the sun had travelled a fair distance through the sky. He turned towards the source of the noise and was surprised to see the unlikely combination of Jorge and Nathalie walking towards him with steady, intent footsteps. Jorge's broad face seemed slightly embarrassed, the gaze averted and the eyebrows knotted in a half frown, as though he was worried that he was about to be responsible for some kind of indiscretion. Nathalie also had an uncertain, hesitant manner as she tucked her dark brown hair behind her ears and looked up at Rafael with solemn, reflective eyes.

His gaze flicked from one to the other as they came to a stop in front of him, an eyebrow curving upwards on his narrow forehead. They stood in silence for a few moments before Jorge began speaking.

"I went to your house when I heard what had happened and found this lady waiting outside. She was looking for you. I guessed you might be here so I offered her a lift."

"Jorge told me what they did to you." Nathalie's words were heavy in the still air. "I thought you might need a friend." Rafael ran a hand across his forehead, rubbing the skin at his temple.

"It's good to see you Nathalie, good to see both of you." His eyes were drawn towards the tomb next to where the three of them stood.

"So this is her," murmured Nathalie, following his gaze and lingering on the picture in its tarnished frame. Rafael nodded softly in response. Jorge considered them from a few paces away, a wry grin playing across his broad mouth.

"I'm going to step over here and leave the two you alone for a bit," he announced before striding away into the yew trees.

225

Nathalie lowered her head and took another pace towards Rafael.

"I'm sorry to intrude like this." She was close enough that the pleasant musky aroma of her hair flickered at the edge of his awareness.

"Jorge knows me better than I thought," replied Rafael, a soft smile at the corners of his lips. "This is where I come when everything's gone wrong and I'm feeling sorry for myself."

"So what are you going to do?" Her eyes flashed brightly, her chin raised in challenge.

"What do you want me to do? What can I do?" Rafael's face was an inscrutable mask.

"You've got to keep looking for Frederico's killers. He's got no-one else."

"I'm not a cop any more Nathalie. They put me back on administrative leave. Most likely Ortega is going to push for me to be forced out of the *Fiscalia*."

"What about justice?" The last word had the full force of her breath behind it and cut through the quiet air like a knife. "God knows there's little enough of it in this country." She folded her arms and her mouth set in a thin line. "But you've got a real chance to do something for once Rafael. You can stop Ortega and Yoposa walking away from this with impunity just because they're rich and have the right connections to the damned oligarchy."

Rafael felt his resistance begin to cave; her determination pushing through the void of his emptiness and irresolution. She was right. There was a chance to make a difference here before he left Bogota for good. What had been done to Frederico was both sinister and compelling. The method seemed so practiced and precise that Rafael was sure that the journalist was not the only victim and that his death was part of some bigger scheme. Whatever that was, he felt certain that he was the first person from outside to step this far along the thread of conspiracy that linked all the pieces together. It was up to him to uncover the truth of Frederico's death and put an end to whatever nefarious activity the Temple was engaged in. Nathalie was right about that; there was no-one else.

"Alright," he grinned at her fiercely, committed now to the course of action. "Let's finish this thing." He felt her slim arms go around him.

"I didn't know her but I think she'd want you to carry on." Her voice was wistful again as they turned away from the tomb. They caught up with Jorge near the remembrance chapel, the anxiety on his face quickly disappeared when Rafael told him their intention. Nathalie lent against Rafael and held him at the elbow as the three of them slowly weaved their way back through the tombs and out of the cemetery.

**

Rafael's fingers slipped on the damp buttons as he entered the code into the dull metal panel. He made a mistake and had to start the sequence from the beginning again. The second time there was a dry click and the bars of the turnstile became slack against the weight of his outstretched arm. He looked over his shoulder to check that the street remained empty and pushed. The cold metal ribs of the gate swung around and swept him silently into the service yard at the back of the *Clinica Merced de Sué*. The air was cool but not chill. Ragged grey clouds covered the black night sky. The darkness in the yard was nearly total and Rafael could barely see the jumble of boxes and clutter that was piled into the narrow, cramped space. Everything was reduced to a shadowy maze of gloomy, indistinct forms that reared up around him, blocking out the glow from the street and leaving him isolated and confused.

He ducked down behind a stack of broken pallets that leaned crazily towards the wall like a drunken man about to lose his balance. The way forward snaked through the debris towards the door he had entered with the doctor at the end of last week. He scuttled closer, darting from one patch of shadows to another, keeping his head down as he approached. The wall of the clinic loomed up out of the darkness as he got closer and Rafael hoped that the black clothing he had changed into would keep him concealed from any unseen watchers. The weight of his dark-grey backpack hung loosely between his shoulders.

He froze in place next to a plastic crate. A security guard lounged against the frame of the door, silhouetted against the light from inside the building. The man appeared to be smoking a cigarette. He made no sign of having seen Rafael. The red tip glowed as he took it from his mouth and blew out a cloud of bitter-smelling smoke. Rafael retreated to the shadows in the

227

corner of the yard and watched soundlessly for a while. The guard wasn't going anywhere. He stubbed the cigarette out against the wall, sending a shower of red sparks cascading onto the floor. Then he rested his hands on his belt and leaned his shoulder against the wall, gazing out at the mass of crowded shapes in front of him.

Rafael cursed himself silently; he had been a fool to think he could just stroll in here the same way as last time. He looked around for something that might help, some means perhaps of distracting the guard. Behind him, in the corner where the wall of the yard met the hospital building proper, Rafael noticed a narrow, wrought iron gate. It was partially concealed under a tangled mass of black ivy. He stepped closer, keeping his movements slow so as not to draw the attention of the guard. Pushing aside the ivy he could see that the bars of the gate were heavy and rusted. It was clear that it had not been used for a long time.

He closed his fist around one of the struts and gave an experimental shove. The grille moved a few centimetres and then jammed against some unseen obstacle on the other side. Flakes of rust and paint peeled away onto his hand. He glanced at the guard but the man continued to be preoccupied by the view of the yard so Rafael put his shoulder up against the doorway and pushed again. There was a dull scraping sound and a muffled creak as the opening widened to the point where Rafael was able to squeeze through sideways.

Ducking under the low archway, he found himself back in the overgrown garden at the front of the clinic. The noise from the gate had seemed painfully loud so he concealed himself in one of the thick bushes at the side of the path and waited to see if the guard had noticed anything. The rich smell of the damp earth filled his nostrils as he lay prone in the undergrowth, making him think momentarily of the vast fields surrounding the army barracks in Tolima where he had spent his early childhood. The farmers planted rice in great green swathes that stretched to the horizon and the smell of the waterlogged soil filled the air as clouds of mosquitos danced and whined in the humid, oppressive sun.

From where he lay, hidden in the undergrowth, he had a wide, unobstructed view across the lawn and path towards the main building. The spiky plants all about him waved in the gentle breeze, making a faint hissing sound as they rustled over each other. Pale moonlight broke through a rent in the clouds, highlighting the clocktower and the roof of the colonnade as though they had been dusted in silver. Rafael was relieved to be out of the yard. The darkness and confined space had seemed to close off any chance of further progress. He had been anticipating that the clinic relied primarily on its towering perimeter walls and the sporadic presence of security guards and orderlies to keep out intruders. There had not been any indications of a more sophisticated security system on his previous visits.

Rafael considered his next move, his eyes scanning the darkness around the main building. Some kind of makeshift scaffolding had been set up against the wall of the colonnade, a collection of flimsy poles and rods bound together with cables and rope. It seemed like a promising option. He waited a few more moments, listening for any sound of disturbance or alarm. All was quiet so he prepared to act. He moved swiftly along the path, keeping close to the wall and staying in the shadows as much as possible. As he got closer the black writing on the reflective tape that wrapped around the scaffold stood out clearly - *precaución pintura fresca.* The chemical tang of the paint lingered in the night.

He scrambled upwards and onto the tiled roof of the colonnade. Dropping to his hands and knees, spreading his weight out as evenly as possible, he started to move clumsily sideways across the slanting mossy surface. From his vantage point he had a view over the ridge of the roof towards the other side of the hospital. Spliced onto the back of the main building, like an extra limb added in some grotesque medical experiment, Rafael caught sight of a sprawling concrete structure. He assumed this was the secure wing of the clinic that he had passed with the doctor on his way to the stairs. Orange lights on the flat roof picked out the detail of what seemed to be a landing pad.

Rafael's foot slid several centimetres across the slippery tiles and he was forced to return all his attention to the act of travelling along the roof. Careful not to dislodge any of the gently curved slates, he approached the windows of the second floor. A sparse heap of dirty cigarette ends was spread out in front of him and piled up in the guttering, indicting that he had reached his intended destination. As he had hoped, the bottom of the sash window had been left open; a narrow slit of blackness against the dull grey frame. He braced himself against the slanted surface of the colonnade roof and pushed the pane upwards. Clambering over the window ledge he hauled himself inside and crouched down with his back against the wall. His muscles ached from the exertion of the awkward sideways motion and Rafael found he was breathing heavily through his mouth. He waited for his eyes to adjust to the deeper gloom inside the building. The narrow outline of Oliviera's office emerged gradually from the darkness.

When the stiffness in his limbs had faded, Rafael unslung his backpack and rummaged inside for the small flashlight he had brought with him. He rose to his feet again and clicked the thin beam on. It was immediately apparent that the office had been stripped bare. The files and papers that had littered the desk and the floor were gone. White squares showed against the yellowed plaster of the walls, where pictures and photographs had been removed. In the dim circle of light Rafael performed a quick search of the filing cabinet and the desk. Both were empty except for a drained bottle of whisky that rolled towards him when he opened the bottom drawer of the desk. There was nothing to be found here. It was time to move on.

He stepped towards the door of the office, clicking the flashlight off as he approached. Turning the handle, he eased it open a crack and checked the landing outside. All was silent and still. The lights were off and the hallway was lost in shadow. He crept along the polished wooden floor towards the desk and the white panelled door at the end. There was a slight rattle as he tried to open it but this time the door would not move at all. Several seconds passed in the darkness as Rafael tried to decide whether to break the lock with the small pry-bar he was carrying in his backpack. Then another thought occurred to him. He turned to the dim outline of the desk in the hallway behind. With a quick glance to check that all remained quiet he turned on the torch again and ran its faint light over the smooth surface. It didn't take him long to locate the key, hidden in a staple box next to a framed photo of the overweight secretary holding her dog. He quietly unlocked the door and stepped through into the room beyond.

The contrast with the space he had just left could not have been more stark. Carolina Florez's office occupied a broad expanse at the end of the building with windows opening on three sides. There was an ornate wooden desk under the central window. A separate meeting table stood to one side with six carved wooden chairs positioned around it. A comfortable-looking sofa occupied the corner nearest the door. Shelves and wooden cabinets for papers and files ran along one of the walls. Pale moonlight shone in through the wide windows, illuminating everything in a steely glow and rendering Rafael's flashlight an unnecessary risk for the moment.

As he advanced into the space his eye was caught by a large oil painting hanging on the wall to his left. Three dark figures towered over a stylised, mythological landscape. A sun and moon with human features lurked in the background, wreathed in clouds. The giant on the left was naked and bent almost double under the weight of an enormous rock. The figure on the right of the painting was bearded with an intelligent piercing stare. The centre of the picture was dominated by an androgynous form, its subtle blend of male and female features gazing down at Rafael with a haughty disdain. The tiny figure of a woman carrying a baby could be seen in the foreground near the giant's feet. In the pallid moonlight the picture appeared in monochrome shades of grey and black, all the colour leeched away by the gloom. Something about the painting made Rafael feel profoundly uneasy. The artist seemed to have rendered a chilling, callous indifference onto the faces of the supernatural beings as they loomed over the helpless, insignificant human figure.

He turned away with a shudder and began to methodically work his way through the cabinets and shelves. Rafael didn't know what he was looking for but he was certain he would recognise it when he found it. He was certain that something in this office could shed light on the real purpose of the clinic and how it was linked to the *Nuevo Templo del Sol*. The cabinets yielded nothing of interest so Rafael turned to the desk. The surface was clear and the drawers contained some miscellaneous personal items including some expensive makeup and an unopened bottle of champagne, but no papers or documents. He stepped back and ran his hand over his hair with quick jerky movements. Disappointment threatened to overwhelm him. To have made the effort to break into the clinic, to have taken all that personal risk and have nothing to show for it was almost heartbreaking. He couldn't accept that. There had to be something here.

The painting caught his eye again with its sinister figures and dreamlike landscape. He was drawn towards it. The canvas was about the width of his outstretched arms. He hesitated for a moment then reached up and lifted the frame from its fastenings. Behind it, recessed into the wall of the office was a sturdy wooden cabinet door. A single black keyhole was embedded in the centre like a dark eye watching him as he rested the painting against the wall. Rafael ran his fingers around the edge of the cabinet, feeling for the gap between the door and the frame. Satisfied, he placed his backpack on the floor and removed the pry-bar from the bag's interior. He jammed it aggressively into the tiny crack and then leaned with his full weight against the free end. There was a dry splintering sound and the door flew open, swinging into the wall next to him with a dull thump.

The inside of the cabinet was lost in shadows and Rafael could make out nothing of the contents. He brought out the torch again and the beam of light split the darkness, picking out a small black book and two cardboard files resting sideways on an inner shelf. His hand trembled slightly as he reached out to take them. The pages of the book were yellowed and curled as he leafed through them under the glow of the torch. A list of names marched down each sheet inscribed in clear, precise handwriting. He thumped his finger on the paper as a jolt of elation ran through his shoulders and neck. There it was, 'Fernandez, F', logged neatly in a column on the left next to a date just before the suitcase has been found on Monserrate. On the other side a large monetary amount had been entered in both Colombian Pesos and US Dollars. Even though he wasn't quite sure what he was looking at yet, a tight grin spread across his face. Here at last was something tangible that seemed to locate Frederico in the clinic just before his gruesome death. An explanation for the payments eluded him for the moment so he turned to the cardboard folders.

Flipping open the first one, he was confronted by the photo of a lean, striking woman staring up at him from the file. There was a quizzical, slightly confused look to her eyes and her face seemed familiar to Rafael. It took him a few moments to work out where he had seen her before, then he remembered. The tall lady who had been talking into the broken mobile phone when he had first visited the clinic. The photo was clipped to a thin stack of printed pages. He ran his finger down the front sheet, reading quickly. Her name was Beatriz Espinosa and the documents seemed to be some kind of medical report with details of height, weight and blood pressure. On the second page the author had been asked to give an opinion on the health of the major organs. The heart, lungs, liver and kidneys were all assessed as in excellent condition. Next to the entry evaluating the kidneys someone had noted a large amount of money in the same neat handwriting that filled the book.

Rafael sat back on his heels in shock, his mind whirring as he tried to process the implications of what he had just read. The similarities between Ignacio's explanation of the Muisca sacrificial rite and Frederico's injuries had led Rafael to believe that the journalist had been killed by the Temple for some kind of ritual purpose. Looking at the papers in front of him, the inescapable conclusion was that a commercial motive was also involved. Could it be that they were harvesting and selling the organs of the clinic's inmates?

His thoughts still reeling, he reached for the second folder. A stack of black and white surveillance photos flopped out onto the floor. The first one was a picture of Ospina and Rafael at the crime scene on Monserrate. Next was Jorge lying in the car in Ciudad Bolivar after being shot. There was one of Ignacio shaking hands with him outside the faculty building in the university and another of him drinking a beer with Dr Oliviera in the tejo club. Near the back was a blurred shot of him walking down the steps outside the *Fiscalia* bunker, which must have been taken yesterday. The final photo was a close up of him and Nathalie sharing an embrace in the cemetery this morning.

Confirmation that he had been watched since the very beginning sent another chill of fear through Rafael as he sat in the dark. They had a photo of Nathalie! What was he going to do? Without a clear idea of where the threat came from it was uncertain how he could protect her against it. He pushed the doubt from his mind and picked up the photos again. Only the truth could bring safety. He had hoped that the interference had ended with the death of Antonio Saloman, but that was clearly not the case. He was certain at least that he hadn't been followed to the clinic or he would never have been allowed to get this far.

The indistinct sound of footsteps and muted conversation in the corridor behind him broke in on his reflections. His heart thumped loudly in his ears. If he was discovered now he had no reasonable justification or authority to fall back on. He would just be another common criminal, a burglar caught in the act. Rafael shoved the papers into his bag and turned to the painting. Fiddling desperately with the frame, he just about managed to wrestle the thing back into place to temporarily conceal the damage he had inflicted on the cabinet. He spun round, eyes scanning the room for a hiding place or a way out as the footsteps advanced down the corridor. The window behind the Directora's desk had also been left open a crack. He rushed towards it, slinging the backpack onto his shoulder. The frames here were stiffer than in Oliveira's office and the glass was jammed tight. His shoulder and back muscles were taut as he heaved upwards. The window jerked open with a groan.

Outside, the cool night air struck his face like a slap as he climbed out onto the roof of the colonnade and quickly pulled it shut behind him. He crouched down to one side of the glass just as the light clicked on in the office behind him. Footsteps sounded in the room, moving towards the desk. Rafael huddled motionless in the darkness on the sloping tiles, not wanting to take the chance of alerting whoever had just entered. The muffled conversation from the hallway resolved itself into the distinctive voices of Carolina Florez and Gael Yoposa.

"We need to move forward," Yopasa was saying in his sing-song lilt. "Our friend in the *Fiscalia* says that Alvarez has nearly figured things out. He's taken steps but can't guarantee that the fool won't try to act against us."

"Well, we have confirmed orders for the next set of assets," Florez replied crisply. "If you and your associates are able to manage the harvesting, we can proceed ahead of schedule." Rafael was aware of her shadow on the window next to him as she sat down at the desk. There was a pause before Yoposa's voice sounded again.

"I've always liked this painting Carolina. I approve of your efforts to increase visibility of our beloved Muisca cosmology.

My one complaint is that holy Sué has been relegated to the background."

"Yes, the artist is a niece of mine. She grew up in Suba with the stories of the Muisca gods." Yoposa continued as though she hadn't spoken.

"Sué should not be represented as subordinate to Chibchacum, punished to carry the world on his shoulders or to bearded Bochica with his tricks and magic." There was a short pause before the *Directora* took up the conversation again. A flat irritated tone had entered her husky voice.

"If you want to argue cosmology, I would point out Furachogua, the mother of the Muisca and the creator of our race in her rightful place at the centre of the picture. How typical of you Gael to overlook the role of women in everything that matters." Rafael took the chance to glance round the corner of the window frame and into the room. Over Florez's shoulder he could see Yoposa with his hands clasped behind his back, gazing up at the canvas. He jerked his head back before he was noticed. Yoposa gave a dry chuckle.

"Fair enough Carolina. I concede. We would all be greatly diminished without our noble mother." There was another pause before Florez spoke again.

"So can you do it or not, Gael? Can you process the organs and have them ready for shipping by tomorrow?" Yoposa seemed to weigh up his options carefully before responding.

"Very well. I'll make the necessary arrangements. The celestial portents are acceptable. We'll proceed at midnight. Bring the subject to my temple at the usual time. Do not be late."

"Agreed. After tonight though I want any traces of our operations cleared away until we've taken steps to protect ourselves. You need to find a way to neutralise this investigator and his friends before he becomes a real menace."

"Certainly. This will be the last offering for a while until we've taken care of our investigator problem. One way or another, everything will be finished tonight."

**

235

25. Veinticinco

Rafael blinked and tried to focus on the shifting swathe of light that spread out in front of him. Vague, indistinct, shapes rushed past in the blackness, picked out momentarily in the twin cones of luminescence from the headlights. The window of the car was open and the rush of cool air helped him concentrate as he wrestled with the steering wheel, trying to keep the Landcruiser's tyres out of the storm drain that ran alongside the narrow dirt track. Getting free of the clinic had proved a slow and frustrating task and Rafael had been forced to stop and conceal himself regularly to avoid detection by the security guards and orderlies. After getting out through the garden and the turnstile gate he had rushed straight for the car but by the time the engine growled into life Yoposa and Florez were long since gone.

He had decided to avoid the direct route up the *Autopista del Norte* to Chia that he had taken to get to Boyerino and the Temple last time. A diversion through the northern suburb of Bello Horizonte and into the narrow, winding tracks that climbed up into the hills to the east of the city had seemed like the more prudent choice to ensure his car wouldn't be seen and recognised. He had rummaged in the backpack for his phone, wedging it between his shoulder and chin as he called Jorge while weaving through the narrow streets. His friend's voice had sounded confused and distant as Rafael had blurted a few scattered details about the surveillance, about keeping Nathalie safe and about where he was going and why.

A thin mist was rising as he climbed higher into the hills. All colour seemed to have been bleached from the world around him. A procession of trees, bushes and fence posts connected by strings of barbed wire marched past in empty shades of black and grey. After the orange haze of Bogota had disappeared behind him he was left with the impression that he was all alone in the darkness, the last man left alive, careering desperately through a black void. He wondered for a moment what he was doing, what he was going to find when he arrived and whether he would be able to achieve some kind of disruption to Yoposa's plans. Rafael realised he was clinging to this course of action as though it were the only thing that would stop him from drowning, the only choice that remained.

Up ahead the sporadic lights of the village winked into existence on the dark hills to the north. From this distance the concrete bulk of the Temple and its squat, ugly tower were concealed behind the ridge line. The road dipped into a valley and passed through a shadowy stand of trees. Rafael slowed the car looking for an opening. The headlights dipped and lurched as he guided the Landcruiser off the track and in among the trunks, picking his way carefully around the silent black pillars before stopping some distance from the road. The air was heavy with the scent of dead pine needles as he climbed from the car.

Pain lanced through his forehead forcing his eyes to close. He raised both hands to his face, pushing against his brow while he waited for it to subside. The familiar craving swept through him, the voices whispering that he needn't struggle alone and that help wasn't far away. He reached into his pocket and pulled out the small plastic bag that contained the last of his pills. It had been a while since he had taken one now, not since last weekend when he had discovered Frederico's identity and broken into the archive room in the bunker; before he had met Nathalie.

He stared at the bag hanging from his grasp in the shadowy moonlight under the trees. After a long moment his jaw tightened. He had come this far without their help and he wasn't going to give in now. Whatever happened next, for good or ill, he was determined to experience it without the dulling filter of the pills. He felt he owed himself that much. Before he could reconsider he turned away and hurled the pills as far as he could into the dense undergrowth. For good measure he yanked the broken watch off his arm and threw it after the pills. Feeling somehow lighter, he pulled the backpack onto his shoulders and began to jog back towards the track and the village. All was silent apart from the crunch of his feet on the loose ground and the sound of his own ragged breathing, loud in his ears.

It was getting close to midnight by the time the first whitewashed houses came into view and Rafael paused to study the way ahead. His memory of the layout of the village suggested that the track he was on would lead back to the centre before taking him out to where the Temple was located. He stepped forward, senses scanning the gloomy street in front of him for any sign of danger. Swarms of insects gathered at the few widely-spaced street lamps, shimmering in and out of the light like shoals of fish. He wondered briefly if he was being observed from any of the darkened windows all around him and then realised there was very little he could do about it if he was.

Further up the road Rafael could see that the way ahead was blocked. An SUV had been positioned sideways across the lane and he ducked down out of sight behind a parked car. Glancing over the bonnet he saw something move in the shadows next to the car. A moment later the squawk of a radio sounded in the silent street and the silhouette of a man holding an automatic rifle moved forward into the light. Rafael remained motionless holding his breath. The sentry gazed intently along the road, his face lost in shadow under his black baseball cap. After what seemed an eternity the radio squawked again and the man turned away, pacing slowly back to the SUV.

Rafael worked his way back up the street, keeping to the darkness and out of sight. Whatever was happening in Boyerino tonight the Temple were clearly taking no chances. The village was far enough from the main roads that the odds of a casual driver trying to pass through in the middle of the night were low. Even so, it was obviously important enough to justify armed sentries to keep people out and ensure that they were not disturbed. He expected that the guards had been provided with his description and pushed bleakly past the thought of what would probably happen to him if he was discovered.

He had to find a way past the man and get to the Temple. To his left a high wall ran along the street while the houses on the right were separated by narrow alleyways, presumably leading to yards or open space at the back. He darted towards the nearest entry, stepping over the low gate that closed it off. Past the corner of the house a neglected garden stretched out under the moonlight in front of him, the grass and bushes grown wild and scrubby. A path made of uneven concrete slabs led past a gnarled tree with a broken swing hanging from one of its lower branches. The house itself seemed empty with no light showing from anywhere inside. One of the windows at the back had been broken and left un-repaired. The ground sloped gently down away from the house and Rafael followed the path past a series of damaged wire cages that he guessed had once contained chickens or other small animals.

At the end of the garden a track ran along the back of the properties, parallel to the street that was blocked by the man with the gun. The ground here was soft and mud clung to his shoes as he hurried forward. Towering conifer trees shadowed the track and the darkness here was deeper than in the open. Rafael decided against using the flashlight in case other unseen watchers lurked in the night. The screening trees allowed occasional glimpses through into gardens and the backs of other buildings. Most seemed long unoccupied and as run down as the house where he had entered the track. He wondered if the Temple was responsible for the partial abandonment of the village, if Yoposa and his organisation had been involved in forcing the inhabitants to leave. On the other hand, perhaps the people had simply left of their own will, pushed out by the usual worries about security and poverty that had left so much of rural Colombia a desolate wasteland.

Ahead the track ran up to a wooden fence before curving away over open ground. Rafael estimated that he was somewhere near the centre of the village now and following the track further would take him away from where he needed to go. He waited for a moment, listening to the sounds of the night and then jumped up, grabbing the top of the fence with his hands. Grunting with effort, he hauled himself upwards, feet scraping and sliding on the loose, slippery wood. At the top his tired arms gave out and he overbalanced, falling forward into darkness on the other side. He managed to twist round but landed awkwardly on his leg, sprawling to the ground. A stab of pain shot through his ankle and he closed his eyes, willing it to pass.

At the edge of his hearing a soft rustling, slithering noise whispered through the shadows and Rafael jerked his eyes open. A low growling came from somewhere in front on him. Then the night exploded with savage barking and the rapid click of running paws drumming over hard ground. Against the

239

gloom Rafael could see a large brown dog coming straight for where he lay prone on the dry, packed mud. Its lips were pulled back with teeth fixed in a vicious snarl as it sprinted towards him.

For a moment he was frozen in place, unable to move as the distance was eaten up by the animal's bounding strides. Recovering, he scrabbled back towards the fence, putting up an arm to shield his face. Then there was a strangled yelp and the dog jerked upwards and backwards. It had reached the end of the chain that attached its neck to a post sunk into the concrete. His heart beating wildly, Rafael picked himself up, not quite believing his own luck that the dog's teeth were not fixed into his arm. It continued its angry barking, wrenching at the chain as it prowled back and forth at the limit of its reach.

Rafael moved away quickly following the line of the fence. No one had yet come to check what had alarmed the dog but it was clear that this area was not abandoned in contrast to most of what he had seen of the village. A row of tangled, thorny bushes screened away what Rafael supposed was the main building. He could make out a solid shadow against the deeper purple of the night sky and the hint of a roofline through the gently waving leaves. The hard mud underfoot was replaced by a concrete yard and Rafael passed the decaying remains of a rusting tractor. A storage tank to his left gave off a strong chemical smell. The dog had settled down now that he was out of sight. It still let out an occasional sullen bark which was picked up and echoed by the few other dogs nearby in the village before fading into silence.

A ramshackle wooden outbuilding blocked the way forward at the end of the yard. Hanging from nails driven into the planks, a row of machetes caught the rays of the moon and gave off a cold sparkle the colour of ice. As he got closer the night air was permeated by the pungent, ammonia reek of urine and human waste. The shack clearly served as a basic outdoor toilet and Rafael wrinkled his nose as he followed the wall round towards a narrow opening that led between the side of the main building and its immediate neighbour. The glow of street lights could be seen at the end of the passage and as he approached, Rafael became aware of a low buzz, a babble of indistinct, hushed conversation. He crept through the shadowy chasm with his back to the wall, pausing at the edge of the building.

The stonework was cold against his face as he peered carefully round the corner.

Rafael's eyes widened as he took in the scene in front of him. An area of open ground spread out where a number of the village streets converged. In the middle of the space Rafael could see the strange standing stone monument topped with the bronze sphere that he had noticed on his previous visit. Milling about the monument, conversing quietly in twos and threes, groups of shadowy figures paced around or sat on benches. There were about twenty of them in total and each was wearing a striking purple robe with a golden sun device emblazoned on the chest. From the faces he could see, they seemed to be mainly corpulent middle-aged men with dull eyes and hard faces. Lurking in the darkness near the monument he recognised the bulky form of Yoposa's enforcer, Ernesto.

Each of the men carried a rounded, helmet-like object and some of them had begun to put them on, concealing their faces from view. When one of them stepped into the yellowish glow of the street lights Rafael had the surreal experience of seeing that the man's head had been replaced by that of a roaring animal; a jaguar frozen in a stylised expression with its mouth open and teeth bared. As the man passed through the light, Rafael realised that it was in fact a ceremonial metal mask, but whether it was built to conceal the wearer's identity or allow him to take on another was unclear. The effect was both sinister and slightly ridiculous at the same time. He shook his head, wondering at the arcane pageantry of it all.

Looking further round the corner to his right Rafael could see that a trestle table had been set up close to the front of the building. A full-figured, sullen woman wearing a printed dress and a hat pulled down low over her scowling features stood behind the table, serving ceramic bowls filled with some kind of drink that she dipped from a container beside her. The bowls were handed over with a muttered, ritual blessing. Suddenly he understood exactly where he was; alongside the cafe that had been closed last week, looking out at the small plaza with the monument.

Rafael still didn't have a clear idea of what he was going to do next when one of the figures turned abruptly and began to move towards where he was concealed in the alley. The man's jowly face and thick, fleshy neck were covered in a sheen of sweat that glistened in the half-light as he approached. He tossed the bowl he was holding onto the table without a glance at the serving woman, wiping his hand on the purple robe as he headed straight for the dark opening from where Rafael watched. Recalling the unpleasant stench from the outbuilding Rafael was fairly certain of the man's destination.

He retreated up the passage looking for somewhere to hide. The bare concrete space near the outbuilding was virtually empty and offered limited possibilities for concealment. Hefty, lumbering steps echoed off the narrow walls as the man entered the passage. Rafael made a final desperate attempt to get out of sight, pushing himself back into a shadowy corner next to a stone slab that had been propped against the wall. The man was very close now and Rafael could hear his wheezing, laboured breathing just around the corner. A sour, herby smell which must have come from the drink reached his nostrils. Then the man was past him, close-set eyes directed towards the floor, moving steadily towards the building without looking up. Rafael held his breath, willing himself to be invisible, wishing he could melt back into the wall behind him.

A hint of movement flickered through his peripheral vision, drawing his gaze. He watched as slowly, unbelievably, the slab started to move outwards from the wall. While his attention had been fixed on the man, his efforts to crouch down out of sight must have pushed it free. His hand shot out trying to make a desperate grab for the edge but it was far too heavy and slipped past his fingers on its inevitable trajectory towards the floor.

The dull slap resounded like a gunshot in the confined space. The man jolted forward as though he had been struck and whirled round to face the source of the noise. For a second he was too startled to do anything and just stared uncomprehending at Rafael with his dark clothing, frozen in the corner. Then a look of furious anger twisted across his face. His eyes bulged and his lips curled back showing clenched teeth. He snatched one of the wickedly-curved machetes from where it hung on the wall and swung it towards Rafael. Faced with the threat of the blade, Rafael was jarred out of inaction. His reactions were quicker than the bulky, older man's and he ducked in under the clumsy swipe, driving his shoulder into the man's midriff. The man gave a low grunt as the air was knocked out of him. They wrestled for a moment before the man's feet slipped out from under him and they were falling towards the hard ground. There was a sharp crack as the back of the man's head hit the concrete. His eyes rolled upwards and the machete fell from his fingers.

Rafael sat back breathing heavily. A small pool of blood was spreading over the concrete. It was unclear how badly the man was hurt and Rafael was not inclined to linger and find out. The jaguar mask rolled on the floor near his feet. He picked it up, looking into the empty eyeholes. Well, here was an unlooked-for opportunity to get right to the heart of whatever was going on in Boyerino tonight. The risks would be considerable but on balance it seemed worth the gamble. Besides he didn't have a better plan.

Working quickly he stripped off the man's purple robe, careful to avoid the back of his head which was now wet with blood. Underneath he was wearing a dark green suit jacket and an open-necked checked shirt, looking for all the world like a prosperous business man, a member of the oligarchy, spending some well-earned time off at his *finca* in the country. As he bound the man's wrists with a length of frayed electrical cord that he found near the tractor, Rafael noticed another of the heavy, emerald-set gold rings glittering on the little finger of his right hand.

He bundled the man out of sight behind the storage tank and struggled into the robe. The fit was loose and baggy but acceptable. Returning to the alley, he looked out again at the group of bizarrely-dressed figures strolling in the plaza. They were starting to gather near the monument and most of them had their masks on. With a final deep breath, Rafael crammed his own mask over his head and stepped out to join them.

He strode past the woman at the table who didn't give him a second glance. She saw what she was expecting to see and found nothing unusual in the form that moved away from her; even if the build and height were noticeably different from the man who had entered the alley a few minutes before. The narrow eyeholes of the unwieldy mask limited Rafael's visibility to a cramped snapshot of what was immediately in front of him, but he could see he was close to the others now. He shuffled in among the participants as they slowly circled the monument. In the midst of the crowd the sour, herby smell pervaded the air again. It took Rafael a few seconds to work out what it was. Then it came to him. *Chicha*, the homemade fermented maize drink of the Indians and the poor. He supposed that it was all part of the fantasy of connection to an imagined, superior past that these deluded crackpots had constructed for themselves.

As they paced in silence he felt increasingly conspicuous. A growing sense of nervousness rose within him as he looked about. The jaguar-head to his left seemed to be staring straight at him, its dark eyeholes stripping away the layers of his disguise. Had they already worked out he was an imposter? How? What had he done wrong? What subtle sign or action had he missed or performed incorrectly to tip them off? He realised his whole body was tensed, ready to strike the first enemy that came for him, ready to flee with all his strength into the darkness in a desperate bid for freedom.

Just then, when the fear seemed almost unbearable, the masked heads began to turn as one towards the front of the monument and he followed their lead. Ernesto was standing at the front of the crowd with his mask removed, his blocky features seemingly chiseled from stone in the dim light.

"Brothers, it is time," he announced, his rasping voice reverberating through the stillness of the plaza. There was a shuffling and rustling as the jaguar-heads, with Rafael among them, formed a rough line two abreast behind Ernesto. He led them slowly away from the monument and the plaza and into the winding lanes of Boyerino.

Rafael found himself pacing next to another faceless jaguar-man. Looking down he noticed the man's expensive, well-made shoes and wondered if he was walking beside some illustrious dignitary or politician. The metallic masks bobbed up and down in time with the rhythmic steps and Rafael caught a glimpse of another dark SUV that had been moved to one side of the road. A second sentry stood next to the car, his automatic weapon slung on his shoulder. The man bowed his head in a solemn salute as they passed, his fist clenched against his chest, as thought this were some kind of twisted Easter Day parade.

The hulking outline of the Temple loomed out of the darkness ahead, a solid black shape blocking out the stars and the wispy grey clouds of the night sky. An opaque light shone in the narrow spaces of the arched windows, transformed into an ethereal glow by the eerie blue-tinted glass. The effect was as though the building itself was pulsating, like some infernal factory labouring away at a forbidden night shift. As they got closer Rafael could see that the gates in the high metal railing were wide open and the monumental entrance doors to the building had been pulled back. Light spilled out of the cavernous mouth to illuminate the dark streets immediately in front of the Temple. The rich smell of incense floated on the air.

When they crossed the threshold, as though in response to some invisible signal, the jaguar-men started a low, sonorous chanting. The words were beyond Rafael's understanding, a musical mix of sibilant buzzing sounds punctuated by regular, hard plosives. The language had the bearing of an obscure Indian dialect; Chibcha he supposed, recalling Yoposa's discussion of the suppression of the Muisca tongue after the conquest. The frequent vowels that were such a feature of Castilian Spanish were almost entirely absent. Rafael did his best to join in, mumbling low snatches that he hoped sounded convincing, or at least went unnoticed.

The soaring space inside the Temple was filled with the flickering, dancing light of resin-coated wooden torches that had been installed in metal brackets around the walls. Hissing and popping from the burning wood echoed through the gloom, adding a subtle undercurrent to the unearthly chanting. A table draped in a purple cloth had been set up on the raised platform in the centre of the chamber directly beneath the vaulted, elliptical opening where the tower rose into darkness. Rafael pressed forward, concealed among the procession of jaguar-men as they marched into the Temple and assembled around the central platform. He found himself lined up with three of the others in front of a bench, with his back to the entrance doors. The chanting continued, accompanied by a gentle side-to-side swaying.

Rafael had a view of where Ernesto was standing, just to one side of the altar table. The big man raised his hands above his head and clapped twice, the dry slaps cutting through the murmured, rhythmic intonation. All fell silent and simultaneously sat down on the benches. Rafael's eyes were drawn to the raised gallery that ran around the inside of the walls, along which he had been taken to meet with Yoposa in his inner sanctum. Near where he was seated, a broad imposing

245

stairway ran down from the upper level to end close to the edge of the raised platform. He had not noticed it in the shadows on the other side of the hall when Ernesto had marched him across the floor at gunpoint last week.

There was a flurry of movement at the top of the stairs and Gael Yoposa emerged into the dancing light of the torches. He was wearing a shimmering white mantle decorated with swirling designs picked out in golden thread. Gold ornaments had been woven into his long hair. His face was transformed into a fierce rictus with eyes wide open, head tilted back slightly and chin thrust out in front. In his right hand, Yoposa clutched the ornately decorated handle of the unwieldy, hemispherical knife, the sacrificial *tumí*. A simple wooden bowl rested in the upward-facing palm of the other. He paced slowly down the stairs and onto the platform, taking up a position at the centre of the altar.

Yoposa's fiery glare swept round the room, taking in the silent congregation of jaguar-heads staring back at him impassively.

"Welcome my brothers," he declared in his dissonant, fluctuating intonation. "It is with joy in my heart that I look out at you, at the assembly of the twenty elders of the new Muisca nation and all that we represent." Rafael adopted the pose of the man to his immediate left, with his hands on his knees and spine straight, resting against the back of the bench. The weight of the metal mask was beginning to make the muscles of his neck and shoulders ache.

"The twenty of you were selected from among the ranks of our most devoted servants and have been chosen to be a perfect reflection of the sacred Muisca number of twenty, the full number of digits on the human body as brought into being by our holy creator Sué." Glancing round the benches, Rafael suddenly realised that he was the only member of the gathering not wearing one of the conspicuous emerald rings that he had seen on the finger of the man whose robes he had taken. He shifted his right hand to conceal it under his thigh.

"I am proud of what our society represents," Yoposa continued, moving his hands as he spoke. "Proud of what we have built in this place where before there was nothing. Proud of what we have done to re-establish the influence of our noble, glorious culture in its eternal, ancestral and rightful homeland."

He paused, looking down at where the knife and bowl rested on the altar table. "I am also proud and thankful for the ceremony we will conduct here tonight and the honour it will bring to our beloved Sué."

As Yoposa stopped talking, Rafael became aware of a scraping, shuffling sound growing louder in the darkness near the walls. Then, from a recessed doorway directly opposite the grand staircase down which Yoposa had made his entrance, two contrasting forms stepped out into the circle of light near the altar. The first was tall and muscular, dressed in the high-buttoned, white jacket of a hospital orderly. It took Rafael several seconds to recall where he had seen the man's wide nose and angular features before, but then he realised he was looking at Ramirez, the muscular guard who had escorted him from the clinic after Carolina Florez had interrupted his meeting with Doctor Oliviera.

Ramirez was clutching the other figure by the upper arm, almost dragging the person towards where the spectators waited silently. Rafael closed his eyes under the mask, as he recognised the face of Beatriz Espinosa, the mobile phone lady whose photo he had seen in the file at the clinic earlier that evening. She stumbled and tripped, seemingly unaware of her surroundings or what was going on around her. Her hair was dishevelled and her eyes blinking and unfocused as she leaned heavily against Ramirez and peered groggily around the temple.

Yoposa turned towards them and raised both arms above his head.

"O great Sué," he intoned, an expression of savage ecstasy taking over his face, as he turned it upwards towards the ceiling. "By the powers I possess as the living representation of Idacansas, the greatest of the Muisca prophets and priests, I decree that you have been granted the honour of being sent to join with Sué, in accordance with the ritual practices set down in our laws and traditions." Beatriz looked bemused as this bizarre pronouncement was made.

"Where's my phone?" she squawked. "I'm expecting an important call."

There was a muted, metallic clash which seemed to come from outside. As the sound died away, Rafael watched the colossal doors at the back of the temple jerk smoothly open. A line of wooden torches lit up the ground outside, fixed onto long stakes that had been driven into the earth. By their wavering light Rafael could make out the paved area at the back of the temple and the vague, shadowy outline of the wooden hut structure at the far end of the path. Yoposa gestured and the Jaguar-men, with Rafael among them, stood again. He led them out into the cool night air to take up positions around the circular court in the middle of the grounds. Four more attendants, naked to the waist and well-muscled, stepped forward from the shadowed colonnade of the hut. Their faces were hidden behind stylised sun masks and each of them clutched a long wooden spear with a glimmering, golden spike at the end.

From where he was standing Rafael could see the two circular stone slabs that he had noted at his last visit. This time, near the spot where the two stones almost touched, a curious framework had been constructed over the paved area. Three tall cross-beams had been set up to lean against each other and lashed together at the top. From the place where they intersected a short length of chain connected the frame to another pole that hung free over the stones. The hanging pole was about the height of a person, or slightly taller. Rafael's eyes were drawn to the end which had been tapered to a point. Underneath it, as he knew it would be, rested a deep-red clay vessel shaped like a reclining man. The face leered up at him in the gloom and the stick-thin arms clutched the swollen belly around a wide black hole that had been positioned directly underneath, to catch the blood of the sacrifice as it dripped down.

Yoposa gazed round the audience, his eyes shining.

"Brothers," he began again, his voice catching slightly from prolonged use. "We have established the perfect location for our gift. It is here, mid-way between our recreation of the ancient Temple of Sué as it appeared in the days of our ancestors and the church we have built to re-establish His holy reign on this earth." He raised his face to the sky. "Mighty Sué, we bring you this offering under the light of Chía, your holy wife-moon. Accept our sacrifice of human blood and life essence, which will be poured out for your greater glory and satisfaction."

The unseen gong clashed again and Ramirez pulled his captive forward into the open space formed by the circle of jaguar-men. Rafael found himself powerless, rooted to the spot, watching with horrified fascination as Beatriz was led passively towards the waiting sacrificial framework. He tried desperately to think how he could intervene to prevent the horrific torture and death that he was certain was about to be inflicted. Steeling himself, he prepared to step forward and do something, anything to disrupt the inevitable sequence of events that would start with the thrusts of the golden spears and end with a final downward slice of the *tumi*.

At the moment he was ready to act, the faint but unmistakable rattle of automatic weapons drifted through the night air. There was silence for a few seconds and then it sounded again, closer this time, before it was consumed into the distant whine of police sirens. The jaguar-heads started to shift and turn towards each other. A nervous murmur began to make its way round the circle. Yoposa raised a calming hand and all eyes were drawn towards him.

"Brothers," he called out. "The agents of the false government are coming for us. We knew this day would come but sadly it seems that it has arrived sooner than we thought and we must leave our work here unfinished." He nodded at Ramirez, who promptly led Beatriz, still swaying and weaving, away into the darkness. "We have made our preparations. Now, it is time to leave. You know what to do." He turned away and marched towards the wooden hut. The sun-masked attendants fell into step around him and Ernesto followed a short distance behind.

Rafael couldn't quite believe what was happening but he pushed in among the other jaguar-men as they fled back towards the entrance and out into the night. He caught a final glimpse of the deserted temple grounds as he was bustled away, with the sacrificial pole swinging gently in the breeze above the stones. Outside, his anonymous companions scattered in different directions, quickly leaving Rafael alone on the dark street. The clatter of gunshots seemed to intensify behind him as he passed through the plaza, jogging now to escape Boyerino as quickly as possible. He tossed the robe and the mask into the bushes as he made his way back to the car.

**

249

26. Veintiséis

The sun was coming up by the time Rafael got back to the city, a dull red ball hanging over the blanket of grey smog that clung to the densely packed buildings and streets. Jorge had phoned him on the drive from Boyerino.

"What the hell happened, Jorge? What was that all about?" he had demanded frantically, one hand on the wheel.

It transpired that his friend had called in some favours and managed to cajole the recalcitrant *commandante* Azuero to agree to the exploratory deployment of a small task force of *Policia Nacional* to Boyerino on the strength of Jorge's concerns. Riding in the second car of the four-car unit, Jorge had been with them as the convey came into the village. The stone-faced professionals of the police tactical unit had proved to be more than a match for the thinly-stretched sentries and they had quickly secured the area, mopping up the sporadic resistance.

"It wasn't enough though, Rafael." Jorge's voice sounded weary and disappointed. "We took out a few of the guards but we got nothing conclusive. Whoever might have been there, they'd all melted away into the night. By the time we reached the Temple it was empty. We found the lady wandering the streets. She doesn't remember anything and it seems she isn't very coherent at the best of times. I'm sorry Rafael, there's not much more I can do."

A dull, thumping ache had started in his temples as the frustration and fatigue threatened to overwhelm him. He'd just had time to say goodbye to Jorge before the battery on the phone died.

The panorama of the vast cityscape stretched out below him, the rumble of the traffic audible even from this distance, a constant, never-ending beat. His mind wandered, turning the road in front of him to a blur, as he tried to determine what courses of action remained open to him. He passed a goat chewing pensively in the litter at the side of the kerb as he came down from the mountains. An overloaded lorry was grinding up the slope in the other direction, belching out great clouds of black smoke and dust. It was clear that these people would not stop until he was dead and he clutched desperately to his determination to put an end to this investigation, before it ended him.

The transition into Bogota from the east was always a somewhat jarring experience. One moment the mountainous roadside was bordered by open space, trees and grass. Then, round the next bend decaying shacks lined the street again and people crowded in from all directions. Two viable strands remained to the investigation as Rafael saw it. Everyone else who had been sucked into its insidious grip was either dead, run to ground or beyond reach. One was unknowable and uncontrollable. The other was a remote chance but at least it remained within his power to try to do something about it.

Grey clouds were rising up from the west and the sun began to fade away like a bar of soap dissolving into dirty water. The rain had started by the time he drove up into the twisting streets of Suba, a steady, insistent drizzle that soaked into everything and washed away the patina of dust and grit that coated cars and shops. Forests of umbrellas sprouted on the sidewalks and people in brightly-coloured raincoats splashed through the puddles. As Rafael slipped into the yard behind the tejo club, he could see that the owner was taking a delivery. The main entrance had been blocked by a mud-spattered truck and the driver was busy unloading the cargo, wrestling with wet crates of beer bottles and slippery steel barrels. The canvas side curtains were pulled back revealing further precarious stacks of cases and packages crammed into every available inch of the space.

Rafael's approach caused the surly proprietor to look up from the damp sheet of paper he was using to check off the items on his order. The stale smell of spilled beer and old cigarette smoke reeked off the man's clothes. He nodded when Rafael showed him the faded photo of Oliviera that he had taken from the case file.

"Yeah, I recognise that guy. Who wants to know anyway?" Without his *Fiscalia* credentials Rafael was forced to resort to more expensive means to get the information he sought. He pulled out a couple of fifty thousand peso bills and pressed them into the man's grubby outstretched palm. "Your friend used to be one of the regulars. Some kind of doctor over at that clinic up in the hills. That's what I heard." The man folded the money and stuffed it into his shirt pocket.

"I really need to talk to him." Rafael turned his pale stare on the man's blotchy face. "I don't suppose you know where he is right now?"

"He doesn't come in here any more, at least he hasn't done for a while now." Rafael held up another fifty thousand. A hungry glint flickered momentarily over the man's s beady eyes as he considered what to say. His thin hair was plastered to his forehead with the rain. "I heard one of the guys in our tejo team saw him over in the park that runs alongside the Tibabuyes lake." He snatched the money and secreted it away with the rest. "It's where you go when you need a fix in this neighbourhood. But look, I can sort you out here without all that hassle if that's what you want." Rafael shook his head and stepped away, returning quickly to the rainy streets.

The lake wasn't far so he decided to walk. After a couple of blocks the road petered out. The tarmac ran right up to a high chainlink fence and stopped. A gate had been let into the fence and a dirt track continued on the other side, disappearing into tall grasses, scrubby bushes and trees made hazy in the drizzle. Ramshackle houses were packed into the space in front of the fence with unfinished top floors hanging out over the wetland itself. On the ground, a broken padlock and a length of chain lay abandoned next to the entrance. Further up the street, a rusty blue pickup truck drove slowly past in the spray. A pale face watched him from a ground floor window.

With a final look around, Rafael pushed through the gate and plunged into the expanse of open ground. The sounds of the city seemed to fade away quickly as though the fence marked off the boundary to a mysterious world that was somehow cut off from the sprawling urban landscape all around it. A yellow panel next to the path ahead explained that he was in a *Parque Ecologico* and made all sorts of wild promises about the rare and unique animals that he might be lucky enough to encounter, ranging from frogs and snakes to guinea pigs and birds. Much of the writing had been overpainted by jagged gang signs and a heap of abandoned construction material had been left to one side.   After a short walk, during which he saw no-one, he arrived at a flimsy wooden footbridge, really just a couple of planks thrown down over the shrunken ditch that held the brownish trickle of the Arzobispo river.

On his right, the surface of the lake emerged from behind a stand of stunted trees.   The water was slate grey and dappled with rain spots.   The piercing cry of a water bird reverberated through the haze.   A few seconds later Rafael saw the unfortunate creature wading its way through a mass of plastic bags and bottles.   The park was on the southern shore and now that he had crossed the bridge he could see that the path alongside the lake was picked out in red brick paving.   The grass was cut short and wiry palm trees had been planted at regular intervals along its length.   Shifty figures loitered in the tenuous shelter provided by the dripping fronds or gathered half-concealed in the bushes, following his progress across the park with darting, furtive glances before turning back to their dubious business.   He showed a few of them the photo and handed over some more money, getting occasional nods and muttered comments for his efforts.   Finally, a gaunt, emaciated man, his   face almost lost in the covering of his shapeless hooded top, pointed Rafael in the direction of a wrecked children's playground.

In among the broken climbing frames and empty swings, Oliviera was slumped on a bench like a misshapen sack of refuse.   He started to his feet as Rafael approached, shuffling quickly in the opposite direction, away from the investigator.

"Wait Oliviera! We need to talk," he called out, the words unnaturally loud in the drizzly stillness. The doctor seemed not to hear and hurried on with his head down. He passed behind a screen of hedges surrounding the playground and Rafael lost sight of him.   Covering the distance swiftly, Rafael jogged to the corner where the doctor had disappeared.   He glanced left and right, peering through the pale curtain of limply falling rain. The ungainly figure of the doctor was hastening across a stretch of barren carpark towards a complex of low-rise apartment buildings. Rafael started after him again, desperate to close the gap. His fear that one of his only remaining contacts was about to disappear into the chaotic maze of Bogota streets was almost palpable and spurred him on.

Panic flitted across Oliviera's face when Rafael caught up to him, clutching at his shoulder to spin him round. His eyes went wide and he brought up a hand to protect himself.

"Don't hurt me," he cringed. "I didn't tell them anything. I've got nothing left to take."

"Doctor, it's me. It's Rafael Alvarez. I need your help."

"I thought you were dead," said the doctor, peering sceptically at Rafael. "Everyone else seems to be dead." A bark of inane laughter escaped his waxy lips. Rafael could smell the alcohol on the doctor's breath. He imagined he made an intimidating sight in his torn and mud-stained black clothing.

"We never finished, at the clinic, when I came to see you last week," he said, studying the doctor's face, his sharp eyes intense. "You were almost ready to tell me something. You need to tell me now." The doctor looked back at him vacantly, swaying slightly and blinking in confusion. He flinched when Rafael reached into his pocket for some money. "Come on man. Let me get you some breakfast."

As they walked Rafael caught sight of his own haggard reflection in the window of a parked car. Black lines were carved deep under his eyes and his pale complexion was darkened by beard shadow. He looked almost as dishevelled as the doctor.

A selection of colourful food trailers had pitched up in a bleak corner of the carpark, the owners looking more hopeful than prosperous in the damp morning air. The doctor weaved his way towards a battered cart decorated with a smiling cartoon Mexican in an exaggerated sombrero hat. Rafael handed over some coins and two lukewarm foil parcels were passed down from the serving hatch.

Clutching the soggy tortilla, Rafael followed the doctor away from the carpark towards a scrubby area which had been designated for the construction of more apartments. Oversized advertising panels depicted perfect families living happy, fulfilled lives in flawless, sunlit surroundings. Rafael and Oliviera sat side by side on a rusty metal drum that had been laid lengthways in the bristly grass. The food seemed to sober Oliviera up, to the point where his responses became more coherent than single syllable grunts or laughter, so Rafael tried to probe him again.

"I know you don't work at the clinic any more," he began as the doctor wolfed down the last of the burrito. "I was there last night and I saw what was left of your office. I was in Florez's office too and I found her file on Beatriz Espinosa." Oliviera remained silent and fiddled absently with his food wrapper. "Okay, let's try something different. I'll talk and you tell me if what I'm saying is true or false."

Rafael rubbed a hand over his forehead, closing his eyes for a moment before speaking again.

"You got kicked out of the clinic the day after I came to see you there. Florez knew who I was and she threatened to reveal your past if you tried to go against her." The doctor blinked and looked down at this hands. "You knew Frederico Fernandez. He checked himself into the clinic to investigate the links with the missing artefacts from the Museum of Culture and Heritage. After Florez and Yoposa found out about him, you helped keep him sedated and locked up in the secure wing while they decided what to do with him."

Oliviera's shoulders slumped. He nodded gently, his mouth twisting into a bitter pout of self-disgust.

"Yoposa owns the clinic," Rafael continued. "There are plenty of patients that no-one will miss and that are too crazy to understand what's going on. Florez chooses them and Yoposa gets to kill them at one of his deranged ceremonies at the Temple, to keep his pack of faithful maniacs happy. But that's not all; after they're dead their organs are removed and sold on to the highest bidder on the black market. It's a tidy little arrangement that works for everyone and keeps the cash flowing in."

The doctor jerked to his feet, leaving the packaging from the food to fall to the ground as he paced away over the damp grass. Rafael was left non-plussed for a moment then briskly rose to follow him, lengthening his stride to keep pace alongside the taller man as they approached a gently curving back road.

"All of what you said is true, but you'll never be able to prove any of it," the doctor said, his voice little more than a whisper. "I worked for them. I helped them cut out the organs and get rid of the bodies. So many now I'm afraid I've lost count."

"But Frederico wasn't mad. He figured out what was going on and they had to get rid of him quickly because people would have listened to him and believed him. Jesus! I've seen with my own eyes what they were going to do to Beatriz, what they did to Frederico. These people are insane. They have to be stopped."

"You can't stop them Rafael." Oliviera's eyes were dead and flat as they paced along.

Concrete fence posts marched along their right hand side. The tops had been slanted to lean over the street and strands of barbed wire had been strung between them.

"It was you, wasn't it?" said Rafael glancing sideways at the doctor. "You sent the note to the *Fiscalia* that led me to Frederico." Oliviera nodded, his gaze fixed on the ground. The road had not yet been covered with tarmac and rainwater pooled and flooded across its broken surface, gathering in wide yellow puddles.

"Did you ever ask yourself how Frederico's remains came to be found on Monserrate?" the doctor asked as they stepped around a pile of loose bricks and concrete slabs that had been left in the middle of the path.

"Yes. His body was in a case that was stolen by a gang of *Rateros*."

"But stolen from where Rafael? They couldn't get rid of the bodies at the clinic; the risk was too great. After I removed the organs, what was left was always taken away. Before you ask, it was a part of the operation with which I had no involvement. However, if you can find an answer to my question, you might stand a chance of uncovering something unequivocal and ending this nightmare once and for all."

The backstreet had led them out onto a major road junction. Rafael didn't recognise the spot but guessed they were probably somewhere along Calle Ochenta. The path was sloping gently upwards now, leading onto a footbridge over the traffic. Ragged canvas shelters had been set up along the approach, to shield the cluster of street vendors who hawked their wares to the passing pedestrians. A sullen young man stood smoking a cigarette next to a cart submerged under crisps and soft drinks. To one side a wooden panel had been set up, covered rather optimistically in cheap plastic sunglasses.

"You don't owe them anything doctor," Rafael said shaking his head. "They're going to come for you just like they did for Ignacio Perez." He made a grab for the doctor's forearm.

"You've got to come with me. I can protect you from them."
The doctor gave a bitter laugh, shaking him off. They were at
the centre of the bridge now. Cars roared past on the motorway
below, kicking up billowing clouds of spray. Oliviera had
stopped pacing and turned to face Rafael.

"I know you can't protect me Rafael. No one can." A fixed
look came over the doctor's face. His jaw tightened and his
eyes went hard. Before Rafael could react, he grabbed the
painted yellow handrail and vaulted over the barrier to balance
precariously on the ledge above the speeding streams of traffic.

"You're right," the doctor roared over the booming stream of
cars below. "I do need to get out, but I'm doing it on my own
terms. This is my exit. Goodbye."

"Come on Juan. Don't do this," Rafael pleaded, taking a
step towards him. Too late. He rushed to the edge of the bridge
just as the doctor let go of the rail and toppled forward into the
void. He was caught in mid-flight by a monstrous juggernaut
loaded down with shapeless black sacks. A red spray tinged the
mist and the stream of vehicles skidded to a messy, juddering
halt. A symphony of horns and shouting rose up from the
roadway below. Rafael watched for a moment, numb as people
clustered round the shredded remains of Oliviera, then he turned
away with a hopeless emptiness gnawing at his insides.

**

257

27. Veintisiete

The ponderous shape of the airplane dropped from the dirty clouds like a giant, ungainly seagull. Its landing wheels were splayed out underneath and the running lights blinked out a compulsive rhythm as it hurtled towards the unseen runway to the north. The shrieking roar of the engines broke over Rafael like a wave as he trudged along the drab, nearly-empty streets of Fontibon. His time living near the airport had long since inured him to the noise of the low-flying planes and the thunderous wail with its shrill insistent pitch washed over him unnoticed.

Hunched over, with hands shoved deep into his pockets, he barely perceived the houses passing on either side. His mind was empty, a blank void, submerged with fatigue. The only impulse keeping him moving was the basic need to get home, have a shower, change clothes and then sleep. The rain had stopped but the sky remained low and grey. The pavement was covered with a slick greasy sheen.

He had been forced to park the Landcruiser up on the kerb some distance from his apartment. The nearby roads had been closed off for resurfacing work, a rare enough occurrence in Bogota where streets could remain unpaved or un-repaired for months or even years. It was widely known that an impenetrable system of kickbacks and facilitation payments determined the allocation of public works contracts, under the auspices of INVIAS, the Transport Ministry's inscrutable National Roads Agency.

The results were often surprising and inconsistent, this site being a case in point. Red and white barriers closed off the roads for several blocks around and various pieces of lumbering construction equipment had been hauled into place, but there were no workers visible anywhere. The sole and slightly baffling exception was a single operative who had taken up station at the street corner, bundled up in a reflective vest with a clam-like hard hat jammed down low on his head. His job was to hold up an octagonal sign that read *'Pare'*, as though anyone masochistic enough to try and drive near the byzantine tangle of the roadworks needed a reminder to stop.

Rafael shook his head in disgust as he stepped up to the front door, groping in the backpack for his keys. The whirr of power tools came from behind the folding metal panels closing off the garage on the ground floor. His neighbour was busy working on a car and Rafael caught brief snatches of pulsing accordion *vallenato* music coming from the radio in the intervals when the tools paused.

The air inside the narrow passage and up the stairs was damp and smelled of raw onions and old cooking oil. A faint patch of brown mould had sprung up in the corner of the ceiling near his apartment door. He stared at the black panelled wood for a long moment as though trying to remember what to do next before reaching out with his key to unfasten the lock.

The familiar perspective of the hallway greeted him as the door swung open. He advanced over the threshold, struggling out of the stained jacket before letting it drop to the floor. Unbidden, a vivid image of the doctor's torso disintegrating under the impact of the truck forced its way into his consciousness. It was just the latest in the series of violent, traumatic incidents Rafael had experienced since he'd stood next to the case on the desolate path to Monserrate. The murder of Ignacio Perez, gunned down at the university, the attack by the unknown assailant in Frederico's apartment, the fear of being discovered while witnessing the bizarre ceremony at the Temple in Boyerino. Suddenly the images, the death, the violence, the tension all crowded in on him at the same time, threatening to overwhelm him.

He fell to one knee. An uncontrollable shaking started in his shoulders and quickly spread to the rest of his body. He covered his face with his hands as a deep, wrenching sob escaped him. How had it come to this? Where had he lost sight of his plans to leave all this madness behind? In his stubbornness to prove that he was capable of solving the puzzle of Frederico's murder he'd unleashed a torrent of savagery and carnage. What had he been thinking trying to take on an organisation backed by the deep-seated, insidious power of the Bogota oligarchy? Why hadn't he listened to Ortega and just gone through the motions to close the case quietly? Well it was too late now. He'd run out of moves to make and the only choice left for him was to sit around waiting for the Temple's *sicarios* to come and kill him too.

For a moment he felt like he couldn't breathe. His limbs were impossibly light and he thought he was going to pass out. Then he forced himself to concentrate on a single moment at a time, taking in deep lungfuls of air. His composure returned slowly and he wiped his face as the last of the panic subsided. The inside of his mouth felt dry and sticky so he turned to the kitchen eager, for a glass of water. Pushing aside the partially shut door he stepped inside without really paying attention to what he was doing. He looked around absently, his mind on calling Jorge later that afternoon, following some much needed sleep.

He froze in place with his hand stretched halfway to one of the uneven cabinets as his tired brain tried to absorb the scene in front of him. The windowpane next to the sink had been broken inwards and jagged shards of glass were strewn across the tiled floor. Through the open frame he had a clear view out over the flat roof above the garage with its mysterious clusters of aerials and cables. A muffled thump came from the direction of the lounge at the other end of the passageway, making him start. Fear rose in his throat like vomit. So this was it. They had found him already. He should have known it was too much of a risk to return home after seeing the surveillance photos at the clinic.

Squaring his shoulders and raising his chin, he felt an unexpected reserve of rage flow from somewhere deep inside, outstripping the terror and fatigue. He reached for the handle of the pistol that still rested in the waistband at the back of his trousers and slipped back into the hallway, moving silently on the balls of his feet. Whatever was waiting for him in the lounge he vowed to make a fight of it. They would regret the brazenness with which they had broken into his home without even bothered to conceal their presence. He refused to be snuffed out with such casual, dismissive contempt.

The wooden floor creaked under his feet as he crept along. A shuffling sound came from inside the room in front of him. Rafael's heart was pulsing and his chest was tight as he reached the door. The gun was a dead weight in his hand, sweat from his palm slick against the grip. All in one motion he lifted his foot and struck the door in the middle, swinging the barrel of the gun into the room as he plunged through the opening.

A startled, fragile young man was cowering in the corner, his hands outstretched in front of his thin, wiry frame as he backed away. His anxious hazel eyes were frozen open in fear and his narrow, pinched features were pale and fixed. He flinched away instinctively from the levelled muzzle of the pistol, disturbing a low stack of boxes that had been piled up next to the sofa. The topmost one slid forward, spilling its jumbled contents across the floor between the two of them. A wave of papers, old photos and bric-a-brac spread out near their feet. The dull bronze and green ribbon of Rafael's *Orden de Estrella* medal was shuffled in among the debris.

The youth and the man stared at each other in mutual incomprehension for several heartbeats before Rafael lowered the gun, pointing the barrel to one side.

"Jesus! Paulito, is that you? You shared the shit out of me! What the hell are you doing here?" The slender young man dropped his gaze to the floor and gave a half shrug.

"I didn't know where else to go," he muttered in a quiet, lost voice. As he recovered his composure, Rafael started to appreciate the unexpected measure of good fortune that he'd suddenly been dealt. He moved across the room, inclining his head to look the boy in the eyes and placing a hand on his scrawny shoulder.

"You're in exactly the right place *muchacho*," he declared, a broad grin spreading over his face. "You can't imagine how pleased I am to see you again." Paulito was filthy and bedraggled to the point where he would stand out even in a rundown neighbourhood like Fontibon. The black and purple stains of old bruises and cuts criss-crossed his pale face. Rafael settled him on the sofa and went back to the kitchen to hunt for some food. Between mouthfuls of cold chicken and rice served out of a tinfoil takeaway container, Paulito told Rafael what had befallen him and his brother.

The big man with the tattoo on his hand, who Rafael now knew was Ernesto had continued to pursue them relentlessly across Ciudad Bolivar. He seemed to be one step behind them at every turn, running them to ground like a shark scenting blood. Every refuge they reached, every place they stayed, everyone who sheltered them, it seemed it was only a matter of time before they were discovered and had to run for their lives again. The big man had been helped by another; a stocky man with a close-cropped beard. Sometimes they had been together, sometimes alone but Paulito was sure that the bearded man had connections to the police. From the descriptions Paulito gave, Rafael was certain he was talking about Antonio Saloman. He told Paulito as much, letting the youth know that Saloman would not be in a position to trouble him again. Paulito nodded, a tight smile playing across his thin lips as he continued with his story.

One day near the end of last week, the Barraca brothers had run out of luck. Ernesto had cornered them at one of the half-finished abandoned shacks that clustered along the winding, broken lanes of Mirador El Paraiso, not far from where the canyon gouged its way through the rugged, dry ground at the edge of the city. He had stalked in upon them unaware, while they were both sleeping, having finally succumbed to exhaustion from the constant running and hiding. Passed out in a corner, huddled under some plastic sheeting, they had not realised the danger until it was too late. Ernesto had kicked them awake and then knocked Ruben senseless with the butt of his gun while Paulito watched helpless.

Their hands had been fastened with plastic cable ties and then the questioning had begun.

"Why did you steal my case? How did you know I would be there? Who put you up to it?" Ernesto's demands had been insistent and repetitive, with little attention paid to the answers, as though the point was purely to wear them down, to get them accustomed to giving a response of some kind, even if they all knew that nothing said was of any practical use or value. As Ernesto continued, with intermittent interruptions for further beatings and threats, the focus had shifted noticeably towards the *Fiscalia*.

"More than anything he wanted to know if we'd had any contact with you," Paulito continued, his voice a low, dejected whisper in the tatty living room. "He had a photo of you, that he held in front of my face as he asked his questions. How did we know you? What had we said to you? When were we going to see you again? There was a point where I was sure we were both going to die."

262

Paulito leaned forward over his knees and wrapped his arms around himself.

"I remember Ruben turned to look at me as we knelt there in that empty hut and then he launched himself at our captor. There wasn't much he could do with his hands tied but he managed to knock the guy over. I knew I wouldn't get another chance so I ran while they were wrestling on the ground. That was the last time I saw him." Paulito hung his head, staring intently at the threadbare carpet. "He's dead. I know that. You don't need to tell me. If he'd managed to escape he would have found a way to get back to me again." Rafael gave a slight nod.

"I saw what that animal did to him. There was nothing you could have done Paulito." The young man's jaw tightened and he nodded in return, his hazel eyes momentarily clouded by a damp sheen. He shook his head and turned to look at Rafael again.

"But I don't understand. What were they so worried I would tell you about? What is it that I'm supposed to know?"

"It all started with that suitcase the three of you took. All the lies, all the deception, all the killing. Everything comes from that moment. I want you to think back; tell me everything you can remember. It might be our only way out of this."

"I wish I'd never seen that fucking case!" Paulito raged suddenly as his voice cracked and tears rolled down his cheeks. Rafael was suddenly stuck by how young Paulito really was, not much more than twelve or thirteen at the most, and how much suffering he'd had to endure. The lines of it were graved deep into his smooth face and his eyes had a dark, haunted look. He put a hand on the boy's shoulder again, until the crying subsided.

"These are bad men Paulito. They've killed a lot of people and they're going to carry on doing it unless we can find a way to stop them." Paulito sniffed and stood up, shaking off his sorrow like a dog.

"Alright, let's get these assholes," he declared. "They deserve to pay for what they did to my brother."

Pacing back and forth in Rafael's living room, blurting out the details as they came into his head, Paulito recalled the night of the robbery, while the investigator sat silent and still, listening intently on the sofa. He told how together with Angel and Ruben he had headed to the Candelaria with some *burundunga* powder and a half baked plan to rob some tourists. How they had seen Ernesto with the case and decided to target him. How Ernesto had resisted the effects of the powder and Angel had been stabbed in the struggle. Finally, how Ruben and Paulito had been forced to run for their lives with the case, leaving their friend behind in the alley.

"But where, Paulito? Where did this all happen?" Rafael insisted thinking back to his last conversation with the doctor.

"I'm not sure. Somewhere near the edge of the Candelaria, south of Calle Seis. We were at the back of a restaurant. There was a shop. They came out of it. It was dark and we had to run."

"Come on Paulito. Think deeper. What about the shop? There must be something you remember." The youth closed his eyes and his forehead creased with concentration.

"Some kind of jewellery store. Something about emeralds." He blinked and turned his face towards Rafael again. "That's all I know man, I swear." Rafael hoped it would prove to be enough.

**

28. Veintiocho

Stepping out onto the grey expanse of Plaza Bolivar, Rafael was faced with an unexpected, almost dizzying perspective opening up through the tight grid of teeming streets. The church of Monserrate seemed to float above the mass of jumbled buildings in the early afternoon haze like the shimmering form of a mirage. It hovered disconcertingly over the opposite corner of the square, almost bisecting the space between the honey-coloured *Palacio de Justicia* with its rigid, precise angles and lines and the dirtier but more ornate *Catedral Primada*.

Fatigue had made Rafael whimsical and discontented and he found himself thinking that the wispy, insubstantial image of the church was a perfect emblem for the shifting dreams and fixations of the groaning city below.

The bleak, windswept altiplano seemed to be awash with an unstable series of obsessions and passing infatuations that had successively afflicted the people who had chosen to make their homes here. The Muisca, with their narrow world heavily populated by esoteric gods and demons, had believed themselves to be the unquestioned centre of the universe, only to have their world ripped down around them by the arriving Europeans. The Conquistadores in turn had been gripped by an insatiable desire for gold and had never been able to free themselves of the compulsion to continue searching for the mythical golden city of El Dorado.

Simón Bolívar had shaken off the grip of the Spanish empire only to see his own dreams of building a Gran Colombia, unified with Ecuador, Panama and his Venezuelan homeland, shattered in turn. The shadowy members of the Bogota oligarchy continued to delude themselves that a territory as fractured and diverse as Colombia could be micromanaged from behind the steel gates of their high-security compounds and apartment complexes, while all around them the fabric of the country continued to unravel in a spiral of violence and death.

The city itself seemed to be founded on a bedrock of delusions, with lies and half-truths pervading every fibre of its being. He supposed his own set of delusions were no less absurd. That there was some meaningful way to fight the forces ranged against him and that he was capable of finding a small measure of justice for Frederico's killing. But like all delusions its pull was irresistible. Clear sightedness was no defence. Knowing it was unreal didn't prevent the compulsion to strive towards it, in the hope that this time, maybe this time it would prove to be true.

Rafael turned away from the translucent church resting atop its gauzy green mountain, where just over two weeks ago the mutilated torso in the case had set this whole tumultuous train of events in motion. His own fixation was calling out to him again with its siren tones and he found himself ready, almost eager to continue the pursuit, wherever it might decide to lead him this time.

He followed the streets, working through the grid, moving south past the Congress building and the elegant wrought-iron gates of the *Casa de Nariño* where the president huddled away behind his guards, spouting empty platitudes about winning the war.

Rather than take the car into the maze of narrow, one-way lanes at the centre of the city, Rafael had opted to ride the Transmilenio. Getting off, he had pushed his way through the crowds of distracted afternoon commuters at the angular, grey pavilion of the Avenida Jimenez station and walked the short distance to Plaza Bolivar.

Rafael had been happy to leave Paulito in the apartment. There was nothing worth stealing and from Paulito's perspective it was certainly preferable to running and hiding on the street.

"Stay here. Lock the door and don't open it for anyone apart from me," he had instructed as he left. Paulito had nodded mutely in response and returned to the lounge to devour what was left of the chicken and rice.

A shower and a change of clothes had refreshed him but the grinding tiredness remained, like a shadow behind his eyes, clutching his brain in its numbing grip. As he moved south towards where the broad band of *Calle Seis* snaked through the Candelaria's rigid grid pattern like a lost river bursting its banks, the character of the structures began to change. The gentrified colonial-era buildings with second-floor balconies and full-length windows became interspersed with decrepit single-storey houses, their chipped and peeling plaster facades written over with graffiti tags. Imposing government buildings and graceful, pillar-fronted museums were replaced with decaying grocery stores and vacant lots strewn with rubbish.

The afternoon began to draw towards early evening and Rafael still hadn't found what he was looking for. Shadows lengthened in the narrow street. A scrawny dog raised its head from investigating the corner of a filthy doorway to stare at Rafael with blank indifference as he passed.

From a building up ahead a green awning thrust out over the pavement, undulating gently in the light breeze. Picked out on the faded cloth in sloping white letters were the words *comidas rapidas y jugos naturales*. Rafael was sure he was close to the area Paulito had described, but as yet there was no sign of anything matching the jewellery shop the young man had talked about. The run-down streets around him looked like an unlikely location for selling anything of value. Besides, the main centre of the emerald trade in Bogota was several kilometres north, around the San Victorino market.

He shook his head in frustration as he stepped out onto the road to move round a pile of broken furniture that had been left on the pavement. There was a sharp, insistent beep from behind him and Rafael jumped backwards as a moped swerved past him, almost overbalancing under the weight of the formless plastic-wrapped bundles that were piled high in the space behind the rider.

The moped pulled up onto the pavement under the green awning. He watched as the driver dismounted, untied the cable securing the bundles to the back of his bike and began to ferry them through the door of the cafe. A sign fixed across a window revealed the name of the place to be *El Rinconito Paisa*.

Rafael's stomach growled and he suddenly realised that the last thing he had eaten had been the flimsy tortilla that he had shared with Doctor Oliviera. He blinked away a momentary image of the man's gruesome suicide and strode towards the restaurant. The moped rider glared at him from inside his helmet as he approached, as though expecting some kind of confrontation for the near-miss. Instead, Rafael walked past him and down the short flight of stairs that led into the restaurant.

A few widely-spaced windows were set high up around the room, screened off behind dirty lace curtains. The walls had been inexpertly panelled in dark-painted wood which had also been shaped into a series of irregular booths and nooks. Gaps showed between the planks revealing the bare concrete underneath.

Faded photos had been nailed up in the booths and behind the bar depicting traditional Colombian *Fincas* set in the rolling, wooded hills of Anitoquia. Random trinkets and souvenirs had been crammed onto much of the remaining flat space; an antique coffee grinder, a porcelain bell, a tin model of a tram. The effect was a little like stepping into the living room of an elderly relative with the dusty, stale smell to match.

The place was nearly empty at this early hour. Two men in suits stood at the bar discussing in hushed voices the latest political scandal that was developing around a distinguished senator. The only other customer was an emaciated old man who sat in the corner slowly sipping a cup of coffee. The owner rose heavily from the stool he had stationed at one end of the bar and waved Rafael towards one of the battered wooden tables near the back of the room. Gathering up some cutlery and a menu he shuffled over to where Rafael had settled himself.

"*A la orden señor.*" The man's nasal accent, revealed him to be the *Paisa* from which the restaurant took its name. He hovered near the table while Rafael scanned through the offerings before ordering a *picada* and a glass of beer. Dim lights in dusty brass housings cast patches of soft yellow light in the intimate gloom.

As Rafael sipped the beer, his thoughts drifted towards Nathalie. He was surprised and pleased by his attraction to her. Their moments together had involved an unexpected level of intimacy that filled him with exhilaration and scared him with its intensity. He had shared things with her that he thought had been lost forever after Gabriella's death.

An overwhelming need to put an end to this chaotic series of events and lift the cloud of uncertainty that seemed to hang over them flowed through him. Once that was achieved they'd both have the chance to work through their feelings and see if this was going to be a viable relationship. It felt like the beginning of the healing process.

The owner slouched back to the table again carrying a plate piled high with perfectly charred hunks of fried meat, sausage and plantain. The savoury, salty aroma of the food pervaded the booth and made him think of the meal Claudia and Jorge had cooked for him on the roof terrace in San Cristobal. His mouth watered with anticipation.

"Are you waiting for someone else?" the owner asked as he unloaded a selection of condiments from the tray. Rafael shook his head. "*Mejor solo que mal acompañado*," the man grinned at him. A bitter smile twisted over Rafael's face in turn at the use of the well-known Colombian adage. 'Better alone than in bad company' indeed he thought to himself. "What brings you here anyway *jefe*?" said the owner, scratching his fleshy nose idly. "Most of the people that come to my restaurant are either tourists or politicians. You look like neither."

Rafael looked up sharply but could see no guile in the man's broad, good-natured face. His eyes were distracted and neutral; he was merely curious, talkative, bored.

"I think I'm on a fool's errand," Rafael replied, forcing a levity into his voice that he did not feel. "My employer is in the emerald business." The lie was as effortless and unpremeditated as the mist that came down from the mountains. "Someone told him that a new dealer has set up shop in this part of the city. He sent me down here to take a look, to check out the competition. I've been wandering around all afternoon but not seen a sign of the place. I'm not even sure if it exists." He finished with an exaggerated shrug and slipped another piece of the plantain into his mouth.

"Maybe you mean the old *Palacio de Esmereldas*, next block over," replied the owner his bushy eyebrows drawing together. "I wouldn't get your hopes up though. The place has been closed for years." He stepped away from the table to attend a group of scruffy young backpackers who had just strolled down the stairs. The old man grinned toothlessly at him from the other side of the room and raised his coffee cup in an ironic salute.

Rafael ate quickly, working through the plate until his hunger was sated. He drained the beer, left some money on the table and headed towards the back of the restaurant. A narrow passage, partially blocked with stacks of cardboard boxes, led towards the toilet. Through a hatch in the wall he could see into the kitchen where a hatchet-faced worker with a bandana pulled down over his forehead was busy scrubbing pots in time to the music blaring from the radio. The fire escape door at the end of the passage had been wedged open with one of the boxes. After a cursory visit to the toilet, Rafael decided to head out this way rather than trek back through the restaurant.

He stepped into a tapering, rubbish-strewn alley that twisted between the buildings for a short distance before joining back onto the main street. The ground underfoot was rough and unpaved. An unpleasant miasma drifted up from a drainage grill next to where he was standing. It was that fickle hour between sunset and night when the sky was a dusky orange and everything seemed in flux. The alley was bathed in a spectral twilight glow and the cool, early evening air seemed pregnant with possibilities.

At the corner, as the restaurant owner had promised, Rafael caught sight of the crumbling facade of the jewellery store. His chest tightened with excitement. This was the place now, he felt certain of it. He must have been standing in the alley where Paulito had waited with Ruben and Angel. It must have been from here that they watched Ernesto struggling up the street carrying the case with Frederico's torso stuffed inside. The faint, dark stain discolouring the concrete a few metres from where he was standing must have been where Angel had bled out on the pavement.

His attention returned to the *Palacio de Esmereldas*. It was a squat, single-story building with uneven, broken tiling on the low roof. The yellow-painted plaster that covered the front was chipped and flaking, showing the bricks underneath in several wide patches. A faded green trim had been painted around the single door and two wide display windows that faced onto the street. Heavy metal security shutters closed off the doorway, the pitted surface plastered over with peeling adverts and spidery graffiti. The glass had been smashed out from both windows and someone had tried to prise away the rusted metal bars that closed off the openings.

Rafael waited for a few more moments in the alley to see if anything would happen. The street remained deserted. The houses all around were shuttered and silent. He was uncertain what might be waiting for him inside, but if the doctor had been right, there would be some tangible, definitive evidence that could be used to put an end to Yoposa's bloodthirsty schemes once and for all.

Now the time had come, Rafael found himself reluctant to move. The tiredness returned, no doubt fuelled by the beer and the food, but also supplemented by another unexpected sensation. His stomach felt tight and there was a tingling lightness behind his ears as he scanned the building looking for a way in. Oliviera had hinted at some kind of dumping ground for what was left of the bodies once they had been stripped of their valuable organs.

The idea filled him with quiet dread, both from the thought of finding the bodies themselves and fear of what might have been put in place to protect them. Then another notion flitted through his exhausted mind. What if there was nothing there? What if it was just another empty, broken building? That would leave him with no more moves to make. He would be at the mercy of the *sicarios*, waiting around for them to catch up with him sooner or later.

He drew in a long, deep breath, pushed the welter of feelings to one side and stepped out into the darkening street. He hadn't come this far to cower in a squalid alley. It was time to move on and see what secrets this decaying workshop concealed.

With a final glance along the empty street he strode over to the window with the loose bar. Taking a firm grip of the metal he jerked it forward and backwards, trying to work it clear of the frame. After a couple of good yanks the partially-severed iron rod came away in his hands. He grabbed the bars to either side, put his foot on the sill and hauled himself through the opening he had made.

Inside, he was forced to remain on his hands and knees while he navigated the cramped and filthy space of the display cabinet mounted to the window. A few scattered stands for holding up pieces of jewellery blocked the way forward. He pushed them aside as he clambered down into the main room where the shop had once been.

The broad, low-ceilinged chamber was filled with shadows, the walls grey and indistinct. Dust spun lazily in the last of the sunlight streaming in through the window behind him. A row of

271

display cases, broken and empty now, marched off into the darkness. He wiped his hands on his shirt, leaving black streaks behind on the material. Dirt and grime coated his trousers. The smell of rotten wood and mould were heavy in the air.

He circled the room, half-heartedly examining the debris as he went, looking for anything that might link this place to the Temple or give any indiction whether human remains had been stored or disposed of here. While he was poking at some old newspapers in a fire-blackened corner, a pigeon burst out of a pile of dirty cardboard boxes close to his feet, making him start and jump backwards. The clumsy slap of its wings echoed through the gloom until it found its way out through a gap in the roof tiles.

He sat down heavily on a swivel chair that someone had left near the door. It shifted under his weight where one of the runners had been broken off. It was apparent that while the place was empty and disused it had not been abandoned entirely. Some half-eaten food sat quietly decomposing in a plastic bag on the counter at the back of the shop. Rafael gazed at the ground, lost in thought. As well as his own footsteps in the dust circling the room, he could just make out the faint marks of other tracks in the powdery dirt coating the uneven wooden floor boards. Looking at the trail more closely he could see that it led behind the counter to a line of cabinets along the back wall.

Rising from the damaged chair, he moved swiftly to examine the flimsy-looking wood and glass cupboards that had been ranged at the back of the shop. He ran his hands along the shelves and tapped the thin panels, looking for for something, anything that was out of place. About half way along the wall, a faint breeze caressed his face as it emanated from the gap between two of the cupboards. He hesitated for a moment then heaved the cabinet out of the way, grunting with the effort needed to move the uncooperative piece of furniture from its place in the line.

Peering round the corner of the cupboard, Rafael was confronted by the sight of a ragged, door-shaped hole that had been knocked through the brickwork. A sharp, acidic smell drifted out from the darkness beyond. His hand trembled slightly as he approached the opening but whether it was due to exertion from shifting the cabinet or from excitement at finding the concealed entrance was unclear to him. He paused at the threshold, straining his eyes to penetrate the gloomy half-light on the other side.

The improvised doorway emerged through an opening mid-way up a concrete-lined wall. The space that opened out in front of him seemed immense after the narrow confines of the dusty shop, almost like an aircraft hanger but on a smaller scale. Stretching above him, the ceiling was constructed of rusting metal plates overlaying the timber roofing beams. Occasional sheets of rigid, clear plastic were interspersed among them, letting in a dirty grey light, tinged orange now from the sunset. The air felt cool and crisp against the exposed skin of his face and hands.

The lower half of the room was lost in shadows but Rafael could make out several bulky clusters of lumpy, indistinct shapes spread out across the floor. Each mound seemed to be about the size of a small car and had been covered over loosely by a grimy tarpaulin. A makeshift flight of wooden stairs had been built up against the wall towards where the door hole broke through. The stairway was flush with the concrete wall on one side. On the other a shaky handrail led down into the darkness.

Rafael slipped from the doorway onto the stairs, feeling like an insect emerging into some long forgotten cave. The rickety steps creaked under his weight as he descended. At the bottom the acrid tang was noticeably stronger; a thick, cloying vapour that hung in the air and seemed to coat the back of his nose and throat. The stench emanated most strongly from near the wall to his right.

Turning that way and peering through the gloom he caught sight of a row of strange, ghostly pillars looming up towards the distant ceiling. As he crept closer the pillars resolved themselves into stacks of white plastic barrels piled up high against the wall. A few of the drums had been lowered from the main accumulation and heaped into a series of smaller piles across the floor. He brushed the dirt off the nearest one, revealing a stencilled row of alarming warning labels involving exclamation marks, flames and dissolving hands. A long, unpronounceable chemical name had been stamped out in neat black letters under the labels. He wondered if Miriam would recognise it from one of her environmental crimes investigations.

Rafael stepped away, following the wall with the tips of his fingers as he approached the nearest of the tarpaulin-covered mounds. The steady drip of water from an unseen pipe beat out an unfaltering rhythm in the darkness. Closer up he had a partial view through the grimy, faintly transparent material; enough to get a basic sense of the shape underneath. It took him a few seconds to work out that he was looking at a row of deep ceramic basins that must have originally been used for some kind of industrial laundry.

The interior of the tanks remained indistinguishable in the murk and Rafael found himself wishing he'd had the sense to bring his flashlight. He reached out to grasp the tarpaulin. The material was cold and slippery under his touch. Lifting the cloth he leaned out over the hollow, his face tense and his nostrils pinched as he looked down. He coughed deeply and jerked his head back, blinking away the fleeting image of a cluster of heads floating serenely in the briny liquid, features in various stages of decomposition.

The acidic smell was overpowering and he staggered backwards trying to cough the stench out of his lungs. As he backed away he felt something behind him jar into the flesh near his lower spine and the surprise of the impact made him jolt forward again.

Without realising it though, his foot had become tangled in the tarpaulin of the mound behind him and he sprawled to the ground pulling the covering with him. The greasy material slithered aside to reveal a low platform lined with yellowing ceramic tiles. From where he lay on the stained, concrete floor he had a clear view of the partially dismembered torso that rested silent and still in the dim, grey light. A small pile of human arms lay to one side next to a compact hacksaw with a fouled and dirty blade.

He hauled himself to his feet, heart hammering wildly. This had to be enough to call down the forces of the law on the Temple and its associates. Even the most obtuse of his opponents in the *Fiscalia* couldn't ignore a pile of chopped-up human corpses that was enough to revive memories of the worst excesses of the narco cartels in the 1980s. He turned towards the stairs, anxious now to be free of this room of death and its grisly contents.

As he placed his foot on the first of the steps, the distant rasp of the metal shutters scraping open reached his ears followed by an indistinct buzz of animated conversation. He retreated into the darkness, taking refuge behind a nearby pile of the white chemical barrels. A silhouette appeared outlined against the doorway above him.

"There's somebody in here man. I told you," the dark shape shouted over its shoulder. Rafael frantically scanned the area around his hiding place, eyes darting along the smooth, high concrete walls. There was no way out of here. He was trapped.

"Come out! Show yourself *pendejo!*" the figure yelled into the darkness. From where he was concealed Rafael could see that the man had a gun in his hand now and had begun to step cautiously down the staircase. Another silhouette appeared in the doorway above him. Rafael reached back to remove his own gun from where it rested in his waistband. He took careful aim at the man on the stairs, lining up through a gap between two of the barrels and then squeezed the trigger.

The blast ripped through the thin, stagnant air, shattering the stillness with a crack like a firework. The man on the stairs fell back, clutching his shoulder.

Rafael swung the gun towards the doorway but the other man had already ducked back out of sight.

"*Policia! Agente de Fiscalia,*" he bellowed at the opening. "Put down your weapons." The order was more out of habit than from any real hope that he would be obeyed. The only response he got was a spattering of return fire and it was Rafael's turn to crouch down, listening to the dull thump of the bullets hitting the thick plastic of the barrels around him.

From the corner of his eye he spotted the dark stain of liquid leaking across the concrete. The fluid was thick and viscous and he shifted away to avoid touching it.

He tried to change position, planning to make a run to the next stack of drums, closer to the stairway. The moment he lifted his head, the ground around him was peppered with more bullets, the barking retorts dry and forceful in the enclosed space. A splinter of concrete struck him in the forehead with a sharp spark of pain.

The smell from the spilled chemical was becoming overpowering. He felt his head spinning from the fumes. He swung the gun up again to send one more burst of shots towards the doorway in a desperate attempt to clear a way out. Another volley of bullets pushed him back again.

Rafael fell to the ground, gagging and choking on the acidic vapours, his eyes streaming, fighting for breath. As he drifted into unconsciousness a voice from somewhere deep within him whispered that he was dead.

**

29. Veintinueve

Rafael came awake with a shudder. His mouth was dry and his body was cold, the muscles aching and stiff. His vision swam gradually back into focus revealing a patch of chipped concrete wall with a cast-iron drainage grate running oddly up towards the ceiling. After a moment of confusion, he worked out that the disorienting angle was in fact a consequence of him lying on his side and that thankfully the drainage grate ran along at floor level like normal.

He was no longer in the hidden room at the back of the *Palacio de Esmereldas*, there could be no doubt of that. The chemical reek had gone and the dim shadows had been replaced by a harsh brightness that caused him to blink and squint. For the moment at least he was still alive, but where was he?

He tried to move; something was wrong. He jerked his shoulders and his arms didn't work, wouldn't respond to the impulses of his brain. Stifling the panic that threatened to rise within him, he glanced down to see that his limbs had been confined in tubes of cloth and strapped securely across his body.

He gave up struggling with the strait-jacket and sat up slowly, fighting to overcome a sudden rush of dizziness and nausea. His eyes adjusted to the unaccustomed glare and after a few more seconds he was able to make out the shape and dimensions of the room.

He was slumped in the corner of a tiny, almost featureless cell. A solid metal door with a cramped observation window closed off most of the wall facing him. The ceiling soared up higher than the floor was wide, giving the impression of being at the bottom of a pit or shaft. If he'd been able to move his arms he would have been able to touch both the sidewalls simultaneously without difficulty. A narrow ventilation grille mounted high up in the wall showed a sliver of black night sky. A single bare bulb in a metal cage cast a dim shadow like a spider's web on the floor and walls around him.

A hard, tight, ball of dread formed in his stomach. He had a pretty good notion now of where he had been confined and for the moment there seemed to be nothing he could do about it.

He waited then. There was no way of knowing how much time passed as he stared at the concrete wall, a jumble of thoughts and images cycling through his mind. The sky through the grille above seemed faintly lighter when his ears caught the rhythmic slap of footsteps in the corridor. He sat up against the wall as the flap closing the observation window jerked open. A stern face flashed into view for a moment followed by the rattling of keys in the lock.

The door swung outwards and Emilio Ortega stalked into the cell, a white-uniformed orderly hovering behind his shoulder out in the corridor. The sight of the prosecutor standing over him left Rafael feeling breathless, as though a heavy weight had been dropped on his chest.

"What a mess you've got yourself into Alvarez," he drawled with an irritating smirk. "All that sneaking around other people's private property has resulted in an unfortunate accident. The fumes from the chemical spill you maliciously caused in our storage operations have driven you quite mad and my good friend Gael Yoposa has kindly agreed to take you in at his humble treatment facility." Rafael's jawline hardened as he glared up at his captor.

"You're finished Ortega. I've seen your dirty secret. As soon as someone from the *Fiscalia* comes for me all this will be over." Even to himself, the defiance sounded childishly optimistic as he said the words. Sure enough, Ortega responded with a bark of dismissive laughter.

"No-one is coming for you, you stupid little shit." Ortega squatted down, so that he was level with Rafael. "Now if it was up to me we wouldn't be here having this conversation at all, but when we found out that you'd been careless enough to allow yourself to be captured, Yoposa insisted that it had to be some sort of sign from his sun god." The prosecutor's sinuous red tongue darted out of his mouth to moisten his thin lips. "You are to be sacrificed at sunrise," he declared. "It is a great honour, apparently. Far greater than you deserve."

Rafael slumped back against the wall. He could feel the blood draining from his face as he recalled the torn and mutilated bodies strewn about in the makeshift mortuary.

"It was you, wasn't it," Ortega began again, peering at Rafael with his head tilted slightly to one side. "You were responsible for the interruption to the ceremony last night." Rafael let his gaze drop to the floor, saying nothing. "Well you're going to get another chance to see Yoposa in action and this time you'll have the best view in the room." Another bark of laughter escaped from Ortega's sneering mouth. "If only you'd done what I told you Alvarez and found a way to close the case then none of this would have been necessary." Rafael raised his face, his yellow eyes bitter as they fixed on the prosecutor.

"Why are you helping him, Ortega?" His voice was a grating whisper. "He's completely mad."

"Oh I know that." The twisted smirk flashed back into place on Ortega's lean, predatory face. "But he's useful and rich so I let him do what he wants." He shrugged dismissively. "When you strip everything back the only things that really matter are money and power. Everything else is just another delusion. Yoposa and his friends are trying to recreate a Muisca world that doesn't exist, that has never existed. You're lost in some abstract ideal of justice, as though such a thing could ever happen in this sad and broken country. It's an amazing thing, the lies we tell ourselves," he mused shaking his head. "The things we do to survive."

"I pity you Ortega. You're an empty shell of a man, so full of greed and cynicism that you can no longer see anything else. Did you ever stop to think about the damage you've done? To think about the men and women whose lives you took away before you had their organs sliced out and sold on to the highest bidder like some kind of disposable commodity; like a goddam bag of Colombian coffee!" Rafael felt his voice rising in line with his anger.

"Open your eyes Alvarez. These are not people that anyone wants or needs. No one is looking for them. They are barely alive at all."

"That's where you're mistaken. The fact I'm sitting here with you, that I came so close to bringing this all down proves you're wrong." The prosecutor shrugged again and rose to his feet in a single fluid motion.

"Well, you failed and it's all over." He moved towards the open cell door and the waiting orderly. "Enjoy your last few

279

hours before Yoposa comes for you." He turned back at the doorway looking down over his shoulder at Rafael. "One more thing. We picked up your new girlfriend as well. She's going to join you for Yoposa's silly pagan ceremony in a few hours. The two of you are going to be killed together to appease the all-powerful sun god." Sarcasm and contempt were thick on Ortega's voice. Rafael struggled and thrashed against the restraints holding his arms in place, using the wall to lever himself upright.

"She's got nothing to do with this. Leave her out of it."

"You should have thought of that yourself before you involved her in your sad little mission." He shook his head, a wry grin on his face. "Another death on your conscience. You really were a crap investigator Alvarez."

With a final chuckle he stepped out of the cell and the door slammed shut behind him. Rafael threw himself after the prosecutor and crashed into the door just as it closed. He was yelling incoherently now, about Nathalie, about the *Fiscalia,* about whatever came into his head. Random, snarling noises that gave voice to his rage and frustration. Then, with a monumental effort of will he brought himself under control again. He felt tremors running through his body as he slid back to the floor, wondering if there was anything left he could do. The hissing of the grimy bulb seemed to fill the bare concrete room as his thoughts circled a mute abyss of panic and despair.

A short while later, Rafael was stirred from his despondence by a faint clanging and shouting that echoed down the low-ceilinged passage and into his claustrophobic prison. Looking up, he noticed for the first time that the observation window had been left open and he now had a restricted view out into the corridor. Scrambling awkwardly to his feet he pressed his face against the narrow opening. The sound was louder now and he had an oblique perspective of two figures at the end of the corridor coming slowly towards him.

His first thought was that it was Nathalie and he nearly called out to her but then he realised that both the voices were masculine and he stopped himself short. The figures were closer now and he could perceive the stern-faced orderly pushing another patient along in front of him. The man's hands and feet were bound with metal shackles and he shuffled along with an awkward stumbling motion. As he got closer, Rafael caught sight of his chubby, round face and wide vacant eyes. He realised that what he had first thought was an odd deformity of the man's forehead was in fact a red plastic helmet.

Their eyes met for an instant and a flash of recognition passed over Edgar's confused, agitated features. He paused his incoherent shouting for a second, stopping where he stood to stare fixedly at the section of Rafael's face that was visible at the narrow observation window. Out of the wheelchair he was surprisingly tall and stocky. Even stooped over and restrained by the shackles he was a good head taller than his guard. Then the orderly shoved him from behind and Edgar staggered forward again.

"Come on. Keep moving you big moron," the man shouted at him striking him across the back of the head with the cudgel he carried. The blow glanced off the helmet but Edgar fell to his knees wailing. "Stop your shouting and get up. You're in here now until you calm down again."

Rafael watched as Edgar was pushed into the neighbouring cell and locked in. The orderly casually closed the hatch on the observation window as he went back up the corridor without pausing to glance inside. The guard's manner sent a shiver through Rafael, as though he had been rendered invisible, a person the staff had been instructed not to see.

A thick silence descended across the cell block again. Then Rafael caught the faint sounds of Edgar's sobbing drifting up through the drainage grate that ran along the base of the wall. As he moved towards the noise he noticed a small length of pipe near the corner that had been sawn off flush with the wall. Perhaps it had once been fixed to a radiator that had long since been removed. Squinting down the grime-encrusted length of tube gave him a tiny circle of vision into the next cell. He could see a small section of Edgar's head and upper arm as the big man hunched forward over his knees. His shoulders heaved and shuddered as he sobbed and muttered quietly to himself. Rafael leaned forward and placed his mouth close to the pipe.

"Edgar, are you alright? What happened to you?" he called out in a hoarse whisper. There was no reaction from the man in the other cell. He continued his quiet weeping, seemingly oblivious to Rafael's attempts at contact. "It's me, Rafael Alvarez," he persisted. "You showed me your paintings in the crafting studio last week, with Doctor Oliviera. Do you

281

remember?" At the mention of Oliviera's name, Edgar lifted his head from his knees and rubbed the tears from his cheeks with the back of his hand.

"I, I don't understand what I did wrong," he muttered looking around the room, his heavy forehead criss-crossed by lines. "I wanted to speak to my, my doctor. To doctor Oliviera. No-one will tell, tell me where he is."

"What did they do to you Edgar?" Rafael asked again.

"My, my demon Viruñas came back to me. I had to break, break some things. I think I hurt people too. I don't remember."

"Listen to me Edgar. Oliviera is dead. I was with him when he died. The people that run this place drove him to kill himself. He can't help you any more. I'm sorry Edgar." Rafael rested his forehead against the cold, concrete wall. There was a quiet pause from the other side.

"No, no, that can't be right. Viruñas told me that the doctor was coming to look after me. He was going to give me my medicine and make me better. What have you done with him? Why have you taken him away?" Edgar's voice was degenerating into frenzied babbling as he continued speaking.

"We've got to save ourselves now Edgar," Rafael urged. "We have to get out of these cells. I can get us some help if I can just get out of here." But it was no good. The shouting and wailing had started again. Rafael sank back against the wall, trying to shut out the meaningless ranting. "We're going to die in here unless we can find a way to get out," he muttered to himself. "And I have no idea how we're going to do that."

Hopelessness threatened to overwhelm him then. His breathing became shallow and difficult. An empty buzzing insinuated itself at the threshold of his hearing and the dizziness and nausea returned. His thoughts constantly spun back round to what might be happening to Nathalie and how to get out of the cell, with no answer to either question emerging from the tired fog in his brain.

He was trying to work the straps loose from the jacket without any real hope of success when he heard a dry rustling, followed by a faint, surreptitious whisper.

"Rafael, is that you? Are you down there?"

His heart thumped wildly in his chest. For a moment he thought he really was going mad, that his desperation had driven him to start hearing voices like Edgar. Then his eyes followed the voice upwards and he saw the thin pale face of Paulito Barraca framed against the solid black bars of the ventilation grille above him, blinking like an owl in the sharp light from cell.

**

Having spent most of his young life on the hostile streets of Bogota, Paulito was well used to hiding in the shadows and making himself invisible when it was necessary to do so. However, even his extensive talent for stealth and concealment had been stretched to the limit by his efforts get into the clinic and locate Rafael's underground prison. He knelt down in the dry grass at the bottom of the blank, concrete wall and peered past the bars, down into the tiny room. An expression of disbelief and joy was etched on the face tilted up to stare at him. Rafael's pale eyes were wide open and his eyebrows arched high up his forehead. He looked even more haggard and desperate than the last time Paulito had seen him. A cut had opened up above his right eye and dried blood was caked across the side of his face. His skin was almost translucent and he looked thinner, almost as though he'd been very sick.

"Paulito, is that really you?" Rafael called up from the cramped cell. "That's the second time today you've appeared like a ghost out of nowhere. Do I owe you money, or something?" A grin spread across the investigator's face. Paulito found himself grinning too. "You can't imagine how good it is to see you again *muchacho*. How on earth did you manage to get up there?"

"They came to your apartment," Paulito recounted in an excited whisper. "I managed to get out just in time and watched them from the roof outside the kitchen. One of them got a call while they were searching through your things. I overheard them saying you had been captured and were being held somewhere." He leaned forward putting one hand on the bars. "It was dark and they didn't see me climb into the back of their pickup truck. I hid underneath a blanket. When they stopped I found myself here. I waited till everything was quiet again and then started looking for you."

"Paulito, you've got to help me get out of here. Try and steal some keys or see if you can create a distraction or something, anything that gives me half a chance to get out of this cell." A thread of desperation had entered the investigator's voice. "All our lives depend on it now."

"I won't let you down, Rafael." The youth nodded, his chin thrust forward, his hazel eyes firm. With a final glance through the bars he turned away and followed the wall back round the building, pulling up the hood of his dark grey sweater. He slipped through the shadows, moving quickly with Rafael's warning resonating through his head. The night was clear and crisp. A swirl of stars spread across the inky sky above him. The eastern horizon was stained with a faint pink tinge where the sun was due to rise behind the jagged ridge-line of the mountains in a couple of hours.

This part of the clinic seemed to be almost unoccupied compared to the other areas he'd searched through. Earlier, he'd had to stop every couple of minutes to conceal himself from orderlies and security guards as he'd combed the buildings looking for Rafael. Now though, he appeared to be alone as he stalked along a narrow path between the concrete bunker in which Rafael was imprisoned and the featureless expanse of the outer wall. Dim lights had been fixed to the wall at widely-spaced intervals and he darted from one patch of darkness to the next, his ears tuned to the night sounds, scanning for any sense of movement or danger.

The path turned a corner and ended in a bin storage area. Rich, cloying smells rose up from the ranks of metal skips that had been jammed into the gloomy claustrophobic enclosure, shut in by a rickety wooden fence. Plastic bags had been piled up in the spaces between the skips and Paulito could hear the rustling of rats from in among the rubbish. He wove his way between the bins looking for a way through. The metal wheels on the underside of the skips squealed sharply as he shoved them aside, clearing a narrow pathway through the storage area.

He was not far from the fence when he first noticed the continuous purring roar over the other noises of the night. The sound quickly grew louder, rising to an overwhelming staccato thump that seemed to come from all around him. He froze in place, cowering down among the skips as a dark shape swept across the narrow wedge of open sky above him. The flashing lights and sweeping rotors of the helicopter were unmistakable at that short distance.

He could hear it hovering and buzzing close by like a giant angry insect. It must have been coming in to land on the roof of the concrete bunker next to him. Paulito had never seen a helicopter from so close before and he wondered what it was doing in this malign place. He felt a sense of rising unease from its presence and pushed ahead with added urgency.

At the far side of the bin yard a low archway led through to the cluttered service area and carpark where he had first emerged from the back of the pickup truck. From the safety of the archway he scanned the gloomy shapes in front of him. The jumbled space seemed quiet and deserted. The pickup truck was still parked in among the stacks of crates and boxes that filled the yard.

Some steps climbed up to a raised area in front of a metal-framed glass door that led further into the clinic. He crossed the yard quickly and tried the handle. It was locked. Stepping back, he could see the roof above the entrance was flat and low. If he could just get up there, he was certain he could find a way into the building. There would be some kind of alarm he could activate or something he could do to help Rafael.

The edge of the roof loomed above him, tantalising but out of reach. Glancing around for something to climb on, his eyes fixed on a round steel bin that had been placed to one side of the doors. A wisp of smoke twisted up from the inside, most likely from a discarded cigarette judging by the profusion of crushed ends littered around the door and steps. He wrestled the bin towards the wall, ignoring the acrid smell that drifted up towards his face and made his eyes water.

Clambering precariously on top he leaned forward, his finger-tips reaching upwards for the edge. So close, he almost had it, just a little further. Suddenly the bin lurched sideways and Paulito found himself falling forward into space. With a final lunge of his arms he grasped hold of the strip of plastic that ran along the side of the roof while behind him the crashing clatter of the bin toppling over resounded like a set of pans falling to the floor. He scrabbled against the wall with his feet but there was no purchase on the slippery brickwork. The strength drained from his fingers and he hung there for a few seconds longer before dropping back to the ground next to the door.

Turning round he saw a bright tongue of flame flickering inside the bin. The cigarette must have set fire to whatever else had been thrown away in there. His first instinct was to flee and he had already taken several steps back towards the archway. Then the idea flashed like an arc light through his brain and he stopped where he was. He searched through the chaotic stacks of crates and boxes for a few moments before finding what he wanted. Holding the plank of dry wood that he had broken off from one of the pallets he returned to the bin. He thrust one end into the embryonic flames kindling inside the metal canister.

The wood caught quickly, crackling and popping as the fire curled along its edges. Carrying the plank before him like a glowing standard he moved quickly back to the archway and the metal skips. Working his way backwards through the bins he waved the burning board over the piles of plastic bags and touched it to the shapeless junk overflowing from the tops of the dumpsters, lingering at each spot for a few seconds to make sure the fire took hold. The flames leaped across the greasy refuse sending out great plumes of smoke and Paulito was forced to back away from the raging furnace he had created in the bin yard. He grinned and slipped back into the shadows as the fire licked up towards the roof.

**

30. Treinta

Rafael stared at the narrow sliver of pink sky through the bars. His eyes were fixed desperately on the thin wisps of cloud that were starting to materialise in the growing light as though he could read in them the truth of what the future might hold for him.   Paulito had been discovered and captured or worse. Yoposa and his fanatics were going to come stomping down the corridor and into his cell any moment now, he was sure of it.

It was all over. At least he would be reunited with Gabriella at the end of it all, see his beautiful, beloved wife again.   He hung his head as his thoughts jumped to Nathalie and the damage he had inflicted on her by making her a part of his investigation. Because of his actions Victor would grow up as an orphan, deprived of the love and protection of his mother in an indifferent and often callous world. The shame and guilt of his selfishness and failure to consider the consequences burned bright inside him. He shut his eyes watching the circle of light behind his eyelids shrink to a pinprick. Would this be like the moment of death he wondered.

At that moment an unexpected smell brushed at his nostrils. A trace of a pungent, ashy aroma that flickered on the air like burnt food and caught at the back of his throat.   There it was again, stronger now and Rafael let out an involuntary cough as the odour forced its way deeper into his lungs.   Opening his eyes, the air in his cell seemed faintly hazy and there was no mistaking now the distant jangling of alarms and bells from the hallways and rooms above him.

A choking blanket of smoke started to fill the corridor, drifting under the gap between the door of the cell and the concrete floor. He wriggled over to the pipe linking him to Edgar's cell. Perhaps Paulito had prevailed after all and there would be one last desperate chance when the door was opened as it surely must be. He bent his face towards the tube hoping his words could get through to the distraught schizophrenic on the other side of the wall.

"Edgar, this smoke gives us a chance. Try and pull yourself together and get ready for when they come for us. I know you can do it Edgar. Oliviera might have gone, but I believe in you." There was no response from the other side of the wall but the sobbing and muttering had settled down.

Rafael levered himself upright and stepped over to the steel door. He began kicking it with all the effort he could muster, the metal clanging and reverberating under the force his blows.

"Hey! We need help down here! Something's on fire!" he yelled between loud coughs. A few minutes later, the clack of hurrying footsteps sounded from the corridor outside, moving past where he stood listening and stopped at the entrance to Edgar's cell. He heard the door creak open.

"Come on you. On your feet, you big monkey. You need to move." The gruff voice of the guard was clearly audible through the wall. "Oh, so you don't want to listen to me. You really are as stupid as you look. I'm going to knock some sense into that thick skull of yours. No-one's going to care what I do to you anyway."

There was the sound of a struggle from the other room, a deep grunting and the repeated thumps of heavy blows. Then silence returned as the smoke continued to thicken in the choking air. Rafael backed away from the door. What had happened to Edgar? What had the guard done to him? If the man came for Rafael there was little he could do with his arms immobilised by the straitjacket. He readied himself for a wild, head-first charge. Perhaps if he could knock the man off balance he might have a chance to get out into the corridor. It sounded hopeless even to him.

The keys turned in the lock with a sharp clicking sound. Rafael steeled himself for the expected pain of the coming beating. The door swung open and instead of an agitated guard ready to strike, Edgar was standing in the entrance grinning like a maniac. A smear of gore was spattered across his face and the red safety helmet was cracked above his right eye.

"I, I did it Rafael. I found a way to get, get us out!" Rafael took an involuntary step backwards, his eyes wide.

"What did you do Edgar?"

"He, he hit me and I hit him back. Viruñas told me to keep hitting him. He's not moving any more." Edgar's gaze shifted to the ground for a moment, then a happy grin flashed across his thick features. "But look! I've, I've got all the keys," he added holding up a jangling set that had previously been attached to the guard's belt. Rafael's shoulders slumped in relief and his face softened into a weary smile to match Edgar's.

"Good work Edgar." He let out a long breath of relief. "Help me out of this thing and let's go before this smoke gets worse." Edgar fiddled with the straps at the back of the jacket and the hateful garment fell to the floor. Rafael flexed his arms, rubbing the circulation back into his stiff limbs. He placed his hand on Edgar's shoulder for a moment before stepping past him and out into the corridor. Smoke billowed thickly on the other side of the door and he put his hand over his mouth and nose. It was time to find Nathalie quickly and get out.

He turned to glance through the open door of Edgar's cell. The guard lay face down on the floor, motionless. His head had been reduced to a bloody, wet mess. Rafael shuddered and turned to see Edgar looking at him, his eyes sad.

"Viruñas made me do it. I wanted to stop but he wouldn't let me."

"It's okay Edgar. You did what you had to. He was trying to do the same to you, remember?" The big man nodded, his gaze dropping to the floor.

Rafael turned back to the guard, dropping to one knee beside him. He ran his hands down the man's sides, patting the pockets of the uniform as he searched for anything else that might help them escape. At the man's waist, he unclipped the leather holster and removed the pistol from inside. He checked the clip and slid a bullet into the chamber before stepping away.

With the gun ready at his side he led Edgar down the murky corridor towards a set of concrete stairs at the end. It was getting hard to see in the dense, grey fog that smelled strongly of burning as they moved forward close to the ground. The thick air was almost unbreathable now. Rafael was forced to feel his way up the steps as they curved round a corner and out onto another corridor. He had a dim view of a wooden table and a grid of iron bars blocking the way forward. With a flash of recognition he suddenly realised where they were.

The entrance to the secure wing that he had seen briefly with the doctor looked different from this side but there was no mistaking the passage that led to the way out of the hospital. He stumbled forward, taking the keys from Edgar. It took several attempts before he found the correct one and slid it smoothly into the lock. The bars swung open and they moved on again.

At the corner Rafael paused to scan the way ahead. A regular, pulsing thump like an accelerated heartbeat pushed its way into his consciousness, even over the insistent blaring of the alarms. The image of the helicopter pad on the roof of the building that he had glimpsed when he had been here last time jumped unbidden into his mind. With a sudden certainty he knew where he would find Nathalie, Ortega and probably Yoposa too. He pulled Edgar close.

"I have to go and find my friend. Follow this corridor and you should get to the exit. Thanks for getting me out. I'll see you outside when all this is done." Edgar nodded and Rafael watched his companion's bulky form disappear into the swirling, silvery smoke like a swimmer diving underwater, before he turned the other way down the corridor.

The heavy fire escape was where he remembered it and he barrelled through, barely pausing for breath. The stairwell on the other side seemed to be empty and he took the steps two at a time as he rushed upwards. Away from the corridor the smoke was thinner and Rafael passed the door he had taken last time with the doctor as he stalked grimly toward the roof. Round the next turn the stairs ended at a tight concrete platform. He had reached the top; there was nowhere else to go. A door to his right presumably provided access out onto the roof and he paused with his hand on the horizontal opening bar.

The noise had been building as he had risen up the stairwell and now he found himself enveloped in a shaking, deafening maelstrom that drove out every other sound, every other thought, leaving his consciousness scraped raw. All that was left was the bitter sense of fear, like a cold hand clutched somewhere between the bottom of his throat and the top of his chest.

He had been so intent on escape, so sure that he needed to get to the roof that he hadn't really thought about what he would do when he got there. Whatever was on the other side of the door he knew that he had to face it, to bring this harrowing business to an end once and for all. He had faced down his fears and doubts so many times since he'd stood with Frederico's torso on Monserrate that he'd almost become accustomed to what was required of him. He took a final deep breath, readied the gun and shoved the door open.

The wall of sound climbed another octave of intensity as he emerged from the smoky gloom of the stairwell into the pink-tinged blue of a flawless Bogota dawn. A gentle breeze was cool against the flushed skin of his soot-smeared face. Silhouetted against the coral sky, the sleek black form of the helicopter was skewed awkwardly across the roof some distance away from him.

A small group of hunched figures was assembled near the machine, buffeted by the relentless downwash as they waited among the low stacks of crates and boxes that had been spread out over the landing zone. To Rafael's left, smoke boiled up from the side of the building in an angry black cloud. A faint hint of wailing sirens drifted across the crisp morning air from somewhere below and far away.

He was unnoticed at first as he prowled through the forest of antennas and satellite dishes that colonised the section of the roof leading up to the helipad. Orange lights strobed across the flat surface of the pad and Rafael had the opportunity to pick out the hulking form of Ernesto. The burly enforcer was heaving a box into the helicopter. Next to him stood Gael Yoposa gesturing impatiently, his long hair whipped about him by the wind.

As Rafael watched, Carolina Florez stepped out from the other side of the helicopter and approached Yoposa, bending close to discuss something with him. She was clutching a sheaf of papers that flapped wildly as she tried to hold them down. Ortega slumped inside the helicopter looking bored and impatient and there, strapped into the seat beside him, was Nathalie.

Her hands had been bound in front of her and her head was thrown back as she glared at Ortega with a look somewhere between contempt and disgust. Even from this distance Rafael could see the fragility of the spark of defiance to which she clung. He took another step forward, holding the gun low.

"This ends now," he roared at the top of his voice over the thumping of the rotating blades. "You need to let her go and stop this madness." Ernesto was the first to react. As he caught sight of Rafael he dropped the white crate he was carrying and his hand snaked up towards his jacket. The crate split as it hit the floor and Rafael's eyes flicked involuntarily to the glistening red and brown contents that sloshed out across the surface of the helipad. When he looked up again Ernesto had a gun in his hand.

Rafael dived behind a protruding air-conditioning duct a split second before the barking retort of Ernesto's pistol cracked through the dancing air. The bullets hammered into the thin metal, thudding and clunking all around him.

Rafael clutched his gun in both hands, willing himself to move. He spun sideways away from the shelter of the steel pipeline to take his shot. Ernesto fell backwards, a bright spray of arterial blood pumping from his neck.

A snarl of hatred twisted over Yoposa's angular face. He had snatched up a shotgun from the helicopter and now he swung the barrel towards Rafael. The investigator barely had time to scramble backwards before part of the duct behind which he was hiding disintegrated in a hail of pellets.

He peered furtively round the edge of the damaged metal in time to see Florez pull a snub-nosed pistol from the expensive handbag she carried at her side. Ortega cowered back in the helicopter but Nathalie was no longer next to him. Rafael glanced across the narrow section of the helipad within his field of vision but couldn't catch sight of her before another burst of shots caused him to pull back again.

Yoposa and Florez unleashed a steady stream of fire at Rafael's flimsy hiding place. The two of them had him pinned down now. Every time he showed himself another thunderous volley forced him back behind the shredded remains of the air-conditioning vent.

He fired blind in response, lifting his hand above the ragged metal to spray bullets in a desperate attempt to keep them away. A stray shot thudded into some crucial part of the intricate mechanism operating the helicopter. The engine housing belched black smoke and the spinning rotors whined to a gradual stop.

In the restless stillness that followed, Rafael could hear the furtive shuffling as his two attackers advanced around the sides of his hiding place. It was a matter of moments before one of them would be able to take a clear shot at him.

His eyes scanned the desolate roofscape, darting from one side to the other as he searched for some means of escape. It was no use, the nearest shelter was too far to reach without exposing himself and the moment he tried to move he would present an unmissable target.

He saw with a sudden clarity that this was where things ended for him. The bitterness of coming so close only to fail rose up within him like bile. He wondered how good a shot Yoposa was and if he would hear the blast that killed him. Cradling the pistol he readied himself to try for a final attack when the moment presented itself, without any real hope that he would be given the chance.

When the gunfire came, it was from further away than he had expected. The salvo of shots sounded as though it had been discharged from near the helicopter rather than the the jumbled heaps of boxes and crates where Yoposa and Florez were preparing to gun him down.

Rafael hesitated for a split second, surprised to find himself still alive, then peered out from his hiding place. The corpse of Yoposa sprawled on the floor on top of the shotgun he had been carrying, a wide wet crater blasted into the small of his back. A few meters away Florez lay motionless on her side, a dark pool of blood spreading slowly away from her across the level surface of the roof.

He looked up to see Nathalie standing by the broken helicopter, her eyes wide with shock, tremors juddering through her body. The pistol that she had taken from Ernesto was held loosely in her trembling hands. As their eyes met she let the unwieldy weapon fall to the floor.

"I had to do it. They were going to shoot you. I've never killed anyone before." Her voice wavered and she raised a hand to her mouth as her eyes jerked back to the two contorted figures lying still on the ground in front of her.

He was on his feet in an instant, running to her, impatient to close the distance between them. Then she was in his arms, pressed close against his body, the rich smell of her hair shutting out the burning stench all around them. He ran a hand along the soft skin of her face, gazing into her liquid hazel eyes. She kissed him passionately, her lips firm against his, the cinnamon taste of her mouth engulfing his senses.

"I thought I'd lost you," he whispered resting his cheek against her smooth forehead. "Did they hurt you? Are you ok?"

"I'm alright," she replied taking a deep shuddering breath. "Rafael, what is this all about?" She pushed her hair back from her face and looked him directly in the eye. "Why did this happen?"

How could he explain? How was he ever going to explain any of this madness to anyone? He was silent for a moment, trying to put his turbulent thoughts into some kind of coherent order.

"They wanted the organs," he began hesitantly, gesturing at the spilled remains on the landing pad. "Yoposa owned this asylum. Florez chose which inmates to provide for his mad cult to sacrifice. Then they removed the organs from the victims and sold them on the black market for transplants." Rafael lowered his head. "That's what happened to Frederico. The trail from the missing Muisca objects led him to the Temple. I think he managed to infiltrate the organisation, getting that tattoo to prove his allegiance, but then they discovered who he really was. He was sent here, drugged and confined in the secure wing and then, when the time was right they offered him up at one of their bizarre ceremonies. I found the records of the money they made from him when I broke in here the night before last."

Rafael wrapped his arms around her more tightly. She clung to him fiercely and he felt the wetness of her tears through his shirt.

"I'm sorry Nathalie. It's over now. They were going to kill us too. So you really didn't have a choice." His eyes moved back to the two corpses. "You did what you had to do," he asserted, a note of firmness in his voice.

He was interrupted by a muffled thump of falling boxes coming from behind the helicopter. They drew apart quickly and turned to face it. Rafael raised the gun again.

Emilio Ortega stepped out from behind the crippled machine with his hands held in the air. His well-tailored suit looked rumpled and was caked in dust.

"Well done Alvarez," he sneered, his cultured voice heavy with irony. "You've got the whole thing figured out. I suppose I underestimated you." Ortega's shifty, reptilian eyes darted from side to side, unwilling to meet Rafael's gaze. A damp sheen of perspiration glistened on his pale forehead.

"Stay where you are," Rafael warned, levelling the gun at him.

"I'm going to tell you what happens now," Ortega cut across him. "The responsibility for all this unpleasantness is going to land fully on the two *guevones* lying dead over there. You're going to put the gun down and I'm going to walk away."

"You're mad Ortega. Why would I want to do that?"

"Come on Alvarez." A pleading desperation had crept into Ortega's voice. "There must be something you want or need. Don't you understand the value of doing a favour for me? I can make things happen for you, but only if you let me go." He was edging round the two of them now, heading for the stairs and the way off the roof. "I miscalculated." The prosecutor shrugged dismissively. "Believe me, I will be in your debt for this. Don't think of it as an end Alvarez, think of it as a new beginning."

For the briefest of moments Rafael considered the prosecutor's offer, turning over in his mind the advantages of being able to rely on a senior patron in the Fiscal's office. The opportunity for advancement, the ability to circumvent the numerous obstacles that were an inevitable part of working for a sprawling bureaucracy like the *Fiscalia*. These were tempting propositions. He lowered the gun slowly.

Ortega had been waiting for an opening and the moment Rafael's gaze dropped with the gun he kicked the melting sludge from the spilled organs towards Rafael's face. He instinctively raised an arm to protect himself and when he looked up again, Ortega was reaching down to take the compact pistol from the lifeless, outstretched hand of Carolina Florez.

Rafael's first urge was to offer Ortega the same mercy that the prosecutor had shown to him in the basement earlier and he felt his finger begin to tighten on the trigger. But then, at the last second, he dropped his aim before firing. Ortega collapsed sideways clutching his leg with a a yell of surprise and pain. A crimson stain seeped through the light grey material of his suit just above the knee.

The sirens were louder now and from his vantage point on the rooftop, Rafael could see the first of the squad cars arriving outside the walls of the clinic closely followed by a long red fire truck. He looked over at Nathalie.

"Someone has to answer for what was done to Frederico and for all the rest of this chaos. I can't think of anyone better, can you?" She nodded, an enigmatic smile playing across her lips. Rafael hauled the groaning figure of Ortega to his feet and dragged him across the roof to face his retribution in the light of the newly risen sun.

**

Epilogue

Rafael and Nathalie stood side by side in the garden, behind the perimeter tape that had been hastily set up by the arriving firefighters. The remains of the clinic continued to burn fiercely in front of them, with bright bursts of flame showing at the windows and thick billows of smoke pouring from great gaping holes in the walls. They could hear glass shattering as the windows burned away and the crackle of wood as the floors fell through.

To one side a group of patients milled about among the trees as the orderlies shepherded them away from the burning structure. A flash of red from his protective helmet showed that Edgar was among them. He waved happily at the two of them and Rafael raised his arm in reply. As they watched the air grew thick with ashes and smoke, obscuring the clinic from view.

There was a flicker of movement near where the administrative building had once stood and Paulito emerged from the swirling smoke. A plastic bag stuffed with medical supplies that he had pilfered from the clinic's pharmacy was held in both hands close to his chest. He glanced around and headed furtively towards the gateway, keeping his distance from anyone who might notice what he was doing.

Catching sight of Rafael and Nathalie across the lawn he stopped moving. Paulito stood as still as a statue, clutching the medical supplies. He looked at Rafael and Nathalie with wide, solemn eyes. Rafael extended his hand and, after a moment, Paulito came running, letting the bag fall to the ground. The three of them linked hands, Rafael and Nathalie on either side and Paulito in the middle. They walked away from the clinic without looking back as the smoke rose into the clear blue sky.

**

Adrien Trarieux studied archaeology and anthropology at Oxford University. He lived in Paris before starting a career working in the financial services industry in London. The Bogota Delusion is his first novel. He lives in London with his Colombian wife and young family.

Printed in Dunstable, United Kingdom

64397466R00171